THE KING BEYOND THE GATE

A man's scream broke the dawn silence and flocks of birds rose from the trees screeching in panic. Tenaka leapt to his feet.

'It came from over there,' shouted Renya, pointing north-east. Tenaka's sword flashed into the sunlight and he began to run.

In the centre of a narrow clearing ringed by snow-covered oak, a man was crouching at the base of a tree, his tunic covered with blood and his leg hideously slashed. Before him stood a huge Joining.

Tenaka shouted as the creature lunged for the wounded man, and it twisted, its blood-red eyes turning on the warrior. He knew he was looking into the eyes of Death, for no man could stand against this beast and live.

'Run!' shouted the man. 'Please leave me!'

Tenaka said nothing and the beast charged, sending a bloodchilling roar echoing through the trees. He crouched, his violet eyes fixed on the awesome creature bearing down upon him.

As its shadow fell across him he leapt forward, screaming a Nadir war-cry.

And the beast vanished.

THE KING BEYOND THE GATE

David A. Gemmell

Arrow Books Limited
20 Vauxhall Bridge Road, London SW1V 2SA

An imprint of Random Century Group

London Melbourne Sydney Auckland
Johannesburg and agencies throughout
the world

First published by Century 1985
Arrow edition 1986

7 9 11 12 10 8 6

Photoset by Input Typesetting Ltd, London

Printed and bound in Great Britain by
Cox & Wyman Ltd, Reading, Berkshire

ISBN 0 09 947010 1

This book is dedicated with love to my children Kathryn and Luke, as a small return for the gift of their company.

Acknowledgements:
Without the help of friends there would be no joy in writing. Many thanks to Tom Taylor for his help with the story, Stella Graham for the proof-reading, and Jean Maund for the copy-editing. Thanks also to Gary, Russ, Barbara, Philip, George, John D., Jimmy, Angela, Jo, Lee and Iona and all the staff of the *Hastings Observer* who created the good years.

And to Ross Lempriere for storming the stairs.

Prologue

The trees were laced with snow and the forest lay waiting below him like a reluctant bride. For some time he stood among the rocks and boulders, scanning the slopes. Snow gathered on his fur-lined cloak and on the crown of his wide-brimmed hat, but he ignored it, as he ignored the cold seeping through his flesh and numbing his bones. He could have been the last man alive on a dying planet.

He half wished that he were.

At last, satisfied that there were no patrols, he moved down from the mountainside, placing his feet carefully on the treacherous slopes. His movements were slow and he knew the cold to be a growing danger. He needed a camp-site and a fire.

Behind him the Delnoch range reared under thickening clouds. Before him lay Skultik forest, an area of dark legend, failed dreams and childhood memories.

The forest was silent, save for the occasional crack of dry wood as thickening ice probed the branches, or the silky rushing of snow falling from overburdened boughs.

Tenaka turned to look at his footprints. Already the sharp edges of his tracks were blurring and within minutes they would be gone. He pushed on, his thoughts sorrowful, his memories jagged.

He made camp in a shallow cave away from the wind and lit a small fire. The flames gathered and grew, red shadow-dancers swaying on the cave walls. Removing his woollen gloves he rubbed his hands above the blaze; then he rubbed his face, pinching the flesh to force the blood to flow. He wanted to sleep, but the cave was not yet warm enough.

The Dragon was dead. He shook his head, and closed his eyes. Ananais, Decado, Elias, Beltzer. All dead. Betrayed because they believed in honour and duty above all else. Dead because they believed that the Dragon was invincible and that good must ultimately triumph.

Tenaka shook himself awake, adding thicker branches to the fire.

'The Dragon is dead,' he said aloud, his voice echoing in the cave. How strange, he thought – the words were true, yet he did not believe them.

He gazed at the fire shadows, seeing again the marbled halls of his palace in Ventria. There was no fire there, only the gentle cool of the inner rooms, the cold stone keeping at bay the strength-sapping heat of the desert sun. Soft chairs and woven rugs; servants bearing jugs of iced wine, carrying buckets of precious water to feed his rose garden and ensure the beauty of his flowering trees.

The messenger had been Beltzer. Loyal Beltzer – the finest Bar-ranking warrior in the Wing.

'We are summoned home, sir,' he had said, standing ill-at-ease in the wide library, his clothes sand-covered and travel-stained. 'The rebels have defeated one of Ceska's regiments in the north and Baris has issued the call personally.'

'How do you know it was Baris?'

'His seal, sir. His personal seal. And the message: "The Dragon calls".'

'Baris has not been seen for fifteen years.'

'I know that, sir. But his seal . . .'

'A lump of wax means nothing.'

'It does to me, sir.'

'So you will go back to Drenai?'

'Yes, sir. And you?'

'Back to what, Beltzer? The land is in ruins. The Joinings are undefeatable. And who knows what foul, sourcerous powers will be ranged against the rebels? Face it, man! The Dragon was disbanded fifteen years ago and we are all older men. I was one of the younger officers and I am now forty. You must be nearer fifty – if the Dragon still survived you would be in your pension year.'

'I know that,' said Beltzer, drawing himself stiffly to attention. 'But honour calls. I have spent my life serving the Drenai and now I cannot refuse the call.'

'I can,' said Tenaka. 'The cause is lost. Give Ceska time and he will destroy himself. He is mad. The whole system is falling apart.'

'I am not good with words, sir. I have ridden two hundred miles to deliver the message. I came seeking the man I served, but he is not here. I am sorry to have troubled you.'

'Listen, Beltzer!' said Tenaka, as the warrior turned for the door. 'If there was the smallest chance of success, I would go with you gladly. But the thing reeks of defeat.'

'Do you not think I know that? That we all know it?' said Beltzer. And then he was gone.

The wind changed and veered into the cave, gusting snow to the fire. Tenaka cursed softly. Drawing his sword he went outside, cutting down two thick bushes and dragging them back to screen the entrance.

As the months passed he had forgotten the Dragon. He had estates to minister, matters of importance in the real world.

Then Illae had fallen sick. He had been in the north, arranging cover patrols to guard the spice route, when word had reached him and he hurried home. The physicians said she had a fever that would pass and that there was no cause for concern. But her condition worsened. Lung blight, they told him. Her flesh melted away until at last she lay in the wide bed, her breathing ragged, her once beautiful eyes shining now with the image of death. Day after day he sat beside her, talking, praying, begging her not to die.

And then she had rallied and his heart leapt. She was talking to him about her plans for a party, and had stopped to consider whom to invite.

'Go on,' he had said. But she was gone. Just like that. Ten years of shared memories, hopes and joys vanished like water on the desert sand.

He had lifted her from the bed, stopping to wrap her in a white woollen shawl. Then he carried her into the rose garden, holding her to him.

'I love you,' he kept saying, kissing her hair and cradling her like a child. The servants gathered, saying nothing, until after an hour two of them had come forward and separated them, leading the weeping Tenaka to his room. There he found the sealed scroll that listed the current state of his business investments, and beside it a letter from Estas, his accountant. These letters contained advice about areas of investment, with sharp political insights into places to ignore, exploit or consider.

Unthinking he had opened the letter, scanning the list of Vagrian settlements, Lentrian openings and Drenai stupidities until he came to the last sentences:

Ceska routed the rebels south of the Sentran Plain. It appears he has been bragging about his cunning again. He sent a message summoning old soldiers home; it seems he has feared the Dragon since he disbanded it fifteen years ago. Now his fears are behind him – they were destroyed to a man. The Joinings are terrifying. What sort of world are we living in?

'Living?' Tenaka said. 'No one is living – they are all dead.'

He stood up and walked to the western wall, stopping before an oval mirror and gazing at the ruin of his life.

His reflection stared back at him, the slanted violet eyes accusing, the tight-lipped mouth bitter and angry.

'Go home,' said his reflection, 'and kill Ceska.'

1

The barracks buildings stood shrouded in snow, the broken windows hanging open like old, unhealed wounds. The square once trodden flat by ten thousand men was now uneven, as the grass pushed against the snow above it.

The Dragon herself had been brutally treated: her stone wings smashed from her back, her fangs hammered to shards and her face daubed with red dye. It seemed to Tenaka as he stood before her in silent homage that she was crying tears of blood.

As Tenaka gazed at the square, memory flashed bright pictures to his mind: Ananais shouting commands to his men, contradictory orders that had them crashing into one another and tumbling to the ground.

'You dung-rats!' bellowed the blond giant. 'Call yourselves soldiers?'

The pictures faded against the ghostly white emptiness of reality and Tenaka shivered. He moved to the well where an old bucket lay, its handle still tied to a rotting rope. He dropped the bucket into the well and heard the ice break, then hauled it up and carried it to the dragon.

The dye was hard to shift, but he worked at it for almost an hour, scraping the last traces of red from the stone with his dagger.

Then he jumped to the ground and looked at his handiwork.

How could they visit their hatred upon the descendant of the Drenai's greatest hero? It was not easy for them, but they managed it.

Goat's blood was daubed on his pillow, scorpions hidden in his boots. Saddle-straps were severed and finally a viper was placed in his bed.

It almost killed him as he rolled upon it, its fangs sinking into his thigh. Snatching a dagger from his bedside table, he killed the snake and then slashed a cross-cut by the fang marks, hoping the rush of blood would carry the venom clear. Then he lay very still, knowing any movement would accelerate the poison in his system. He heard footsteps in the corridor and knew it was Ananais, the officer of the guard, returning to his room after completing his shift.

He did not want to call out, for he knew Ananais disliked him. But neither did he want to die! He called Ananais' name, the door opened and the blond giant stood silhouetted in the doorway.

'I have been bitten by a viper,' said Tenaka.

Ananais ducked under the doorway and approached the bed, pushing at the dead snake with his boot. Then he looked at the wound in Tenaka's leg.

'How long ago?' he asked.

'Two, three minutes.'

Ananais nodded. 'The cuts aren't deep enough.'

Tenaka handed him the dagger.

'No. If they *were* deep enough you would sever the main muscles.'

Leaning forward, Ananais put his mouth over the wound and sucked the poison clear. Then he applied a tourniquet and left to get the surgeon.

Even with most of the poison flushed out, the young Nadir prince almost died. He sank into a coma that lasted four days and when he awoke Ananais was at his bedside.

'How are you feeling?'

'Good.'

'You don't look it. Still, I am glad you're alive.'

'Thank you for saving me,' said Tenaka, as the giant rose to leave.

'It was a pleasure. But I still wouldn't want you marrying my sister,' he said, grinning as he moved to the door. 'By the way, three young officers were dismissed from the service yesterday. I think you can sleep soundly from now on.'

'I shall never do that,' said Tenaka. 'For the Nadir, that is the way of death.'

'No wonder their eyes are slanted.' said Ananais.

*

Renya helped the old man to his feet, then heaped snow upon the small fire to kill the flames. The temperature plummeted as the storm-clouds bunched above them, grim and threatening. The girl was frightened, for the old man had ceased shivering and now stood by the ruined tree staring vacantly at the ground by his feet.

'Come, Aulin,' she said, slipping her arm around his waist. 'The old barracks are close by.'

'No!' he wailed, pulling back. 'They will find me there. I know they will.'

'The cold will kill you,' she hissed. 'Come on.'

Meekly he allowed her to lead him through the snow. She was a tall girl, and strong, but the going was tiring and she was breathing heavily as they pushed past the last screen of bushes before the Dragon Square.

'Only a few more minutes,' she said. 'Then you can rest.'

The old man seemed to gain strength from the

promise of shelter and he shambled forward with greater speed. Twice he almost fell, but she caught him.

She kicked open the door of the nearest building and helped him inside, removing her white woollen burnoose and running a hand through her sweat-streaked, close-cropped black hair.

Away from the biting wind, she felt her skin burning as her body adjusted to the new conditions. She unbelted her white sheepskin cloak, pushing it back over her broad shoulders. Beneath it she wore a light blue woollen tunic and black leggings, partially hidden by thigh-length boots, sheepskin-lined. At her side was a slender dagger.

The old man leaned against a wall, shaking uncontrollably.

'They will find me. They *will*!' he whimpered. Renya ignored him and moved down the hallway.

A man came into sight at the far end and Renya started, her dagger leaping to her hand. The man was tall and dark and dressed in black. By his side was a longsword. He moved forward slowly, yet with a confidence Renya found daunting. As he approached she steadied herself for the attack, watching his eyes.

They were, she noticed, the most beautiful violet colour, and slanted like those of the Nadir tribesmen of the north. Yet his face was square-cut and almost handsome, save for the grim line of his mouth.

She wanted to stop him with words, to tell him that if he came any closer she would kill him. But she could not. There was about him an aura of power – an authority which left her no choice but to respond.

And then he was past her and bending over Aulin.

'Leave him alone!' she shouted. Tenaka turned to her.

'There is a fire in my room. Along there on the right,' he said calmly. 'I will take him there.' Smoothly he lifted the old man and carried him to his quarters, laying him on the narrow bed. He removed the man's cloak and boots, and began to rub gently at his calves where the skin was blue and mottled. Turning he threw a blanket to the girl. 'Warm this by the fire,' he said, returning to his work. After a while he checked the man's breathing – it was deep and even.

'He is asleep?' she asked.

'Yes.'

'Will he live?'

'Who can say?' said Tenaka, rising and stretching his back.

'Thank you for helping him.'

'Thank you for not killing me,' he answered.

'What are you doing here?'

'Sitting by my fire and waiting for the storm to pass. Would you like some food?'

They sat together by the blaze, sharing his dried meat and hardcake biscuits and saying little. Tenaka was not an inquisitive man and Renya intuitively knew he had no wish to talk. Yet the silence was far from uncomfortable. She felt calm and at peace for the first time in weeks, and even the threat of the assassins seemed less real, as if the barracks were a haven protected by magic – unseen but infinitely powerful.

Tenaka leaned back in his chair, watching the girl as she in turn gazed into the flames. Her face was striking, oval-shaped with high cheekbones and wide eyes so dark that the pupils merged with the iris. Overall the impression he gained was one of strength, undermined by vulnerability, as if she held a secret fear or was tormented by a hidden weakness. At another time he would have been attracted by her. But when he reached inside himself he could find no emotions, no desire . . . No life, he realised with surprise.

'We are being hunted,' she said at last.

'I know.'

'How would you know?'

He shrugged and added fuel to the fire. 'You are on a road to nowhere, with no horses or provisions, yet your clothes are expensive and your manner cultured. Therefore you are running away from something or someone, and it follows that they are pursuing you.'

'Does it bother you?' she asked him.

'Why should it?'

'If you are caught with us, you will die too.'

'Then I shall not be caught with you,' he said.

'Shall I tell you why we are hunted?' she enquired.

'No. That is of your life. Our paths have crossed here, but we will both go on to separate destinies. There is no need for us to learn of one another.'

'Why? Do you fear it would make you care?'

He considered the question carefully, noting the anger in her eyes. 'Perhaps. But mainly I fear the weakness that follows caring. I have a task to do and I do not need other problems in my mind. No, that is not true – I do not *want* other problems in my mind.'

'Is that not selfish?'

'Of course it is. But it aids survival.'

'And is that so important?' she snapped.

'It must be, otherwise you would not be running.'

'It is important to him,' she said, pointing at the man in the bed. 'Not to me.'

'He cannot run from death,' said Tenaka, softly. 'Anyway there are mystics who maintain there is a paradise after death.'

'He believes it,' she said, smiling. 'That is what he fears.'

Tenaka shook his head slowly, then rubbed his eyes.

'That is a little too much for me,' he said, forcing a smile. 'I think I will sleep now.' Taking his blanket, he spread it on the floor and stretched himself out, his head resting on his pack.

'You are Dragon, aren't you?' said Renya.

'How did you know?' he asked, propping himself on one elbow.

'It was the way you said "my room".'

'Very perceptive.' He lay down and closed his eyes.

'I am Renya.'

'Goodnight, Renya.'

'Will you tell me your name?'

He thought of refusing, considering all the reasons why he should not tell her.

'Tenaka Khan,' he said. And slept.

*

Life is a farce, thought Scaler, as he hung by his fingertips forty feet above the stone courtyard. Below him a huge Joining sniffed the air, its shaggy head swinging ponderously from side to side, its taloned fingers curled around the hilt of the saw-edged sword. Snow swept in icy flurries, stinging Scaler's eyes.

'Thanks very much,' he whispered, transferring his gaze to the dark, pregnant storm-clouds above. Scaler was a religious man, who saw the gods as a group of Seniles – eternals playing endless jokes on humanity with cosmic bad taste.

Below him the Joining sheathed its sword and ambled away into the darkness. Taking a deep breath, Scaler hauled himself over the window-sill and parted the heavy velvet curtains beyond. He was in a small study furnished with a desk, three chairs of oak, several chests and a row of bookshelves and manuscript holders. The study was tidy – obsessively so, thought Scaler, noting the three quill pens placed exactly parallel at the centre of the desk. He would have expected nothing less of Silius the Magister.

A long silvered mirror, framed in mahogany, was fixed to the far wall, opposite the desk. Scaler advanced towards it, drawing himself up to his full height and pulling back his shoulders. The black face-mask, dark tunic and leggings gave him a forbidding look. He drew his dagger and dropped into a warrior's crouch. The effect was chilling.

Perfect, he told his reflection. I wouldn't want to meet you in a dark alley! Replacing the dagger, he moved to the study door and carefully lifted the iron latch, easing the door open.

Beyond was a narrow stone corridor and four doors – two on the left and two on the right. Scaler padded across to the furthest room on the left and slowly lifted the latch. The door opened without a sound and he moved inside, hugging the wall. The room was warm, though the log fire in the grate was burning low, a dull red glow illuminating the curtains around the large bed. Scaler moved forward to the bed, pausing to look down on fat Silius and his equally fat mistress. He lay on his stomach, she on her back; both were snoring.

Why am I creeping about? he asked himself. I could have come in here beating a drum. He stifled a chuckle, found the jewel box in its hidden niche below the window, opened it and poured the contents into a black canvas pouch tied to his belt. At full value they would keep him in luxury for five years. Sold, as they must be, to a shady dealer in the southern quarter, they would keep him for barely three months or six if he didn't gamble. He thought of not gambling but it was inconceivable. Three months, he decided.

Re-tying his pouch, he backed out into the corridor and turned . . .

Only to come face to face with a servant, a tall, gaunt figure in a woollen nightshirt.

The man screamed and fled.

Scaler screamed and fled, hurtling down a circular stairway and cannoning into two sentries. Both men tumbled back, shouting as they fell. Scaler hit the floor in a tumbler's roll, came to his feet and sprinted left, the sentries close behind. Another set of steps appeared on his right and he took them three at a time, his long legs carrying him at a terrifying speed.

Twice he nearly lost his footing before reaching the next level. Before him was an iron gate – locked, but the key hung from a wooden peg. The stench from beyond the gate brought him to his senses and fear cut through his panic.

The Joinings' pit!

Behind him he could hear the sentries pounding down the stairs. He lifted the key, opened the gate and stepped inside, locking it behind him. Then he advanced into the darkness, praying to the Seniles to let him live for a few more of their jests.

As his eyes grew accustomed to the darkness of the corridor he saw several openings on either side; within, sleeping on straw, were the Joinings of Silius.

He moved on towards the gate at the far end, pulling off his mask as he did so.

He was almost there when the pounding began

behind him and the muffled shouts of the sentries pierced the silence. A Joining stumbled from its lair, blood-red eyes fastening on Scaler; it was close to seven feet tall, with huge shoulders and heavily-muscled arms covered with black fur. Its face was elongated, sharp fangs lining its maw. The pounding grew louder and Scaler took a deep breath.

'Go and see what the noise is about,' he told the beast.

'Who you?' it hissed, the words mangled by the lolling tongue.

'Don't just stand there – go and see what they want,' ordered Scaler sharply.

The beast brushed past him and other Joinings came into the corridor and followed it, ignoring Scaler. He ran to the gate and slipped the key in the lock. As it turned and the gate swung open, a sudden bellowing roar blasted in the confines of the corridor. Scaler twisted round to see the Joinings running towards him, howling ferociously. With shaking fingers he dragged free the key and leapt through the opening, pulling the gate shut behind him and swiftly locking it.

The night air was crisp as he ran up the short steps to the western courtyard and on to the ornate wall, scaling it swiftly and dropping into the cobbled street beyond.

It was well after curfew, so he hugged the shadows all the way to the inn, then climbed the outer trellis to his room, rapping on the shutters.

Belder opened the window and helped him inside.

'Well?' asked the old soldier.

'I got the jewels,' stated Scaler.

'I despair of you,' said Belder. 'After all the years I spend on you, what do you become? A thief!'

'It's in the blood,' said Scaler, grinning. 'Remember the Earl of Bronze?'

'That's Legend,' replied Belder. 'And even if it's true, not one of his descendants has ever lived a less than honourable life. Even that Nadir-spawn Tenaka!'

'Don't speak ill of him, Belder,' said Scaler softly. 'He was my friend.'

2

Tenaka slept and the familiar dreams returned to haunt him.

The Steppes rolled away from him like a green, frozen ocean, all the way to the end of the world. His pony reared as he dragged the rawhide rein, then swung to the south with hooves drumming the hard-packed clay.

With the dry wind in his face Tenaka grinned.

Here, only here, was he his own man.

Half-Nadir, half-Drenai, wholly nothing – a product of war, a flesh-and-blood symbol of uneasy peace. He was accepted among the tribes with cool courtesy, as befitted one in whose veins ran the blood of Ulric. But there was little camaraderie. Twice the tribes had been turned back by the strength of the Drenai. Once, long before, the legendary Earl of Bronze had defended Dros Delnoch against Ulric's hordes. Twenty years ago the Dragon had decimated Jongir's army.

Now here was Tenaka, a living reminder of defeat.

So he rode alone and mastered all the tasks they set him. Sword, bow, spear, axe – with each of these he was skilled beyond his peers, for when they ceased practice to enjoy the games of childhood he worked on. He listened to the wise – seeing wars and battles on a different plane – and his sharp mind absorbed the lessons.

One day they would accept him. If he had patience.

But he had ridden home to the city of tents and seen his mother standing with Jongir. She was crying.

And he knew.

He leapt from the saddle and bowed to the Khan, ignoring his mother, as was fitting.

'It is time for you to go home,' said Jongir.

He said nothing, merely nodded.

'They have a place for you within the Dragon. It is your right as the son of an Earl.' The Khan seemed uncomfortable, and did not meet Tenaka's steady gaze. 'Well, say something,' he snapped.

'As you wish, Lord, so let it be.'

'You will not plead to stay?'

'If you desire me to.'

'I desire nothing of you.'

'Then when shall I leave?'

'Tomorrow. You will have an escort – twenty riders, as befits my grandson.'

'You honour me, Lord.'

The Khan nodded, glanced once at Shillat and then walked away. Shillat opened the tent-flap and Tenaka entered their home. She followed him and once inside he turned to her and took her in his arms.

'Oh, Tani,' she whispered through her tears. 'What more must you do?'

'Maybe at Dros Delnoch I shall truly be home,' he said. But hope died within him as he said it, for he was not a fool.

*

Tenaka awoke to hear the storm hissing and battering at the window. He stretched and glanced at the fire – it had faded to glowing coals. The girl slept in the chair, her breathing deep. He sat up and then moved to the fire, adding fresh wood and gently blowing the flames to life. He checked the old man; his colour was not good. Tenaka shrugged and left the room. The corridor was icy, the wooden boards creaking under his boots. He made his way to the old kitchen and the indoor well; it was hard to pump, but he enjoyed the exercise and was rewarded when water jetted to the wooden bucket. Stripping off his dark jerkin and grey woollen shirt, he washed his upper body, enjoying the near-pain of the ice-touched water on his sleep-warm skin.

Removing his remaining clothes, Tenaka moved out into the gym area beyond. There he twirled and leapt, landing lightly – first his right hand slicing the air, then his left. He rolled to the floor, then arched his back and sprang to his feet.

From the doorway Renya watched him, drawing back into the shadows of the corridor. She was fascinated. He moved like a dancer, yet there was something barbaric in the scene: some primordial element that was both lethal and yet beautiful. His feet and hands were weapons, flashing and killing invisible opponents, yet his face was serene and devoid of all passion.

She shivered, longing to withdraw to the sanctuary of his room but unable to move. His skin was the colour of gold under sunlight, soft and warm, but the muscles beneath strained and swelled like silver steel. She closed her eyes and stumbled back, wishing she had never seen him.

Tenaka washed the sweat from his body and then dressed swiftly, hunger eating at him. Back in his room he sensed the change in the atmosphere. Renya avoided meeting his eyes as she sat by the old man, stroking his white hair.

'The storm is breaking,' said Tenaka.

'Yes.'

'What is the matter?'

'Nothing . . . except that Aulin is not breathing well. Will he be all right, do you think?'

Tenaka joined her at the bedside. Taking the old man's frail wrist between his fingers he felt for the pulse. It was weak and irregular.

'How long since he has eaten?' he asked.

'Two days.'

Tenaka delved in his pack, producing a sack of dried meat and a smaller pack of oats. 'I wish I had sugar,' he said, 'but this will have to do. Go and fetch some water and a cooking pot.'

Without a word Renya left the room. Tenaka smiled. So that was it – she had seen him exercising and for some reason it had unsettled her. He shook his head.

She returned with an iron pot brimming with water.

'Throw half of it away,' he told her. She splashed it in the hallway and he took the pot to the fire, slicing the meat with his dagger. Then he carefully placed the pot on the flames.

'Why did you not speak this morning?' he asked, his back towards her.

'I don't know what you mean.'

'When you saw me exercising?'

'I did not see you.'

'Then how did you know where to fetch the pot and get the water? You did not go past me in the night.'

'Who are you to question me?' she snapped.

He turned to her. 'I am a stranger. You do not need to lie to me, or pretend. Only with friends do you need masks.'

She sat down by the fire, stretching her long legs to the flames.

'How sad,' she said, softly. 'Surely it is only with friends that one can be at peace?'

'It is easier with strangers, for they touch your life but for an instant. You will not disappoint them, for you owe them nothing, neither do they expect anything. Friends you can hurt, for they expect everything.'

'Strange friends you have had,' she said.

Tenaka stirred the broth with his dagger blade. He was uncomfortable suddenly, feeling that he had somehow lost control of the conversation.

'Where are you from?' he asked.

'I thought you did not care.'

'Why did you not speak?' Her eyes narrowed and she turned her head.

'I did not want to break your concentration.'

It was a lie and they both knew it, but the tension eased and the silence gathered, drawing them together. Outside the storm grew old and died, whimpering where once it had roared.

As the stew thickened Tenaka added oats to further swell the mixture, and finally salt from his small store.

'It smells good,' said Renya, leaning over the fire. 'What meat is it?'

'Mule, mostly,' he told her.

He went to fetch some old wooden platters from the kitchen and when he returned Renya had wakened the old man and was helping him to sit up.

'How are you feeling?' Tenaka enquired.

'You are a warrior?' asked Aulin, his eyes fearful.

'Yes. But you need not fear me.'

'Nadir?'

'Mercenary. I have prepared you some stew.'

'I am not hungry.'

'Eat it anyway,' ordered Tenaka. The old man stiffened at the authoritative tone, then averted his eyes and nodded. Renya fed him slowly as Tenaka sat by the fire. It was a waste of food, for the old man was dying. Still, he did not regret it and could not understand why.

With the meal over, Renya collected the platters and the pot. 'My grandfather wishes to speak with you,' she said and left the room.

Tenaka moved to the bedside, staring down at the dying man. Aulin's eyes were grey and bright with the beginnings of fever.

'I am not strong,' said Aulin. 'I never was. I have failed everyone who ever trusted me. Except Renya . . . I never failed her. Do you believe me?'

'Yes,' Tenaka answered. Why was it that weak men always felt the need for confession?

'Will you protect her?'

'No.'

'I can pay.' Aulin gripped Tenaka's arm. 'Just take her to Sousa. The city is only five, six days south.'

'You are nothing to me. I owe you nothing. And you cannot pay me enough.'

'Renya says you were Dragon. Where is your sense of honour?'

'Buried under desert sands. Lost in the swirling mists of time. I don't want to talk to you, old man. You have nothing to say.'

'Please listen!' Aulin begged. 'When I was a younger man I served the Council. I supported Ceska, worked for his victory. I believed in him. So I am, at least in part, responsible for the appalling terror he has visited on this land. I was a Source priest once. My life was in harmony. Now I am dying and I don't know anything any more. But I cannot die leaving Renya to be taken by the Joinings. I *cannot*. Don't you see? My whole life has been a failure – my death *must* achieve something.'

Tenaka pulled away the old man's hand and stood.

'Now you listen,' he said. 'I am here to kill Ceska. I do not expect to live beyond the deed, but I have neither the time nor the inclination to take on your responsibilities. You want to see the girl get to Sousa, then recover. Use your will.'

Suddenly the old man smiled, tension and fear falling from him. 'You want to kill Ceska?' he whispered. 'I can give you something better than that.'

'Better? What could be better?'

'Bring him down. End his reign?'

'Killing him should achieve that.'

'Yes, indeed, but one of his generals would only take over. I can give you the secret which would destroy his empire and free the Drenai.'

'If this is to be a tale of enchanted swords or mystic spells, do not waste your time. I have heard them all.'

'No. Promise me you will protect Renya as far as Sousa.'

'I will think about it,' said Tenaka. Once more the fire was dying and he fed the last of the wood to the flames before leaving the room in search of the girl. He found her sitting in the cold kitchen.

'I don't want your help,' she said, without looking up.

'I haven't offered it yet.'

'I don't care if they take me.'

'You are too young not to care,' he said, kneeling before her and lifting her chin. 'I will see that you get safely to Sousa.'

'Are you sure he can pay you enough?'

'He says that he can.'

'I don't like you very much, Tenaka Khan.'

'Welcome to the majority view!' he said.

Leaving her, he returned to his room and the old man. Then he laughed and moved to the window, throwing it wide to the winter air.

Before him the forest stretched on for a white eternity.

Behind him the old man was dead.

*

Hearing his laughter Renya entered the room. Aulin's arm had slid from the bed and his bony fingers now pointed at the wooden floor. His eyes were closed and his face peaceful.

She went to him and touched his cheek gently. 'No more running, Aulin. No more fear. May your Source bring you home!'

She covered his face with a blanket.

'Now your obligation is over,' Renya told the silent Tenaka.

'Not yet,' he said, pulling shut the window. 'He told me he knew of a way to end Ceska's reign. Do you know what he meant?'

'No.' She turned away from him and gathered her cloak, her heart suddenly empty. Then she stopped, her cloak falling from her hands as she stared at the dying fire and shook her head. Reality receded. What was there to live for?

Nothing.

What was there to care for?

Nothing.

She knelt by the fire, staring unblinking as a terrible ache filled the emptiness within. Aulin's life had been a steady tale of small kindnesses, tenderness and caring. Never had he been intentionally cruel or malicious; never greedy. But he had ended his life in a deserted barracks – hunted as a criminal, betrayed by his friends and lost to his god.

Tenaka watched her, no hint of emotion in his violet eyes. He was a man used to death. Quietly he stowed his gear in the canvas pack, then lifted her to her feet, fastened her cloak and pushed her gently through the doorway.

'Wait here,' he said. Returning to the bed, he pulled his blanket clear of the corpse. The old man's eyes had opened and he seemed to be staring at the warrior.

'Sleep truly,' whispered Tenaka. 'I will take care of her.' He closed the dead eyes and folded his blanket.

Outside the air was crisp. The wind had died and the sun shone weakly in a clear sky. Tenaka took a slow deep breath.

'Now it is over,' whispered Renya. Tenaka glanced round.

Four warriors had left the screen of trees and were walking forward with swords in hand.

'Leave me,' she said.

'Be silent.'

He loosed his pack, lowering it to the snow, then pushed back his cloak from his shoulders, revealing the scabbard sword and hunting-knife. Walking forward ten paces he waited for the warriors, gauging each man in turn.

They wore the red and bronze breastplates of Delnoch.

'What do you seek?' asked Tenaka, as they drew near.

None of the soldiers spoke, which marked them as veterans, but they spread out slightly – ready for any aggressive action from the warrior.

'Speak, or the emperor will have your heads!' said Tenaka. That stopped them and their eyes flickered to a sharp-featured swordsman on the left; he stepped forward, his blue eyes cold and malevolent.

'Since when does a northern savage make promises on behalf of the emperor?' he hissed.

Tenaka smiled. They had all stopped and were waiting for an answer; they had lost their momentum.

'Perhaps I should explain,' he said, maintaining the smile and moving towards the man. 'It's like this . . .' His hand flashed out and up, fingers extended, smashing the man's nose. The thin cartilage sliced up into the brain and he dropped without a sound. Then Tenaka whirled and leapt, his booted foot hammering into the throat of a second man. Even as he leapt he drew the hunting-knife. Landing on the balls of his feet he spun, parried a thrust and buried his blade in his opponent's neck.

The fourth man was running towards Renya, sword raised. She stood still, watching him without interest.

Tenaka hurled the hunting-knife, which hit the man hilt-first at the base of the helm. Unbalanced, the warrior tumbled in the snow, losing his grip on his sword. Tenaka ran forward as he scrambled to rise, then threw himself on the man's back and he pitched forward once more, his helm tumbling from his head. Tenaka grabbed his hair, tugging the head back, then took hold of the man's chin and wrenched it to the left. His neck snapped like dry wood.

Recovering his knife, Tenaka wiped it clean and replaced it. He scanned the clearing. All was silent.

'Nadir we,' he whispered closing his eyes.

'Shall we go?' asked Renya.

Puzzled, he took her arm, gazing down into her eyes.

'What is the matter with you? Do you want to die?'

'No,' she said absently.

'Then why did you just stand there?'

'I don't know. Shall we go?'

Tears welled in her night-dark eyes, spilling to her cheek, but her pale face remained impassive. Reaching up, he smoothed a tear from her skin.

'Please don't touch me,' she whispered.

'Now you listen to me. The old man wanted you to live; he cared for you.'

'It doesn't matter.'

'It mattered to him!'

'Does it matter to *you*?' The question caught him cold, like a blow. He absorbed it and searched himself swiftly for the right answer.

'Yes, it does.' The lie came easily, and only when it was spoken did he realise it was not a lie.

She looked deeply into his eyes, then nodded.

'I will come with you,' she said. 'But know this: I am a curse to all who love me. Death haunts me, for I should never have tasted life.'

'Death haunts everyone, and never fails,' he said.

Together they walked to the south, stopping by the stone dragon. Icy rain had stung her flanks, giving her a diamond sheen. Tenaka's breath caught in his throat as he gazed upon her face – the water had run to the ruined fangs of her upper mouth, forming new teeth of sparkling ice, renewing her grandeur, restoring her power.

He nodded, as if hearing a silent message.

'She is beautiful,' said Renya.

'Better than that,' said Tenaka softly, 'she is alive.'

'Alive?'

'In here,' he answered, touching his heart. 'She is welcoming me home.'

*

Throughout the long day they pushed on towards the south. Tenaka said little, concentrating on the snow-hidden trails and keeping a wary eye for patrols. He had no way of knowing if the four soldiers were the full complement of hunters, or whether there were several groups pursuing the girl.

In a strange way he did not care. He forced the pace, rarely looking back to see if Renya was struggling. When he did pause, to check out skylines or scan stretches of open ground, she was always just behind him.

For her part Renya followed quietly, eyes fixed on the tall warrior, noting the sureness of his movements and the care with which he chose the route. Again and again two scenes played in her mind: the naked dance in the deserted gymnasium, and the dance of death with the soldiers in the snow. One scene overlaid the other . . . blending, merging. The same dance. The movements were so smooth, almost liquid, as he leapt and turned. The soldiers by comparison seemed ungainly, disjointed, like Lentrian puppets with knotted string.

And now they were dead. Did they have families? Probably. Did they love their children? Probably. They had walked into that clearing as confident men. And yet, in a matter of icy moments, they were gone.

Why?

Because they chose to dance with Tenaka Khan.

She shivered. The light was failing and long shadows crept from the trees.

Tenaka chose a site for his fire against a jutting

of rock, sheltered from the wind. It was set in a hollow surrounded by gnarled oaks and the fire was well-screened. Renya joined him, gathering dead wood and stacking it carefully. A sense of unreality gripped her.

All the world should be like this, she thought, ice-covered and cleansed: all plants sleeping, waiting for the golden perfection of spring; all evil withering under the purifying ice.

Ceska and his demon-spawned legions would fade away like the nightmares of childhood and joy would return to the Drenai, like the gift of dawn.

Tenaka removed a pot from his pack and placed it on the fire, scooping handfuls of snow into the container until it was half-full with warming water. Then, from a small canvas sack he poured a generous mixture of oats into the liquid, adding salt. Renya watched him in silence, fixing her gaze on his slanted violet eyes. Once again, sitting with him by the fire, she felt at peace.

'Why are you here?' she asked.

'To kill Ceska,' he replied, stirring the porridge with a wooden spoon.

'*Why* are you here?' she repeated.

Moments passed, but she knew he was not ignoring her and waited, enjoying the warmth and the closeness.

'I have nowhere else to go. My friends are dead. My wife . . . I have nothing. The reality is that I have always had . . . nothing.'

'You had friends . . . a wife.'

'Yes. It's not easy to explain. There was a wise man once, in Ventria, near where I lived. I spoke with him often about life, and love, and friendship. He chided me, made me angry. He talked about clay diamonds.' Tenaka shook his head and lapsed into silence.

'Clay diamonds?' she asked.

'It doesn't matter. Tell me about Aulin.'

'I do not know what he planned to tell you.'

'I accept that,' he said. 'Just tell me of the man.' Using two sticks he lifted the pot from the flames and set it on the ground to cool. She leaned forward, adding fresh wood to the fire.

'He was a peaceful man, a Source priest. But he was also an Arcanist and liked nothing better than to scour the land for relics of the Elders. He gained a name for his abilities. He told me that when Ceska first came to power he supported him, believed all the promises about a better future. But then the terror began. And the Joinings . . .'

'Ceska always loved sorcery,' said Tenaka.

'You knew him?'

'Yes. Go on.'

'Aulin was one of the first to explore the Graven site. He found the hidden door below the forest and the machines that lay there. He told me his research proved the machines had been created to heal certain diseases suffered by the Elders. But instead of using them in this fashion, Ceska's adepts created the Joinings. At first they were used only in the arenas, tearing each other to pieces to thrill the crowds; but soon they began appearing on the streets of Drenan wearing armour and the markings of Ceska's guard.

'Aulin blamed himself and journeyed to Delnoch, ostensibly to examine the Chamber of Light beneath the Keep. From there he bribed a sentry and tried to escape through Sathuli lands. But the chase began and we were forced south instead.'

'Where do you come into the story?' he asked.

'You did not ask about me, but about Aulin.'

'I am asking now.'

'May I have some porridge?'

He nodded, tested the pot and handed it to her. She ate in silence and then passed the remains to Tenaka. Finishing the meal, the warrior leaned back against the cold rock.

'There is a mystery around you, lady. But I will leave it lie. The world would be a sad place without mysteries.'

'The world *is* a sad place,' she said, 'full of death and terror. Why is evil so much stronger than love?'

'Who says that it is?' he responded.

'You have not been living among the Drenai. Men like Aulin are hunted down like criminals; farmers are butchered for failing to reach absurd crop levels; the arenas are packed with baying crowds who laugh while animals rip and tear women and children. It is vile! All of it.'

'It will pass,' he said gently. 'And now it is time to sleep.' He held out his hand to her, but she shrank back, her dark eyes suddenly fearful. 'I will not harm you, but we must let the fire die. We will share warmth, but that is all we will share. Trust me.'

'I can sleep alone,' she said.

'Very well.' He untied the blanket and passed it to her, then wrapped himself in his cloak and leaned his head back to the rock, closing his eyes.

Renya stretched herself out on the cold ground, pillowing her head on her arm.

As the fire died so the night cold grew, seeping into her limbs. She awoke shivering uncontrollably and sat up, rubbing warmth into her numbed legs.

Tenaka opened his eyes and held out his hand. 'Come,' he said.

She moved to him and he opened his cloak, wrapping it around her and pulling her in to his chest before covering them both with the blanket. She nestled against him still shivering.

'T-t-tell me about c-c-clay diamonds,' she asked.

He smiled. 'The wise man was called Kias. He said that too many people go through life without pausing to enjoy what they have and he told of a man who was given a clay jug by a friend. The friend said, "Examine it when you have the time." But it was just a simple clay jug and the man put it aside and forged on with his life, spending his time acquiring riches. One day, when he was old, he took the jug and opened it. Within was a huge diamond.'

'I do not understand.'

'Kias claimed that life was like that clay jug. Unless we examined it and understood it, we could not enjoy it.'

'Sometimes understanding robs you of joy,' she whispered.

He said nothing, transferring his gaze to the night sky and the distant stars. Renya fell into a dreamless sleep, her head tipping forward, dislodging the woollen burnoose that covered her close-cropped hair. Tenaka reached up to replace it, then stopped as his hand touched her head. The hair was not close-cropped – it had grown as long as it would grow. For it was not hair but dark fur, soft as sable. Gently he pulled the burnoose into place and closed his eyes.

The girl was a Joining, half-human, half-animal.

No wonder she did not care for life.

Were there diamonds in the clay for such as she? He wondered.

3

At the Dragon barracks a man pushed his way past the screen of bushes before the parade ground. He was a big man, broad shoulders tapering to lean hips and long legs, was dressed in black and carried an iron-tipped ebony quarterstaff. Hooded, his face was covered by a shaped mask in black leather. He moved easily – the rolling, fluid gait of the athlete – yet he was wary, his bright blue eyes flickering to every bush and shadow-haunted tree.

When he saw the bodies he circled them slowly, reading the brief battle in the tracks.

One man against four.

The first three had died almost instantly and that spoke of speed. The fourth had run past the lone warrior. The tall man followed the track and nodded.

So. Here was a mystery. The lone warrior was not alone – he had a companion who took no part in the fray. The footprints were small, yet the stride long. A woman?

Yes, a woman. A tall woman.

He glanced back at the bodies.

'That was well done,' he said aloud, the voice muffled by the mask. 'Damn well done.' One against four. Not many men could survive against such odds, yet this man had not only survived but won the day with skill to spare.

Ringar? He was a lightning killer with astonishing

reflexes. Yet he barely chanced a neck cut, more often choosing the lower torso: the disembowelling cut.

Argonin? No, he was dead. Strange how a man could forget such a thing.

Who then? An unknown? No. In a world where skill with arms was of paramount importance, there were few unknowns of such bewildering talent.

He studied the tracks one more, picturing the battle, seeing at last the blurred print at the centre. The warrior had leapt and spun in the air like a dance before hammering home the death blow.

Tenaka Khan!

Realisation struck the big man like a blow to the heart. His eyes glittered strangely and his breathing grew ragged.

Of all the men in the world who he hated, Tenaka had pride of place.

Or was that still true? He relaxed and remembered, his thoughts tracing his memories like salt over a festering wound.

'I should have killed you then,' he said. 'None of this would have happened to me.'

He pictured Tenaka dying, his blood seeping into the snow. It gave him no joy, but still he hungered for the deed.

'I will make you pay,' he said.

And set off to the south.

*

Tenaka and Renya made good progress on the second day – seeing no one, nor any track made by man. The wind had died down and the clean air held the promise of spring. Tenaka was silent through most of the day and Renya did not press him.

Towards dusk as they clambered down a steep incline, she lost her footing and pitched forward, tumbling and rolling to the foot of the hill and striking her head on a gnarled tree-root. Tenaka ran to her side, pulling free her burnoose and examining the seeping gash on her temple. Her eyes flared open.

'Don't touch me,' she screamed, clawing at his hands.

He moved back, handing her the cotton burnoose.

'I don't like to be touched,' she said apologetically.

'Then I shall not touch you,' he answered. 'But you should bandage that wound.'

She tried to stand, but the world spun and she fell to the snow. Tenaka made no move to help her. Glancing around for a place to camp, he spotted a likely site some thirty paces away to the left: a natural screen of trees blocking the wind, with overhanging boughs to halt any storm snow. He made his way to it, collecting branches as he went. Renya watched him walk away and struggled to rise, but felt sick and began to tremble violently. Her head throbbed, the pain a rhythmic pounding which sent waves of nausea through her. She tried to crawl.

'I . . . don't need you,' she whispered.

Tenaka prepared the fire, blowing the tinder until tiny flames shivered above the snow. Then he added thicker twigs and finally branches. When the blaze was well set he returned to the girl, stooping to lift her unconscious body. He laid her by the fire, then climbed a nearby fir tree to hack away green boughs with his short sword. Gathering them he made a bed for her, lifted her on to it and then covered her with the blanket. He examined the wound – there was no fracture as far as he could tell, but an ugly bruise was forming around an egg-sized lump.

He stroked her face, admiring the softness of her skin and the sleekness of her neck.

'I will not harm you, Renya,' he said. 'Of all the things that I am, of all the deeds I have done that shamed me, I have never harmed a woman. Nor a child. You are safe with me . . . Your secrets are safe with me.'

'I know what it is like, you see. I too am between worlds – half-Nadir, half-Drenai, wholly nothing. For you it is worse. But I am here. Believe in me.'

He returned to the fire, wishing he could say those words when her eyes were open but knowing he would not. In all his life he had opened his heart to only one woman: Illae.

Beautiful Illae, the bride he had purchased in a Ventrian market. He smiled at the memory. Two thousand pieces of silver and he had taken her home only to have her refuse to share his bed.

'Enough of this nonsense,' he had stormed. 'You are mine. Body and soul! I bought you!'

'What you bought was a carcass,' she retorted. 'Touch me and I will kill myself. And you too.'

'You will be disappointed if you try it in that order,' he said.

'Don't mock me, barbarian!'

'Very well. What would you have me do? Re-sell you to a Ventrian?'

'Marry me.'

'And then, I take it, you will love and adore me?'

'No. But I will sleep with you and try to be good company.'

'Now there is an offer that's hard to refuse. A slave girl who offers her master less than he paid for, at a much greater price. Why should I do it?'

'Why should you not?'

They had wed two weeks later and ten years of

their life together had brought him joy. He knew she did not love him, but it didn't matter. He did not need to *be* loved, he needed to *love*. She had seen that in him from the first, and played on it mercilessly. He never let her know that he understood the game, he merely relaxed and enjoyed it. The wise man, Kias, had tried to warn him.

'You give too much of yourself to her, my friend. You fill her with your dreams and your hopes, and your soul. If she leaves or betrays you, what will you have left?'

'Nothing,' he had answered truthfully.

'You are a foolish man, Tenaka. I hope she stays by you.'

'She will.'

He had been so sure. But he had not bargained for death.

Tenaka shivered and drew his cloak about him as the wind picked up.

He would take the girl to Sousa and then head on for Drenan. It would not be hard to find Ceska, nor to kill him. No man is so well protected that he becomes safe. Not as long as the assassin is prepared to die. And Tenaka was more than prepared.

He desired death, longed for the bleak emptiness and the absence of pain.

By now Ceska would know Tenaka was on his way. The letter would have reached him within the month, travelling as it did by sea to Mashrapur and then north-east to Drenan.

'I hope you dream of me, Ceska. I hope I walk in your nightmares.'

'I don't know about him,' said a muffled voice, 'but you walk in mine.'

Tenaka spun to his feet, his sword flashing into the air.

Before him stood the giant in the black mask.

'I have come to kill you,' he said, drawing his longsword.

*

Tenaka edged away from the fire, watching the man, his mind clearing and his body easing into the smooth confident fluidity of combat.

The giant twirled his sword and spread his arms wide for balance. Tenaka blinked as recognition hit him.

'Ananais?' he said.

The giant's sword whistled for his neck, but Tenaka blocked the cut and jumped back.

'Ananais, *is* it you?' he said again.

The giant stood silently for a moment. 'Yes,' he said, at last. 'It is I. Now defend yourself!'

Tenaka sheathed his sword and walked forward. 'I could not fight you,' he said. 'And I know not why you should desire my death.'

Ananais leapt forward, hammering a fist to Tenaka's head and pitching him to the snow.

'Why?' he shouted. 'You don't know *why*? Look at me!'

He wrenched the leather mask from his face and in the flickering firelight Tenaka saw a living nightmare. There was no face, only the twisted, scarred ruin of features. The nose was gone, and the upper lip, jagged white and red scars criss-crossing the remaining skin. Only the blue eyes and the tightly-curled blond hair showed evidence of humanity.

'Sweet gods of light!' whispered Tenaka. 'I didn't do that . . . I never knew.'

Ananais moved forward slowly, lowering the point of his sword to touch Tenaka's neck.

'The pebble that caused the landslide,' said the giant cryptically. 'You know what I mean.'

47

Tenaka lifted his hand and slowly pushed aside the sword-blade.

'You will have to tell me, my friend,' he said, sitting up.

'Damn you!' shouted the giant, dropping his sword and hauling Tenaka to his feet, dragging him forward until their faces were inches apart. '*Look* at me!'

Tenaka gazed steadily into the ice-blue eyes, sensing the edge of madness lurking there. His life hung on a thread.

'Tell me what happened,' he said softly. 'I am not running away. If you desire to kill me, so be it. But tell me.'

Ananais released him and turned, seeking his mask, presenting his broad back to Tenaka. And in that moment Tenaka knew what was required of him. Sadness filled him.

'I cannot kill you,' he said.

The giant turned again, tears flowing from his eyes.

'Oh, Tani,' he said, his voice breaking, 'look what they did to me!' As he sank to his knees, hands covering the ruined face, Tenaka knelt beside him in the snow and embraced him. The giant began to weep, his chest heaving, his sobbing loud and painful. Tenaka patted his back as if he were a child and felt his pain as if it were his own.

Ananais had come not to kill him, but to die at his hand. And he knew why the giant blamed him. On the day the order to disband the Dragon had been served, Ananais had gathered the men ready to march on Drenan and depose Ceska. Tenaka and the Dragon Gan, Baris, had defused the situation, reminding the men that they had lived and fought for democracy. Thus the revolution was over before it had begun.

And now the Dragon was destroyed, the land in ruins and terror stalked the Drenai.

Ananais had been right.

Renya watched silently until the sobbing ceased, then she stood and walked to the two men, pausing to add fuel to the dying fire. Ananais glanced up and saw her, then scrabbled for his mask.

She moved to his side, kneeling by him, then gently touched the hands that held the mask in place. Curling her fingers around his hands, she pulled the mask clear, her dark eyes fixed only to the giant's own.

As the ruined face came into view Ananais closed his eyes and bowed his head. Renya leaned forward and kissed his brow, then his scarred cheek. His eyes opened.

'Why?' he whispered.

'We all have scars,' she said. 'Better by far for them to be worn on the outside.' She rose and returned to her bed.

'Who is she?' asked Ananais.

'She is hunted by Ceska,' Tenaka told him.

'Aren't we all?' commented the giant, replacing his mask.

'Yes, but we will surprise him,' said Tenaka.

'That would be nice.'

'Trust me, my friend. I mean to bring him down.'

'Alone?'

Tenaka grinned. 'Am I still alone?'

'No! Do you have a plan?'

'Not yet.'

'Good. I thought perhaps the two of us were going to surround Drenan!'

'It might come to that! How many of the Dragon still live?'

'Precious few. Most followed the call. I would

have done so too, had it reached me in time. Decado still lives.'

'That is good news,' said Tenaka.

'Not really. He has become a monk.'

'A *monk*? Decado? He lived to kill.'

'Not any more. Are you thinking of gathering an army?'

'No, it would do no good against the Joinings. They are too strong, too fast – too everything.'

'They can be beaten,' said Ananais.

'Not by men.'

'I defeated one.'

'You?'

'Yes. After we disbanded I tried farming. It didn't work out. I had heavy debts and Ceska had opened the arenas for combat games, so I became a gladiator. I thought I would have maybe three fights and earn enough to settle my debts. But I enjoyed the life, you know? I fought under another name, but Ceska found out who I was. At least, that's what I assume. I was due to fight a man named Treus, but when the gates opened there stood a Joining. Gods – he must have been eight feet tall.

'But I beat him. By all the demons in Hell, I beat him!'

'How?'

'I had to let him come in close and think he had won. Then I gutted him with my knife.'

'That was an awful risk,' said Tenaka.

'Yes.'

'But you got away with it?'

'Not quite,' answered Ananais. 'He tore off my face.'

*

'I really thought I could kill you, you know?' said Ananais as they sat together by the fire. 'I really believed it. I hated you. The more I saw the nation suffer, the more you came into my mind. I felt cheated – as if all I had ever lived for had been ruined. And when the Joining . . . when I was injured . . . I lost my mind. My courage. Everything.'

Tenaka sat silently, his heart heavy. Ananais had been a vain man, but gifted with humour that was always self-mocking; it took the edge from his vanity. And he had been handsome, adored by the ladies. Tenaka did not interrupt him. He had the feeling that a long, long time had passed since Ananais had sat in company. The words flowed like a torrent, but always the giant returned to his hatred of the Nadir prince.

'I knew it was irrational, but I couldn't help it, and when I found the bodies at the barracks and knew it was you, I was blind with rage. Until I saw you sitting there. And then . . . then . . .'

'Then you thought to let me kill you,' said Tenaka softly.

'Yes. It seemed . . . fitting.'

'I am glad we found each other, my friend. I just wish some of the others were here.'

The morning was bright and fresh and the warmth of the promise of spring kissed the forest, lightening the hearts of the travellers.

Renya watched Tenaka with new eyes, remembering not only the love and understanding he had shown to his scarred friend, but the words he had said to her before the giant arrived: 'Believe in me.'

And Renya believed.

But more than this. Something in his words touched her heart and the pain in her soul eased.

He knew.

And yet he cared. Renya did not know what love

51

was, for in all her life only one man had ever cared for her, and that was Aulin, the ancient Arcanist. Now there was another. He was not ancient.

Oh, no. Not ancient at all!

He would not leave her in Sousa. Or anywhere else. Where Tenaka Khan walked, there would be Renya. He was unaware of it as yet. But he would learn.

That afternoon Tenaka stalked a young deer – bringing it down with a dagger hurled twenty paces – and the companions ate well. They slept early, making up for the late night before, and the following morning sighted the spires of Sousa to the south-east.

'You'd best stay here,' Ananais advised. 'I should imagine your description has been circulated throughout Drenai by now. Why ever did you write that damned letter? It's not the sensible thing to let the victim know the assassin is on his way!'

'On the contrary, my friend. Paranoia will *eat* at him. It will keep him awake – on edge – he will not think clearly. And for every day that there is no news of me, his fears will grow. It will make him uncertain.'

'You think,' said Ananais. 'Anyway, I will take Renya into the city.'

'Very well. I shall wait here.'

'And does Renya have nothing to say about this arrangement?' said the girl sweetly.

'I did not think it would displease you,' answered Tenaka, nonplussed.

'Well it does!' she snapped. 'You do not own me; I go where I will.' She sat down on a fallen tree and folded her arms, staring into the trees.

'I thought you wanted to go to Sousa,' said Tenaka.

'No. Aulin wanted me there.'

'Well, where do you want to go?'

'I am not sure yet. I will let you know.'

Tenaka shook his head and turned to the giant, spreading his hands.

Ananais shrugged. 'Well, I will go in anyway. We need some food – and a little information would not go amiss. I shall see what I can find out.'

'Stay out of trouble,' warned Tenaka.

'Don't worry about me, I will blend in. I shall just find a large crowd of tall black-masked men and stick with them.'

'You know what I mean.'

'Yes. Don't worry! I will not risk fifty per cent of our new army on one reconnaissance.'

Tenaka watched him walk away and returned to the girl, sweeping the snow from the trunk and sitting down beside her.

'Why did you not go with him?'

'Did you want me to?' she countered, turning to look into his violet eyes.

'Want you to? What do you mean?'

She leaned into him. He caught the musky perfume of her skin and noticed again the sleekness of her neck and the dark beauty of her eyes.

'I want to stay with you,' she whispered.

He closed his eyes, shutting out the magic of her beauty. But the perfume lingered.

'This is insane,' he said, pushing himself to his feet.

'Why?'

'Because I am not going to live very long. Don't you understand? Killing Ceska is not a game. My chances of survival are one in a thousand.'

'It is a game,' she said. 'A man's game. You don't

need to kill Ceska – it is not for you to take on the burden of the Drenai.'

'I know that,' he said. 'It is personal. But I will see it through and so will Ananais.'

'And so will I. I have as much reason to hate Ceska as both you and your friend. He hounded Aulin to death.'

'But you are a woman,' he said desperately.

She laughed at him, a rich, pealing sound which was full of humour. 'Oh, Tenaka, how I have longed for you to say something foolish. You are always so right. So clever. A woman, indeed! Yes, I *am*. And more than that. Had I wished, I could have slain those four soldiers myself. My strength is as great as yours, possibly greater, and I can move just as fast. You know what I am: a Joining! Aulin knew me in Drenan, where I was a cripple with a twisted back and a ruined leg. He took pity on me and brought me to Graven, where he used the machines as they were intended. He healed me, by blending me with one of Ceska's pets. You know what he used?'

'No,' whispered Tenaka.

In a blur of motion she sprang from the fallen trunk. His arms came up as she hit him and he fell to the snow, air exploding from his lungs. Within seconds she had pinned him to the ground. He struggled, but could not move. Holding his arms flat to the snow, she twisted her body until she was lying on top of him, her face inches from his own.

'He blended me with a panther,' she said.

'I would still have believed it if you had merely said it,' he told her. 'The demonstration was unnecessary.'

'Not for me,' said Renya. 'For now I have you at my mercy.'

He grinned . . . arched his back and twisted. With

a scream of surprise Renya was hurled to the left. Tenaka swivelled and dived on her, pinning her arms beneath her.

'I am seldom at anyone's mercy, young lady,' he said.

'Well?' she asked him, raising an eyebrow. 'Now what will you do?'

His face reddened and he did not answer. Nor did he move. He could feel the warmth of her body, smell the perfume of her skin.

'I love you,' she said. 'Truly!'

'I have no time, I cannot. I have no future.'

'Neither do I. What is there for a Joining? Kiss me.'

'No.'

'Please?'

He did not answer. He could not. For their lips touched.

4

Scaler stood in the crowd and watched the girl as they tied her to the stake. She did not struggle or cry out, and only contempt showed in her eyes. She was tall and fair-haired – not beautiful, but striking. As the guards piled brushwood against her legs they did not look at her, and Scaler sensed their shame.

It matched his own.

The officer climbed to the wooden platform beside the girl and surveyed the crowd. He felt their sullen anger wash over him and rejoiced in it. They were powerless.

Malif adjusted his crimson cloak and removed his helm, tucking it neatly into the crook of his arm. The sunshine felt good and the day promised to be fine. Very fine.

He cleared his throat.

'This woman has been accused of sedition, witchcraft, dealing in poisons and theft. On all counts she has been righteously condemned. But if there be any to speak for her, let them do so now!'

His eyes flickered to the left, where a movement began among the watchers. An old man was being restrained by a younger. No sport there!

Malif swept his arms to the right, pointing at a Joining in the red and bronze livery of Silius the Magister.

'This servant of the law has been appointed to defend the decision of the court. If any should wish to champion the girl, Valtaya, let him first gaze upon his opponent.'

Scaler gripped Belder's arm. 'Don't be a fool!' he hissed. 'You will be killed; I will not allow it.'

'Better to die than see this,' said the old soldier. But he ceased to struggle and with a weary sigh turned away and pushed his way back through the crowd.

Scaler glanced up at the girl. Her grey eyes were looking into his and she was smiling. There was no hint of mockery in the smile.

'I am sorry,' he mouthed, but she had looked away.

'May I speak?' she asked, her voice clear and strong.

Malif turned to her. 'The law says that you may, but let there be nothing seditious in your words or I shall have you gagged.'

'My friends,' she began, 'I am sorry to see you here today. Death means nothing but the absence of joy is worse than death. Most of you I know. And I love you all. Please go from here and remember me as you knew me. Think of the laughter and put this evil moment from your minds.'

'No need for that, lady!' someone shouted. The crowd parted and a tall man dressed in black moved to the open space before the pyre.

Valtaya looked down into the man's bright blue eyes. His face was covered by a mask of shining black leather and she wondered if a man with such beautiful eyes could possibly be the executioner.

'Who are you?' demanded Malif. The man removed his leather cloak, carelessly tossing it into the crowd.

'You requested a champion, did you not?'

Malif smiled. The man was massively built, but even he was dwarfed by the Joining.

What a fine day, to be sure!

'Remove your mask, so that we may see you,' he ordered.

'That is not necessary, nor is it part of the law,' replied the man.

'Indeed it is not. Very well. The contest will be decided in hand-to-hand combat, without weapons.'

'No!' shouted Valtaya. 'Please sir, reconsider – it is madness! If I must die, then let it be alone. I am reconciled to it, but you only make it more difficult.'

The man ignored her as from his broad black belt he tugged a pair of leather gauntlets.

'Is it permitted for me to wear these?' he asked.

Malif nodded and the Joining ambled forward. It was almost seven feet tall, with a hugh vulpine head. Its hands ended in wickedly curved talons. A low growl issued from its maw, and its lips curled back to show gleaming fangs.

'Are there any rules to this combat?' asked the man.

'None,' replied Malif.

'Fine,' said the man, hammering a fist into the beast's mouth. One fang snapped under the impact and blood sprayed into the air. Then he leapt forward, blows thundering to the beast's head.

But the Joining was strong, and after the initial shock it roared its defiance and sprang to the offensive. A fist snapped its head back, then its taloned claw flashed out. The man jumped back, his tunic slashed, blood seeping from shallow cuts in his chest. The two circled each other.

Now the Joining leapt and the man threw himself into the air feet first, his boots thundering into the beast's face. The Joining was hurled to the ground and the man rolled to his feet, running forward to aim a kick, but the Joining swept up an arm and knocked him to the ground. The beast reared up to its full height, then staggered, with eyes rolling and tongue lolling. The man jumped forward, hurling blow after blow to the creature's head, and the Joining toppled face-first into the dust of the market square. The man stood above it, chest heaving; then he turned to the stunned Malif.

'Cut the girl loose!' he said. 'It is over.'

'Sorcery!' shouted Malif. 'You are a warlock. You will burn with the girl. Take him!'

An angry roar rose from the crowd and they surged forward.

Ananais grinned and leapt to the platform as Malif stumbled back, scrabbling for his sword. Ananais hit him and he flew from the platform. The guards turned and ran and Scaler climbed to the stake, slicing his dagger through the ropes.

'Come on!' he yelled, taking Valtaya by the arm. 'We must get out of here. They will be back.'

'Who has my cloak?' bellowed Ananais.

'I have it, general,' shouted a bearded veteran. Ananais swirled the cloak around his shoulder, fixing the clasp, then lifted his hands for silence.

'When they ask who freed the girl, tell them it was the army of Tenaka Khan. Tell them the Dragon is back.'

'This way, quickly!' shouted Scaler, leading Valtaya to a narrow alley. Ananais leapt lightly from the platform and followed them, pausing to glance down at the lifeless Malif, his neck grotesquely twisted. He must have fallen badly, thought Ananais. But then if the fall had not killed him, the poison would have done so. Carefully he removed his gauntlets, pressing the hidden stud and sliding the needle covers in place over the knuckles. Tucking them into his belt, he raced after the man and the girl.

They ducked through a side door off a cobbled street and Ananais found himself in a darkened inn, the shutters closed and the chairs stacked on tables. The man and the girl were standing by the long bar.

The landlord – a short, balding fat man – was pouring wine into clay jugs. He glanced up as Ananais walked forward out of the shadows and the carafe fell from his trembling fingers.

Scaler spun round, his eyes fearful.

'Oh, it's you!' he said. 'You certainly move quietly for a big man. It's all right, Larcas; this is the man who rescued Valtaya.'

'Pleased to meet you,' said the landlord. 'Drink?'

'Thanks.'

'The world's gone mad,' said Larcas. 'You know, during the first five years that I ran this inn there was not one murder. Everyone had at least a little money. It was a joy in those days. The world's gone mad!'

He poured wine for Ananais, refilling his own glass which he drained at a single swallow. 'Mad! I hate violence. I came here for the quiet life. A corn city just off the Sentran Plain – no trouble. And look at us now. Animals that walk like men. Laws no one can understand, let alone obey. Informers, thieves, murderers. Break wind during the anthem and you are dubbed a traitor.'

Ananais pulled a chair from a table and sat down with his back to the trio. Gently he lifted his mask and sipped the wine. Valtaya joined him and he turned his head away, then finished the wine and replaced his mask. Her hand reached out and covered his own.

'Thank you for the gift of life,' she said.

'It was my pleasure, lady.'

'Your scars are bad?'

'I have not seen worse.'

'Have they healed?'

'Mostly. The one under my right eye opens now and then. I can live with it.'

'I will heal it for you.'

'It is not necessary.'

'It is a small thing. I would like to do it for you. Have no fear. I have seen scars before.'

'Not like these, lady. I have no face beneath this mask. But I was handsome once.'

'You are handsome still,' she said. His blue eyes blazed and he leaned forward, fist clenched.

'Do not make a fool of me, woman!'

'I merely meant . . .'

'I know what you meant – you meant to be kind. Well, I do not need kindness. Or understanding. I was handsome and I enjoyed it. Now I am a monster and I have learned to live with it.'

'Now *you* listen,' ordered Valtaya, leaning forward on her elbows. 'What I was going to say was that looks mean nothing to me. Deeds paint better pictures of a man than skin hanging from tendons and bones. What you did today was handsome.'

Ananais leaned back in his chair, folding his arms across his broad chest.

'I am sorry,' he said. 'Forgive me.'

She chuckled and reached forward, gripping his hand.

'There is nothing to forgive. We just know each other a little better.'

'Why did they seek to burn you?' he asked, laying his hand on hers and enjoying the warmth of her skin.

She shrugged: 'I deal in herbs and medicines. And I always speak the truth.'

'That accounts for witchcraft and sedition. What about theft?'

'I borrowed a horse. Tell me about you.'

'Little to tell. I am a warrior in search of a war.'

'Is that why you came back to Drenai?'

'Who knows?'

'Do you really have an army?'

'A force of two. But it's a beginning.'

'It's optimistic anyway. Does your friend fight as well as you?'

'Better. He's Tenaka Khan.'

'The Nadir prince. The Khan of Shadows.'

'You know your history.'

'I was raised at Dros Delnoch,' she said, sipping her wine. 'I thought he would be dead with the rest of the Dragon.'

'Men like Tenaka do not die easily.'

'Then you must be Ananais. The Golden One?'

'I once had that honour.'

'There are legends surrounding you both. The two of you routed twenty Vagrian raiders a hundred miles west of Sousa. And later you surrounded and destroyed a large group of slavers near Purdol in the east.'

'There were not twenty raiders, only seven – and one was sick with fever. And we outnumbered the slavers two to one.'

'And did you not rescue a Lentrian princess from Nadir tribesmen, travelling hundreds of leagues to the north?'

'No, but I often wondered how that story came about. All this happened before you were born – how do you know so much about it?'

62

'I listen to Scaler; he tells wonderful stories. Why did you save me today?'

'What kind of question is that? Am I not the man who travelled hundreds of leagues to rescue a Lentrian princess?'

'I am not a princess.'

'And I am no hero.'

'You took on a Joining.'

'Yes. But then from my first blow he was dying. I have poison spikes in my gauntlets.'

'Even so, not many men would have faced it.'

'Tenaka would have killed it without the gauntlets. He's the second fastest man I've ever known.'

'The *second*?'

'You mean you have never heard of Decado?'

*

Tenaka built up the fire and then knelt beside the sleeping Renya. She was breathing evenly. He touched her face gently with one finger, stroking the skin of her cheek. Then he left her and walked to the top of a nearby rise to stare out over the rolling hills and plains to the south as the dawn sun crested the Skeln mountains.

Forests, rivers and long meadows swept on into a distant blue haze, as if the sky had melted and linked with the land. To the south-west the defiant Skoda mountains pierced the clouds like dagger points, red as blood and shining proud.

Tenaka shivered and pulled his cloak about him. Void of human life, the land was beautiful.

His thoughts drifted aimlessly, but always Renya's face returned to his mind's eye.

Did he love her? Could love be born with such speed, or was it just the passion of a lonely man for a child of sorrow?

She needed him.

But did he need her?

Especially now, with all that lay before him?

You fool, he told himself, as he pictured life with Renya in his Ventrian palace – it is too late for that. You are the man who stepped off the mountain.

He sat down on a flat rock and rubbed his eyes.

What is the sense to this hopeless mission, he asked himself, an edge of bitterness washing over him. He could kill Ceska – of that there was no doubt. But what would be the point? Would the world change with the death of one despot?

Possibly not. But the course was set.

'What are you thinking about?' asked Renya, moving up to sit beside him and curling her arm around his waist. He opened his cloak, lifting it around her shoulders.

'I was just dawn-dreaming,' he said. 'And admiring the view.'

'It is beautiful here.'

'Yes. And now it is perfect.'

'When will your friend be back?'

'Soon.'

'Are you worried about him?'

'How did you know?'

'The way you told him to stay out of trouble.'

'I always worry about Ananais. He has an instinct for the dramatic and a sublime belief in his physical talents. He would tackle an army, convinced he could win. He probably could too – a small army anyway.'

'You like him a great deal, don't you?'

'I love him.'

'Not many men can say that,' said Renya. 'They feel the need to add "like a brother". It's nice. Have you known him long?'

'Since I was seventeen. I joined the Dragon as a cadet and we became friends soon after.'

'Why did he want to fight you?'

'He didn't really. But life has dealt harshly with him and he blamed me for it – at least in part. A long time ago, he wanted to depose Ceska. He could have done it. Instead I helped to stop him.'

'Not an easy thing to forgive,' she said.

'With hindsight, I agree.'

'Do you still mean to kill Ceska?'

'Yes.'

'Even if it means your own death?'

'Even then!'

'Then where do we go from here? To Drenan?'

He turned to her, lifting her chin with his hand.

'You still wish to travel with me?'

'Of course.'

'It's selfish, but I am glad,' he told her.

A man's scream broke the dawn silence and flocks of birds rose from the trees screeching in panic. Tenaka leapt to his feet.

'It came from over there,' shouted Renya, pointing north-east. Tenaka's sword flashed into the sunlight and he began to run, Renya only yards behind him.

A bestial howling mingled now with the screams and Tenaka slowed his run.

'It's a Joining,' he said, as Renya caught up.

'What shall we do?'

'Damn!' he said. 'Wait here.'

He ran forward, over a small rise and into a narrow clearing ringed by snow-covered oak. At the centre a man was crouching at the base of a tree, his tunic covered with blood and his leg hideously slashed. Before him stood a huge Joining.

Tenaka shouted as the creature lunged for the

man and the beast twisted, its blood-red eyes turning on the warrior. He knew he was looking into the eyes of Death, for no man could stand against this beast and live. Renya ran to his side, her dagger held before her.

'Get back!' order Tenaka.

She ignored him. 'What now?' she asked coolly.

The beast reared up to a full nine feet tall and spread its taloned paws wide. It was obviously part bear.

'Run!' shouted the wounded man. 'Please leave me!'

'Good advice,' said Renya.

Tenaka said nothing and the beast charged, sending a blood-chilling roar echoing through the trees. He crouched, his violet eyes fixed on the awesome creature bearing down upon him.

As its shadow fell across him he leapt forward, screaming a Nadir war-cry.

And the beast vanished.

Tenaka fell to the snow, dropping his sword. He rolled to his feet instantly to face the wounded man, who was standing now, and smiling. There was no trace of wounds upon his blue tunic or his body.

'What the devil is happening here?' demanded Tenaka.

The man shimmered and vanished. Tenaka swung to Renya, who was standing wide-eyed and staring at the tree.

'Someone played us for fools,' said Tenaka, brushing snow from his tunic.

'But why?' asked the girl.

'I don't know. Let us away – the forest has lost its magic.'

'They were so real,' said Renya. 'I thought we were finished. Were they ghosts, do you think?'

'Who knows? Whatever they were they left no tracks, and I have little time for such mysteries.'

'But there must have been a reason,' she persisted. 'Was it done just for us?'

He shrugged, then helped her up the steep incline back to their camp.

*

Forty miles away four men sat silently in a small room, their eyes closed and their minds open. Then one by one they opened their eyes, leaning back in their chairs and stretching as if awakening from deep sleep.

Their leader, the man who had appeared to be under attack in the clearing, stood and walked to the narrow stone window, gazing out over the meadow below.

'What do you think?' he asked, without looking round. The other three exchanged glances and then one, a short stocky man with a thick yellow beard, said, 'He is worthy at least. He did not hesitate to aid you.'

'Is that important?' asked the leader, still gazing from the window.

'I believe it is.'

'Tell my why, Acuas.'

'He is a man with a mission, yet he is a humanist. He was willing to risk his life – no, throw it away – rather than let a fellow human suffer alone. Light has touched him.'

'What do you say, Balan?'

'It is too early for judgements. The man may just be rash,' answered a taller, slimmer man with a shock of dark curly hair.

'Katan?'

The last man was slender, his face long and ascetic, his eyes large and sorrowful. He smiled.

'Were it my choice, I would say yes. He is worthy. He is a man of the Source, although he knows it not.'

'Then we are – in the main – agreed,' said the leader. 'I think it is time we spoke with Decado.'

'But should we not be more sure, Lord Abbot?' asked Balan.

'Nothing in life is sure, my son. Except the promise of death.'

5

It was an hour past curfew and the streets of Drenan were deserted, the vast white city silent. A three-quarter moon hung in a clear sky, its reflection glinting from a thousand rainwashed cobbles on the Street of Pillars.

From the shadows of a tall building came six men in black armour, dark helms covering their faces. They walked swiftly, purposefully towards the palace, looking neither to right nor left.

Two Joinings, armed with massive axes, barred their path and the men stopped. Six pairs of eyes fastened on the beasts and they howled in pain and fled.

The men walked on. From behind shutters and heavily curtained windows eyes watched their progress and the marchers felt the stares, sensing the curiosity turning to fear as they were recognised.

They moved on in silence until they reached the gates, where they waited. After several seconds they heard the grating movement of the bar beyond, and the gate opened. Two sentries bowed their heads as the black-armoured men marched forward across the courtyard and on into the main torchlit corridors lined with guards. All eyes avoided them. At the far end the double doors of oak and bronze slid open, the leader raised his hand and his five companions halted, turning on their heels to stand before the doors with black-gloved hands resting on ebony sword-hilts.

The leader lifted his helm and entered the room beyond.

As he had expected, Ceska's chief minister Eertik waited alone at his desk. He looked up as the warrior appeared, his dark, heavy-lidded eyes fixing on the knight.

'Welcome, Padaxes,' he said, his voice dry and faintly metallic.

'Greetings, counsellor,' answered Padaxes, smiling. He was a tall man, square-faced, with eyes the grey of a winter sky. His mouth was full-lipped and sensual, yet he was not handsome. There was about his features a strangeness – a taint hard to define.

'The emperor has need of your services,' said Eertik. As he stood and moved round the desk of oak, his dark velvet garments rustled. Padaxes registered the sounds, considering them not dissimilar to a snake moving through dry grass. He smiled again.

'I am always at the emperor's command.'

'He knows that, Padaxes, just as he knows you value his generosity. There is a man who seeks harm to the emperor. We have had word that he is in the north and the emperor wishes him taken or slain.'

'Tenaka Khan,' said Padaxes.

Eertik's eyes opened wide in surprise. 'You know of him?'

'Obviously.'

'May I ask how?'

'You may not.'

'He is a threat to the empire,' said Eertik, masking his annoyance.

'He is a walking corpse from the moment I leave this room. Did you know that Ananais was with him?'

'I did not,' said Eertik, 'although now you say it, I understand the mystery. Ananais was thought to be dead of his wounds. Does this intelligence pose a problem for your Order?'

'No. One, two, ten or one hundred. Nothing can stand against my Templars. We will ride in the morning.'

'Can I aid you in any way?'

'Yes. Send a child to the Temple in two hours. A girl child under ten years. There are certain religious rites which must be performed. I must commune with the power that holds the universe.'

'It shall be done.'

'Our temple buildings are in need of repair. I was considering a move to the country and the commissioning of a new temple – something larger,' said Padaxes.

'The emperor's thoughts exactly,' said Eertik. 'I will have some plans drawn up for your return.'

'Convey my thanks to the Lord Ceska.'

'I will indeed. May your journey be swift and your return joyful.'

'As the Spirit wills it,' answered Padaxes, replacing his black helm.

*

From his high tower window the Abbot gazed down into the upper garden where twenty-eight acolytes knelt before their trees. Despite the season the roses thrived, the perfume of their blooms filling the air.

The Abbot closed his eyes and soared, his spirit rising and flowing. Gently he descended to the garden, coming to rest beside the slender Katan.

Katan's mind opened to receive him and the Abbot joined the acolyte, flowing within the fragile stems and capillary systems of the plant.

The rose welcomed them. It was a red rose.

The Abbot withdrew and, one by one, joined each of the acolytes in turn. Only Balan's rose had failed to flower, but the buds were full and he was but a little way behind the rest.

The Abbot returned to his body in the high tower, opening his eyes and breathing deeply. He rubbed his eyes and moved to the southern window, looking down to the second level and the vegetable garden.

There, kneeling in the soil, was a priest in a dirty brown cassock. The Abbot walked from the room, descending the circular stair to push open the door to the lower level. He stepped out on to the well-scrubbed flagstones of the path and descended the stone steps to the garden.

'Greetings, brother,' he said.

The priest looked up, then bowed. 'Greetings, Lord Abbot.'

The Abbot seated himself on a stone bench nearby.

'Please continue,' he said. 'Do not let me disturb you.'

The man returned to his work, weeding the soil, his hands black with dirt and his fingernails cracked and broken.

The Abbot looked about him. The garden was well-tended, the tools sharp and cared-for, the pathways clean and clear of weeds.

He gazed fondly on the priest. The man had changed greatly since that day five years ago when he had walked into the monastery declaring his wish to become a priest. Then he had been dressed in garish armour, two shortswords strapped to his thighs and a baldric belt across his chest bearing three daggers.

'Why do you wish to serve the Source?' the Abbot had asked.

'I am tired of death,' he had replied.

'You live to kill,' said the Abbot, staring into the haunted eyes of the warrior.

'I want to change,'

'You want to hide?'

'No.'

'Why did you choose this monastery?'

'I . . . I prayed.'

'Did you receive an answer?'

'No. But I was heading west and after praying I changed my mind and came north. And you were here.'

'You think that is an answer?'

'I don't know,' answered the warrior. 'Is it?'

'Do you know what order this is?'

'No.'

'The acolytes here are gifted beyond other men and they have powers you could not comprehend. Their whole lives are given over to the Source. What do you offer?'

'Only myself. My life.'

'Very well. I will take you. But hear this and mark it well. You will not mix with the other acolytes. You will not walk to the upper level. You will live below in a crofter's hut. You will put aside your weapons and never touch them again. Your tasks will be menial and your obedience total. You will not speak to anyone at any time – only when I address you, may you answer.'

'I agree,' said the warrior without hesitation.

'I will instruct you each afternoon and I will gauge your progress. If you fail in any way, I will dismiss you from the monastery.'

'I agree.'

For five years the warrior had obeyed without question, and as the seasons passed the Abbot watched the haunted expression fade from his dark eyes. He had learned well, though never could he master the release of the spirit. But in all other things the Abbot was pleased.

'Are you happy, Decado?' the Abbot asked now. The priest leaned back and turned.

'Yes, Lord Abbot.'

'No regrets?'

'None.'

'I have news of the Dragon,' said the Abbot, watching him carefully. 'Would you care to hear it?'

The priest looked thoughtful. 'Yes, I would. Is that wrong?'

'No, Decado, it is not wrong. They were your friends.'

The priest remained silent, waiting for the Abbot to speak.

'They were wiped out in a terrible battle by the Joinings of Ceska. Although they fought valiantly and well, they could not stand against the power of the beasts.' Decado nodded and returned to his work.

'How do you feel?'

'Very sad, Lord Abbot.'

'Not all your friends perished. Tenaka Khan and Ananais have returned to the Drenai and they plan to kill Ceska – to end his terror.'

'May the Source be with them.' said Decado.

'Would you like to be with them?'

'No, Lord Abbot.'

The Abbot nodded. 'Show me your garden,' he said. The priest rose and the two men walked among the plants, coming at last to the tiny hut that housed Decado. The Abbot walked around the outside. 'You are comfortable here?'

'Yes, Lord Abbot.'

Behind the hut the Abbot stopped, staring down at a tiny bush and the single flower that grew there.

'And what is this?'

'It is mine, Lord Abbot. Have I done wrong?'

'How did you come by it?'

'I found a seedpod someone had thrown from the upper level and I planted it three years ago. It's a beautiful plant; it usually flowers much later.'

'Do you spend much time with it?'

'When I can, Lord Abbot. It helps me to relax.'

'We have many roses on the upper levels, Decado. But none of this colour.'

It was a white rose.

*

Two hours after dawn Ananais returned to the campsite, bringing with him Valtaya, Scaler and Belder. Tenaka watched them approach. The older man, he could see, was a veteran who moved carefully, hand on sword-hilt. The woman was tall and well-made and she stayed close to the black-garbed Ananais. Tenaka grinned and shook his head. Still the Golden One, he thought. But the young man was interesting. There was about him something familiar, yet Tenaka was sure they had never met. Athletic and tall, clear-eyed and handsome, his long dark hair was held in place by a black metal circlet adorned with an opal at the centre. He wore a leaf-green cloak and calf-length brown walking boots. His tunic was of soft leather and he carried a shortsword in his hand. Tenaka sensed his fear.

He stepped from the trees to greet them.

Scaler looked up as he appeared. He wanted to rush forward and embrace him, but resisted the urge. Tenaka would never recognise him. The Nadir prince had changed little, he thought, save for the few grey hairs glinting in the sunlight. The violet eyes were still piercing, the stance still unconsciously arrogant.

'You cannot resist surprises, my friend,' said Tenaka.

'So true,' answered Ananais. 'But I have breakfast in the pack, and explanations can wait until I have eaten.'

'Introductions cannot,' said Tenaka softly.

'Scaler, Valtaya and Belder,' said Ananais, waving an arm at the trio. With that he strode past Tenaka and on towards the fire.

'Welcome!' said Tenaka lamely, spreading his hands.

Scaler walked forward. 'Our presence in your camp is temporary,' he said. 'Your friend helped Valtaya and it was vital that we left the city. Now that she is safe, we shall return.'

'I see. Join us for food first,' offered Tenaka.

The silence around the fire was uncomfortable, but Ananais ignored it, taking his food to the edge of the trees and sitting with his back to the group so that he could remove his mask and eat.

'I have heard much of you, Tenaka,' said Valtaya.

He turned to her. 'Much of what people say is untrue.'

'There is always a grain of truth at the centre of such sagas.'

'Perhaps. Where did you hear the stories?'

'From Scaler,' she replied. Tenaka nodded and turned to the young man, who was blushing furiously.

'And where did you hear them, my friend?'

'Here and there,' replied Scaler.

'I was a soldier. Nothing more. My ancestry gave me fame. I could name many better swordsmen, better riders, better men. But they had no name to carry before them like a banner.'

'You are too modest,' said Scaler.

'It is not a question of modesty. I am half-Nadir of the line of Ulric and half-Drenai. My great-grand-father was Regnak, the Earl of Bronze. And yet I am neither Earl nor Khan.'

'The Khan of Shadows,' said Scaler.

'How did such a thing come about?' asked Valtaya.

Tenaka grinned. 'It was the Second Nadir War and Regnak's son Orrin made a treaty with the Nadir. Part of the price was that his son, Hogun, should marry the Khan's daughter, Shillat. It was not a marriage of love. It was a grand ceremony, I am told, and the union was consummated near the Shrine of Druss on the northern plain before Delnoch. Hogun took his bride back to the fortress, where she dwelt unhappily for three years. I was born there. Hogun died in a riding accident when I was two and his father sent Shillat home. It was written into the marriage contract that no child of the union could inherit Dros Delnoch. And as for the Nadir, they desired no half-breed to lead them.'

'You must have been very unhappy,' said Valtaya.

'I have known great joys in my life. Do not feel pity for me, lady.'

'How did you come to be a Dragon general?'

'I was sixteen when the Khan, my grandfather, sent me to Delnoch. Again it was part of the marriage contract. My other grandfather was there to greet me. He told me he had arranged a commission in the Dragon. It is that simple!'

Scaler stared into the fire, his mind flowing back.

Simple? How could such a terrible moment be described as simple?

It was raining, he remembered, when the guard on the Eldibar tower sounded the trumpet. His grandfather Orrin had been in the keep, engaged in a war-game with their guest. Scaler was perched on a high chair, watching them roll the dice and move the tiny regiments, when the trumpet call echoed eerily in the storm winds.

'The Nadir spawn has arrived,' said Orrin. 'He picked the right day for it.'

They dressed Scaler in a cloak of oiled leather and a wide-brimmed leather hat, then began the long walk to Wall One.

Once there, Orrin gazed down on the twenty riders and the dark-haired youth on the white shaggy pony.

'Who seeks entry to Dros Delnoch?' called Orrin.

'The son of Shillat,' yelled the Nadir captain.

'He only may enter,' said Orrin.

The great gates creaked open and the Nadir troop wheeled their mounts, riding swiftly back to the north.

Tenaka did not turn to watch them go, and no word passed between them. The youth touched his heels to the pony and cantered into the gate tunnel and up on to the green field between Walls One and Two. There he slid from the saddle and waited for Orrin to approach.

'You are not welcome here,' said Orrin, 'but I will stand by my bargains. I have arranged a commission in the Dragon and you will leave in three months. Until then you will learn Drenai ways. I want no relative of mine eating with his fingers in the officers' mess.'

'Thank you, grandfather,' said Tenaka.

'Don't call me that,' snapped Orrin. 'Not ever!

You will call me "My Lord" or in company "Sir". Do you understand?'

'I believe that I do, grandfather. And I shall obey you.' Tenaka's gaze flickered to the child.

'This is my true grandson,' said Orrin. 'All my children are dead. Only this little lad survives to continue my line. His name is Arvan.'

Tenaka nodded and turned to the dark-bearded man to Orrin's left.

'And this is a friend of the House of Regnak – the only counsellor worth his salt in the entire country. His name is Ceska.'

'Delighted to meet you,' said Ceska, reaching out his hand. Tenaka clasped it firmly, his gaze locking to the man's dark eyes.

'Now let us get inside and out of this damned rain,' muttered Orrin. Lifting the child to his broad shoulders, the white-bearded Earl strode away towards the distant keep. Tenaka gathered the reins of his pony and followed, Ceska beside him.

'Do not be upset by his manner, young price,' said Ceska. 'He is old and set in his ways. But he is a fine man, truly. I hope you will be happy among the Drenai. If ever there is anything I can do for you, do not hesitate to tell me.'

'Why?' asked Tenaka.

'I like you,' said Ceska, clapping him on the shoulder. 'And who knows – you may be Earl some day.'

'That is unlikely.'

'True, my friend. But the House of Bronze has been unlucky of late. As Orrin said, all his children are gone. Arvan alone survives.'

'He looks a strong child.'

'Indeed he does. But looks can be so deceptive, can they not?'

Tenaka was not sure he understood the meaning of Ceska's words, but he knew there were undercurrents of dark promises. He said nothing.

*

Later Tenaka listened in silence as Valtaya talked of the rescue in the marketplace, and of their bribing a night sentry to let them pass through the northern postern gate of the city. Ananais had brought a huge pack of food, plus two bows and eighty shafts in doeskin quivers. Valtaya had extra blankets and a rolled canvas sheet for a small tent.

After they had eaten, Tenaka took Ananais into the trees. They found a secluded spot and cleared the snow from some rocks before sitting down to talk.

'There is an uprising in Skoda,' said Ananais. 'Two villages were sacked by Ceska's Legion. A local named Rayvan gathered a small army and destroyed the raiders. They say men are flocking to him, but I don't think he can last. He's a common man.'

'Not of the Blood, you mean,' said Tenaka dryly.

'I have nothing against common men. But he has not the training to plan a campaign.'

'What else?'

'Two risings in the west – both ruthlessly put down. All the men crucified, fields sewn with salt. You know the system!'

'What about the south?'

'Difficult to say. News is scarce. But Ceska's there. On hand. I don't think they will rise. It is said that there is a secret society against Ceska, but that is likely to be no more than talk.'

'What do you suggest?' asked Tenaka.

'Let us go to Drenan, kill Ceska and then retire.'

'That simple?'

'The best plans are always simple, Tani.'

'What about the women?'

Ananais shrugged. 'What can we do? You say Renya wants to be with you? Let her come. We can leave her with friends in Drenan. I still know one or two people I think we can rely on.'

'And Valtaya?'

'She won't stay with us – there is nothing for her. We will leave her in the next town.'

Tenaka raised an eyebrow. 'Nothing for her?'

Ananais looked away. 'Not any more, Tani. Once, maybe.'

'All right. We will head for Drenan, but angle to the west. Skoda should be beautiful at this time of the year.'

Side by side they returned to the camp, where they found three strangers waiting. Tenaka spoke softly: 'Scout around, Ani. See how many other surprises are in the offing.' Then he walked forward. Two of the men were warriors, both about the same age as Tenaka himself. The third was an old man, blind and wearing the tattered blue robes of the Seekers.

The warriors approached him. They were uncannily alike, black-bearded and stern of eye, though one was fractionally taller than the other. It was the shorter man who spoke.

'I am Galand and this is my brother, Parsal. We have come to join you, general.'

'For what purpose?'

'To put down Ceska. Why else?'

'I need no help for that, Galand.'

'I don't know what game this is, general. The Golden One was in Sousa and he told the crowd the Dragon was back. Well, if that is so, then I reckon I am back too. You don't recognise me, do you?'

'In truth I do not,' said Tenaka.

'I was not bearded then. I was Bar Galand of the Third Wing under Elias. I was the Sword Master and I beat you in a tourney once.

'I remember. The half-moon riposte! You would have ripped out my throat. As it was I had a ghastly bruise.'

'My brother is a good a man as I. We want to serve.'

'There is nothing to serve, my friend. I plan to kill Ceska. That is the work of an assassin – not an army.'

'Then we will stick by until the deed is done! I was sick with fever when the call came and the Dragon re-formed. I have been sick with sorrow since. A lot of fine men were lured into that trap. It does not seem right.'

'How did you find us?'

'I followed the blind man. Strange, don't you think?'

Tenaka moved to the fire and sat down opposite the Seeker.

The mystic's head lifted. 'I seek the Torchbearer,' he said, his voice a dry whisper.

'Who is he?' asked Tenaka.

'The Dark Spirit is over the land, like a great shadow,' whispered the man. 'I seek the Torchbearer, from whom all shadows flee.'

'Who is this man you seek?' persisted Tenaka.

'I don't know. Is it you?'

'I doubt it,' answered Tenaka. 'Will you eat with us?'

'My dreams told me the Torchbearer would bring me food. Is it you?'

'No.'

'There are three,' said the man. 'Of Gold, and

Ice, and Shadow. One is the Torchbearer. But which one? I have a message.'

Scaler moved forward to crouch at the man's side.

'I seek the truth,' he said.

'I have the truth,' replied the mystic, extending his hand. Scaler dropped a small silver coin into his palm.

'Of Bronze you sprang, haunted and hunted, drawn on your father's path. Kin to shadow, never resting, never silent. Dark spears hover, black wings to devour. You will stand when others flee. It is in the red you carry.'

'What does it mean?' asked Tenaka. Scaler shrugged and moved away.

'Death calls me. I must answer,' whispered the mystic. 'And yet the Torchbearer is not here.'

'Give me the message, old man. I will pass it on, I promise you.'

'Dark Templars ride against the Prince of Shadows. He cannot hide, for the torch is bright against the night. But thought is faster than arrows, and truth is sharper than blades. The beasts can fall, but only the King Beyond the Gate can bring them down.'

'Is that all?' asked Tenaka.

'You are the Torchbearer,' said the man. 'Now I see you clearly. You are chosen by the Source.'

'I am the Prince of Shadows,' said Tenaka. 'But I do not follow the Source, or any god. I believe in none of them.'

'The Source believes in you,' said the old man. 'I must go now. My rest is near.'

As Tenaka watched him hobble from the camp, his bare feet blue against the snow, Scaler joined him.

'What did he say to you?'

'I did not understand it.'

'Tell me the words,' said Scaler and Tenaka repeated them. Scaler nodded. 'Some of it is easy to decipher. The Dark Templars, for example. Have you heard of The Thirty?'

'Yes. Warrior priests who spend their lives becoming pure in the heart before riding off to die in a distant war. The Order died out years ago.'

'The Dark Templars are an obscene parody of The Thirty. They worship the Chaos Spirit and their powers are dark, yet deadly. Every form of vileness is pleasure to them, and they are formidable warriors.'

'And Ceska has sent them against me?'

'It would seem so. They are led by a man named Padaxes. There are sixty-six warriors in each temple, and ten temples. They have powers beyond those of normal men.'

'They will need them,' said Tenaka grimly. 'What of the rest of his words?'

'Thought is faster than arrows? That you must outthink your enemies. The King Beyond the Gate is a mystery. But you should know.'

'Why?'

'Because the message was for you. You must be part of it.'

'And what of your message?'

'What about it?'

'What did it mean?'

'It meant I must travel with you, though I do not desire it.'

'I don't understand,' said Tenaka. 'You have free will – you may go where you please.'

'I suppose so,' said Scaler, smiling. 'But it is time I found my path. You remember the old man's words to me? "Of Bronze you sprang"? My ancestor was also Regnak the Wanderer. "Kin to Shadow"? That is you, cousin. "Dark spears hover"? The Templars. The red I carry? The blood of the Earl of Bronze. I have run long enough.'

'Arvan?'

'Yes.'

Tenaka placed his hands on the young man's shoulders. 'I have often wondered what became of you.'

'Ceska ordered me slain and I ran away. I have spent a long time running away. Too damned long! I'm not much of a swordsman, you know.'

'No matter. It is good to see you again.'

'And you. I followed your career and I kept a diary of your exploits. It is probably still at Delnoch. By the way, there was something else the old man said, right at the beginning. He said that there were three. Of Gold, and Ice, and Shadow. Ananais is the Golden One. You are the Khan of Shadows. Who is Ice?'

Tenaka turned away, staring through the trees.

'There was a man once. He was known as the Ice Killer, since he lived only for death. His name is Decado.'

*

For three days the companions skirted the forest, moving south and west towards the Skoda mountains. The weather was growing warmer, the snow retreating before the spring sunshine. They moved warily and on the second day they found the body of the blind seeker, kneeling by a twisted oak. The ground was too hard to attempt a burial and they left him there.

Galand and his brother paused by the corpse.

'He doesn't seem too unhappy,' said Parsal, scratching his beard.

'It's hard to know whether he's smiling, or whether death has pulled his face into a grin.' said Galand. 'He won't look too happy in about a month.'

'Will *we*?' whispered Parsal. Galand shrugged and the brothers moved on to follow the others.

Galand had been luckier than most and considerably more astute than many Dragon warriors. When the order to disband was given he had moved south, keeping his background to himself. He bought a small farm near Delving forest, south-west of the capital. When the terror began, he was left alone. He married a village girl and started a family, but she had disappeared on a bright autumn day six years before. It was said that the Joinings stole women, but Galand knew she had never loved him . . . and a village lad named Carcas had disappeared on the same day.

Rumours came to Delving about the round-up of former Dragon officers, and it was said that Baris himself had been arrested. This did not surprise Galand – he had always suspected Ceska would prove a tyrant.

Man of the people! Since when did one of his stinking class care about the people?

The small farm had prospered and Galand bought an adjoining parcel of land from a widower. The man was leaving for Vagria – he had a brother in Drenan who had warned him about impending changes – and Galand had bought him out for what seemed a peppercorn price.

Then the soldiers arrived.

A new law meant that non-titled citizens could own only four acres of land. The state acquired the rest at a price that made peppercorn seem a king's ransom. Taxes were increased and crop levels set.

These were impossible to meet after the first year, for the land was robbed of its goodness. Fallow fields were planted and the yields dropped.

Galand took it all, never voicing complaints.

Until the day his daughter died. She had run out to see the horsemen canter and a stallion had kicked out at her. Galand watched her fall and ran to her, cradling her to him.

The horseman dismounted. 'Is she dead?' he asked.

Galand nodded, unable to speak.

'Unfortunate,' said the rider. 'It will increase your tax level.'

The rider died with Galand's dagger buried in his heart. Then Galand dragged the man's sword clear of its scabbard and leapt at a second horseman, whose mount shied; the man toppled to the ground, where Galand killed him with a throat-cut. The other four wheeled their mounts and rode back some thirty paces. Galand turned to the dark stallion which had killed his daughter and hammered the sword two-handed across its neck. Then he ran to the second mount, vaulted into the saddle and rode for the north.

He had located his brother in Vagria, where he worked as a stonemason.

Now Parsal's voice cut through his thoughts, as they walked some thirty paces behind the others.

'What did you say?'

'I said I never thought I would ever follow a Nadir.'

'I know what you mean; it makes the blood run cold. Still, he wants the same as us.'

'Does he?' whispered Parsal.

'What does that mean?'

'They're all the same breed: the warrior elite. It's just a game to them – they don't *care*.'

'I don't like them, brother. But they are Dragon, and that means more than blood. I cannot explain it. Though we are worlds apart, they would die for me – and I for them.'

'I hope you're right!'

'There are few things in life I am sure about. That is one of them.'

Parsal was not convinced but he said nothing, staring ahead at the two warriors.

'What happens when we kill Ceska?' he asked suddenly.

'How do you mean?'

'I don't know really. I mean – what do we do?'

Galand shrugged. 'Ask me when his body lies bleeding at my feet.'

'Strikes me that nothing will change.'

'Maybe not, but I will have had my payment.'

'It doesn't bother you that you may die getting it?'

'No! Does it you?' asked Galand.

'Damn right!'

'You don't have to stay.'

''Course I do! I've always looked after you. Can't leave you with a Nadir, can I? Why does the other one wear that mask?'

'I think he has scars or something. He was an arena warrior.'

'We've all got scars. Bit vain, isn't it?'

'Nothing suits you at the moment, does it?' said Galand, grinning.

'Just a thought. Those other two seem an odd pair,' muttered Parsal, flicking a glance at Belder and Scaler as they walked beside the women.

'You can't have anything against them – you don't even know them.'

'The old boy looks handy.'

'But?'

'I don't think the young one could fight his way through a fog.'

'While we're at it, I don't suppose you would care to criticise the women?'

'No,' said Parsal, smiling. 'Nothing at all to criticise there. Which do you fancy?'

Galand shook his head and chuckled. 'I'm not getting into this,' he said.

'I like the dark one,' said Parsal, unabashed.

They made camp in a shallow cave. Renya ate sparingly and then walked out into the night to watch the stars. Tenaka joined her and they sat together, wrapped in his cloak.

He told her of Illae and Ventria and the beauty of the desert. And while he spoke he stroked her arm and her back, and kissed her hair.

'I cannot say if I love you,' he said suddenly.

She smiled. 'Then do not say it.'

'You don't mind?'

She shook her head and kissed him, curling her arm up and around is neck.

You are a fool, Tenaka Khan, she thought. A wonderful, loving fool!

6

The black man was enjoying himself. Two of the robbers were down and another five remained. He hefted the short iron bar and twirled the chain attached to it. A tall man with a quarterstaff leapt forward and the black man's hand flashed out, the chain whipping round the staff. As he tugged, his attacker stumbled – into a crunching left upper-cut. He slumped to the ground.

Two of the remaining four robbers dropped their clubs, pulling curved daggers from their belts. The other two ran back into the trees, fetching longbows.

This was getting serious. Up to now the black man had killed no one, but that would have to change. He discarded the mace and pulled two throwing knives from his boots.

'Do you really want to die?' he asked them, his voice deep and sonorous.

'No one is going to die,' said a voice from the left and he turned. Two more men stood at the edge of the trees; both had bows bent, aimed at the outlaws.

'A timely intervention!' commented the black man. 'They killed my horse.'

Tenaka gently released the pressure on the bowstring and came forward.

'Put it down to experience,' he told the man. Then he turned to the outlaws. 'I suggest you put away your weapons – the fight is over.'

'He was more trouble that he was worth, anyway,' said the leader, walking over to check the fallen.

'They are all alive,' said the black man, replacing his knives and collecting the mace chain.

A scream sounded from the woods and the outlaw leader jerked to his feet.

Galand, Parsal and Belder moved into view.

'You were right, general,' said Galand. 'There were two more of them creeping in.'

'Did you kill them?' asked Tenaka.

'No. Sore heads, though!'

Tenaka swung to the outlaw. 'Are we likely to have any more trouble with you?'

'You are not going to ask for my word, are you?' replied the man.

'Is it worth anything?'

'Sometimes!'

'No, I don't want your word. Do as you please. But the next time we meet, I will see you all dead. That is *my* word!'

'The word of a barbarian,' said the man. He hawked and spat.

Tenaka grinned. 'Exactly so.' Turning his back, he walked back to Ananais and then on into the trees. Valtaya had prepared a fire and was talking to Scaler. Renya, dagger in hand, returned to the clearing as Tenaka arrived; he smiled at her. The others followed, except Galand who was keeping an eye on the outlaws.

The black man arrived last, carrying two saddlebags across one broad shoulder. He was tall and very powerful, dressed in a tight-fitting tunic of blue silk under a sheepskin cloak. Valtaya had never seen anyone like him, though she had heard stories of dark races far to the east.

'Greetings to you, my friends,' he said, dumping

his saddlebags to the ground. 'Many blessings be upon you all!'

'Will you eat with us?' asked Tenaka.

'That is kind, but I have my own provisions.'

'Where are you headed?' asked Ananais as the black man delved into his bags, pulling out two apples which he polished on his tunic.

'I am visiting your fine land. I have no set destination for the moment.'

'Where are you from?' asked Valtaya.

'A far way, my lady, many thousand of leagues east of Ventria.'

'You are on a pilgrimage?' enquired Scaler.

'You could say that. I have a small mission to perform and then I shall return home to my family.'

'How are you called?' asked Tenaka.

'I fear my name would be difficult to you to pronounce. However, one of the robbers called me something that touched a chord. You may call be Pagan.'

'I am Tenaka Khan.' Swiftly he introduced the others.

Ananais held out his hand; Pagan took it in a firm clasp and their eyes met. Tenaka leaned back, watching them. Both men were from the same mould, immensely powerful and inordinately proud. They were like two prize bulls, each gauging the other.

'Your mask is dramatic,' said Pagan.

'Yes. It makes us look like brothers, black man,' replied Ananais and Pagan chuckled, a deep rolling sound full of good humour.

'Then brothers we are, Ananais!' he said.

Galand appeared and moved to Tenaka. 'They've gone north. I don't think they will be back.'

'Good! That was fine work back there.' Galand

nodded and moved to sit beside his brother. Renya signalled to Tenaka and the two of them moved away from the fire.

'What is it?' he asked.

'The black man.'

'What about him?'

'He carries more weapons than anyone I have ever seen. He has two knives in his boots; a sword and two bows that he left in the trees back there. And there's a broken axe under his horse. He's like a one-man army.'

'So?'

'Did we meet him by accident?'

'You think he might be hunting us?'

'I don't know. But he is a killer, I can sense it. His pilgrimage has to do with death. And Ananais doesn't like him.'

'Don't worry,' he said softly.

'I am not Nadir, Tenaka. I'm not a fatalist.'

'Is that all that's worrying you?'

'No. Now you mention it – the two brothers; they don't like us. We don't belong together and we are none of us close – just a group of strangers thrown together by events.'

'The brothers are strong men and good warriors. I know about these things. I also know they regard me with suspicion, but there's nothing I can do about that. It has always been the way. But we share a common goal. And they will come to trust me. Belder and Scaler? I don't know. But they will do us no harm. And as for Pagan – if he is hunting me, I will kill him.'

'If you can!'

He smiled. 'Yes. If I can.'

'You make it sound easy. I don't see it that way.'

'You worry too much. The Nadir way is better:

tackle each problem as it arises and worry about nothing.'

'I shall never forgive you if you let yourself be killed,' she said.

'Then you watch out for me, Renya. I trust your instincts – I mean that, truly. You are right about Pagan. He is a killer and he may be hunting us. It will be interesting to see what action he now takes.'

'He will offer to travel with us,' she said.

'Yes, but that would make sense. He is a stranger in our land and has already been attacked once.'

'We should refuse him. We are conspicuous enough with your giant friend and his black mask. But to add a black man in blue silk?'

'Yes. The gods – if such there be – are in humorous mood today.'

'I am not laughing,' said Renya.

*

Tenaka awoke from a dreamless sleep, his eyes flaring open and fear touching him like a cold caress. He rose to his feet. The moon was unnaturally bright, glowing like an eldritch lantern, and the branches of trees rustled and swayed though there was no breath of wind.

He looked around him – his companions were all sleeping. Then he glanced down and shock hit him hard: his own body lay there, wrapped in its blankets. He began to shiver.

Was this death?

Of all the cruel jests fate could play . . .

A faint stirring, like the memory of yesterday's breeze, caused him to turn. At the edge of the trees stood six men in dark armour, their black swords in their hands. They advanced on him, spreading out in a half-circle. Tenaka reached for his own blade but could not touch it; his hand passed through the hilt as if it were mist.

'You are doomed,' said a hollow voice. 'The Chaos Spirit calls.'

'Who are you?' asked Tenaka, ashamed that his voice quavered.

Mocking laughter came from the dark knights.

'We are Death,' they said.

Tenaka backed away.

'You cannot run. You cannot move,' said the first knight. Tenaka froze. His legs would not obey him and still the knights came closer.

Suddenly a feeling of peace swept over the Nadir prince and the knights halted their slow advance. Tenaka glanced left and right. Beside him stood six warriors in silver armour and white cloaks.

'Come then, you dogs of darkness,' said the silver warrior nearest him.

'We will come,' replied a dark knight. 'But not when you call.' One by one they backed away into the trees.

Tenaka turned slowly, lost and frightened, and the silver warrior who had spoken placed his hand on the Nadir prince's shoulder.

'Sleep now. The Source will protect you.'

Darkness settled over him like a blanket.

*

On the morning of the sixth day they cleared the trees and entered the broad plains stretching from Skultik to Skoda. In the distance, to the south, was the city of Karnak, but only the tallest spires could be seen as white pinpoints against a green horizon. The snow lay in white patches now, the spring grass groping for the sunlight.

Tenaka held up his hand as he saw the smoke.

'It cannot be a grass fire,' said Ananais, shielding his eyes from the harsh sunlight.

'It's a village burning,' said Galand, walking alongside. 'Such sights are all too common these days.'

'Yours is a troubled land,' said Pagan, dumping his huge pack on the ground at his feet and laying his saddlebags upon it. Attached to the pack was a bronze-edged shield of stiffened buffalo hide, an antelope horn bow and calf-hide quiver.

'You carry more equipment than a Dragon platoon,' muttered Ananais.

'Sentimental reasons,' answered Pagan, grinning.

'We'd best avoid the village,' said Scaler. His long hair was greasy with sweat and his lack of fitness was telling on him. He sat down beside Pagan's pack.

The wind shifted and the sound of drumming hooves came to them.

'Spread out and lie low,' said Tenaka. The companions ran for cover, dropping to their bellies in the grass.

A woman crested the top of a small hill, running at top speed, her auburn hair flowing behind her. She was dressed in a skirt of green wool and wore a brown shawl. In her arms she carried a small babe whose piping screams carried to the travellers.

As the woman ran on, she cast occasional panic-stricken glances over her shoulder. The haven of the trees was an eternity away as the soldiers cantered into view, but still she ran, cutting towards the hidden Tenaka.

Ananais swore and stood up. The woman screamed and veered left – into the arms of Pagan.

The soldiers reined their mounts and the leader dismounted. He was a tall man, dressed in the red cloak of Delnoch, his bronze armour burnished to a sheen.

'Thank you for your help,' he said, 'though we did not need it.' The woman was quiet now and in her despair she buried her head against Pagan's broad chest.

Tenaka smiled. There were twelve soldiers, eleven of them still mounted. There was nothing to be done except to hand back the woman.

Then an arrow flashed into the neck of the nearest rider and he pitched from the saddle. Tenaka's eyes flared in shock. A second arrow buried itself in the chest of another soldier and he too fell back, his horse rearing and hurling him from the saddle. Tenaka drew his sword, plunging it into the officer's back, for the man had turned as the arrows struck home.

Pagan pushed the woman from him and dropped to his knee, drawing the throwing-knives from his boots. They flew from his hands and two more soldiers died as they tried to control their mounts. Tenaka ran forward, leaping into the saddle of a riderless horse, scooping up the reins and heeling the beast forward. The seven remaining soldiers had drawn their weapons and two charged at Pagan. Tenaka's mount crashed into the remaining five and one horse fell, the others rearing and whinnying madly. As Tenaka's sword sliced down, an arrow whipped by him, taking a rider through the left eye-socket.

Pagan drew his shortsword, then dived left as the horses thundered by him, rolling to his feet once more as the riders dragged their mounts to a halt. Running forward, he blocked a wild slashing cut and buried his blade in the rider's side. As the man screamed and fell from the saddle, Pagan vaulted to the beast's back; then he hurled himself at the second rider, carrying the man clear of his horse. They fell heavily and Pagan broke the man's neck with a single blow.

Renya hurled aside her bow and, dagger in hand, ran from cover to where Tenaka, joined by Ananais, was battling the remaining soldiers. She leapt to a horse's back behind its rider and hammered her dagger between his shoulder-blades. The man screamed and tried to twist round but Renya punched him behind the ear. His neck snapped and he tumbled clear.

The last two soldiers turned their mounts and spurred them clear of the fray, riding back towards the hill. But Parsal and Galand stepped out in their paths and the horses reared, throwing one man from the saddle. The other clung on grimly until Galand's sword opened his throat. Parsal pulled his blade clear of the downed rider.

'I'll say this,' he called, grinning broadly. 'It's not been dull since we came back.'

Galand grunted. 'We're damned lucky, is all I'll say.' Wiping his sword on the grass, he gathered the reins of the two horses and walked back to the main group.

Tenaka hid his anger and called out to Pagan, 'You fight well!'

'I think it must be all the practice I am getting,' answered the black man.

'What I want to know is, who fired that arrow?' shouted Ananais.

'Forget it – it's done,' said Tenaka. 'Now we had best move from here. I suggest we ride back to the forest until nightfall. Now that we have mounts, we can make up the time.'

'No!' said the woman with the babe. 'My family. My friends. They're being butchered back there!'

Tenaka went to her, placing his hands on her shoulders. 'Listen to me. Unless I am mistaken these soldiers were part of a half-century, which means there are almost forty men in your village. It is too many – we cannot help you.'

'We could try,' said Renya.

'Be silent!' snarled Tenaka and Renya's mouth dropped open, but she said no more. He turned back to the woman. 'You are welcome to stay with us and we will come to the village tomorrow. We will do what we can.'

'Tomorrow will be too late!'

'It is probably already too late,' said Tenaka and she pulled away from him.

'I would not expect help from a Nadir,' she said, tears flowing. 'But some of you are Drenai. Please help me!'

'Dying will not help anyone,' said Scaler. 'Come with us. You escaped – so may others. And anyway, there is nowhere else for you to go. Come on, I will help you to a horse.'

The companions mounted and headed for the forest. Behind them the crows circled and wheeled.

That night Tenaka called Renya to him and they went from the camp-site and into the trees. No word had passed between them all afternoon.

Tenaka's manner was cold and distant. He walked to a moonlit clearing, then turned on the girl.

'You loosed that arrow! Don't ever act again without my order.'

'Who are you to order me?' she snapped.

'I am Tenaka Khan, woman! Cross me again and I will leave you behind.'

'They would have killed that woman and baby.'

'Yes. But because of your action we might all be dead. What would that have achieved?'

'But we are *not* dead. And we saved her.'

'Through luck. A soldier may need luck on occasion, but we would rather not have to rely on it. I am not asking you, Renya, I am telling you: you will not do it again!'

'I do as I please,' she said. He struck her open-handed across the face. She hit the ground hard, but rolled to her feet with eyes blazing, fingers curled into talons. Then she saw the knife in his hand.

'You would kill me, wouldn't you?' she whispered.

'Without a thought!'

'I loved you! More than life. More than anything.'

'Will you obey me?'

'Oh, yes, Tenaka Khan, I will obey you. Until we reach Skoda. And then I will leave your company.' She turned on her heel and strode back to the campsite.

Tenaka sheathed his dagger and sat down on a boulder.

'Still the loner, eh, Tani?' said Ananais, stepping from the shadows of the trees.

'I don't want to talk.'

'You were hard on her, and quite right too. But you went a little far – you wouldn't have killed her.'

'No. I would not.'

'But she frightens you, doesn't she?'

'I said I didn't want to talk.'

'True, but this is Ananais – your crippled friend who knows you well. As well as any man. You think that because we risk death there is no place for love? Don't be a fool – enjoy it while it's there.'

'I cannot,' said Tenaka, head bowed. 'When I came here, I could see nothing but Ceska. But now I seem to spend more time thinking of . . . you know.'

'Of course I know. But what happened to your Nadir code? Let tomorrow look to itself.'

'I am only half-Nadir.'

'Go and talk to her.'

'No. It is better this way.'

Ananais stood up and stretched his back. 'I think I'll get some sleep.' He ambled away back to the camp, stopping where Renya sat staring miserably into the fire.

He squatted down beside her. 'It is a strange thing about some men,' he said to her. 'In matters of business or war, they can be giants; wise to a fault. In matters of the heart, they are like children. Now women are a different matter; they see the child in a man for what it is.'

'He would have killed me,' she whispered.

'Do you really think so?'

'Do you?'

'Renya, he loves you. He couldn't hurt you.'

'Then why? Why say it?'

'To make you believe it. To make you hate him. To make you go.'

'Well, it worked,' she said.

'That's a shame. Still . . . you shouldn't have loosed that arrow.'

'I know that!' she snapped. 'You don't need to tell me. I just . . . couldn't see them kill a baby.'

'No, I wasn't over-keen myself.' He glanced across the fire to where the woman lay sleeping. The black giant, Pagan, sat with his back to a tree, holding the babe against his chest. The child had reached a pudgy hand from its blanket and curled it around Pagan's finger, while he was speaking to it in low, gentle tones.

'Good with children, isn't he?' said Ananais.

'Yes. And with weapons.'

'A real man of mystery. Still, I am watching him.'

Renya glanced at the bright blue eyes beyond the black mask. 'I like you, Ananais. I really do.'

'Like me, like my friends,' he said, nodding towards the tall figure of Tenaka Khan as he made his way to his blankets.

She shook her head and returned her gaze to the fire.

'That's a shame,' he said again.

*

They rode into the village two hours after dawn. Galand had scouted ahead and reported that the soldiers were setting off towards the south and the distant spires of Karnak. The village was gutted, charred timbers oozing dark plumes of smoke. Bodies lay here and there, while around the edge of the burnt-out buildings ten crosses had been erected, from which hung the village council. They had been whipped and beaten before being nailed to the beams, finally their legs had been broken, causing their battered frames to slump and cut off the air supply to the lungs.

'We have become barbarians,' said Scaler, turning his mount away from the scene. Belder merely nodded, but he followed the young Drenai to the grass fields beyond.

Tenaka dismounted at the village square, where the mass of bodies lay – more than thirty women and children.

'There is no sense to it,' he said as Ananais joined him. 'Now who will work the fields? If this is happening all over the empire . . .'

'It is,' said Galand.

The woman with the babe lifted her shawl over her head and closed her eyes. Pagan glimpsed the movement and rode alongside her, taking the reins from her hands.

'We will wait for you outside the village,' he said. Valtaya and Renya followed them.

'It is a strange thing,' said Ananais. 'For centuries the Drenai have turned back enemies who would have done this to our land. And now we do it ourselves. What breed of men are they recruiting now?'

'There are always those who love this kind of work,' answered Tenaka.

'Among your people, maybe,' said Parsal softly.

'What does that mean?' snarled Ananais, turning on the black-bearded warrior.

'Forget it!' ordered Tenaka. 'You are right Parsal; the Nadir are a vicious people. But the Nadir did not do this. Nor did the Vagrians. As Ananais has said, we are doing it to ourselves.'

'Forget I said it, general,' murmured Parsal. 'I am just angry. Let's get away from here.'

'Tell me something,' said Galand suddenly. 'Will killing Ceska change all this?'

'I don't know,' Tenaka replied.

'He needs to be smashed.'

'I don't think six men and two women can bring down his empire. Do you?'

'A few days ago,' said Ananais, 'there was only one man.'

'Parsal is right, let us get away from here,' said Tenaka.

At that moment a child began to cry and the four men ran to the bodies, hauling them aside. At last they reached an old fat woman, her dead arms curled protectively around a girl of five or six. The woman's back bore three terrible wounds and she had obviously crouched down over the child to shield her from the weapons. But a lance had ripped through her body and into that of the child beyond. Parsal lifted the girl clear, then blanched as he saw the blood that had soaked her clothing. He carried her out of the village to where the others had dismounted and Valtaya ran forward to relieve him of the slender burden.

As they laid her gently to the grass her eyes opened; they were blue and bright.

'I don't want to die,' she whispered. 'Please?' Her eyes closed and the woman from the village knelt by her, lifting her head and cradling the child in her lap.

'It's all right, Alaya; it's me, Parise. I have come back to look after you.'

The child smiled weakly, but then the smile froze and twisted into a grimace of pain. The companions watched life depart.

'Oh no! Please, no!' murmured Parise. 'Sweet gods of light, no!' Her own babe began to cry and Pagan lifted it from the ground to hold it against his chest.

Galand turned away and fell to his knees. Parsal moved to his side and Galand looked up at his brother, tears streaming from his eyes. He shook his head, for no words would come.

Parsal knelt beside him. 'I know, brother, I know,' he said gently. Galand took a deep breath and drew his sword.

'I swear by all that's holy and unholy, by all the beasts that crawl or fly, I will not rest until this land is clean again.' He lurched to his feet, waving his sword in the air. 'I'm coming for you, Ceska!' he bellowed. Hurling aside his blade, he stumbled away towards a small grove of trees.

Parsal turned apologetically to the others. 'His own daughter was killed. A lovely child . . . a child of laughter. But he meant what he said, you know. And . . . and I'm with him.' His voice was thick with emotion and he cleared his throat. 'We're not much, him and me. I wasn't even good enough for the Dragon. We're not officers or anything. But when we say a thing we mean it. I don't know what the rest of you want out of all this. But those people back there – they are my people, mine and Galand's. Not rich and noble. Just dead. That old fat woman died to protect that child. And she failed. But she tried . . . gave her life trying. Well, so will I!' His voice broke then and he swore. Turning he walked quickly to the grove.

'Well, general,' said Ananais, 'what are you going to do with your army of six?'

'Seven!' said Pagan.

'See, we are growing all the time,' said Ananais and Tenaka nodded.

'Why will you join us?' he asked the black man.

'That is my business, but our ends are the same. I came thousands of miles to see Ceska fall.'

'We will bury the child and head for Skoda,' said Tenaka.

They rode warily throughout the long afternoon, Galand and Parsal riding wide on the flanks. Towards dusk a sudden storm burst over the plains and the companions took refuge in a deserted stone tower on the banks of a fast-flowing stream. They picketed the horses in a nearby field, gathered what wood they could find near a cluster of trees and cleared an open space within the tower on the first level. The building was old and square, and had once housed twenty soldiers; it was a watchtower from the days of the First Nadir War. There were three levels, the top being open to the sky where sharp-eyed scouts would watch for Nadir or Sathuli raiders.

Around midnight, as the others slept, Tenaka

called Scaler to him and led him up the winding stair to the turret.

The storm had moved on to the south and the stars were bright. Bats circled around the tower, dipping and wheeling, and the night wind was chill as it swept down from the snow-clad Delnoch range.

'How are you faring, Arvan?' Tenaka asked Scaler as they sat beneath the battlements away from the wind.

Scaler shrugged. 'A little out of place.'

'That will pass.'

'I am no warrior, Tenaka. When you tackled those soldiers, I just lay in the grass and watched. I froze!'

'No, you didn't. Everything happened at once and those of us standing just reacted more quickly. We are trained for it. Take the brothers: they moved to the only spot the soldiers would break for and stopped any survivors from escaping to bring help. I didn't tell them to do it, they're soldiers. Now, the whole skirmish lasted maybe two minutes. What could you have done?'

'I don't know. Drawn my sword. *Helped!*'

'There will be time for that. What is the situation at Delnoch?'

'I don't know. I left there five years ago and before that I had spent ten years in Drenan.'

'Who rules?'

'No one of the House of Bronze. Orrin was poisoned and Ceska put in his own man. His name is Matrax. Why do you ask?'

'My plans have changed.'

'In what way?'

'I was intending to assassinate Ceska.'

'And now?'

'Now I plan something even more foolish. I am going to raise an army and bring him down.'

'No army in the world can stand against the Joinings. Gods, man, even the Dragon failed – they didn't even come close!'

'Nothing in life is easy, Arvan. But it's what I am trained for. To lead an army. To bring death and destruction on my enemies. You heard Parsal and Galand; what they said was right. A man must stand against evil wherever he finds it and he must use all his talents. I'm not an assassin.'

'And where will you find this army?'

Tenaka smiled. 'I need your help. You must take Delnoch.'

'Are you serious?'

'Deadly!'

'You want me to take a fortress single-handed? A fortress that has withstood two Nadir hordes? It's insane!'

'You are of the House of Bronze. Use your head. There is a way.'

'If you have already thought of a plan, why don't *you* do it?'

'I cannot. I am of the House of Ulric.'

'Why so cryptic? Tell me what to do.'

'No. You are a man and I think you sell yourself short. We will stop in Skoda and see how the land lies. Then you and I will bring an army.'

Scaler's eyes widened and his mouth dropped open.

'A Nadir army?' he whispered, blood draining from his face. 'You would bring the *Nadir*?'

'Only if you can take Dros Delnoch!'

7

In the dark of the library the Abbot waited patiently, leaning forward on his desk, his fingers steepled and his eyes closed. His three companions sat opposite him, immobile, like living statues. The Abbot opened his eyes and regarded them all:

Acuas, the strong one, compassionate and loyal.

Balan, the sceptic.

Katan, the true mystic.

All were travelling, their spirits entwined as they sought the Dark Templars and threw a veil of mind mist over the movements of Tenaka Khan and his companions.

Acuas returned first. He opened his eyes, rubbing his hands over his yellow beard; he seemed tired, drained.

'This is not easy, my Lord,' he said. 'The Dark Templars have great power.'

'As have we,' said the Abbot. 'Go on.'

'There are twenty of them. They were attacked in Skultik by a bank of outlaws but slew them with arrogant ease. They are truly formidable warriors.'

'Yes. How close are they to the Torchbearer?'

'Less than a day. We cannot deceive them for much longer.'

'No. A few more days will be invaluable,' said the Abbot. 'Have they tried another night attack?'

'No, my Lord, though I think it likely.'

'Rest now, Acuas. Fetch Toris and Lannad to relieve you.'

The Abbot left the room and the long corridor beyond, making his way slowly to the second level and the garden of Decado.

The dark-eyed priest welcomed him with a smile. 'Come with me, Decado. There is something for you to see.'

Without another word he turned on his heel and led the priest to the steps and the oak doors above. Decado hesitated in the doorway – during all his years in the monastery he had never ascended these steps.

The Abbot turned. 'Come!' he said and stepped into the shadows beyond. A strange sense of fear gripped the gardener, as if his world was slipping away from him. He swallowed and began to tremble. Then, taking a deep breath, he followed the Abbot.

He was led through a maze of corridors, but he looked neither to left nor right, focusing his gaze on the grey cassock of the man walking before him. The Abbot halted before a door shaped like a leaf; there was no handle.

'Open,' whispered the Abbot and the door slid silently into a recess. Inside was a long chamber containing thirty sets of silver armour, draped with cloaks of dazzling white. Before each set was a small table bearing scabbarded swords placed in front of helms crowned with plumes of white horse-hair.

'Do you know what these represent?' asked the Abbot.

'No.' Decado was sweating freely. He wiped his eyes and the Abbot noticed with concern that the haunted look had returned to the former warrior.

'This is the armour worn by The Delnoch Thirty,

led by Serbitar – the men who fought and died during the First Nadir War. You have heard of them?'

'Of course.'

'Tell me what you have heard.'

'Where is this leading, my Lord Abbot? I have duties in the gardens.'

'Tell me of The Delnoch Thirty,' ordered the Abbot.

Decado cleared his throat. 'They were warrior priests. Not like us. They trained for years and then chose a distant war in which to die. Serbitar led The Thirty at Delnoch, where they advised the Earl of Bronze and Druss the Legend. Together they turned back the hordes of Ulric.'

'But why would priests take up weapons?'

'I don't know, Lord Abbot. It is incomprehensible.'

'Is it?'

'You have taught me that all life is sacred to the Source, and that to take life is a crime against God.'

'And yet evil must be opposed.'

'Not by using the weapons of evil,' answered Decado.

'A man stands above a child with spear poised. What would you do?'

'I would stop him – but not kill him.'

'You would stop him with a blow, perhaps?'

'Yes, perhaps.'

'He falls badly, strikes his head and dies. Have you sinned?'

'No . . . yes. I don't know.'

'He is the sinner, for his action ensured your reaction, and therefore it was his action that killed him. We strive for peace and harmony, my son – we long for it. But we are of the world and subject to its demands. This nation is no longer in harmony.

Chaos controls and the suffering is terrible to behold.'

'What are you trying to say, my Lord?'

'It is not easy, my son, for my words will cause you great pain.' The Abbot moved forward, placing his hands on the priest's shoulders. 'This is a Temple of The Thirty. And we are preparing to ride against the darkness.'

Decado pulled back from the Abbot. 'No!'

'I want you to ride with us.'

'I believed in you. I *trusted* you!' Decado turned away and found himself facing one of the sets of armour. He twisted round. '*That* is what I came here to escape: death and slaughter. Sharp blades and torn flesh. I have been happy here. And now you have robbed me of it. Go ahead – play your soldier's games. I will have none of it.'

'You cannot hide for ever, my son.'

'Hide? I came here to change.'

'It is not hard to change when your biggest problem is whether the weeds prosper in a vegetable patch.'

'What does that mean?'

'It means that you were a psychopathic killer – a man in love with death. Now I offer you the chance to see if you have changed. Put on the armour and ride with us against the forces of Chaos.'

'And learn to kill again?'

'That we shall see.'

'I don't want to kill. I wish to live among my plants.'

'Do you think I want to fight? I am nearing sixty years of age. I love the Source and all things that grow or move. I believe life is the greatest gift in all the Universe. But there is real evil in the world, and it must be fought. Overcome. Then others will have the opportunity to see the joy of life.'

'Don't say any more,' snapped Decado. 'Not another damned word!' Years of suppressed emotion roared through him, filling his senses, and forgotten anger lashed him with whips of fire. What a fool he had been – hiding from the world, grubbing in the soil like a sweating peasant!

He moved to a set of armour placed to the right of the rest and his hand reached down to curl round the ivory hilt. With one smooth movement he swept the blade into the air, his muscles pulsing with the thrill of the weapon. Its blade was silver steel and razor-sharp, and the balance was perfection. He turned to the Abbot, and where he had once seen a Lord he now saw an old man with watery eyes.

'This quest of yours, does it involve Tenaka Khan?'

'Yes, my son.'

'Don't call me that, priest! Not ever again. I don't blame you – I was the fool for believing in you. All right, I will fight with your priests, but only because it will aid my friends. But do not seek to give me orders.'

'I will not be in a position to order you, Decado. Even now you have moved to your own armour.'

'*My* armour?'

'You recognise the rune on the helm?'

'It is the number One in the Elder script.'

'It was Serbitar's armour. You will wear it.'

'He was the leader, was he not?'

'As you will be.'

'So that is my lot,' said Decado, 'to lead a motley crew of priests as they play at war. Very well; I can take a joke as well as any man.'

Decado began to laugh. The Abbot closed his

eyes and mouthed a silent prayer, for through the laughter he felt the cry of anguish from Decado's tortured soul. Despair swept through the priest and he left the room, the manic laughter echoing after him.

What have you done, Abaddon? he asked himself.

Tears were in his eyes as he reached his room and, once inside, he fell to his knees.

Decado stumbled from the chamber and returned to his garden, staring in disbelief at the tidy rows of vegetables, the neat hedges and the carefully pruned trees.

He walked on to his hut, kicking open the door.

Less than an hour before, this had been home – a home he loved. Contentment had been his.

Now the shack was a hovel and he left it and wandered to his flower garden. The white rose carried three new buds. Anger coursed through him and he grasped the plant, ready to rip it from the ground. Then he stopped and slowly released it, staring at his hand and then back at the plant. Not one thorn had ripped his flesh. Gently he smoothed out the crushed leaves and began to sob, meaningless sounds which became two words.

'I'm sorry,' he told his rose.

*

The Thirty assembled in the lower courtyard, saddling their mounts. The horses still bore their winter coats, but they were strong mountain-bred beasts and they could run like the wind. Decado chose a bay mare; he saddled it swiftly and then vaulted to its back, sweeping out his white cloak behind him and settling it over the saddle in Dragon fashion. Serbitar's armour fitted him as his own never had – it felt smooth, like a second skin.

The Abbot, Abaddon, stepped into the saddle of a chestnut gelding and moved alongside Decado.

Decado swung in the saddle, watching the warrior priests as they silently mounted – he had to admit that they moved well. Each adjusted his cloak precisely as Decado had done. Abaddon gazed wistfully at his erstwhile disciple; Decado had shaved his chin clean and bound his long dark hair at the nape of his neck. His eyes were bright and alive, and a half-mocking smile was on his lips.

The night before, Decado had been formally introduced to his lieutenants: Acuas, the Heart of The Thirty; Balan, the Eyes of The Thirty; and Katan, the Soul of The Thirty.

'If you want to be warriors,' he had told them, 'then do as I say, when I say it. The Abbot tells me that there is a force hunting Tenaka Khan. We are to intercept it. The men we shall fight are true warriors, so I am told. Let us hope your quest does not end at their hands.'

'It is your quest too, brother,' said Katan, with a gentle smile.

'There is no man alive who can slay me. And if you priests fall like wheat, I shall not stay.'

'Is not a leader obliged to stand by his men?' asked Balan, an edge of anger in his voice.

'Leader? This is all a priestly farce, but very well, I will play the game. But I will not die with you.'

'Will you join us in prayer?' said Acuas.

'No. You pray for me! I have spent too many years wasting my time in that fruitless exercise.'

'We have always prayed for you,' said Katan.

'Pray for yourselves! Pray that when you meet these Dark Templars your bowels do not turn to water.'

With that he had left them. Now he raised his

114

arms and led the troop through the Temple gates
and out over the Sentran Plain.

'Are you sure this choice is wise?' Katan mind-
pulsed to Abaddon.

'It is not my choice, my son.'

'He is a man consumed by anger.'

'The Source knows our needs. Do you remember
Estin?'

'Yes, poor man. So wise – he would have been a
good leader,' said Katan.

'Indeed he would. Courageous, yet kind; strong,
yet gentle; and possessed of intellect without arrogance. But he died. And on the day he died Decado
appeared at our gates seeking sanctuary from the
world.'

'But suppose, Lord Abbot, that it was not the
Source that sent him?'

' "Lord Abbot" no longer, Katan. Merely
"Abaddon".'

The older man severed the mind link and it was
some moments before Katan realised his question
had not been answered.

The years fled from Decado. Once more he was
in the saddle, the wind in his hair. Once more the
drumming of hooves sounded on the plain and the
stirring in his blood brought his youth pounding back
to his mind . . .

The Dragon sweeping down on the Nadir raiders.
Chaos, confusion, blood and terror. Broken men
and broken screams, and crows shrieking their joy
in the dark skies above.

And then later, in one mercenary war after
another in the most far-flung nations of the world.
Always Decado walked away from the battle, not a
wound upon his slender form, while his enemies

journeyed to whatever hells they believed in, shadowed and forgotten.

The image of Tenaka Khan floated in Decado's mind.

Now there was a warrior! How many times had Decado fallen asleep dreaming of a battle with Tenaka Khan? Ice and Shadow in the dance of blades.

They had fought, many times. With wooden blades or tipped foils. Even with blunted sabres. Honours were even. But such contests were meaningless – only when death rested on the blades could a true victor emerge.

Decado's thoughts were interrupted as the yellow-bearded Acuas cantered alongside.

'It will be close, Decado. The Templars have found their trail at some devastated village. They will have made their move by morning.'

'How soon can we reach them?'

'Dawn at the earliest.'

'Back to your prayers, then, yellowbeard. And make them powerful.'

He spurred his horse to a gallop and The Thirty followed him.

*

It was close to dawn and the companions had ridden through most of the night, stopping only for an hour to rest the horses. The Skoda range loomed ahead and Tenaka was anxious to reach their sanctuary. The sun, hidden now beyond the eastern horizon, was stirring and the stars faded as a pink glow painted the sky.

The riders left a grove of trees and emerged on to a broad grassland, swirling in mist. Tenaka felt a sudden chill touch his bones; he shivered and drew his cloak about him. He was tired and discontented.

He had not spoken to Renya since their fight in the forest, yet he thought of her constantly. Far from removing her from his mind by turning on her, he had succeeded only in bringing himself fresh misery. And yet he was incapable of crossing the gulf he had opened between them. He glanced back to where she rode alongside Ananais, laughing at some jest; then turned away.

Ahead, like dark demons out of the past, twenty riders waited in a line. They sat their horses immobile, black cloaks flapping in the breeze. Tenaka reined his mount some fifty paces from the centre of their line and his companions rode alongside.

'What in Hell's name are they?' asked Ananais.

'They are seeking me,' answered Tenaka. 'They came at me in a dream.'

'I don't wish to appear defeatist, but there are rather too many for us to handle. Do we run?'

'From these men you cannot run,' said Tenaka tonelessly as he dismounted.

The twenty riders followed course, walking forward slowly through the mist, and it seemed to Renya they moved like the shades of the dead on a ghostly sea. Their armour was jet, helms covered their faces, dark swords were in their hands. Tenaka went forward to meet them, hand on sword-hilt.

Ananais shook his head. A strange trancelike state had come upon him, leaving him a powerless observer. He slid from the saddle, drew his own sword and joined Tenaka.

The Dark Templars halted and their leader stepped forward.

'We have no commission to kill you yet, Ananais,' he said.

'I don't die easily,' said Ananais. He was about to add an insult, but the words froze in his mouth as a terrible fear struck him like a blast of icy air. He began to tremble and the urge to run rose in him.

'You die as easily as any other mortal,' said the man. 'Go back! Ride away to whatever doom awaits you.'

Ananais said nothing; he swallowed hard and looked at Tenaka. His friend's face was bone-white, and it was obvious that the same fear washed over him.

Galand and Parsal moved alongside them, swords in hand.

'Do you think to stand against us?' said the leader. 'A hundred men could not stand against us. Listen to my words and hear the truth – feel it through your terror.'

The fear increased and the horses grew skittish, whinnying their alarm. Scaler and Belder leapt from the saddles, sensing the beasts were about to bolt. Pagan leaned forward, patting his horse's neck; the beast settled down, but its ears were flat against its skull and he knew it was close to panic. Valtaya and Renya jumped clear as their horses bolted, then helped the village woman, Parise, to dismount.

Shielding her baby who had begun to scream – Parise lay down on the ground, shaking uncontrollably.

Pagan dismounted and drew his sword, walking forward slowly to stand beside Tenaka and the others. Belder and Scaler followed.

'Draw your sword,' whispered Renya, but Scaler ignored her. It was all he could do to muster enough courage to stand alongside Tenaka Khan. Any thoughts of actually fighting beside him were buried under the weight of his terror.

'Foolish,' said the leader, contemptuously, 'like

lambs to the slaughter!' The Dark Templars advanced.

Tenaka struggled to overcome his panic, but his limbs felt leaden as his confidence drained away. He knew dark magic was being used against him, but the knowledge was not enough. He felt like a child stalked by a leopard.

Fight it! he told himself. Where is your courage?

Suddenly, as in his dream, the terror passed and strength flowed to his limbs. He knew without turning that the white knights had returned, this time in the flesh.

The Templars halted their advance and Padaxes cursed softly as The Thirty moved into sight. Outnumbered now, he considered his options. Calling on the power of the Spirit, he probed his enemies, meeting a wall of force that resisted his efforts . . . Except around the warrior at the centre – this man was no mystic. Padaxes was no stranger to the legends of The Thirty – his own temples had been built to parody theirs – and he recognised the rune on the man's helm.

A non-mystic as leader? An idea formed in his mind.

'Much blood will be shed here today,' he called, 'unless we settle this as captains.'

Abaddon grasped Decado's arm as he moved forward. 'No, Decado, you do not understand his power.'

'He is a man, that is all,' answered the other.

'No, he is far more – he has the power of Chaos. If someone must fight him, let it be Acuas.'

'Am I not leader in this force of yours?'

'Yes, but . . .'

'There are no buts. Obey mc!' Pulling himself free

Decado moved on, halting a few feet away from the black-armoured Padaxes.

'What do you suggest, Templar?'

'A duel between captains, the loser's men leaving the field.'

'I want more,' said Decado coldly. 'Far more!'

'Name it.'

'I have studied much of the ways of mystics. It is . . . was . . . part of my former calling. It is said that in ancient wars champions carried the souls of their armies within them, and when they died their armies died.'

'That is so,' said Padaxes, disguising his joy.

'Then that is what I demand.'

'It shall be so. I swear it by the Spirit!'

'Swear nothing to me, warrior. Your oaths count for nothing. Prove it!'

'It will take a little time. I shall conduct the rites first and trust your word that you will follow,' said Padaxes. Decado nodded and walked back to the others.

'You cannot do this thing, Decado,' said Acuas. 'You doom us all!'

'Suddenly the game is not to your liking?' snapped Decado.

'It is not that. This man, your enemy, has powers you do not possess. He can read your mind, sense your every move before you make it. How on earth can you defeat him?'

Decado laughed. 'Am I still your leader?'

Acuas flicked a glance at the former Abbot. 'Yes,' he said, 'you are the leader.'

'Then when he has finished his ritual, you will align the life force of The Thirty to mine.'

'Tell me this before I die,' said Acuas gently. 'Why

are you sacrificing yourself in this way? Why do you doom your friends?'

Decado shrugged. 'Who can say?'

The Dark Templars fell to their knees before Padaxes as he intoned the names of the lower demons, calling on the Chaos Spirit, his voice rising to a scream. The sun breasted the eastern horizon, yet strangely no light fell upon the plain.

'It is done,' whispered Abaddon. 'He has kept his word and the souls of his warriors are within him.'

'Then do likewise,' ordered Decado.

The Thirty knelt before their leader, heads bowed. Decado felt nothing, yet he knew they had obeyed him.

'Dec, is it you?' called Ananais. Decado waved him to silence and advanced to meet Padaxes.

The black sword hissed forward, to be parried instantly by the silver steel in Decado's hand. The battle had begun. Tenaka and his companions watched in awe as the warriors circled and struck, blades clashing and clanging.

Time wore on and desperation became apparent in every move Padaxes made. Fear crept into his heart. Though he anticipated his opponent's every move, such was the speed of the assault that it availed him nothing. He mind-pulsed a terror-thought but Decado laughed, for death held no terror for him. And then Padaxes knew his doom was sealed, and it irked him greatly that a mortal man could bring about his death. Launching a final savage assault, he experienced the horror of reading Decado's mind at the last moment, seeing the riposte in the fraction of a second before it was launched.

The silver steel whiplashed his own sword aside and buried itself in his groin. He sank to the ground, his lifeblood pumping to the grass . . . and the souls of his men died with him.

Sunlight blazed through the darkness and The Thirty rose to their feet, amazed that life still flowed in their veins.

Acuas walked forward.

'How?' he asked. 'How did you win?'

'There is no mystery, Acuas,' said Decado softly. 'He was only a man.'

'But so are you!'

'No. I am Decado. The Ice Killer! Follow me at your peril.'

*

Decado lifted his helm and sucked in a deep breath of cool dawn air. Tenaka shook his head to clear the webs of fear still clinging there.

'Dec!' he called. Decado smiled and walked to him; the men gripped wrists in the warrior's greeting. Ananais, Galand and Parsal joined them.

'By all the gods, Dec, you look fine. Very fine!' said Tenaka warmly.

'And you, general. I am glad we were in time.'

'Would you mind telling me,' said Ananais, 'just why all those warriors died?'

'Only if you will explain about that mask. It's ridiculous for someone as vain as you to hide such classical good looks.'

Ananais looked away while the others stood uneasily, the silence growing.

'Will no one introduce me to our rescuer?' said Valtaya, and the moment passed. The Thirty stood aloof as the conversation began, then split into groups of six and moved about collecting wood for camp-fires.

Acuas, Balan, Katan and Abaddon chose a position by a solitary elm. Katan started the fire and the four of them sat around it, seemingly silent and watching the dancing flames.

'Speak, Acuas,' pulsed Abaddon.

'I am saddened, Abaddon, for our leader is not one of us. I do not mean that arrogantly, but our Order is an ancient one and always we have sought high spiritual ideals. We do not go to war for the joy of killing, but to die in defence of the Light. Decado is purely a killer.'

'You are the Heart of The Thirty, Acuas. For you have always been emotionally charged. You are a fine man – you care . . . you love. But sometimes our emotions can blind us. Do not judge Decado yet.'

'How did he kill the Templar?' asked Balan. 'It was inconceivable.'

'The Eyes of The Thirty and yet you cannot see, Balan. But I will not explain it to you. In time you will tell me. I believe the Source sent Decado to us, and I accepted him. Will one of you tell me why he is the leader?'

Dark-eyed Katan smiled. 'Because he is the least among us.'

'But more than that,' said Abaddon.

'It is his only role,' said Acuas.

'Explain, brother,' asked Balan.

'As a knight he could not communicate with us, nor travel with us. Every move we made would have been a humiliation for him. Yet we go to a war that he understands. As our leader, his lack of talent is counterbalanced by his authority.'

'Very good, Acuas. Now let the Heart tell us where danger lies.'

Acuas closed his eyes and remained mind-silent for several minutes, focusing his concentration.

'The Templars will respond. They cannot suffer

this defeat at our hands and allow the deed to go unavenged.'

'And?'

'And Ceska has sent a thousand men to crush the Skoda rebellion. They will arrive in less than a week.'

Some thirty paces from their fire Decado sat with Tenaka, Ananais, Pagan and Scaler.

'Come on, Dec,' said Ananais. 'How did you become the leader of a gang of warrior wizards? There must be a story to it.'

'How do you know I am not a wizard?' countered Decado.

'No, seriously,' whispered Ananais, glancing at the white-cloaked knights. 'I mean, they are an eerie bunch. None of them is saying anything.'

'On the contrary,' Decado told him. 'They are all talking – mind to mind.'

'Nonsense!' said Ananais, curling his fingers into the sign of the Protective Horn and holding his hand across his heart.

Decado smiled. 'I speak truly.' Turning, he called to Katan who joined them. 'Go on, Ani – ask something,' he ordered.

'I feel foolish,' muttered Ananais.

'Then I shall ask,' said Scaler. 'Tell me, my friend, is it true you knights can talk . . . without talking?'

'It is true,' said Katan softly.

'Would you give us a demonstration?'

'Of what nature?' asked Katan.

'The tall man over there,' said Scaler, pointing and lowering his voice. 'Could you ask him to remove his helm and put it on again?'

'If it would please you,' said Katan and all eyes turned to the warrior some forty paces distant.

Obligingly he removed his helm, smiled and replaced it.

'That's uncanny,' said Scaler. 'How did you do it?'

'It is hard to explain,' said Katan. 'Please excuse me.' Bowing to Decado, he rejoined his companions.

'See what I mean?' said Ananais. 'Eerie, Inhuman.'

'We have men in my land with similar talents,' said Pagan.

'What do they do there?' asked Scaler.

'Very little. We burn them alive,' said Pagan.

'Is that not a little excessive?'

'Perhaps,' answered the black man. 'But then I don't believe in interfering with tradition!'

Tenaka left them talking and moved across to where Renya sat with Valtaya, Parsal and the village woman. As Renya watched him approach, her heart-beat quickened.

'Will you walk with me awhile?' he asked. She nodded and they moved away from the fires. The sun was clear and strong and its light glinted on the silver streaks in his hair. She longed to reach out and touch him, but instinct made her wait.

'I am sorry, Renya,' he said, reaching out and taking her hand. She looked into the slanted violet eyes and read the anguish there.

'Did you speak the truth? Would you have used that dagger on me?'

He shook his head.

'Do you want me to stay with you?' she asked softly.

'Do you want to stay?'

'I desire nothing else.'

'Then forgive me for being a fool,' he said. 'I am

not skilled in these things. I have always been clumsy around women.'

'I am damned glad to hear it,' she said, smiling.

Ananais watched them and his gaze slid to Valtaya. She was talking to Galand, and laughing.

I should have let the Joining kill me, he thought.

8

The journey to Skoda took three days, for the company travelled warily. Acuas told Decado that following the slaying of the soldiers, the Delnoch fortress commander had sent patrols throughout Skultik and the surrounding countryside, while to the south Legion riders scouted the lands for rebels.

Tenaka took time to speak with the leaders of The Thirty, for despite the many legends he knew little of their Order. According to the stories, The Thirty were semi-gods with awesome powers who chose to die in wars against evil. The last time they had appeared was at Dros Delnoch, when the albino Serbitar stood beside the Earl of Bronze and defied the hordes of Ulric, the greatest Nadir warlord of all time.

But though Tenaka questioned the leaders, he learned little.

They were courteous and polite – even distantly friendly – but their answers floated above his head like clouds beyond the grasp of common men. Decado was no different; he would merely smile and change the subject.

Tenaka was not a religious man, yet he felt ill-at-ease among these warrior priests and his mind constantly returned to the words of the Blind Seeker.

'Of Gold and Ice and Shadow . . .' The man had predicted the trio would come together. And they had. He had also foreseen the danger of the Templars.

On the first night of their journey, Tenaka approached the elderly Abaddon and the two walked away from the fire together.

'I saw you in Skultik,' said Tenaka. 'You were being attacked by a Joining.'

'Yes. I apologise for the deceit.'

'What was the reason for it?'

'It was a test, my son. But not merely of you – of ourselves.'

'I do not understand,' said Tenaka.

'It is not necessary that you should. Do not fear us, Tenaka. We are here to help you in whatever way we can.'

'Why?'

'Because it serves the Source.'

'Can you not answer me without religious riddles? You are men – what do you gain from this war?'

'Nothing in this world.'

'You know why I came here?'

'Yes, my son. To purge your mind of guilt and grief – to drown it in Ceska's blood.'

'And now?'

'Now you are caught up in the forces beyond your control. Your grief is assuaged by your love for Renya, but the guilt remains. You did not obey the call – you left your friends to be butchered by the Joinings of Ceska. You ask yourself if it would have been different, had you come. Could you have defeated the Joinings? You torment yourself thus.'

'Could I have defeated the Joinings?'

'No, my son.'

'Can I do it now?'

'No,' said Abaddon sadly.

'Then what are we doing here? What is the point?'

'That is for you to say, for you are the real leader.'

'I am not a torchbearer, priest! I am a man. I choose my own destiny.'

'Of course you do; I did not say otherwise. But you are a man of honour. When responsibility is thrust upon you, can you run from it? No – you never have and you never will. That is what makes you as you are. That is why men follow you, though they hate your blood. They trust you.'

'I am not a lover of lost causes, priest. You may have a desire to die, but I do not. I am not a hero – I am a soldier. When the battle is lost I retreat and regroup; when the war is over I lay down my sword. No last dashing charge, no futile last stand!'

'I understand that,' said Abaddon.

'Then know this: no matter how impossible this war, I shall fight to win. Whatever I have to do, I will do. Nothing could be worse that Ceska.'

'Now you are speaking of the Nadir. You want my blessing?'

'Don't read my mind, damn you!'

'I did not read your mind, only your words. You know the Nadir hate the Drenai – you will merely exchange one bloody tyrant for another.'

'Perhaps. But I shall attempt it.'

'Then we will help you.'

'As simply as that? No pleas, no urgings, no advice?'

'I have told you that your plan with the Nadir carries too many dangers. I shall not repeat myself. But you are the leader – it is your decision.'

'I have told only Arvan. The others would not understand.'

'I shall say nothing.'

Tenaka left him then and walked out into the night. Abaddon sat down with his back against a tree. He was tired and his soul felt heavy. He wondered then if the Abbots before him had known such doubts.

Did the poet Vintar carry such a burden when he rode with The Thirty into Delnoch? One day soon, he would know.

He sensed the approach of Decado. The warrior was troubled, but his anger was fading. Abaddon closed his eyes, resting his head against the rough bark of the three.

'May we talk?' asked Decado.

'The Voice may speak to whomever he pleases,' answered Abaddon, without opening his eyes.

'May we talk as before, when I was your pupil?'

Abaddon sat up and smiled gently. 'Join me then, my pupil.'

'I am sorry for my anger and the harsh words I used.'

'Words are but noises, my son. I put you under great strain.'

'I fear I am not the leader the Source would prefer. I wish to stand down in favour of Acuas. Is that allowed?'

'Wait for a little while. Make no decision yet. Rather, tell me what changed your mind.'

Decado leaned back on his elbows, staring at the stars. His voice was low, barely above a whisper. 'It was when I challenged the Templar and I risked all your lives. It was not a worthy deed and it shamed me. But you obeyed. You put your souls in my hand. And I didn't care.'

'But you care now, Decado?'

'Yes. Very much.'

'I am glad, my boy.'

For a while they sat in silence and then Decado

spoke. 'Tell me, Lord Abbot, how it was that the Templar fell so easily?'

'You expected to die?'

'I thought it a possibility.'

'The man you slew was one of the Six, the rulers of the Templars. His name was Padaxes. He was a vile man, a former Source priest, whose lusts overcame him.

'True, he had powers. They all have. Compared with ordinary men, they are invincible. Deadly! But you, my dear Decado, are no ordinary man. You also have powers, but they lie dormant. When you fight you release those powers and they make you a warrior beyond compare. But add to this the fact that you fought not just for yourself, but for others, and you became invincible. Evil is never truly strong, for it is born of fear. Why did he fall so easily? Because he tested your strength and saw the possibility of death. At that moment, had he possessed true courage, he would have fought back. Instead he froze – and died.

'But he will return, my son. In greater strength!'

'He is dead.'

'But the Templars are not. There are six hundred of them, and many more acolytes. The deaths of Padaxes and his group of twenty will have whiplashed through their Order. Even now they will be mustering, preparing for the hunt. And they have seen us.

'Throughout today I have felt the presence of evil. As we speak, they hover beyond the shield Acuas and Katan have placed over our camp.'

Decado shivered. 'Can we win against them?'

'No. But then we are not here to win.'

'Then why?'

'We are here to die,' said Abaddon.

*

Argonis was tired and not a little hung-over. The party had been fine and the girls . . . oh, the girls! Trust Egon to find the right women. Argonis reined in his black gelding as the scout galloped into view. He lifted his hand, halting the column.

The scout dragged back on his reins and his mount checked its run and reared, pawing the air. The man saluted.

'Riders, sir – about forty of them, heading into Skoda. They're well-armed and they seem military. Are they ours?'

'Let us find out,' said Argonis, lifting his arm and waving on the column. It was conceivable they were a scouting party from Delnoch, but in that case they would not head into the rebels' lair – not with only forty men. Argonis glanced back, seeking reassurance, and received it as his eyes wandered over the hundred Legion riders.

It would be a relief to see action and might even clear his head. Military men, the scout had said. That would make a change from witless villagers hacking about with hoes and axes.

Reaching the crest of a range of hills, Argonis gazed down over a rolling plain almost at the foot of the Skoda range. The scout rode alongside as Argonis shielded his eyes and studied the riders below.

'Ours, sir?' queried the scout.

'No. Delnoch issue red cloaks, or blue for officers – never white. I think they are Vagrian raiders.'

At that moment the column below broke into a canter heading for the sanctuary of the mountains.

'At the gallop!' yelled Argonis, drawing his sabre, and one hundred black-garbed horsemen set off in pursuit, hooves drumming on the hard-packed earth.

With the advantage of the slope, and the fact that

they were cutting towards the enemy at an angle, the gap swiftly narrowed.

Excitement swept through Argonis as he bent low over his horse's neck, the morning breeze fanning his face, his sabre glinting in the sunlight.

'*No prisoners*!' he screamed. He was close enough now to see individual riders and to note that three were women. Then he saw the black man riding alongside one of them, obviously encouraging her – she was not sitting well in the saddle and appeared to be holding something in her arms. Her companion leaned over in the saddle and snatched the bundle from her; with both hands on the reins her mount picked up speed. Argonis grinned – what a futile gesture, for the Legion would be upon them before they reached the mountains.

Suddenly the white-cloaked riders wheeled their mounts. It was a spectacular example of discipline, for they made the move in perfect unison and before Argonis could react they had turned and were charging. Panic struck at Argonis' heart. Here he was, out in front leading the chase, and now thirty madmen were bearing down on him. He dragged on the reins and his men followed suit, confused and uncertain.

The Thirty hit them like a winter storm, silver blades flashing and slicing. Horses reared and men screamed as they fell from the saddle. Then the white-cloaked riders wheeled once more and galloped away.

Argonis was furious. 'After them!' he yelled, but wisely held back his own mount as his men thundered in pursuit. The mountains were nearer now and the enemy had begun the long climb to the first valley. A horse stumbled and fell, pitching a blonde woman to the grass; three riders spurred their horses at her. A tall man dressed in black, his face masked, swung his horse and raced to intercept. Argonis watched fascinated as the masked man ducked under a wild cut and disembowelled the first rider, swinging in the saddle to block an overhead cut from the second. Spurring his horse he cannoned into the third, downing horse and man.

The woman was up now and running. The masked man parried an attack from the second rider, and slashed the man's throat with a reverse cut. Then he was clear. Sheathing his sword, he galloped his horse towards the woman, leaning over in the saddle. His arm swept down to circle her waist and sweep her up in front of him, then they were gone into the Skoda range.

Argonis cantered back to the site of the battle. Thirty-one members of his force were down; eighteen dead, another six mortally wounded.

His men returned, dejected and demoralised. The scout, Lepus, approached Argonis and dismounted. Saluting swiftly, he held Argonis' mount as the officer slid from the saddle.

'Who in Hell's name were they?' asked Lepus.

'I don't know, but they made us look like children.'

'Is that what your report will say, sir?'

'Shut your mouth!'

'Yes, sir.'

'We will have a thousand Legion riders here in a few days. Then we will smoke them out – they cannot defend an entire range. We shall see those white-cloaked bastards again.'

'I'm not sure that I want to,' said Lepus.

*

Tenaka pulled his mount to a stop by a winding stream that trickled through a grove of elm on the western side of the valley. He swung in the saddle, seeking Ananais; he could see the warrior walking his horse, Valtaya sitting side-saddle behind him. They had made it without losing a single member of their party, thanks only to the spectacular skills of The Thirty.

Dismounting, Tenaka left his horse to graze; he loosened the saddle cinch and patted the beast's neck. Renya rode alongside and leapt from her saddle, her face flushed and her eyes bright with excitement.

'Are we safe now?' she asked.

'For the moment,' he answered.

Ananais lifted his leg over the pommel of his saddle and slid to the ground, turning to lift Valtaya clear. She smiled at him and draped her arms over his shoulders.

'Will you always be on hand to save my life?'

'Always is a long time, lady,' he answered, his hands on her waist.

'Did anyone ever tell you that you have beautiful eyes?'

'Not lately,' he said, releasing her and walking away.

Galand watched the scene and then moved to Valtaya.

'I should forget it, girl,' he said. 'The man is not for winning.'

'But you are, eh, Galand?'

'I am, lass! But take your time before saying yes. I'm not exactly a great catch.'

Valtaya laughed. 'You are better than you think.'

'But it's "No" just the same?'

'I don't think you are looking for a wife, are you?'

'If only we had the time,' answered Galand seriously and reaching out, he took her hand. 'You are a fine woman, Val, and I don't think a man could do better. I wish I had known you in better days.'

'Times are what we make them. There are other nations in the world where men like Ceska are shunned. Peaceful nations.'

'I don't want to be a foreigner, Val. I want to live in my own land among my own people. I want . . .' Galand's words tailed away and Valtaya saw the anguish in his eyes. She laid her hand on his arm and he looked away.

'What is it, Galand? What were you going to say?'

'It doesn't matter, lass.' He turned back to her, his eyes clear and his emotions masked. 'Tell me what you see in our scarred companion?'

'I don't know. That is a difficult question for a woman to answer. Come on, let us get some food.'

Decado, Acuas, Balan and Katan left the group at the camp-site and rode back to the mouth of the valley, pausing to gaze down on the green plain where the Legion were ministering to their wounded. The dead had been wrapped in blankets and tied across their saddles.

'You did well,' said Decado, lifting his helm and hooking it over his pommel.

'It was appalling,' said Katan.

Decado swung in the saddle. 'You chose to be a warrior. Accept it!'

'I know that, Decado,' answered the dark-eyes priest. He smiled ruefully and rubbed his face. 'But I cannot revel in it.'

'That's not what I meant. You have chosen to fight against evil and you have just won a small victory. The babe back there would now be dead, but for you and the others.'

'I know that, too. I am not a child. But it is hard.'

The four dismounted and sat on the grass, enjoying the sunshine. Decado removed his white cloak and folded it carefully. He closed his eyes, suddenly aware of a strange sensation like a cool breeze inside his head.

He tried to focus on it and became aware of subtle ebbs and flows within his mind, like the distant echo of rolling waves over shingle. He lay back, drifting and at peace, moving within himself towards the source of the sensation. He was not surprised when the whispering seas became faint voices, and he recognised that of Acuas.

'I still feel Abaddon could be wrong. Did you sense Decado's battle-lust as we struck the riders? The force was so powerful it almost infected me.'

'Abaddon says not to judge.' This from Katan.

'But he is the Abbot no longer.' Balan spoke.

'He will always be the Abbot of Swords. He must be respected.' Katan again.

'It makes me feel uncomfortable,' pulsed Acuas. 'Where is his Talent? In all the long history of The Thirty there has never been a leader who could not Travel and Speak.'

'I think perhaps we should consider the alternatives,' pulsed Katan. 'If Abaddon was misled in his choice of the Voice, then that would mean Chaos has mastered the Source. In turn that would negate every other choice Abaddon has made and render us Outside the Destiny.'

'Not necessarily,' said Balan. 'We are all human. Abaddon could have made merely one mistake. He is Source-guided, but so much depends on interpretation. Estin's death and Decado's arrival could have been either coincidence or dark design.'

'Or Source-inspired?' pulsed Acuas.

'Indeed so.'

Decado opened his eyes and sat up. 'What are

they planning?' he asked aloud, pointing to the Legion.

'They are waiting for the arrival of their army,' said Acuas. 'The leader there, a man named Argonis, is telling his men that we will be smoked out of these mountains and destroyed along with every other rebel in Skoda. He is trying to lift them.'

'But he is not succeeding,' put in Balan.

'Tell us of the Dragon, Decado?' asked Katan and Decado smiled.

'Days of long ago,' he said. 'It seems like another lifetime.'

'Did you enjoy the life?' enquired Acuas.

'Yes and no. More no than yes, I recall. The Dragon was strange. In some way I suppose it created a bond similar to yours except of course that we had no talent and could neither Travel nor Speak as you do. But we were a family. Brothers. And we held the nation together.'

'You must have been saddened when Ceska destroyed your friends,' said Balan.

'Yes. But I was a priest and my life had changed very much. I had my garden and my plants. The world had become a small place indeed.'

'It always amazed me that you produced so many varieties of vegetable in such a small section,' said Balan.

Decado chuckled. 'I grew tomatoes inside potatoes,' he said. 'I placed the seedlings in a potato, and while the tomatoes grew upwards the potatoes grew down. I was quite pleased with the results.'

'Do you miss your garden?' asked Acuas.

'No, I do not. And that makes me sad.'

'Did you enjoy your life as a priest?' said Katan.

Decado looked at the slender young man with the

gentle face. 'Do you enjoy life as a warrior?' he countered.

'No. Not in the least.'

'In some ways I enjoyed my life. It was good to hide for a while.'

'From what were you hiding?' asked Balan.

'I think you know the answer to that. I deal in death, my friend – I always have. Some men can paint, others create beauty in stone or in words. I kill. But pride and shame do not match well and I found the disharmony daunting. In the moment of the kill there was bliss, but afterwards . . .'

'What happened afterwards?' asked Acuas.

'No man alive could match me with the blades, therefore all my enemies became defenceless. I was no longer a warrior, but a murderer. The thrill lessened, the doubts grew. When the Dragon was disbanded I travelled the world seeking opponents, but found none. Then I realised there was only one man who could test me, and I decided to challenge him. On the way to his home in Ventria I was trapped in a sandstorm for three days. It gave me time to think about what I was doing. You see, the man was my friend and yet, had it not been for the storm, I would have killed him. It was then that I returned home to the Drenai and tried to change my life.'

'And what became of your friend?' asked Katan.

Decado smiled. 'He became a Torchbearer.'

9

The council chamber had seen better days; now woodworm pockmarked the inlaid elm around the walls and the painted mosaic showing the white-bearded Druss the Legend had peeled away in ugly patches, exposing the grey of mould growing on the plaster.

Some thirty men and about a dozen women and children were seated on wooden benches, listening to the words of the woman sitting at the Senate chair. She was large, big-boned and broad of shoulder. Her dark hair swept out from her head like a lion's mane and her green eyes blazed with anger.

'Just listen to yourselves!' she roared, pushing herself to her feet and smoothing the folds in her heavy green skirt. 'Talk, talk, talk! And what does it all mean? Throw yourselves on Ceska's mercy? What in hell's name does that mean? Surrender. that's what! You, Petar – stand up!'

A man shuffled to his feet, head bowed and blushing furiously.

'Lift your arm!' bellowed the woman and he did so. The hand was missing and the stump showed evidence still of the tar that had closed the wound.

'*That* is Ceska's mercy! By all the gods, you cheered loud enough when my men of the mountains swept the soldiers from our lands. You couldn't do enough for us then, could you? But now they are coming back, you want to squeal and hide. Well, there *is* nowhere to hide. The Vagrians won't let us cross their borders, and for damn sure Ceska won't forgive and forget.'

A middle-aged man rose to his feet alongside the helpless Petar. 'It's no use shouting, Rayvan. What choices do we have? We cannot beat them. We shall all die.'

'Everybody dies, Vorak,' stormed the woman. 'Or had you not heard? I have six hundred fighting men who say we can defeat the Legion. And there are five hundred more who are waiting to join us when we can lay our hands on more weapons.'

'Suppose we do turn back the Legion,' said Vorak, 'what happens when Ceska sends in his Joinings? What use will your fighting men be then?'

'When the time comes, we shall see,' she promised.

'We shall see nothing. Go back where you came from and leave us to make peace with Ceska. We don't want you here!' shouted Vorak.

'Oh, speaking for everyone now, are we, Vorak?' Rayvan stepped from the dais and marched towards the man. He swallowed hard as she loomed over him, then her hand gripped his collar and propelled him towards the wall. 'Look up there and tell me what you see,' she commanded.

'It's a wall, Rayvan, with a picture on it. Now let me go!'

'That's not just a picture, you lump of dung! That's Druss! That's the man who stood against the hordes of Ulric. And he didn't bother to count them. You make me sick!'

Leaving him, she walked back to the dais and turned on the gathering. 'I could listen to Vorak. I could take my six hundred and vanish back into the mountains. But I know what would happen - you would all be killed. You have no choice but to fight.'

'We have families, Rayvan,' protested another man.

'Yes, and they will die too.'

'So you say,' said the man, 'but we are certain to be killed if we resist the Legion.'

'Do what you want, then,' she snapped. 'But get out of my sight – all of you! There used to be men in this land. Get out!'

Petar turned at the door, the last to leave. 'Don't judge us too harshly, Rayvan,' he called.

'Get *out*!' she bellowed. She wandered to the window and looked out at the city, white under the spring sun. Beautiful, but indefensible. There was no wall. Rayvan put together a string of oaths that rolled from her tongue with rare power. She felt better then . . . but not much.

Beyond the window in the winding streets and open squares people thronged, and although Rayvan could not hear their words she knew the subject of every conversation.

Surrender. The possibility of life. And beyond the words, the driving emotion – fear!

What was the matter with them? Had Ceska's terror eroded the strength of the people? She swung round and stared at the fading mosaic. Druss the Legend, squat and powerful with axe in hand, the mountains of Skoda behind him seeming to echo the qualities of the man – white-topped and indestructible.

Rayvan looked at her hands: short, stubby and still ingrained with the soil of her farms. Years of work, cripplingly hard work, had robbed them of beauty. She was glad there was no mirror. Once she had been the 'maid of the mountains', slim of waist and garlanded. But the years – such good years – had been less than kind. Her dark hair was now shot with silver and her face was hard as Skoda granite. Few men now looked on her with lust, which was just as well. After twenty years of marriage and nine children, she had somewhat lost interest in the beast with two backs.

Returning to the window, she looked out beyond the city to the ring of mountains. Whence would the enemy come? And how would she meet them? Her men were confident enough. Had they not defeated several hundred soldiers, losing only forty men in the process? Indeed they had – but the soldiers had been taken by surprise and they were a gutless bunch. This time would be different.

Rayvan thought long and hard about the coming battle.

Different?

They will cut us to pieces. She swore, picturing again the moment when the soldiers had swept into her lands and butchered her husband and two of their sons. The watching crowd had been subdued until Rayvan, armed with a curved meat cleaver, had run forward and hammered it into the officer's side.

Then it was pandemonium.

But now . . . Now was the time to pay for the dance.

She walked across the hall to stand with hands on hips below the mosaic.

'I have always boasted that I came from your line, Druss,' she said. 'It's not true – as far as I know. But I wish I had. My father used to talk of you. He was a soldier at Delnoch and he spent months studying the chronicles of the Earl of Bronze. He knew more about you than any man living. I wish

143

you could come back . . . Step down from that wall! Joinings wouldn't stop you, would they? You would march to Drenan and rip the crown from Ceska's head. I cannot do it, Druss. I don't know the first thing about war. And, damn it, there is no time to learn.'

The far door creaked open. 'Rayvan?'

She turned to see her son, Lucas, bow in hand. 'What is it?'

'Riders – around fifty of them, heading for the city.'

'Damn! How did they get past the scouts?'

'I don't know. Lake is gathering what men he can find.'

'Why only fifty?'

'They obviously don't hold us in high account,' said Lucas, grinning. He was a handsome lad, dark-haired but grey-eyed; with Lake he was the pick of her litter, she knew.

'They will hold us in higher account when we've met them,' she said. 'Let's move.'

They left the chamber and made their way along the marbled corridor and down the wide stairs to the street. Already the news had spread and Vorak was waiting for them, backed by more then fifty traders.

'That's it, Rayvan!' he shouted as she came into the sunlight. 'Your war is over.'

'What does that mean?' she asked, holding her temper.

'You started all this – it's your fault. Now we're going to hand you over to them.'

'Let me kill him,' whispered Lucas, reaching for an arrow.

'No!' hissed Rayvan, her eyes sweeping the build-ings opposite – in every window was an archer, bow

144

bent. 'Go back into the chamber and get out through Bakers' Alley. Fetch Lake and do what you can to get away into Vagria. Sometime, when you can, avenge me.'

'I won't leave you, mother.'

'You will do as you're told!'

He swore, then backed away through the door. Rayvan walked slowly down the steps, her face set, her green eyes locked on Vorak. He backed away.

'Tie her!' he shouted, and several men rushed forward to pin Rayvan's arms behind her back.

'I shall come back, Vorak. From beyond the grave I shall return,' she promised. He hit her across the face with the flat of his hand. She made no sound, but blood trickled from a split in her lip. They dragged her through the crowd as they made their way to the outer city and the plain beyond where the riders had come into view. The leader was a tall man with a cruel face. He dismounted and Vorak ran forward.

'We have taken the traitress, sir. She led the rebellion, if such you can call it. We are innocent men, all of us.'

The man nodded and approached Rayvan. She stared into his slanted violet eyes.

'So,' she said softly, 'even the Nadir ride with Ceska, do they?'

'Your name, woman?' he said.

'Rayvan. Remember it, barbarian, for my sons will carve it on your heart.'

He turned to Vorak. 'What do you suggest we do with her?'

'Kill her! Make an example. Death to all traitors!'

'But you are loyal?'

'I am. I always have been. It was I who first

reported the rebels in Skoda. You should know of me – I am Vorak.'

'And these men with you, they are also loyal?'

'None more so. Every one is pledged to Ceska.'

The man nodded, turning once more to Rayvan. 'And how did you come to be captured, woman?'

'We all make mistakes.'

The man lifted his hand and thirty white-cloaked riders moved out to surround the mob.

'What are you doing?' asked Vorak.

The man drew his sword, testing the edge with his thumb. He spun on his heel, the blade flashed out and Vorak's head tumbled from his neck, eyes wide with horror.

The head bounced at the man's feet as Vorak's body collapsed to the grass, blood pumping from his neck. The men in the crowd fell to their knees, begging for mercy.

'Silence!' bellowed a black-masked giant who sat a bay gelding. The noise subsided, though here and there the sound of sobbing could still be heard.

'I have no wish to kill you all,' said Tenaka Khan. 'So you will be taken to the valley and released to make your peace with the Legion. I wish you luck – I sincerely believe you will need it. Now get up and move out.'

Herded by The Thirty, the men began to walk to the east as Tenaka untied Rayvan's arms.

'Who are you?' she asked.

'Tenaka Khan, of the line of the Earl of Bronze,' he answered, bowing.

'I am Rayvan – of the line of Druss the Legend,' she told him, planting her hands on her hips.

*

Scaler wandered alone in the gardens of Gathere behind the city council hall. He had sat listening as

Tenaka and Rayvan talked of the coming battle, but could find no sensible comments to add. So he had slipped out quietly, his heart heavy. He had been a fool to join them. What could he offer? He was no warrior.

He sat on a stone bench, staring into a rock pool and watching the golden fish dart among the lilies. Scaler had been a lonely child. It had not been easy living with the irascible Orrin, knowing how the old man had pinned his hopes on Scaler becoming a worthy successor. The family had proved ill-fated and Scaler was the last of the line – if you discounted Tenaka Khan. And most people did.

But Arvan – as Scaler then was – had taken to the Nadir youngster, seeking his company at every opportunity, relishing the stories of life on the Steppes. His admiration had changed to hero worship on the night when the assassin climbed into his room.

The man, dressed all in black and hooded, had reached across his bed to clamp a gloved hand over his mouth. Arvan, a sensitive, frightened six-year-old, had fainted in fear, awaking only when the cold winter breeze touched his cheek. When his eyes opened he found himself staring down from the battlements to the cobbles far below. He twisted in the man's grip and felt his fingers loosen.

'If you value your life, don't do it!' said a voice.

The assassin cursed softly, but his hold strengthened.

'And if I let him live?' he asked, his voice muffled.

'Then you live,' said Tenaka Khan.

'You are just a boy. I could kill you too.'

'Then go on with your mission,' said Tenaka. 'And try your luck.'

For several seconds the assassin hesitated. Then

he slowly pulled Arvan back over the battlements and placed him on the stone steps. The man backed away into the shadows and was gone. Arvan ran to Tenaka and the youth sheathed his sword and hugged him.

'He was going to kill me, Tani.'

'I know. But he's gone now.'

'Why did he want to kill me?'

Tenaka had not known the answer. Neither had Orrin, but thereafter a guard was placed at Arvan's door and his life continued with fear as a constant companion . . .

'Good afternoon.'

Scaler looked up to see, standing by the pool, a young woman dressed in a flowing gown of thin white wool. Her hair was dark and gently waved, and her green eyes were flecked with gold. Scaler stood and bowed.

'Why so gloomy?' she asked.

He shrugged. 'I would rather say melancholy. Who are you?'

'Ravenna, Rayvan's daughter. Why are you not in there with the others?'

He grinned. 'I know nothing about wars, campaigns or battles.'

'What do you know about?'

'Art, literature, poetry and all things of beauty.'

'You are out of your time, my friend.'

'Scaler. Call me Scaler.'

'A strange name, Scaler. Do you climb things?'

'Walls, mostly.' He gestured towards the seat. 'Will you join me?' he asked.

'For a little while only. I have errands to run.'

'I am sure they can wait. Tell me, how did a woman come to lead a rebellion?'

'To understand that, you have to know mother.

She is of the line of Druss the Legend, you know, and will not be cowed by anyone or anything. She once drove off a mountain lion with a large stick.'

'A formidable lady,' said Scaler.

'Indeed she is. And she also knows nothing about wars, campaigns and battles. But she will learn. So should you.'

'I would sooner learn more about you, Ravenna,' he said, switching on his winning smile.

'I see there are some campaigns that you understand,' she said, rising from her seat. 'It was nice meeting you.'

'Wait! Could we meet again? Tonight, for instance?'

'Perhaps. If you live up to your name.'

*

That night, as Rayvan lay in her broad bed staring out at the stars, she felt more at peace than at any time during the last few hectic months. She had not realised just how irksome leadership could be. Nor had she ever intended to be a leader. All she had done was to slay the man who killed her husband – but from then on it had been like sliding down an icy mountain.

Within weeks of the campaign Rayvan's slender forces controlled most of Skoda. Those were the heady days of cheering crowds and cameraderie. Then word began to filter into the mountains of an army being gathered, and swiftly the mood changed. Rayvan had felt besieged in the city even before the enemy had arrived.

Now she felt light of heart.

Tenaka Khan was no ordinary man. She smiled and closed her eyes, summoning his image to her mind. He moved like a dancer in perfect control and he wore confidence like a cloak. The warrior born!

Ananais was more enigmatic but, by all the gods, he had the look of eagles about him. Here was a man who had been over the mountain. He it was who had offered to train her fledgling fighters and Lake had taken him back into the hills where they camped. The two brothers Galand and Parsal had travelled with them – solid men, with no give in them.

The black she was unsure of. He looked like a damned Joining, she thought. But for all that, he was a handsome devil. And there was little doubt he could handle himself.

Rayvan turned over, punching a little comfort into the thick pillow.

Send in your Legion, Ceska. We shall stove in their damned teeth!

Down the long corridor, in a room facing east, Tenaka and Renya lay side by side, an uncomfortable silence between them.

Tenaka rolled on to his elbow and looked down at her, but Renya did not return his gaze.

'What is the matter?' he asked.

'Nothing.'

'That is palpably untrue. Please, Renya, speak to me.'

'It was the man you killed.'

'You knew him?'

'No, I didn't. But he was unarmed – there was no need.'

'I see,' he said, swinging his long legs from the bed. He walked to the window, and she lay there staring at his naked form silhouetted against the moonlight.

'Why did you do it?'

'It was necessary.'

'Explain it to me.'

'He led the mob and he was obviously Ceska's man. By killing him suddenly, it cowed them. You saw them – all armed, many with bows. They could have turned on us, but his death stunned them.'

'It certainly stunned me – it was butchery!'

He turned to face her. 'This is not a game, Renya. Many men will die, even before this week is out.'

'It still was not right.'

'*Right*? This isn't a poem, woman! I am not some gold-armoured hero righting wrongs. I reasoned that his death would allow us to remove a cancer from the city without loss to ourselves. And anyway, he deserved to die.'

'It doesn't touch you, does it? Taking life? You don't care that he might have had a family, children, a mother.'

'You are right; I don't care. There are only two people in the world that I love – you are one and Ananais is the other. That man had made his decision. He chose sides and he died for it. I don't regret it and probably I would have forgotten it within the month.'

'That is a terrible thing to say!'

'You would prefer it if I lied to you?'

'No. I just thought you were . . . different.'

'Don't judge me. I am only a man doing my best. I know no other way to be.'

'Come back to bed.'

'Is the argument over?'

'If you want it to be,' she lied.

In the room above them Pagan grinned and moved away from the window.

Women were strange creatures. They fell in love with a man and then sought to change him. Mostly they succeed – to spend the rest of their lives wondering how they could have married such boring conformists. It is the nature of the beast, Pagan told himself. He thought of his own wives, running their faces past his mind's eye, but he could picture only about thirty of them. You are getting old, he told himself. He often wondered how he had allowed the numbers to become so great. The palace was more crowded than a bazaar. Ego. That was it! There was no getting away from it. Just as there was no getting away from his forty-two children. He shuddered. Then he chuckled.

A faint shuffling noise disturbed his thoughts and he moved back to the window, peering out into the shadows.

A man was climbing the wall some twenty feet to the right – it was Scaler.

'What are you doing?' asked Pagan, keeping his voice low.

'I am planting corn,' hissed Scaler. 'What do you think I'm doing?'

Pagan glanced up to the darkened window above. 'Why didn't you just climb the stairs?'

'I was asked to arrive this way. It's a tryst.'

'Oh, I see. Well, goodnight!'

'And to you.'

Pagan ducked back his head through the window. Strange how much effort a man would make just to get himself into trouble.

'What's going on?' came the voice of Tenaka Khan.

'Will you keep your voice down?' snarled Scaler.

Pagan returned to the window, leaning out to see Tenaka staring upwards.

'He is on a tryst . . . or something,' said Pagan.

'If he falls he will break his neck.'

'He never falls,' said Belder, from a window to the left. 'He has a natural talent for not falling.'

'Will someone tell me why there is a man climbing the wall?' shouted Rayvan.

'He is on a tryst!' yelled Pagan.

'Why couldn't he climb the stairs?' she responded.

'We have been through all that. He was asked to come this way!'

'Oh. He must be seeing Ravenna then,' she said.

Scaler clung to the wall, engaged in his own private conversation with the Senile Eternals.

Meanwhile in the darkened room above. Ravenna bit her pillow to stop the laughter.

Without success.

*

For two days Ananais walked among the Skoda fighters, organising them into fighting units of twenty and pushing them hard. There were five hundred and eighty-two men, most of them tough and wolf-lean. Men to match the mountains. But they were undisciplined and unused to organised warfare. Given time, Ananais could have produced a fighting force to equal anything Ceska could send against them. But he did not have time.

On his first morning with the grey-eyed Lake, he had mustered the men and checked their weapons. There were not one hundred swords among them.

'It's not a farmer's weapon,' said Lake. 'But we have plenty of axes and bows.' Ananais nodded and moved on. Sweat trickled under his mask, burning against the scars that would not heal, and his irritation grew.

'Find me twenty men who could make leaders,' he said, then walked swiftly back to the crofter's cottage he had made his quarters. Galand and Parsal followed him.

'What's wrong?' asked Galand as the three men sat down in the cool of the main room.

'Wrong? There are nearly six hundred men out there who will be dead in a few days. That is what's wrong.'

'A little defeatist, aren't you?' said Parsal evenly.

'Not yet. But I am close,' admitted Ananais. 'They are tough and they are willing. But you cannot send a mob against the Legion. We don't even have a bugle. And if we did, there is not one man out there to understand a single call.'

'Then we shall have to cut and run – hit them hard and move away,' proposed Galand.

'You were never an officer, were you?' said Ananais.

'No. I didn't come from the right background,' snapped Galand.

'Whatever the reason, the simple fact is that you were not trained to lead. We cannot hit and run because that would mean splitting our force. Then the Legion would come after us piecemeal and we would have no way of knowing what was happening to the rest of the army. Equally, it would allow the Legion to enter Skoda and embark on a killing campaign against the cities and villages.'

'Then what do you suggest?' asked Parsal, pouring water from a stone jug and passing the clay goblets to the other two.

Ananais turned away and lifted his mask, noisily sipping the cool water. Then he turned back to them. 'To be truthful, I don't know yet. If we stay together they will cut us to pieces in a single day. If we split up, they will cut the villagers to pieces. The choices are not attractive. I have asked Lake to supply me with rough maps of the terrain. And we have maybe two days to drill the men so that they will respond to rudimentary calls – we will use hunting horns and work out simple systems. Galand, I want you to go among the men and find the best two hundred – I want men who will stand firm against horsemen. Parsal, you check the bowmen. Again I want the best brought together as one unit. I shall also want to know the finest runners. And send Lake to me.'

As the two men left, Ananais gently removed the black leather mask. Then he filled a bowl with water and dabbed the red, angry scars. The door opened and he swung round, turning his back on the newcomer. Having settled the mask in place, he offered Lake a chair. Rayvan's eldest son was a fine-looking man, strong and lean; his eyes were the colour of a winter sky and he moved with animal grace and the confidence of the man who knows he has limits, but has not yet reached them.

'You are not impressed with our army?' he said.

'I am impressed by their courage.'

'They are mountain men,' said Lake, leaning back in his chair and stretching out his long legs on to the table top. 'But you did not answer my question.'

'It was not a question,' replied Ananais. 'You knew the answer. I am not impressed. But then they are not an army.'

'Can we turn back the Legion?'

Ananais considered the question. With many another man he would have lied, but not with this one. Lake was too sharp.

'Probably not.'

'And will you still stay?'

'Yes.'

'Why?'

'A good question. But I cannot answer it.'

'It seemed simple enough.'

'Why will you stay?' countered Ananais.

'This is my land and they are my people. My family brought them to this.'

'Your mother, you mean?'

'If you like.'

'She is a fine woman.'

'Indeed she is. But I want to know why you will stay.'

'Because it is what I do, boy. I fight. I'm Dragon. Do you understand?'

Lake nodded. 'So the war between good and evil does not concern you?'

'Yes, it does, but not greatly. Most wars are fought for greed but we are luckier here – we fight for our lives and the lives of the people we love.'

'And the land,' said Lake.

'Rubbish!' snapped Ananais. 'No man fights for dirt and grass. No, nor mountains. Those mountains were here before the Fall and they will be here when the world topples again.'

'I don't see it that way.'

'Of course not – you're young and full of fire. Me – I'm older than the sea. I have been over the mountain and looked into the eye of the Serpent. I have seen it all, young Lake. And I am not too impressed.'

'So! We understand one another, at least,' said Lake, grinning. 'What do you want me to do?'

'I want men sent now to the city. We have only seven thousand arrows and that is not enough. We have no armour – get some. I want the city scoured. We need food, oats, meal, dried beef, fruit. And I want horses – up to fifty. More if you can get them.'

'And how will we pay for all this?'

'Give them notes.'

'They will not accept promises from dead men.'

'Use your head, Lake. They will accept – because if they don't, you will take what you want. Any man

156

who refuses will be branded a traitor and dealt with accordingly.'

'I am not going to kill a man because he won't let us rob him.'

'Then go back to your mother and send me a man who wants to win,' stormed Ananais . . .

The weapons and food began to arrive on the morning of the third day.

*

By the morning of the fourth day Galand, Parsal and Lake had chosen the two hundred men Ananais had requested to stand against the Legion. Parsal had also organised the finest of the archers into a single group of just under one hundred.

As the sun cleared the eastern peaks, Ananais gathered the men together in an open meadow below the camp. Many of them now carried swords, by courtesy of the city armourer. All the archers carried two quivers of arrows, and even the occasional breastplate was to be seen among Ananais' new foot soldiers. With Parsal, Lake and Galand flanking him, Ananais climbed to the back of a cart and stood with hands on hips, eyes scanning the warriors seated around him.

'No fine speeches, lads,' he told them. 'We heard last night that the Legion is almost upon us. Tomorrow we will be in position to greet them. They are heading for the lower eastern valley, which I am told you call the Demon's Smile.

'There are about twelve hundred fighting men, all well-armed and well-horsed. Two hundred of them are archers – the rest lancers and swordsmen.' He paused to let the numbers sink in and watched men exchange glances, noting with pleasure the absence of fear in their faces.

'I have never believed in lying to the men under

my command, and so I tell you this: our chances of victory are slim. Very slim! It is important we understand that.

'You know me by reputation. As yet you do not know me as a man. But I ask you to listen to what I say now, as if your own fathers were whispering in your ears. Battles are won in many cases by the actions of a single man. Each one of you could represent the difference between victory and defeat.

'Druss the Legend was such a man. He turned the battle for Skeln Pass into one of the greatest Drenai victories of all time. But he was just a man – a Skoda man.

'On the day one of you, or ten of you, or a hundred of you, will turn the battle. A moment's panic, or a single second of heroism.' He paused again and then lifted his hand, one finger pointing to the sky. 'One single second!'

'Now I am going to ask for the first act of courage from some of you. If there be any men here who believe they could fail their friends in tomorrow's fight, let them leave the camp before today's end.

'I swear by all I hold precious that I will look down on no man who does this. For tomorrow it is vital that the men who look into the eyes of death should not falter.

'Later today we will be joined by a warrior second to none on the face of this earth – the most skilful general I have ever known and the deadliest fighting man under the sun. He will have with him a group of soldiers having very special talents; these warriors will be split up among you and their orders are to be obeyed without hesitation. And I *mean* that!

'Lastly, I ask for something for myself. I was the Wing Gan of the finest army in the world – the Dragon. They were my family, my friends, my brothers. And they are dead, betrayed and lost to this nation. But the Dragon was more than an army, it was an ideal. A dream, if you like. It was a force to stand against Darkness, formed by men who would march into Hell with a bucket of water, knowing they would put out the fire.

'But you don't need glittering armour or a battle standard to be the Dragon. You just need to be willing.

'The forces of Darkness are marching against us, like storm winds against a lantern. They think to find us cowering in the mountains like sheep. But I want them to feel the Dragon's breath on their necks and the Dragon's teeth in their guts! I want those black-garbed, high-riding sons of sluts to burn in the Dragon's fire!' He was shouting now, his fists clenched and punching the air for emphasis. He took a deep breath, then another, and suddenly swung out his arm to encompass them all.

'I want you to *be* the Dragon. I want you to *think* Dragon. When they charge I want you to *fight* like Dragon!

'Can you do it? Well, CAN YOU?' he bellowed, pointing at a man in the front row.

'Damn right!' shouted the man.

'Can you?' said Ananais, pointing to a warrior several rows back. The man nodded. 'Use your voice!' stormed the general.

'I can!' the man called.

'And do you know the Dragon's roar?'

The man shook his head.

'The Dragon's roar is death. Death. DEATH! Let's hear you – you alone!'

The man cleared his throat and began to shout. He was blushing furiously.

'Give him some support, the rest of you!' Ananais, joining in with the man.

'Death, Death, DEATH . . .' and the sound grew, rolling across the meadow to echo in the white-capped mountains, growing in strength and confidence, hypnotic as it drew the men together.

Ananais stepped from the wagon, pulling Lake to him.

'Now you get up there, lad. And give them your fighting-for-the-land speech. They're ready for it now, by thunder!'

'No fine speeches, indeed,' said Lake, grinning.

'Get up there, Lake, and lift their blood!'

10

Pagan took the village woman Parise to an inn at the southern quarter of the city, where he passed three gold coins to the innkeeper. The man's eyes bulged at the sight of the small fortune glittering in his palm.

'I want the woman and the babe to receive your best,' said Pagan softly. 'I will leave more gold with friends, should this amount prove insufficient.'

'I will treat her like my own sister,' said the man.

'That is good,' said Pagan, smiling broadly and leaning over him. 'Because if you do not, I shall eat your heart.'

'There is no need to threaten me, black man,' said the stocky balding innkeeper, drawing back his shoulders and clenching his powerful fists. 'I require no instructions on how to treat a woman.'

Pagan nodded. 'These are not good times to rely on trust alone.'

'No, that's true enough. Will you join me for a drink?'

The two men sat together nursing their ale, while Parise fed the babe in the privacy of her new room. The innkeeper's name was Ilter and he had lived in the city for twenty-three years, ever since his farm failed during the great drought.

'You know you have given me too much money, don't you?' he said.

'I know,' answered Pagan. Ilter nodded and drained the rest of his ale.

'I have never seen a black man before.'

'In my land, beyond the dark jungles and the Mountains of the Moon, the people have never seen a white man, though there are legends that speak of such.'

'Strange world, isn't it?' said Ilter.

Pagan stared into the golden depths of his drink, suddenly homesick for the rolling veldt, the sunsets of scarlet and the coughing roar of the hunting lion.

He remembered the morning of the Day of Death. Would he ever forget it? The ships with black sails had beached in White Gold Bay and the raiders had swiftly made their way inland to his father's village. The old man had gathered his warriors swiftly, but there were not enough and they had been butchered at the last before the old king's kraal.

The raiders had come in search of gold, for legends were many concerning the people of the bay, but the old mines had been long worked out and the people had turned to the growing gold of maize and corn. In their fury the raiders took the women and tortured many, raping and murdering them at the last. In all four hundred souls passed over on that day – among them Pagan's father, mother, three sisters, a younger brother and four of his daughters.

One child escaped during the opening moments of the attack and ran like the wind, finding Pagan and his personal guard hunting in the High Hills.

With sixty men he raced barefoot over the veldt, his long-bladed spear resting on his shoulder. They reached the village soon after the raiders had left. Taking in the scene at a glance Pagan read the tracks. Three hundred men or more had attacked his father's kraal – too many for him to handle. Taking his spear, he snapped it across his knee, discarding the long shaft and hefting the stabbing blade like a short sword. His men followed suit.

'I want many dead – but one alive,' said Pagan. 'You, Bopa, will take the live one and bring him to me. For the rest, let us drink blood.'

'We hear and obey, Kataskicana,' they shouted, and he led them into the jungle and on to the bay.

Moving like black ghosts, they came upon the party singing and laughing as they made their way back to their ships. Pagan and his sixty fell upon them like demons of hell, hacking and stabbing. Then they were gone into the jungle.

Eighty raiders died in that one attack and one man was missing, presumed dead. For three days he wished that were so.

Pagan took the man to the ruined village and there he used all the barbarous skills of his people until at last the thing that had been a man gave up his soul to the void. Then Pagan had the carcass burned.

Returning to his palace, he called his counsellors to him and told them of the attack.

'My family blood calls to me for revenge,' he told them, 'yet our nation is too distant for war. The killers came from a land called Drenai, sent by their king to gather gold. I am a king and I carry the heart of my people in my hand. Therefore I alone shall carry this war to the enemy. I shall seek out their king and destroy him. My own son, Katasi, will sit on my throne until I return. If I am gone for longer than three years . . .' He turned to the warrior beside him. 'It is time for you to rule, Katasi. I was king at your age.'

'Let me go in your place, father,' pleaded the young man.

'No. You are the future. If I do not return, I do not wish my wives to burn. It is one thing for them to follow a king on the day of his death and at the place of his passing. But if I am to die it may be that it will happen soon. I cannot have my wives waiting three years only to be lost in the mists. Let them live.'

'To hear is to obey.'

'Good! I believe I have taught you well, Katasi. Once you hated me for sending you to Ventria to study – even as I hated my father. Now I think you will find those years to your benefit.'

'May the Lord Shem rest his soul upon your sword,' said Katasi, embracing his father.

It had taken Pagan more than a year to reach the lands of the Drenai, and cost him half the gold he carried. He had soon realised the enormity of his task. Now he knew the gods had given him his chance.

Tenaka Khan was the key.

But first they must defeat the Legion.

*

For the last forty hours Tenaka Khan had been camped in the Demon's Smile, riding and walking over the terrain, studying each curve and hollow, memorising details of cover and angles of possible attack.

Now he sat with Rayvan and her son Lucas at the highest point of the curving valley, staring out on to the plain beyond the mountains.

'Well?' said Rayvan, for the third time. 'Have you come up with anything?' Rubbing his tired eyes, Tenaka discarded the sketch he had been working on and turned to the warrior woman, smiling. Her ample frame was now hidden beneath a long mailshirt and her dark hair was braided beneath a round black helm.

'I hope you are not still intending to stand with the fighters, Rayvan,' he said.

'You cannot talk me out of it,' she replied. 'My mind is made up.'

'Don't argue, man,' advised Lucas. 'You will be wasting your breath.'

'I got them into this,' she said, 'and I will be damned if I let them die for me without being with them.'

'Make no mistake about it, Rayvan, there will be a deal of dying. We can achieve no cheap victory here; we shall be lucky if we don't lose two-thirds of our force.'

'That many?' she whispered.

'At least. There is too much killing ground.'

'Can't we just pepper them with arrows from the high ground as they enter the valley?' asked Lucas.

'Yes. But they would just leave half their force to keep us pinned down and then attack the city and the villages. The bloodshed would be terrible.'

'Then what do you suggest?' said Rayvan.

He told her and she blanched. Lucas said nothing. Tenaka folded the parchment notes and sketches and tied them with a strip of leather. The silence grew between them.

'Despite your tainted blood,' said Rayvan at last, 'I trust you, Tenaka. From any other man, I would say it was madness. Even from you . . .'

'There is no other way to win. But I accept it is fraught with dangers. I have marked out the ground where the work must be done, and I have made maps and charted distances for the archers to memorise. But it is up to you, Rayvan. You are the leader here.'

'What do you think, Lucas?' she asked her son.

He waved his hands. 'Don't ask me! I'm not a soldier.'

'You think *I* am?' snapped Rayvan. 'Give me an opinion.'

'I don't like it. But I cannot give you an alternative. As Tenaka says, if we cut and run we open Skoda to them. And we cannot win that way. But two-thirds . . .'

Rayvan pushed herself to her feet, grunting as her rheumatic knee half gave way beneath her. She walked away down the slope to sit beside a ribbon stream that rushed over white pebbles, glinting like pearls inches below the surface.

Burrowing in the pocket of her mailshirt she found a hard-cake biscuit. It had broken into three pieces against the iron rings.

She felt a fool.

What was she doing here? What did she know of war?

She had raised fine sons and her husband had been a prince among men, big and gentle and soft as goosedown. When the soldiers cut him down she had reacted in an instant. But from then on she had lived a lie – revelling in her new role as a warrior queen, making decisions and directing an army. But it was all a sham, just like her claim to Druss' line. Her head bowed and she bit the knuckle of her thumb to stop the tears flowing.

What are you, Rayvan? she asked herself.

A fat, middle-aged woman in a man's mailshirt.

Tomorrow, or at most the day after, four hundred young men would die for her . . . their blood on her hands. Among them would be her surviving sons. Dipping her hands into the stream, she washed her face.

'Oh, Druss, what should I do? What would you do?'

There was no answer. Nor did she expect one. The dead were dead – no golden shades in ghostly palaces gazing fondly down on their descendants. There was no one to hear her cry for help, no living thing. Unless the stream itself and the pearl-like stones beneath could hear her, or the soft spring grass and the purple heather. She was alone.

In a way this had always been so. Her husband, Laska, had been a great comfort and she had loved him well. But never with that all-consuming love she had dreamed about. He had been like a rock, a solid steadfast mountain of a man she could cling to when no others could see her. He had inner strength, and he didn't mind when she lorded it over him in public and appeared to be making all the family decisions. In reality she listened to his advice in the quiet of their room and, more often than not, acted upon it.

Now Laska was gone, and with him her other son, Geddis, and she sat alone in a ridiculous mailshirt. She gazed out at the mountains at the opening of the Demon's Smile, picturing the dark-cloaked Legion riders as they rode into the valley, remembering again the blow that had felled Laska. He had not expected an attack and was sitting by the well talking to Geddis. There must have been two hundred Skoda men in the area, waiting for the cattle auction. She had not heard what passed between the officer and her husband, for she was thirty feet away, chopping meat for the barbecue. But she had seen the sword flash into the air and watched the blade as it cut deep. Then she had been running, the meat cleaver in her hand . . .

Now the Legion were coming back for revenge – not just on her but on the innocents of Skoda. Anger flickered inside her – they thought to ride into her mountains and stain the grass with the blood of her people!

Pushing herself to her feet, she slowly made her way back towards Tenaka Khan. He sat motionless like a statue, watching her without emotion in those violet eyes. Then he rose. She blinked, for his movement was swift and fluid; one moment he was still, the next in motion. There was perfection in that movement and it gave her confidence, though she could not imagine why.

'You have made a decision?' he asked.

'Yes. We will do as you advise. But I stay with the men in the centre.'

'As you wish, Rayvan. I shall be at the mouth of the valley.'

'Is that wise?' she asked. 'Is that not very dangerous for our general?'

'Ananais will take the centre, Decado the right flank. I shall come back to cover the left. If I fall, Galand shall cover for me. Now I must seek Ananais, for I want his men working through the night.'

*

The leaders of The Thirty met together in a sheltered hollow on the eastern slopes of the Demon's Smile. Below in the bright moonlight four hundred men were toiling, stripping turf and digging channels into the soft black earth beneath.

The five priests sat in a tight circle, saying nothing as Acuas travelled, receiving reports from the ten warriors watching over the preparations. Acuas soared high into the night sky, revelling in the freedom of the air; there was no gravity here, no necessity for breath, no chains of muscle and bone. Here, above the world, his eyes could see for ever and his ears hear the sweet song of the solar winds. It was intoxicating and his soul swelled with the extravagance of the beauty of the universe.

It was an effort to return to his duties, but Acuas was a man of discipline. He thought-flew to the outer scouts holding the shield against the Templars, and felt the malice beyond the barrier.

'How goes it, Oward?' he pulsed.

'It is hard, Acuas. They are growing in strength all the time. We will not be able to hold them for much longer.'

'It is imperative the Templars do not see the preparations.'

'We are almost at our limits, Acuas. Much more and they will be through. Then the deaths will begin.'

'I know. Hold them!'

Acuas sped down and on past the mouth of the valley to where the Legion were camped. Hovering there was the warrior Astin.

'Greetings, Acuas!'

'Greetings. Any change?'

'I don't believe so, Acuas, but the Templars have now closed us off and I can no longer intercept the leader's thoughts. But he is confident. He does not expect serious opposition.'

'Have the Templars tried to get through to you?'

'Not as yet. The shield holds. How fare Oward and the others?'

'They are being pushed to the limit. Do not wait too long, Astin. I do not want to see you cut off.'

'Acuas,' pulsed Astin as the other made to leave.

'Yes?'

'The men we escorted from the city . . .'

'Yes?'

'They have all been slain by the Legion. It was ghastly.'

'I feared it would be so.'

'Are we responsible for their deaths?'

'I don't know, my friend; I fear so. Be careful.'

Acuas returned to his body and opened his eyes. He outlined the situation to the others and waited for Decado to speak.

'There is no more we can do,' said Decado, 'it is set. It will be dawn in less than three hours and the Legion will strike. As you know, Tenaka requires five of us to join his forces. The choice of men I will leave to you, Acuas. The rest of us will stand with Ananais at the centre. The woman, Rayvan, will be with us – Ananais wishes her protected at all costs.'

'No easy task,' said Balan.

'I didn't say it was easy,' answered Decado. 'Merely to try. Psychologically she is vital, for the Skoda men fight for her as well as for the land.'

'I understand that, Decado,' said Balan smoothly. 'But we can guarantee nothing. We will be on open ground with no horses and nowhere to run.'

'Do you imply criticism of Tenaka's plan?' asked Abaddon.

'No,' said Balan. 'We are all students of war here, and tactically his battle strategy is sound – technically brilliant, in fact. However, at best it has a thirty-per-cent chance of success.'

'Sixty,' said Decado.

Balan lifted an eyebrow. 'Really? Explain.'

'I accept you have skills beyond ordinary men. I accept also that your understanding of strategy is exceptional. But beware of pride, Balan.'

'In what way?' asked Balan, the hint of a sneer on his face.

'Because your training has been merely that –

training. If we mapped out the battle as a game of chance, then thirty per cent is correct. But this is not a game. Down there you have Ananais, the Golden One. His strength is great and his skill greater. But more than this he has a power over men that comes close to your own psychic talents. Where he stands others will stand – he holds them with the power of his will. It is what makes him a leader. Any estimate of success in such a scheme will depend on the willingness of the line to hold, and the men to die. They may be beaten and slain, but they will not run.

'Add to this the speed of thought of Tenaka Khan. Like Ananais he has great skill and his understanding of strategy is beyond compare. But his timing is immaculate. He does not have Ananais' leadership qualities, but only because of his mixed blood. Men of the Drenai will think twice before following a Nadir.

'Lastly there is the woman, Rayvan. Her men will fight the stronger because she is with them. Revise your estimate, Balan.'

'I will reconsider, adjusting the points to incorporate your suggestions,' said the priest.

Decado nodded and then turned to Acuas. 'How far away are the Templars?'

'They will not arrive for tomorrow's battle, thank the Source! There are one hundred of them two days' ride from here. The rest are in Drenan while the leaders, the Six, meet with Ceska.'

'Then that is a problem for another day,' said Decado. 'I think I will rest now.'

Dark-eyed Katan spoke for the first time. 'Will you not lead us in prayer, Decado?'

Decado smiled gently. There was no hint of criticism from the young priest.

'No, Katan. You are closer to the Source than I and you are the Soul of The Thirty. You pray.'

Katan bowed and the group closed their eyes in silent communion. Decado relaxed his mind, listening for the faint sea roar. He drifted until the 'voice' of Katan grew and he floated towards it. The prayer was short and perfect in its sincerity, and Decado was touched to hear the young priest mention him by name, calling on the Lord of the Heavens to protect him.

Later, as Decado lay staring up at the stars, Abaddon came and sat beside him. The slim warrior sat up and stretched his back.

'Are you looking forward to tomorrow?' the Abbot asked.

'I am afraid that I am.'

The old man leaned back against a tree and closed his eyes. He looked tired, drained of all strength; the lines on his face – once as delicate as web threads – now seemed chiselled deep.

'I have compromised you, Decado,' whispered the Abbot. 'I have drawn you into a world you would not otherwise have seen. I have prayed about you constantly. It would be pleasant to know I was right. But that is not to be.'

'I cannot help you, Abaddon.'

'I know that. Every day I watched you in your garden and I wondered. In truth it was more hope than certainty. We are not a true Thirty – we never were. The Order was disbanded in my father's day but I felt – in my arrogance – that the world had need of us. So I scoured the continent, seeking out those children of special gifts. I did my best to teach them, praying the Source would guide me.'

'Perhaps you were right,' said Decado softly.

'I don't know any more. I have watched them all

tonight, joined them in their thoughts. Where there should be tranquillity there is excitement, and even a lust for battle. It began when you killed Padaxes and they joyed in your victory.'

'What did you expect of them? There is not a man among them over twenty-five years of age! And they have never lived ordinary lives . . . been drunk . . . kissed a woman. Their humanity has been suppressed.'

'Think you so? I would prefer to think their humanity has been enhanced.'

'I am out of my depth in this conversation,' admitted Decado. 'I don't know what you expect from them. They will die for you – is that not enough?'

'No. Not by far. This grimy little war is meaningless against the vast scope of human endeavour. Don't you think these mountains have seen it all before? Does it matter that we may all die tomorrow? Will the world spin any less fast? Will the stars shine any more brightly? In a hundred years, not a man here today will still be alive. Will that matter? Many years ago, Druss the Legend stood and died on the walls of Dros Delnoch to stop a Nadir invasion. Does that matter now?'

'It mattered to Druss. It matters to me.'

'But why?'

'Because I am a man, priest. Simply that. I don't know if the Source exists and I don't really care. All I have is myself, and my own self-respect.'

'There must be more. There must be the triumph of Light. Man is so beset by greed, lust and the pursuit of the ephemeral. But kindness, understanding and love are equally parts of humanity.'

'Are you now saying we should love the Legion?'

'Yes. And we must fight them.'

'That is too deep for me,' said Decado.

'I know. But I hope one day you will understand. I shall not be there to see it. Yet I pray for it.'

'Now you are getting morbid. That happens on the eve of a battle.'

'I am not morbid, Decado. Tomorrow is my last day on this earth. I know it. I have seen it. It doesn't matter . . . I just hoped that tonight you could convince me that I was right – at least with you.'

'What do you want me to say?'

'There is nothing you *can* say.'

'Then I cannot help you. You know what my life was before I met you. I was a killer and I revelled in death. I do not wish to sound weak, but I never asked to be that way – it was just me. I had neither the strength nor the inclination to change. You understand? But then I almost killed a man I loved. And I came to you. You gave me a place to hide and I was grateful. Now I am back where I belong, with a sword near to hand and an enemy close by.

'I don't deny the Source. I just don't know what game He is playing – why he allows the Ceskas of this world to survive. I don't want to know. While my arm is strong I shall oppose Ceska's evil, and at the end of all things if the Source says to me, "Decado, you do not deserve immortality," then I shall reply, "So be it." There will be no regrets.

'You could be right. You might die tomorrow. If the rest of us survive, I shall look after your young warriors. I shall try to keep them to your path. I think they will not let you down. But then you will be with your Source, and you must ask Him to lend a hand.'

'And what if I was wrong?' asked the Abbot, leaning forward and gripping Decado's arm. 'What if I resurrected The Thirty because of my own arrogance?'

'I don't know, Abaddon. But you acted in faith with no thought of gain. Even if you are wrong, your God should forgive you. If he does not, then he is not worth following. If one of your priests commits an indiscretion, do you not forgive him? Are you then more forgiving than your God?'

'I don't know. I'm not certain of anything any more.'

'You once told me that certainty and faith do not belong together. Have faith, Abaddon.'

'It is not easy, Decado, to be confident on the day of your death.'

'Why did you seek me out with this? I cannot help you to find faith. Why did you not speak to Katan, or Acuas?'

'I felt you would understand.'

'Well, I do not. You were always so sure – you radiated harmony, tranquility. You had stars in your hair and your words were wisdom. Was it all a façade? Are these doubts so sudden?'

'I once accused you of hiding in your garden. Well, I also hid. It was easy to suppress doubts when the monastery walls were firm around us. I had my books and I had my pupils; it seemed then a grand project of the Light. But now men are dead and the reality is different. Those fifty men who sought to capture Rayvan: they were frightened and they wanted to live, but we marched them from the city and out on to the plain to be slaughtered. We did not let them say farewell to their wives and children. We just led them like cattle to the slaughterhouse.'

'Now I understand,' said Decado. 'You saw us as White Templars marching against evil, cheered by the crowds: a small band of heroes in silver armour and white cloaks. Well, it could never be like that, Abaddon. Evil lives in a pit. If you want to fight it

– you must climb down in the slime to do so. White cloaks show the dirt more than black, and silver tarnishes. Now leave me and commune with your God – He has more answers than I.'

'Will you pray for me, Decado?' pleaded the Abbot.

'Why should the Source listen to me if he does not want to listen to you? Pray for yourself, man!'

'Please! Do this for me.'

'All right. But go and rest now.'

Decado watched the old man move away into the darkness. Then he lay back and gazed up at the lightening sky.

11

As the dawn sun rose in blood, Tenaka Khan stood on the high ground overlooking the plain. With him were one hundred men armed with bows, swords and axes. Only about thirty of them had shields, and these warriors Tenaka placed in the open ground facing the dip into the plain. Mountains towered on either side of the small force, while behind them the Demon's Smile widened on both sides, becoming wood-covered hills.

The men were becoming restless now and Tenaka had no words for them. They moved warily around the Nadir warrior, casting suspicious glances at him; they would fight alongside him, but only because Rayvan had asked it of them.

Tenaka raised a hand to shield his eyes and saw that the Legion were moving. He could make out the sunlight glittering on their spear-points and flashing from their polished breastplates.

After the Dragon, the Legion were the finest fighting men among the Drenai. Tenaka drew his sword and tested the edge with his thumb. Taking a small whetstone, he honed the blade once more.

Galand moved alongside him. 'Good luck, general!' he said.

Tenaka grinned and cast his eyes over his small force. Their faces were set, determined; there was no give in them. For countless centuries men like these had held the Drenai empire together, turning back the greatest armies in the world: the hordes of Ulric, the Immortals of Gorben and the ferocious raiders from Vagria in the Chaos Wars.

Now they stood again to face impossible odds.

The rolling thunder of hooves on the dry plain floated into the mountains, echoing like the drums of doom. To the left of the men with shields Rayvan's son, Lucas, notched an arrow to his bow. Swallowing hard, he wiped a sleeve across his brow; he was sweating heavily – strange how so much moisture could form on his face, while his mouth was so dry. He glanced back at the Nadir general to see him standing calmly with sword in hand, his violet eyes fixed on the charging horsemen. There was no trace of sweat on his brow.

Bastard, thought Lucas. Inhuman bastard!

The horsemen had reached the slope before the Smile and their charge slowed fractionally.

A single arrow soared out to meet them, falling short of the riders by thirty paces.

'Wait until you hear the order,' bellowed Galand, switching his gaze to the impassive Tenaka.

The riders thundered on, lances levelled.

'Now?' asked Galand, as the leading horsemen passed the mark made by the first arrow. Tenaka shook his head.

'Face front!' shouted Galand, as nervous archers craned their necks to see the command given.

The Legion were riding fifty abreast in twenty-five ranks. Tenaka gauged the gap between each rank as around six lengths. It was a well-disciplined charge.

'Now!' he said.

'Give them Hell!' screamed Galand and a hundred arrows flashed into the sunlight. The first line of horsemen disappeared as the shafts hammered home into their mounts. Men were hurled headlong on to the rocks as screaming horses reared and fell. The second line faltered, but the gap between ranks allowed the riders to adjust in time to leap the fallen. But they leapt into a second volley of arrows that killed, crippled or maimed their mounts. As the dazed riders rose to their feet, more shafts flashed death to them, slicing into exposed flesh. But still the charge continued and the horsemen were almost upon them.

With one shaft left, Lucas rose from his knees. A lancer broke the line and Lucas loosed the shaft without aiming. It bounced from the horse's skull, causing the beast to rear in pain, but the rider clung on. Lucas dropped his bow and ran forward, dragging his hunting knife into his hand. He leapt to the beast's back and struck the rider in the chest, but the man threw himself to the right and the combined weight of the two warriors toppled the horse. Lucas landed atop the rider, the fall combining with his weight to bury the blade to the hilt. The man groaned and died; Lucas strained to drag the knife clear, but it was buried too deep. Drawing his sword, he ran at a second lancer.

Tenaka ducked under a stabbing thrust and then leapt at the rider, dragging him from the saddle. A backhand cut to the throat left the man choking on his own blood.

Tenaka clambered into the saddle. The archers had dropped back from the mouth of the pass and were peppering the Legion as they breasted the rise. Men and horses jammed the mouth of the valley. All was chaos. Here and there riders had forced their way through and Skoda warriors armed with swords and axes hacked and hammered at them from the ground.

'Galand!' shouted Tenaka. The black-bearded

warrior, fighting alongside his brother, despatched his opponent and turned to the call. Tenaka pointed forward at the mass and Galand waved his sword in acknowledgement.

'To me, Skoda!' he bellowed. 'To me!' With his brother and about twenty warriors, he charged the milling men. The riders dropped their lances, scrabbling for swords as the fighting wedge struck them. Tenaka heeled his horse and charged in to fight alongside them.

For several bloody minutes the battle continued, then a bugle sounded from the plain and the Legion wheeled their mounts and rode from the carnage.

Galand, scalp bleeding from a shallow cut, ran to Tenaka. 'They will turn immediately for another charge,' he said. 'We'll not hold them.' Tenaka sheathed his sword. He had lost almost half his force.

Lucas ran alongside. 'Let us get the wounded back,' he pleaded.

'No time!' said Tenaka. 'Take positions – but be ready to run when I give the word.' Kicking his horse forward, he rode to the rise. The Legion had turned at the foot of the slope and were re-forming into lines fifty abreast.

Behind him the Skoda archers were desperately gathering shafts, pulling them clear of bodies. Tenaka lifted his arm, calling them forward, and they obeyed without hesitation.

The bugle sounded once more and the black-cloaked riders surged forward. No lances this time, bright swords shone in their hands. Once more the thunder of charging hooves echoed in the mountains.

At thirty paces Tenaka lifted his arm. 'Now!' he yelled. Hundreds of shafts thudded home. 'Away!' he screamed.

The Skoda warriors turned and ran, sprinting for the transient security of the wooded hills.

Tenaka estimated the Legion had lost nearly three hundred men in the battle, and more horses. He turned his mount and galloped towards the hills. Galand and Parsal were ahead of him, helping Rayvan's injured son. Lucas had been dragging an arrow from the body of a rider, but the man was not dead and had struck out, lashing a cut to Lucas' left leg.

'Leave him to me!' shouted Tenaka as he rode alongside. Leaning over, he pulled Lucas across his saddle horn and glanced back. The Legion had breasted the rise and set off in pursuit of the fleeing warriors. Galand and Parsal sprinted off to the north.

Tenaka angled his run to the north-west and the Legion riders spurred their mounts after him.

Ahead was the first hill, beyond which Ananais waited with the full force. Tenaka urged his horse onward, but with double weight upon him the creature was labouring hard. Atop the hill Tenaka was no more than fifteen lengths clear of his pursuers, but ahead lay Ananais and four hundred men. Tenaka's tired mount galloped on. Ananais moved forward, waving Tenaka to the left. He dragged on the reins, steering the beast through the hazards he himself had organised throughout the long night.

Behind him a hundred Legion riders reined in, waiting for orders. Tenaka helped Lucas from the saddle and then dismounted.

'How did it go?' asked Ananais.

Tenaka lifted three fingers.

'It would have been nice had it been five,' he said.

'It was a disciplined charge, Ani, one rank at a time.'

'You have to give that to them – they were always well-disciplined. Still, the day is yet young.'

Rayvan pushed her way forward. 'Did we lose many?'

'Around forty men at the charge. But more will be caught in the woods,' answered Tenaka. Decado and Acuas made their way to the front.

'General,' said Acuas, 'the Legion leader has now been appraised of our position. He is calling in his outriders for a frontal charge.'

'Thank you. It is what we hoped for.'

'I hope he does it swiftly,' said Acuas, scratching his yellow beard. 'The Templars have breached our defences and soon they will know of your preparations. Then they will convey them to the leader.'

'If that happens, we are dead,' muttered Ananais.

'With all your powers, can you not screen their leader?' asked Tenaka.

'We could,' answered Acuas stiffly, 'but it would be a grave risk to the men charged with the task.'

'It so happens,' snarled Ananais, 'that we are taking no small risk ourselves.'

'It will be done,' said Decado. 'See to it, Acuas.'

Acuas nodded and closed his eyes.

'Well, get to it, lad,' urged Ananais.

'He is doing it now,' said Decado softly. 'Leave him alone.'

The harsh shrieking blasts of the Legion bugles pierced the air and within seconds a line of black-garbed riders rimmed the hill opposite.

'Get back to the centre,' Ananais told Rayvan.

'Don't treat me like a milkmaid!'

'I am treating you like a leader, woman! If you fall in the first charge, then the battle is over.' Rayvan moved back and the men of Skoda readied their bows.

A single bugle blast heralded the charge and the horsemen swept down the low hill. Fear flickered through the ranks of defenders. Ananais sensed it rather than felt it. 'Steady, lads,' he called, his voice even.

Tenaka craned to see the formation: one hundred abreast, single lengths between ranks. He cursed softly. The leading rank reached the bottom of the hill and then continued up toward the defenders, slowing as the gradient increased. This brought the second rank even closer. Tenaka smiled. Thirty paces from the defenders, the first line of horsemen hit the hidden trenches, the soft turf laid upon thin branches. The line went down as if poleaxed by an invisible giant. The second line, too close in, went down with them in a milling mass of writhing horses.

'Charge!' shouted Ananais, and three hundred Skoda warriors dashed forward hacking and cleaving. The hundred that remained sent volleys of arrows over the heads of their comrades into the ranks of lancers beyond – these had pulled up their mounts and presented sitting targets to the archers. From the hill above, the Legion general, Karespa, cursed and swore. Swinging in his saddle he ordered his bugler to sound 'Recall'. The shrill notes drifted over the battling men and the Legion pulled back. Karespa waved his arm, signalling left, and the lancers wheeled their mounts for a flank attack. Ananais pulled back his force to the hilltop.

The Legion charged again – only for their horses to hit the hidden trip-wires in the long grass. Karespa ordered 'Recall' once more. Bereft of choices he ordered his men to dismount and advance on foot, archers to the rear. They moved forward slowly, the men in the front rank hesitant and fearful. They carried no shields and were loth to approach the bowmen among the Skoda defence.

Just out of bowshot the front rank stopped, readying themselves for the hectic race. At that moment Lake and his fifty men rose from the ground behind them, discarding their blankets interwoven with long grass and climbing from the well-hidden trenches beside granite boulders. From his vantage point on the hilltop, Karespa blinked in disbelief as the men appeared, seemingly from the earth itself.

Lake swiftly strung his bow, his men following suit. Their targets were the enemy archers. Fifty arrows screamed home, then fifty more. All was pandemonium. Ananais led his four hundred men in a sudden attack and the Legion wilted under the storm of slashing blades. Karespa swung in the saddle to order his bugler to sound 'Retreat', then his jaw dropped in amazement. His bugler had been dragged from the saddle by a black-bearded warrior, who now stood grinning beside Karespa's mount with a dagger in his hand. Other warriors stood close by, smiling mirthlessly.

Galand lifted the bugle to his lips and sent out the doleful call to surrender. Three times the bugle sounded before the last of the Legion warriors laid down their weapons.

'It is over, general,' said Galand. 'Be so good as to step down.'

'I'll be damned if I will!' snapped Karespa.

'Dead if you don't,' promised Galand.

Karespa dismounted.

In the trough below, six hundred Legion warriors sat on the grass as Skoda men moved among them, relieving them of weapons and breastplates.

Decado sheathed his sword and moved to where

Acuas knelt beside the fallen Abaddon. There was no mark upon the Abbot.

'What happened?' asked Decado.

'His was the strongest mind among us. His talents were greater by far than any other's. He volunteered to screen Karespa from the Templars.'

'He knew he would die today,' said Decado.

'He will not die today,' snarled Acuas. 'Did I not say there were risks involved?'

'So a man had died. Many have died today.'

'I am not talking about death, Decado. Yes, his body is slain, but the Templars have taken his soul.'

*

Scaler sat on the high wall of the tower garden, watching the distant mountains for signs of the victorious Legion. He had been relieved when Tenaka had asked him to stay behind, but now he was unsure. Certainly he was no warrior and would have been of little help in a battle. Even so, at least he would have known the result.

Dark clouds bunched above the garden, blocking the sunlight; Scaler pulled his blue cloak around his shoulders and left the wall to wander among the sheltered blooms. Some sixty years before, an ageing senator had built the garden, his servants carrying more than three tons of topsoil to the tower. Now there were trees, bushes and flowers of every kind. In one corner laurel and elderflower grew alongside holly and elm, while elsewhere flowering cherry trees bloomed pink and white against the grey stone walls. Throughout the garden an ornate path wound its way among the flower-beds. Scaler wandered the path, enjoying the fragrance of the blooms.

Renya mounted the circular stairwell, entering the garden just as the sun cleared the clouds. She saw Scaler standing alone, his dark hair held in place by a black leather circlet on his brow. He was a handsome man, she thought . . . and lonely. He wore no sword and was studying a yellow flower at the edge of a rockery.

'Good morning,' she said and he glanced up. Renya was attired in a light-green woollen tunic and a rust-coloured silk scarf covered her hair. Her legs were bare and she wore no sandals.

'Good morning, lady. Did you sleep well?'

'No. And you?'

'I fear not. When do you think we will know?'

Renya shrugged. 'Soon enough.'

He nodded his agreement and together they strolled through the garden, drawn at last to the wall facing south towards the Demon's Smile.

'Why did you not go with them?' she asked.

'Tenaka asked me to stay.'

'Why?'

'He has a task for me and does not want me dead before I attempt it!'

'A dangerous task, then?'

'What makes you say so?'

'You said "Attempt it". That sounds as if you doubt your ability to succeed.'

He laughed grimly. 'Doubt? I don't doubt – I *know*. But it doesn't matter. No one lives for ever. Anyway, it may never come to that. First they must defeat the Legion.'

'They will,' said Renya, sitting on a stone bench and drawing up her long legs on to the seat.

'How can you be sure?'

'They are not the men to be beaten. Tenaka will find a way to win. And if he has asked you to help him, then he must be sure you have a chance.'

'How simply women view the world of men,' commented Scaler.

'Not at all. It takes men to make the simplest things sound complex.'

'A deadly riposte, lady. I am undone!'

'Are you defeated so easily, Scaler?'

He sat down beside her. 'I am easily defeated, Renya, because I don't care too much about winning. Just living! I run to survive. When I was young, assassins were all around me. My family all died at their hands. It was Ceska's doing – I see that now, but then he seemed a friend to my grandfather and myself. For years my rooms were guarded while I slept, my food tasted, my toys checked for hidden needles bearing poison. It was not what you would call a happy childhood.'

'But now you are a man,' she said.

'Not much of one. I frighten easily. Still, there is one consolation. If I was any tougher, I would be dead by now.'

'Or victorious.'

'Yes,' he admitted, 'perhaps victorious. But when they killed Orrin – my grandfather – I ran away. Gave up the earldom and went into hiding. Belder came with me – the last retainer. I have been a great disappointment to him.'

'How did you survive?'

He grinned. 'I became a thief. Hence the name. I climbed into people's homes and stole their valuables. It is said that the Earl of Bronze began his career in this way, so I believe I am merely carrying on the family tradition.'

'Being a thief takes nerve. You could have been caught and hanged.'

'You have never seen me run – I move like the wind.'

Renya smiled and stood to glance over the wall to the south. The she sat down once more.

187

'What does Tenaka require of you?'

'Nothing complex. He merely wants me to become an earl again and re-take Dros Delnoch, subduing ten thousand soldiers and opening the gates to allow a Nadir army through. That's all!'

'Seriously – what *does* he want you to do?'

Scaler leaned forward. 'I have told you.'

'I don't believe you. It's insane!'

'Nevertheless . . .'

'It's impossible.'

'True, Renya, true. However, there is a certain irony to the plan. Consider it: the descendant of the Earl of Bronze, who held the fortress against Ulric, is now commissioned to take the fortress and allow Ulric's descendant to pass through with his army.'

'Where will he get this army? He is hated by the Nadir, even as he is loathed by the Drenai.'

'Ah yes, but he is Tenaka Khan,' said Scaler drily.

'So how will you take the fortress?' she asked.

'I have no idea. I will probably march into the keep, declare my identity and ask them all to surrender.'

'It's a good plan – simple and direct,' she said, straightfaced.

'All the best plans are,' he said. 'Tell me how you came to be mixed up in this business.'

'Just born lucky,' said Renya, standing once more. 'Damn it! Why don't they come?'

'As you said, we shall know soon enough. Will you join me for breakfast?'

'I don't think so. Valtaya is in the kitchens – she will cook you something.'

Sensing she wanted to be alone, Scaler made his way down the stairwell, following the delicious aroma of frying bacon.

He passed Valtaya on her way up and wandered

on to the kitchen where Belder was ploughing his way through a heaped dish of bacon, eggs and long beans.

'A man of your age should have lost his appetite by now,' observed Scaler, slipping into place opposite the gnarled warrior.

Belder scowled at him. 'We should have been with them,' he said.

'Tenaka asked me to stay,' pointed out Scaler.

'I cannot think why,' snapped Belder, sarcasm heavy in his tone. 'Just think how handy we would have been.'

Scaler lost patience. 'I may not have said so before,' he remarked, 'but I am getting pretty sick of you, Belder. Either keep your mouth shut or keep out of my way!'

'The second option sounds like a pleasure,' said the old warrior, eyes blazing.

'Then do it! And forget the sanctimonious lectures. You have been on for years about my profligate ways, my fears and my failings. But you didn't stay with me out of loyalty – you stayed because you are a runner too. I just made it easy for you to hide. Tenaka asked me to stay, but he didn't ask you – you could have gone.'

Scaler pushed himself upright and left the room. The old man leaned forward on his elbows, pushing the plate away.

'I *did* stay out of loyalty,' he whispered.

*

In the aftermath of the battle Tenaka wandered off alone into the mountains, his heart heavy and a terrible melancholy settling over him.

Rayvan watched him walk away and moved to follow, but Ananais stopped her.

'It is his way,' said the giant. 'Leave him be.'

Rayvan shrugged and returned to the business of treating the wounded. Makeshift stretchers had been put together, using the Legion lances and cloaks. The Thirty, stripped of their armour, moved among the wounded using their awesome skills to remove pain while stitches were inserted.

On the open field the dead were laid side by side, Legion lancers alongside Skoda warriors. Six hundred and eleven lancers had died that day; two hundred and forty-six Skoda men lay alongside them.

Rayvan wandered through the ranks of the dead, staring down at the corpses, bringing the names of her warriors to mind and praying over each man. Many had farms and crofts, wives and children, sisters, mothers. Rayvan knew them all. She called Lake to her and told him to fetch paper and charcoal to list the dead.

Ananais washed the blood from his clothes and skin and then summoned the Legion general Karespa to him. The man was sullen and in no mood for conversation.

'I am going to have to kill you, Karespa,' said Ananais apologetically.

'I understand.'

'Good! Will you join me in a meal?'

'No, thank you. My appetite just left me.'

Ananais nodded his understanding. 'Do you have any preference?'

The man shrugged. 'What does it matter?'

'Then it will be a sword-thrust. Unless you would rather do it yourself?'

'Go to the devil!'

'Then I will do it. You have until dawn to prepare yourself.'

'I don't need until dawn. Do it now, while I am in the mood.'

'All right.' Ananais nodded once and pain like the fires of Hell exploded in Karespa's back. He tried to turn, but darkness blanketed his mind. Galand pulled the sword clear and wiped it clean on the general's cloak. Moving forward, he sat beside Ananais.

'Shame about that,' said the black-bearded warrior.

'We couldn't let him go, knowing what he did.'

'I suppose not. Gods, general, but we won! Incredible, isn't it?'

'Not with Tenaka planning it.'

'Come now, anything could have happened. They didn't have to charge – they could have dismounted and sent in the archers to drive us back.'

'Could have. Might have. They did not. They went by the book. According to the Cavalry Manual, the obvious move for horsemen against irregular foot-soldiers is the charge. The Legion are disciplined men and therefore bound to operate by the Manual. You want me to quote chapter and verse?'

'It's not necessary,' muttered Galand. 'I expect you wrote it.'

'No. Tenaka Khan introduced the most recent alterations eighteen years ago.'

'But just suppose . . .'

'What's the point, Galand? He was right.'

'But he couldn't have known where Karespa would wait with his bugler. And yet he told Parsal and me to make for that hill.'

'Where else could Karespa watch the battle from?'

'He might have gone in with his men.'

'And left his bugler to make the decisions?'

'You make it sound so simple, but battles are not like that. Strategy is one thing, heart and skill another.'

'I don't deny it. The Legion didn't fight at their best. There are many good men among them and I don't suppose they relished their task. But that's in the past. For now I am going to ask the men of the Legion to join us.'

'And if they refuse?'

'I shall send them out of the valley – where you will be waiting with one hundred archers. No one man will leave alive.'

'You're a ruthless man, general!'

'I am alive, Galand. And I mean to stay alive.'

Galand heaved himself to his feet. 'I hope you do, general. And I hope Tenaka Khan can produce another miracle when the Joinings arrive.'

'That's tomorrow,' said Ananais. 'Let us enjoy today.'

12

Tenaka found the place of solitude he needed at a sheltered waterfall high in the mountains, where the air was cool and clean and the snow lay in patches on the slopes. Slowly, carefully, he built a fire in a ring of stones and sat watching the flames. He felt no elation at the victory, his emotions washed from him in the blood of the slain. After a while he moved to the stream, remembering the words of Asta Khan, the ancient shaman of the Wolfshead tribe.

'All things in the world are created for Man, yet all have two purposes. The waters run that we might drink of them, but they are also symbols of the futility of Man. They reflect our lives in rushing beauty, birthed in the purity of the mountains. As babes they babble and run, gushing and growing as they mature into strong young rivers. Then they widen and slow until at last they meander, like old men, to join with the sea. And like the souls of men in the Nethervoid, they mix and mingle until the sun lifts them again as raindrops to fall upon the mountains.'

Tenaka dipped his hand into the rushing water. He felt out of place, away from time. A bird hopped on to a rock nearby, ignoring him in its quest for food; it was tiny and brown. Suddenly it dived into the water and Tenaka jerked upright, leaning over the stream to see it flying beneath the surface: an eerie sight. It came to the surface, hopped to a rock and fluttered its feathers; then it returned to the stream. In a strange way Tenaka was soothed by the sight. He observed the bird for a while, then lay back on the grass watching the clouds bunch in the blue sky.

An eagle soared high on the thermals with wings spread, seemingly static as it rose on the warm air.

A ptarmigan fluttered into view, its feathers still mottled and part white – perfect camouflage, for the snow still patched the slopes. Tenaka considered the bird. In winter it was pure white against the snow. In spring it was part white, while in summer the mottling turned slate-grey and brown, allowing it to sit by the boulders – the image of a rock. Its feathers were its only defence.

The ptarmigan rose into the air and the eagle banked sharply, dropping like a stone. But it cut across the sun and its shadow fell athwart the ptarmigan, which swerved just as the talons flashed by. The little speckled bird fled back to the bushes.

The eagle settled on a tree branch close to Tenaka, its dignity ruffled. The Nadir warrior leaned back and closed his eyes.

The battle had been close and the strategy would not work again. They had gained a respite, but that was all. Ceska had sent his Legion to round up a few rebels – had they known Tenaka Khan was here, they would have adopted different tactics. Now they *would* know . . . Now all Ceska's skill would be pitted against Tenaka.

How many men would Ceska range against them now?

There was the rest of the Legion – four thousand men. The regulars numbering ten thousand. The Drenan Pikers, two thousand at the last count. But more terrifying than all the others were the Joinings.

How many now had he created? Five thousand? Ten?

And how could they be rated against common men? One Joining to five? Even that would make them worth 25,000 soldiers.

Ceska would not make the mistake of underestimating the Skoda rebellion a second time.

Weariness settled on Tenaka like a shroud. His first plan had been so simple: kill Ceska and die. Now the complexities of his scheme swirled in his mind like mist.

So many dead, so many still to die.

He moved back to his fire and added fuel; then he lay down beside it, wrapping himself in his cloak. He thought of Illae and his Ventrian home. How good had been the years.

Then Renya's face formed in his thoughts and he smiled. All his life he had been lucky. Sad, lonely, but lucky. To have a mother as devoted as Shillat, that was luck. To find a man like Ananais to stand beside him. To be with the Dragon. To love Illae. To find Renya.

Such good fortune was a gift that more than made up for the loneliness and the pain of rejection. Tenaka began to shiver. Adding more wood, he lay back waiting for the nausea he knew would follow. The headache started first, with bright lights flickering in his eyes. He breathed deeply, calming himself for the onslaught. The pain grew, clawing at his brain with fingers of fire.

For four hours the pain tore at him until he almost wept. Then it receded and he slept . . .

He was in a dark corridor, sloping and cold. At his feet were the skeletons of several rats. He stepped over them and the skeletons moved, bones clicking in the silence. Then they ran into the darkness. Tenaka shook his head, trying to remember where he was. Ahead was a dead man hanging in chains, the flesh decomposed.

'Help me!' said the man.

'You are dead. I cannot help you.'

'Why won't you help me?'

'You are dead.'

'We are all dead. And no one will help us.'

Tenaka walked on, seeking a door, moving ever downward.

The corridor widened into a hall with dark pillars soaring into the void. Shadow-shrouded figures moved into sight, black swords in their hands.

'Now we have you, Torchbearer,' said a voice.

They wore no armour and the leader's face was familiar. Tenaka racked his brains for the man's name, but it remained elusive.

'Padaxes,' said the man. 'Even here I can read your frightened mind. Padaxes, who died under the sword of Decado. And yet am I dead? I am not! But you, Torchbearer – you will be dead, for you have entered the dominion of the Spirit. Where are your Templars? Where are the bastard Thirty?'

'This is a dream,' said Tenaka. 'You cannot touch me.'

'Think you so?' Fire leapt from the blade, scorching Tenaka's shoulders. He threw himself back, fear surging within him. Padaxes' laughter was shrill. 'Think you so *now?*'

Tenaka moved to his feet, drawing his own sword.

'Come, then,' he said. 'Let me see you die a second time.'

The Dark Templars moved forward, spreading in a semi-circle around him. Suddenly Tenaka was aware he was not alone. For a moment, as in his earlier dream, he believed The Thirty had come for him, but when he glanced to his left he saw a power-ful, broad-shouldered Nadir warrior in goatskin tunic. Others moved alongside him.

The Templars hesitated and the Nadir beside Tenaka lifted his sword. 'Drive these shadows away,' he told his warriors. Silently a hundred hollow-eyed tribesmen surged forward and the Templars fled before them.

The Nadir turned to Tenaka. His face was broad and flat, his eyes violet and piercing. There pulsed from him an aura of power and strength that Tenaka had not seen in any living man, and he knew him then. He fell to his knees before him and bent forward his body into a deep bow.

'You know me then, blood of my blood?'

'I do, my Lord Khan,' said Tenaka. 'Ulric, Lord of Hordes!'

'I have seen you, boy. Watched you grow, for my old shaman Nosta Khan is with me still. You have not displeased me . . . But then your blood is of the finest.'

'Not all have felt it so,' said Tenaka.

'The world is full of fools,' snapped Ulric. 'I fought against the Earl of Bronze and he was a mighty man. And rare. He was a man with doubts, who overcame them. He stood on the walls of Dros Delnoch and defied me with his pitiful force, and I loved him for it. He was a fighter and a dreamer. Rare. So very rare!'

'You met him, then?'

'There was another warrior with him – an old man, Druss. Deathwalker, we called him. When he fell I had his body carried to my camp and we built a funeral pyre. Imagine that. For an enemy! We were on the verge of victory. And that night the Earl of Bronze – my greatest enemy – walked into my camp with his generals and joined me at the funeral.'

'Insane!' said Tenaka. 'You could have taken him and the whole fortress.'

'Would you have taken him, Tenaka?'

Tenaka considered the question. 'No,' he said at last.

'Neither could I. So do not worry about your pedigree. Let lesser men sneer.'

'Am I not dead?' asked Tenaka.

'No.'

'Then how am I here?'

'You sleep. Those Templar maggots pulled your spirit here but I will help you return.'

'What hell is this, and how came you here?'

'My heart failed me during the war against Ventria. And then I was here. It is the Nethervoid, pitched between the worlds of Source and Spirit. It seems I am claimed by neither, so I exist here with my followers. I never worshipped anything but my sword and my wits – now I suffer for it. But I can take it, for am I not a man?'

'You are a legend.'

'It is not hard to become a legend, Tenaka. It is what follows when you have to live like one.'

'Can you see the future?'

'In part.'

'Will I . . . will my friends succeed?'

'Do not ask me. I cannot alter your fate, much as I might wish to. This is your path, Tenaka, and you must walk it like a man. You were born to walk it.'

'I understand, Lord. I should not have asked.'

'There is no harm in asking,' said Ulric, smiling. 'Come, close your eyes – you must return to the world of blood.'

*

Tenaka awoke. It was night, yet his fire still burned bright and warm and a blanket had been placed over his sleeping body. He groaned and rolled to his side, raising himself on his elbow. Ananais sat across from the fire, the light flickering on his mask.

'How are you feeling?' asked the giant.

'Good. I needed the rest.'

'Has the pain gone?'

'Yes. Did you bring food?'

'Of course. You had me worried for a while. You turned ghostly white and your pulse was slow as death.'

'I'm all right now.' Tenaka sat up and Ananais tossed him a canvas sack containing dried meat and fruit. They ate in silence. The waterfall glittered like diamonds on sable in the moonlight. Finally Ananais spoke.

'Four hundred of the Legion have joined us. Decado says they will fight true – claims his priests have read their minds. Only three did they turn away. Two hundred others chose to return to Ceska.'

Tenaka rubbed his eyes. 'And?'

'And what?'

'And what happened to those who chose to return?'

'I sent them out of the valley.'

'Ani, my friend, I am back now. I am all right. So tell me.'

'I had them slain in the valley. It was necessary, for they could have given information about our numbers.'

'This was known anyway, Ani – the Templars are watching over us.'

'All right. But even so – it is still two hundred fewer men that they will send against us in the days to come.'

Silence descended again and Ananais lifted his mask gently, probing at the angry scar tissue.

'Take the thing off,' said Tenaka. 'Let the air get to the skin.'

Ananais hesitated, then he sighed and removed the leather. In the red firelight he seemed like a demon, inhuman and terrible. His blue eyes were fixed on Tenaka in a piercing stare, as if he were trying to discern some evidence of revulsion.

'Give me your view of the battle,' said Tenaka.

'It went to plan. I was pleased with Rayvan's men, and her son Lake is an asset. The black man fought well. He is a fine warrior. Given a year, I could rebuild the Dragon around these Skoda men.'

'We don't have a year.'

'I know,' said Ananais. 'I reckon two months.'

'We cannot beat them like this, Ani.'

'You have a plan?'

'Yes. But you won't like it.'

'If it means our winning, I will like it,' promised Ananais. 'What is it?'

'I mean to bring the Nadir.'

'You are right – I *don't* like it. In fact it stinks like rotting meat. If Ceska is bad, the Nadir are worse. Gods, man, at least with Ceska we are still Drenai. Are you out of your mind?'

'It is all we have left, my friend. We have almost a thousand men. We cannot hold Skoda and would be hard-pressed to withstand a single charge.'

'Listen to me, Tani! You know I have never held your blood against you. Not personally. I love you better than a brother. But I hate the Nadir as I hate nothing else on this earth. And I am not alone. No man here will fight alongside them. And suppose you do bring an army? What the hell happens when we win? Do they just go home? They will have beaten the Drenai army; the land will be theirs and we shall have another bloody civil war.'

'I don't see it that way.'

'And how will you bring them? There are no secret ways through the mountains, not even through the Sathuli passes. No army can come from the north save through Delnoch, and even Ulric failed to pass those gates.'

'I have asked Scaler to take Dros Delnoch.'

'Oh, Tani, you have gone mad! He is a fop and a runner who has not joined in one battle so far. When we rescued the village girl, he just buried his head in his hands and lay in the grass. When we found Pagan, he remained with the women. When we were planning yesterday's sortie, he was shaking like grass in a breeze and you told him to stay behind. And *he* will take Delnoch?'

Tenaka added wood to the fire, discarding the blanket from his shoulders. 'I know all these things, Ani. But it can be done. Scaler is like his ancestor, the Earl of Bronze. He doubts himself and he has great fears. But beyond those fears, if he ever sees it, there waits a fine man – a man of courage and nobility. And he is bright and quick-thinking.'

'Our hopes then rest on him?' asked Ananais.

'No. They rest on my judgement of him.'

'Don't play with words. It is the same thing.'

'I need you with me, Ananais.'

Ananais nodded. 'Why not? We are only talking about death. I will stay with you, Tani. What is life if a man cannot count on his friends when he has gone mad?'

'Thank you, Ani. I mean that.'

'I know. And I am worn out. I shall sleep for a while.'

Ananais lay back, resting his head on his cloak.

The night breeze felt good on his scarred face. He was tired – more tired than he could ever remember being. It was the weariness of disappointment. Tenaka's plan was a nightmare, yet there were no alternatives. Ceska held the land within the talons of his Joinings and maybe, just maybe, a Nadir conquest would cleanse the nation. But Ananais doubted it.

From tomorrow he would train his warriors as they had never been trained before. They would run until they fell, fight until their arms ached with weariness. He would drill them hard, preparing a force not only to withstand Ceska's legions, but hopefully one that would live on to battle the new enemy.

Tenaka Khan's Nadir.

*

At the centre of the valley the bodies of the fallen were placed in a hastily dug ditch and covered with earth and rocks. Rayvan said a prayer and the survivors knelt before the mass grave, whispering their own farewells to friends, brothers, fathers and kin.

After the ceremony The Thirty moved away to the hills, leaving Decado and Rayvan and her sons. It was some time before he noticed their absence.

Decado left the fire and went in search of them, but the valley was large and soon he realised the enormity of the task. The moon was high in the sky when he finally came to the conclusion that they had left him behind intentionally: they did not want to be found.

He sat down by a white marble boulder and relaxed his mind, floating down into the whispering realms of the subconscious.

Silence.

Anger nagged at him, dislodging his concentration, but he calmed himself and sought the sanctuary once more.

Then he heard the scream. It came at first as a soft, muted cry and grew into a soul-piercing expression of agony. Decado listened for a while, struggling to identify the source of the sound. Then it came to him. It was Abaddon.

And he knew where The Thirty had travelled: to rescue the Abbot of Swords and free him to die. He also knew that this was folly of the worst kind. He had promised Abaddon that he would look after his charges and now, within a day of the old man's death, they had left him in order to embark on a futile journey, travelling into the realms of the damned.

A terrible sadness assailed Decado, for he could not follow them. So he prayed, but no answer came to him and he expected none.

'What kind of a god are you?' he asked in his despair. 'What do you expect from your followers? You give them nothing and ask for everything. At least with the spirits of darkness there is some communion. Abaddon died for you and still suffers. Now his acolytes will suffer in their turn. Why do you not answer me?'

Silence.

'You do not exist! There is no force for purity. All a man has is his will to do good. I reject you. I want no more to do with you!'

Decado relaxed then and probed deeper into his mind, seeking the mysteries Abaddon had promised him throughout his years of study. He had tried in the past, but never with this sense of desperation. He travelled yet deeper, tumbling and spinning through the roaring of his memories – seeing again the battles and skirmishes, the fears and the failures.

On, on, through the bitter sadness of his childhood, back to his first stirrings in his mother's womb and beyond into separation: seed and egg, driving, waiting.

Darkness.

Movement. The snapping of chains, the soaring freedom.

Light.

Decado floated free, drawn to the pure silver light of the full moon. He halted his rise with an effort of will and gazed down on the curving beauty of the Demon's Smile, but a dark cloud drifted beneath him and obscured the view. He glanced down at his body, white and naked in the moonlight, and joy flooded his soul.

The scream froze him. He remembered his mission and his eyes blazed with cold fire. But he could not travel naked and unarmed. Closing his spirit eyes he pictured armour, the black and silver of the Dragon.

And it was there. But no sword hung at his side, no shield on his arm.

He tried again. Nothing.

The long-ago words of Abaddon drifted back over the years. 'In spirit travel a Source warrior carries the sword of his faith, and his shield is the strength of his belief.'

Decado had neither.

'Damn you!' he shouted into the cosmic night. 'Still you thwart me, even when I am on your business.' He closed his eyes once more. 'If it is faith I need, then I have faith. In myself. In Decado, the Ice Killer. I need no sword, for my hands are death.'

And he flew like a shaft of moonlight, drawn to the scream. He left the world of men with awesome speed, soaring over dark mountains and gloomy plains; two blue planets hovered over the land and the stars were dim and cold.

Below him an ebony castle squatted on a low hill. He halted in his flight, hovering above the stone ramparts. A dark shadow leapt at him and he swerved as a sword-blade flashed by his head. His hand lanced out, gripping the swordsman's wrist, spinning his enemy round. Decado's left hand chopped down at his opponent; the man's neck snapped and he vanished. Decado spun on his heel as a second attacker surged at him. The man wore the dark livery of the Templars. Decado leapt back as the sword cut a glittering semi-circle past his belly. As a back-hand slash hissed at his neck, Decado ducked and dived forward under the blade, ramming his skull under the man's chin. The Templar staggered.

Decado's hand stabbed out, the fingers burying themselves in the Templar's throat. Once more his opponent vanished.

Ahead was a half-open door leading to a deep stair-well. Decado ran forward but then stopped, his senses urging caution. Launching himself feet first, he smashed the door back on its hinges and a man groaned and slumped forward into view. Rolling to his feet, Decado hammered the blade of his foot into the man's chest, caving in the breastbone.

Running on, he took the stairs three at a time to emerge into a wide circular hall. At the centre The Thirty stood in a tight circle, surrounded on all sides by dark-cloaked Templars. Swords clashed silently and no sound issued from the battle. Outnumbered more than two to one, The Thirty were fighting for their lives.

And losing!

They had only one choice left. Flight. Even as he

realised this Decado noticed for the first time that he could no longer soar into the air – as soon as he had touched these grim battlements his powers had left him. But why? In that instant he knew the answer; it lay in the words he had used to Abaddon: 'Evil lives in a pit. If you want to fight it, you have to climb down into the slime to do so.'

They were in the pit and the powers of light were lessened here, even as the powers of darkness failed against the hearts of strong men.

'To me!' yelled Decado. 'Thirty to me!'

For a moment the battle ceased as the Templars paused to check the source of the sound. Then six of them peeled off from the battle to charge him. Acuas cut his way into the gap and led the warrior priests towards the stairs.

The Thirty cut and slashed a path, their silver blades shining like torches in the gloom. No bodies lay on the cold stones – any pierced by sword-blade in that bloodless battle merely vanished as if they had never been. Only nineteen priests still stood.

Decado watched death bear down upon him. His skill was great, but no man alive could tackle six men unarmed and survive. But he would try. A great calm settled upon him and he smiled at them.

Two swords of dazzling light appeared in his hands, and he attacked with blistering speed. A left cut, a parry and riposte, a right slash, a left thrust. Three down and gone like smoke in the breeze. The remaining three Templars fell back – into the eldritch blades of The Thirty.

'Follow me!' shouted Decado. Turning, he ran up the stairs ahead of them and out on to the battlements. Leaping to the wall, he gazed down on the jagged rocks so far below. The Thirty came out into the open.

'Fly!' ordered Decado.

'We shall fall!' shouted Balan.

'Not unless I tell you to, you son of a slut! Now move!'

Balan hurled himself from the battlements, swiftly followed by the other sixteen survivors. Last of all Decado leapt to join them.

At first they fell, but once clear of the pull of the castle they soared into the night, hurtling back to the realities of Skoda.

Decado returned to his body and opened his eyes. Slowly he walked towards the eastern woods, drawn by the pulsing mood of despair emanating from the young priests.

He found them in a clearing between two low hills. They had laid out the eleven bodies of the slain and now they prayed, heads bowed.

'Get up!' ordered Decado. 'On your feet!' Silently they obeyed him. 'My, how ridiculous you are! For all your talents you are but children. Tell me, how did the rescue go, children? Have we freed Abaddon? Are we going to have a celebration party? Look me in the eyes, damn you!'

He moved to Acuas. 'Well, yellowbeard, you have excelled yourself. You have achieved what neither the Templars nor the forces of Ceska could accomplish. You have destroyed eleven of your comrades.'

'That is not fair!' shouted Katan, tears in his eyes.

'Be silent!' thundered Decado. 'Fair? I am talking about reality. Did you find Abaddon?'

'No,' said Acuas softly.

'Have you worked out why?'

'No.'

'Because they never had his soul – that would be a feat beyond them. They lured you into their trap by deceit, which is something at which they excel. Now eleven of your brothers are slain. And you carry that burden.'

'And what about you?' said Katan, his normally serene face shaking with fury. 'Where were you when we needed you? What sort of a leader are you? You don't believe in our faith. You are just an assassin! There is no heart in you, Decado. You are the Ice Killer. Well, at least we fought for something we believed in, and travelled to die for a man we loved. All right, we were wrong – but we had no leader once Abaddon was dead.'

'You should have come to me,' replied Decado defensively.

'Why? You were the leader and you should have been there. We did seek you. Often. But even when you discovered your talents – talents we had prayed for – you hovered on the edge of our prayers. You never came forward. When do you eat with us, or talk with us? You sleep alone, away from the fire. You are an outsider. We are here to die for the Source. What are you here for?'

'I am here to win, Katan. If you want to die, just fall on your sword. Or ask me – I will do it for you, I will end your life in an instant. You are here to fight for the Source, to ensure that evil does not triumph in this land. But I will talk no more. I am the leader chosen and I require no oaths from you. No promises. Those who will obey me will come to me in the morning. We will eat together – aye, and pray together. Those who wish to follow their own road may do so. And now I leave you to bury the dead.'

*

Back in the city the populace cheered the victorious army from the fields a half-mile south, right through to the city centre and the makeshift barracks. But the cheers were muted, for the question remained on everyone's mind: What now? When will Ceska come with his Joinings?

Tenaka, Rayvan, Ananais, Decado and other leaders of the new army met together in the Senate Hall, while Rayvan's sons Lake and Lucas produced maps of the terrain to the east and south.

After an afternoon of heated discussion, it became obvious that much of Skoda was indefensible. The pass at the Demon's Smile could be walled and manned, but it would need a thousand men to hold it for any length of time, while to the north and south some six other passes gave entrance to the valleys and meadows of Skoda.

'It's like trying to defend a rabbit warren,' said Ananais. 'Ceska – even without his Joinings – can put into battle fifty times as many men. They could hit us on any of sixteen fronts. We simply cannot cover the ground.'

'The army will grow,' said Rayvan. 'Even now more men are coming down from the mountains. Word will spread outside Skoda and rebels will flock to join us.'

'Yes,' admitted Tenaka, 'but in that there is a problem. Ceska will send spies, agents, alarmists – they will all filter in.'

'The Thirty will help where they can and ferret out traitors,' said Decado. 'But if too many are allowed in, we will not be able to deal with them.'

'Then we must man the passes, spread The Thirty among the men,' said Tenaka.

And so it went on. Some men wanted to return to their farms to ready the fields for summer, others merely wished to return home with news of their victory. Lake complained that the food supplies were inadequate. Galand told of fights breaking out between Skoda men and the new Legion volunteers.

Throughout the long afternoon and into dusk, the leaders sought answers to the problems. It was agreed, finally, that half the men would be allowed home, so long as they promised to work on the farms of those who stayed behind. At the end of the month the first half would return, to be replaced at home by the others.

Ananais bristled with anger. 'And what of training?' he stormed. 'How in the devil's name do I get them ready for war?'

'They are not regular soldiers,' said Rayvan softly. 'They are working men, with wives and children to feed.'

'What about the city treasury?' asked Scaler.

'What about it?' queried Rayvan.

'How much is there?'

'I have no idea.'

'Then we should check. Since we rule Skoda, the money is ours. We could use it to buy food and stores from the Vagrians. They may not let us pass their borders, but they will not turn back our money.'

'Curse me for a fool!' said Rayvan. 'Of course we must. Lake, check the treasury now – if it has not been already bled dry.'

'We have had a guard on it, mother,' said Lake.

'Even so, get down there now and count it.'

'That will take all night!'

She flashed him an angry look and he sighed.

'All right, Rayvan,' he said. 'I'm going. But be warned – the moment I have finished I shall wake you with the total!'

Rayvan grinned at him and then turned to Scaler.

'You have a good brain in your head – will you go to Vagria and buy what we need?'

'He cannot,' said Tenaka. 'He has another mission.'

'Hasn't he just!' muttered Ananais.

'Well, I suggest,' interposed Rayvan, 'that we call a halt to tonight's meeting and break for supper. I could eat the best part of a horse. Can't we get together again tomorrow?'

'No,' said Tenaka. 'Tomorrow I leave Skoda.'

'Leave?' said Rayvan, astonished. 'But you are our general.'

'I must, lady – I have an army to find. But I shall return.'

'Where will you find an army?'

'Among my people.'

The silence in the Senate Hall was devastating. Men exchanged nervous glances and only Ananais seemed unmoved; he leaned back in his chair, placing his booted feet on the table top.

'Explain yourself,' murmured Rayvan.

'I think you know what I mean,' said Tenaka coolly. 'The one people with enough warriors to trouble Ceska are the Nadir. If I am lucky, I will raise an army.'

'You would bring those murderous savages into the Drenai? They are worse than Ceska's Joinings,' said Rayvan, pushing herself to her feet. 'I will not have it – I will die before those barbarians set foot on Skoda Land.'

All around men hammered their fists on the table in support. Then Tenaka stood up, raising his hands for silence.

'I appreciate the sentiments of everyone here. I was raised among the Nadir and I know their ways. But they do not eat babies, nor do they mate with demons. They are men, fighting men who live for war. It is their way. And they have honour. But I am not here to defend my people – I am here to give you a chance of staying alive through the summer.

'You think you have won a great victory? You won nothing but a skirmish. Ceska will throw fifty thousand men against you, come the summer. With what will you reply?

'And if you are defeated, what will happen to your families? Ceska will turn Skoda into a desert, and where there were trees there will be gibbets: a land of cadavers, desolate and tormented.

'There is no guarantee that I can raise an army among the Nadir. To them I am tainted by round-eye blood – accursed and less than a man. For they are no different from you. Nadir children are raised on stories of your debaucheries, and our legends are filled with tales of your genocides.

'I do not seek your permission for what I do. To be truthful, I don't give a damn! I leave tomorrow.'

He sat down to silence and Ananais leaned over to him.

'There was no need to beat about the bush,' he said. 'You should have given it to them straight.'

The comment produced an involuntary snort from Rayvan, which turned into a throaty chuckle.

Around the table the tension turned to laughter while Tenaka sat with arms folded, his face flushed and stern.

Finally Rayvan spoke. 'I do not like your plan, my friend. And I think I speak for everyone here. But you have played fair by us and without you we would now be crow's meat.' She sighed and leaned over the table, placing her hand on Tenaka's arm. 'You do give a damn, or else you would not be here, and if you are wrong – then so be it. I will stand by you. Bring your Nadir, if you can, and I will embrace the first goat-eating dog-soldier who rides in with you.'

Tenaka relaxed and looked long into her green eyes.

'You are quite a woman, Rayvan,' he whispered.

'You would be wise not to forget it, general!'

13

Ananais rode from the city at dusk, anxious to be free of its noisy confines. Once he had loved the city life, with its endless rounds of parties and hunts. There were beautiful women to be loved, men to be bested at wrestling or mock sword-play. There were falcons and tourneys and dances overlapping one another, as the most civilised western nation indulged in pleasure.

But then he had been the Golden One and the subject of legend.

He lifted the black mask from his torn face and felt the wind ease the angry scar. Riding to a nearby hilltop crowned with rowan trees, there he slid from the saddle and sat staring at the mountains. Tenaka was right – there had been no reason to kill the Legion men. It was proper that they wished to go back – it was their duty. But then hate was a potent force, and Ananais carried hate carved in his heart. He hated Ceska for what he had done to the land and its people and he hated the people for allowing it. He hated the flowers for their beauty and the air around him for granting him breath.

Most of all he hated himself, for not having the courage to end his misery.

What did these Skoda peasants know of his reasons for being among them? They had cheered him on the day of the battle, and again when he arrived in the city. 'Darkmask', they called him – a hero out of the past, built in the image of the immortal Druss.

What did they know of his grief?

He stared down at the mask. Even in this there was vanity, for the front was built out in the shape of a nose. He might just as well have cut two holes in it.

He was a man without a face and without a future. Only the past brought him pleasure – but with that came the pain. All he had now was his prodigious strength . . . and that was failing. He was forty-six years old and time was running out.

For the thousandth time he remembered the arena battle with the Joining. Had there been another way to kill the beast? Could he have saved himself this torment? He watched the battle once more through the eye of memory. There *was* no other way – the beast had been twice as strong and half again as swift as he. It was a miracle that he had slain it at all.

His horse whinnied, its ears flicking up, its head turning. Ananais replaced his mask and waited. Within seconds his keen hearing caught the soft clip-clopping of a walking horse.

'Ananais!' called Valtaya from the darkness. 'Are you there?' He cursed softly, for he was in no mood for company.

'Over here! On the lee of the hill.'

She rode to him and slipped from the saddle, dropping the reins over her mount's neck. The gold of her hair turned silver in the moonlight and her eyes reflected the stars.

'What do you want?' he asked, turning away and sitting down on the grass. She removed her cloak and spread it on the ground, seating herself upon it.

'Why did you ride here alone?'

'To be alone. I have much to think about.'

'Say the word and I shall ride back,' she said.

'I think you should,' he said, but she did not move, as he had known she would not.

'I, too, am lonely,' she murmured. 'But I do not want to be alone. I am alone and I have no place here.'

'I can offer you nothing, woman!' he snapped, his voice rough as the words ripped from him.

'You could let me have your company at least,' she said and the floodgates opened. Tears welled from her eyes and her head dropped; then the sobs began.

'Whisht, woman, there's no call for tears. What have you to cry about? There is no need for you to be lonely. You are very attractive and Galand is well-smitten with you. He is a good man.' But as the sobs continued he moved to her side, curling a huge arm around her shoulder and pulling her to him.

She pushed her head against his chest and the sobbing died down into ragged crying. He patted her back and stroked her hair; her arm crept round his waist and she gently pushed him back to lie upon her cloak. A terrible desire seized Ananais and he wanted her then more than anything life could offer. Her body pressed down on his and he could feel the warmth of her breasts upon his chest.

Her hand moved to his mask, but he grasped her wrist with a swiftness that stunned her.

'*Don't!*' he pleaded, releasing her hand. But slowly she lifted the mask and he closed his eyes as the night air washed over his scars. Her lips touched his forehead, then his eyelids, then both ruined cheeks. He had no mouth to return her kisses and he wept; she held him close then until the crying passed.

'I swore,' he said at last, 'that I would die before a woman would see me this way.'

'A woman loves a man. A face is not a man, any more than a leg is a man, or a hand. I love you, Ananais! And your scars are a part of you. Do you see that?'

'There is a difference,' he said, 'between love and gratitude. I rescued you, but you don't owe me anything. You never will.'

'You are right – I am grateful. But I would not give myself to you out of gratitude. I am not a child. I know you do not love me. Why should you? You had your pick of all the beauties in Drenan and refused them. But I love you and I want you – even for the short time that we have.'

'You know, then?'

'Of course I know! We will not defeat Ceska – we never could. But that is not of consequence. He will die. All men die.'

'You think what we do is a nonsense?'

'No. There will always be those . . . must always be those . . . who will stand against the Ceskas of the world. So that in times to come, men will know that there have always been heroes to stand against the darkness. We need men like Druss and the Earl of Bronze, like Egel and Karnak, like Bild and Iron-latch. They give us pride and a sense of purpose. And we need men like Ananais and Tenaka Khan. It matters not that the Torchbearer cannot win – only that the light shines for a little while.'

'You are well-read, Val,' he said.

'I am not a fool, Ananais.' Leaning over him, she kissed his face once more. Gently she pressed her mouth to his. He groaned and his great arms encircled her.

*

Rayvan could not sleep; the air was oppressive and heavy with the threat of storms. Throwing aside her heavy blanket she left the bed, wrapping a woollen robe about her sturdy frame. Then she opened the window wide, but not a breath of wind travelled over the mountains.

The night was velvet dark and tiny bats skittered and flew around the tower and down into the fruit trees of the garden. A badger, caught in a shaft of moonlight, glared up at her window and then shuffled away into the undergrowth. She sighed – there was such beauty to the night. A flicker of movement caught her eye and from the window she could just make out the figure of a white-cloaked warrior kneeling by a rose bush. Then he stood, and in that fluid motion she recognised Decado.

Rayvan left the window and moved silently through the long corridors, down the winding stairway and out into the courtyard garden. Decado was leaning against a low wall, watching the moonlight on the mountains. He heard Rayvan's approach and turned to meet her, the ghost of a welcoming smile upon his thin lips.

'Engaged in solitude?' she asked him.

'Merely thinking.'

'This is a good place for it. Peaceful.'

'Yes.'

'I was born up there,' she said, pointing east. 'My father had a small farm beyond the timberline – cattle and ponies mostly. It was a good life.'

'We shall not hold any of this, Rayvan.'

'I know. When the time comes we will move

218

further back into the high country, where the passes narrow.'

He nodded. 'I don't think Tenaka will come back.'

'Don't write him off, Decado. He is a canny man.'

'You don't need to tell me – I served under him for six years.'

'Do you like him?'

A sudden smile lit his face, burning the years from him. 'Of course I like him. He is the closest to a friend I have ever had.'

'What about your men, your Thirty?'

'What about them?' he asked guardedly.

'Do you see them as your friends?'

'No.'

'Then why do they follow you?'

'Who knows? They have a dream: a desire to die. It is all beyond me. Tell me about your farm – were you happy there?'

'Yes. A good husband, fine children, a nourished land beneath an open sky. What more can a woman ask on the journey between life and death?'

'Did you love your husband?'

'What kind of question is that?' she snapped.

'I did not mean to give offence. You never mention him by name.'

'That has nothing to do with lack of love. In fact the reverse is true. When I say his name, it brings home to me just what I have lost. But I hold his image in my heart – you understand that?'

'Yes.'

'Why did you never marry?'

'I never wanted to; never had the desire to share my life with a woman. I am not comfortable with people, save on my own terms.'

'Then you were wise,' said Rayvan.

'You think so?'

'I think so. You and your friends are very alike, you know. You are all incomplete men – terribly sad and very alone. No wonder you are drawn together! The rest of us can share our lives, swap jests and tall tales, laugh together, cry together. We live and love and grow. We offer each other small comforts daily and they help us to survive. But you have nothing like that to offer. Instead you offer your life – your death.'

'It is not that simple, Rayvan.'

'Life seldom is, Decado. But then I am but a simple mountain woman and I paint the pictures as I see them.'

'Come now, lady, there is nothing simple about you! But let us suppose – for a moment – that you are right. Do you think that Tenaka, or Ananais, or myself chose to be as we are? My grandfather had a dog. He desired that dog to hate the Nadir, so he hired an old tribesman to come into the farmyard every night and beat the puppy with a switch.

'The puppy grew to hate that old man and any other of his slant-eyed race. Would you blame the dog? Tenaka Khan was raised amid hatred and though he did not respond in kind, still the absence of love left its mark. He bought a wife and lavished all he had upon her. Now she is dead and he has nothing.

'Ananais? You only have to look upon him to know what pain he carries. But even so that is not the whole story. His father died insane after killing Ananais' mother before his eyes. Even before that, the father had bedded Ani's sister . . . she died in childbirth.

'And as for me, my story is even more sordid and sad. So spare me your mountain homilies, Rayvan. Had any of us grown to manhood on the slopes of your mountain, I don't doubt we would have been better men.'

She smiled then and heaved herself on to the wall, swinging round to look down on him. 'Foolish boy!' she said. 'I did not say you needed to be better men. You are the best of men, and I love all three of you. You are not like your grandfather's dog, Decado – you are a man. And a man can overcome his background, even as he can overcome a skilled opponent. Look around you more often: see the people as they touch and show their love. But don't watch coldly, like an observer. Don't hover outside life – take part in it. There are people out there waiting to love you. It is not something you should turn down lightly.'

'We are what we are, lady; do not ask for more. I am a swordsman. Ananais is a warrior. Tenaka is a general beyond compare. Our backgrounds have made us what we are. You need us as you see us.'

'Perhaps. But perhaps you could be even greater.'

'Now is not the time to experiment. Come – I will walk you back to your rooms.'

*

Scaler sat on the broad bed, staring at the dark-stained door. Tenaka was gone now, but he could still see the tall Nadir warrior and hear the softly-spoken commands.

It was a farce – he was trapped here, entangled in this web of heroes.

Take Dros Delnoch?

Ananais could take Dros Delnoch, charging it single-handed with his silver sword flashing in the dawn sun. Tenaka could take it with some improvised plan, some subtle stroke of genius involving a length of twine and three small pebbles. These were men made for Legend, created by the gods to fuel the sagas.

But where did Scaler fit in?

He moved to the long mirror by the window wall. A tall young man stared back at him, dark shoulder-length hair held in place by a black leather brow-circlet. The eyes were bright and intelligent, the chin square, giving the lie to the saga poets. The fringed buckskin jerkin hung well, drawn in to his lean waist by a thick sword-belt. A dagger hung at his left side. His leggings were of softest dark leather and his boots thigh-length after the fashion of the Legion. Reaching for his sword, he slotted it home in the leather scabbard and placed it at his side.

'You poor fool!' the mirror warrior told him. 'You should have stayed at home.'

He had tried to tell Tenaka how ill-equipped he felt, but the Nadir had smiled gently and ignored him.

'You are of the blood, Arvan. It will carry you through,' he had said. Words! Just words. Blood was merely dark liquid – it carried no secrets, no mysteries. Courage was a thing of the soul and not a gift that a man could bestow on his sons.

The door opened and Scaler glanced round as Pagan entered. The black man smiled a greeting and then eased himself into a broad leather chair. In the lantern light he loomed large, the immense sweep of his shoulders filling the chair. Just like the others, thought Scaler – a man to move mountains.

'Come to see me off?' he asked, breaking the silence.

The black man shook his head. 'I am coming with you.'

Relief struck Scaler with almost physical power, but he masked his emotions.

'Why?'

'Why not? I like riding.'

'You know my mission?'

'You are to take a fort and open the gates for Tenaka's warriors.'

'It is not quite so easy as you make it sound,' said Scaler, returning to the bed and sitting down. The sword twisted between his legs as he sat and he straightened it.

'Don't worry about it, you will think of something,' said Pagan, grinning. 'When do you want to leave?'

'In about two years.'

'Don't be hard on yourself, Scaler; it does no good. I know your mission is tough. Dros Delnoch is a city with six walls and a keep. More than seven thousand warriors are stationed there – and some fifty Joinings. But we will do what we can. Tenaka says you have a plan.'

Scaler chuckled. 'That is good of him. He thought of it days ago and waited for me to catch up!'

'So tell me.'

'The Sathuli – they are a mountain and desert people, fierce and independent. For centuries they fought the Drenai over the rights to the Delnoch ranges. During the First Nadir War they aided my ancestor, the Earl of Bronze. In return he gave them the land. I don't know how many there are – possibly ten thousand, maybe less. But Ceska has revoked the original treaty and border skirmishes have begun again.'

'So, you will seek aid from the tribesmen?'

'Yes.'

'But without great hope of success?'

'That's fair comment. The Sathuli have always hated the Drenai and there is no trust there. Worse than that, they loathe the Nadir. And even if they do help, how in Hell's name do I get them to leave the fortress?'

'One problem at a time, Scaler!'

Scaler stood up and the sword twisted again, half-tripping him; he pulled the scabbard from the belt and hurled it to the bed.

'One problem at a time? All right! Let us look at problems. I am no warrior, no swordsman. I have never been a soldier. I am frightened of battles and have never displayed much skill at tactics. I am not a leader and would be hard-pressed to get hungry men to follow me to a kitchen. Which of these problems shall we tackle first?'

'Sit down, boy,' said Pagan, leaning forward and resting his hands on the arms of the chair. Scaler sat, his anger ebbing from him. 'Now listen to me! In my own land, I am a king. I rose to the throne on blood and death, the first of my race to take the Opal. When I was a young man and full of pride, an old priest came to me telling me that I would burn in the fires of Hell for my crimes. I ordered a regiment to build a fire from many trees. It could not be approached closer than thirty paces and the flames beat against the vault of heaven. Then I ordered that regiment to put out the flames. Ten thousand men hurled themselves on the blaze and the fire died. "If I go to Hell," I told the priest, "my men will follow me and stamp out the flames." From the great Sea of Souls to the Mountains of the Moon, I ruled that kingdom. I survived poison in my wine-cup and daggers at my back, false friends and noble enemies, treacherous sons and summer plagues. And yet I will follow you, Scaler.'

Scaler swallowed as he watched the lantern light dance on the ebony features of the man in the chair.

'Why? Why will you follow me?'

'Because the thing must be done. And now I am going to tell you a great truth, and if you are wise you will take it to your heart. All men are stupid. They are full of fear and insecurity – it makes them weak. Always the other man seems stronger, more confident, more capable. It is a lie of the worst kind, for we lie to ourselves.

'Take yourself. When I came in here I was your black friend, Pagan – big, strong and friendly. But what am I now? Now am I not a savage king far above you? Do you not feel ashamed of having forced your tiny doubts upon me?'

Scaler nodded.

'And yet, *am* I a king? Did I truly command my regiment to stamp out a fire? How do you know? You do not! You listened to the voice of your inadequacy, and because you believed you are in my power. If I draw my sword, you are dead!

'And again, when I look at you I see a bright courageous young man, well-built and in the prime of his manhood. You could be the prince of assassins, the deadliest warrior under the sun. You could be an emperor, a general, a poet . . .

'Not a leader, Scaler? Anyone can be a leader, because everyone wants to be led.'

'I am not a Tenaka Khan,' said Scaler. 'I am not of the same breed.'

'Tell me that in a month. But from now on, act the part. You will be amazed at the number of people you fool. Don't share your doubts! Life is a game, Scaler. Play it like that.'

Scaler grinned. 'Why not? But tell me – did you truly send your men into the fire?'

'You tell me,' said Pagan, his face hardening and his eyes glowing in the lamplight.

'No, you did not!'

Pagan grinned. 'No! I will have the horses ready at dawn – I'll see you then.'

'Make sure you pack plenty of honey-cakes – Belder has a fondness for them.'

Pagan shook his head. 'The old man is not coming. He is no good for you and his spirit is gone. He stays behind.'

'If you follow me, then you do as I damn well say,' snapped Scaler. 'Three horses and Belder travels with us!'

The black man's eyebrows rose and he spread his hands. 'Very well.' He opened the door.

'How was that?' asked Scaler.

'Not bad for a start. I'll see you in the morning.'

As Pagan returned to his room, his mood was sombre. Lifting his huge pack to the bed, he spread out the weapons he would carry tomorrow: two hunting-knives, sharp as razors; four throwing-knives to be worn in baldric sheaths; a short sword, double-edged, and a double-headed hand-axe he would strap to his saddle.

Stripping himself naked, he took a phial of oil from his pack and began to grease his body, rubbing hard at the bunched muscles of his shoulders. The damp western air was creeping into his bones.

His mind soared back over the years. He could still feel the heat of the blaze and hear the screams of his warriors as they raced into the flames . . .

*

Tenaka rode down from the mountain onto the slopes of the Vagrian plains. The sun rose over his left shoulder and the clouds bunched above his head. He felt at peace with the breeze in his hair; though mountainous problems reared ahead of him, he felt light and free of burdens.

He wondered if his Nadir heritage had made him uneasy among city dwellers, with their high walls and shuttered windows. The breeze picked up and Tenaka smiled.

Tomorrow death could flash towards him on an arrow point – but today . . . today was fine.

He pushed all thoughts of Skoda from his mind – those problems could be dealt with by Ananais and Rayvan. Scaler too was now his own man, riding for his own destiny. All Tenaka could do was fulfil his particular part in the tale.

His mind swam back to his childhood among the tribes. Spear, Wolfshead, Green Monkey, Grave Mountain, Soul Stealers. So many camps, so many territories.

Ulric's tribe were acknowledged as the premier fighting men: the Lords of the Steppes, the Bringers of War. Wolfshead they were and their ferocity in war was legend. But who ruled the wolves now? Surely Jongir was dead.

Tenaka considered the contemporaries of his youth:

Knifespeaks, swift to anger and slow to forgive. Cunning, resourceful and ambitious.

Abadai Truthtaker, devious and devout in the ways of the shamen.

Tsuboy, known as Saddleskull after he killed a raider and mounted the man's skull on his saddle-horn.

All these were grandsons of Jongir. All descended from Ulric.

Tenaka's violet eyes grew bleak and cold as he brought the trio to mind. Each had showed his hatred of the half-breed.

Abadai had been the most vicious and had even resorted to poison during the Feast of the Long

Knives. Only Shillat, Tenaka's vigilant mother, had observed the placing of the powder in her son's cup.

But none had challenged Tenaka directly, for even by the age of fourteen he had earned the name Bladedancer and was accomplished with every weapon of war.

And he sat for long night hours round the campfires, listening to the old men as they remembered wars past, picking up details of strategy and tactics. At fifteen he knew every battle and skirmish in Wolfshead history.

Tenaka drew on the reins and stared at the distant Delnoch mountains.

> Nadir we,
> youth born,
> axe wielders,
> blood letters,
> victors still.

He laughed and dug his heels into his gelding's flanks. The beast snorted and then broke into a full gallop across the plain, hooves drumming in the early morning silence.

Tenaka let the horse run for several minutes before slowing it to a canter and then a trot. They had many miles to go, and though the beast was game he did not wish to overtire it.

By all the gods, it was good to be free of people! Even Renya.

She was beautiful and he loved her, but he was a man who needed solitude – freedom for his plans to form.

She had listened in silence when he told her of his plan to travel alone. He had expected a bitter row, but she had offered none. Instead she embraced him and they had made love without passion, but with great tenderness.

If he survived this insane venture, he would take her to his heart and his home. If he survived? He calculated the odds against success at hundreds to one; perhaps thousands. A sudden thought struck him. Was he a fool? He had Renya and a fortune waiting in Ventria. Why risk everything?

Did he love the Drenai? He pondered the question, knowing that he did not but wondering just what his feelings were. The people had never accepted him, even as a Dragon general. And the land, though beautiful, had nothing of the savage splendour of the Steppes. So what were his feelings?

The death of Illae had unhinged him, coming so close to the destruction of the Dragon. The shame he felt for spurning his friends had merged with the agony of Illae's passing and in some strange way he saw her death as a punishment for his failure to fulfil his duty. Only Ceska's death – and his own – could wipe away the shame. But now it was different.

Ananais would stand alone if necessary, believing in Tenaka's promise that he would return. And friendship was something infinitely more solid and greatly more sustaining than love of the land. Tenaka Khan would ride across the deepest pit of Hell, endure the greatest hardships under the sun, to fulfil his promise to Ananais.

He glanced back at the Skoda mountains. There would the deaths begin in earnest. Rayvan's band stood upon the anvil of history, staring up defiantly at Ceska's hammer.

Ananais had ridden with him from the city just before dawn, and they had stopped on the brow of a hill.

'Look after yourself, you Nadir slop-swiller!'

'And you, Drenai. Look to your valleys!'

'Seriously, Tani, take care. Get your army and come back swiftly. We don't have long.I should think they will send a Delnoch force against us, to soften us up for the main thrust.'

Tenaka nodded. 'They will probe and cut – tire you out. Use The Thirty; they will be invaluable in the days to come. Have you anywhere in mind for a second base?'

'Yes, we are moving supplies to the high country south of the city. There are two narrow passes we could hold. But if they push us back there, we are finished. There is nowhere to run.'

The two men shook hands and then hugged one another warmly.

'I want you to know . . .' began Tenaka, but Ananais cut him short.

'I know, boy! You must hurry back. You can rely on old Darkmask to hold the fort.'

Tenaka grinned and rode for the Vagrian Plains.

14

For six days there was no sign of hostile activity on the eastern Skoda borders. Refugees poured in to the mountains, bringing tales of torture, starvation and terror. The Thirty screened the refugees as best they could, turning away those found to be lying or secretly sympathetic to Ceska.

But, day by day, the numbers swelled as the outer lands bled of people. Camps were set up in several valleys and the problems of food supply and sanitation plagued Ananais. Rayvan took it in her stride, organising the refugees into work parties to dig latrine trenches and build simple shelters for the elderly and infirm.

Young men came forward hourly to volunteer for the army and it was left to Galand, Parsal and Lake to sift them and find them duties among the Skoda militia.

But always they asked for Darkmask, the black-garbed giant. 'Ceska's Bane', they called him, and among the newcomers were saga poets whose songs floated out in the night from the valley camp-fires.

Ananais found it irksome but he hid it well, knowing how valuable the legends would be in the days to come.

Every morning he rode out into the mountains to study the valleys and the slopes, seeking the passes and gauging distances and angles of attack. He set men to work digging earth-walls and ditches, moving rocks to form cover. Caches of arrows and lances were hidden at various points, along with sacks of food hung high in the branches of trees, screened by thick foliage. Each section leader knew of at least three caches.

At dusk Ananais would call the section leaders to his fire and question them about the day's training, encouraging them to come forward with ideas, strategies and plans. He carefully noted those who did so, keeping them with him when others were dismissed. Lake, for all his idealistic fervour, was a sound thinker who responded intelligently. His knowledge of terrain was extensive and Ananais used him well. Galand too was a canny warrior and the men respected him; he was solid, dependable and loyal. His brother Parsal was no thinker, but his courage was beyond question. To these of the inner circle Ananais added two others; Turs and Thorn. Solitary men who said little, both were former raiders who had earned their living crossing Vagrian lands and stealing cattle and horses to trade in the eastern valleys. Turs was young and full of fire; his brother and two sisters had been killed in the raid that saw Rayvan rebel. Thorn was an older man, leather-tough and wolf-lean. The Skoda men respected them both and listened in silence when they spoke.

It was Thorn who brought news of the herald on the seventh day after Tenaka's departure.

Ananais was scouting the eastern slopes of the mountain Carduil, when Thorn found him and he rode east at speed. Thorn alongside him.

Their horses were well-lathered when Ananais finally reached the valley of the Dawn, where Decado and six of The Thirty waited to greet him. Around them were some two hundred Skoda men, dug into position overlooking the plain beyond.

Ananais walked forward to climb a craggy outcrop of rock. Below him were six hundred warriors wearing the red of Delnoch. At the centre on a white horse sat an elderly man in bright blue robes. His beard was white and long. Ananais recognised him and grinned sourly.

'Who is it?' asked Thorn.

'Breight. They call him the Survivor. I am not surprised – he has been a counsellor for over forty years.'

'He must be Ceska's man,' said Thorn.

'He is anybody's man, but a wise choice to send for he is a diplomat and a patrician. He could tell you that wolves lay eggs and you would believe him.'

'Should we fetch Rayvan?'

'No. I will talk to him.'

At that moment six men rode forward to flank the aged counsellor. Their cloaks and armour were black. As Ananais watched them look up and felt their eyes upon him, ice flowed into his veins.

'Decado!' he shouted as the fear hit him. Instantly the warmth of friendship blanketed him as Decado and his six warriors turned the power of their minds to protect him.

Angry now, Ananais bellowed for Breight to approach. The old man hesitated, but one of the Templars leaned in to him and he spurred his horse forward, riding awkwardly up the steep slope.

'That is far enough!' said Ananais, moving forward.

'Is it you, Golden One?' asked Breight, his voice deep and resonant. The eyes were brown and exceedingly friendly.

'It is I. Say what you have to say.'

'There is no need for harshness between us, Ananais. Was I not the first to cheer when you were honoured for your battle triumphs? Did I not secure your first commission with the Dragon? Was I not your mother's troth-holder?'

'All these things and more, old man! But now you are a lick-spittle lackey to a tyrant and the past is dead.'

'You misjudge my lord Ceska – he has only the good of the Drenai in his heart. These are hard times, Ananais. Bitter hard. Our enemies wage a silent war upon us, starving us of food. Not one kingdom around us wishes to see the enlightenment of the Drenai prosper, for it signals the end of their corruption.'

'Spare me this nonsense, Breight! I cannot be bothered to argue with you. What do you want?'

'I see your terrible wounds have made you bitter and I am sorry for that. I bring you a royal pardon! My lord is deeply offended by your actions against him, yet your past deeds have earned you a place in his heart. In your honour, he has pardoned every man who stands against him in Skoda. Further, he promises to review personally every grievance you have, real or imagined. Can he be fairer than that?'

Breight had pitched his voice to carry to the listening defenders and his eyes scanned the line watching for their reactions.

'Ceska would not know "fair" if it burned his buttocks,' said Ananais. 'The man is a snake!'

'I understand your hatred, Ananais – look at you . . . scarred, deformed, unhuman. But surely there is a shred of humanity left in you? Why should your hatred carry thousands of innocent souls to terrible deaths? You cannot win! The Joinings are now assembling and there is no army on the face of the earth which can stand against them. Will you bring this devastation upon these people? Look into your heart, man!'

'I will not argue with you old man. Down there your men wait, and among them are the Templars – they who feed on the flesh of children. Your semi-human beasts gather in Drenan, and daily thousands of innocents pour into this small bastion of freedom. All of this gives the lie to your words. I am not even angry with you, Breight the Survivor! You sold your soul for a silk-covered couch. But I understand you – you are a frightened old man who has never lived because you never dared to live.

'In these mountains there is life and the air tastes like wine. You are right when you say we may not stand against the Joinings. We know that for we are not fools. There is no glory here; but we are men and the sons of men, and we bend the knee to no one. Why don't you join us, and learn even now of the joys of freedom?'

'Freedom? You are in a cage, Ananais. The Vagrians will not let you move east into their lands, and we wait in the west. You delude yourself. What price your freedom? In a matter of days the armies of the emperor will gather here, filling the plain. You have seen the Joinings of Ceska – well, there are more to come. Huge beasts, blended from the apes of the east, from the great bears of the north, from the wolves of the south. They strike like lightning and they feed on human flesh. Your pitiful force will be swept aside like dust before a storm. Tell me then of freedom, Ananais. I desire not the freedom of the grave.'

'And yet it comes to you, Breight, in every white hair, every decaying wrinkle. death will stalk you and lay his cold hands upon your eyes. You cannot escape! Begone, little man, your day is done.'

Breight looked up at the defenders and opened his arms.

'Don't let this man deceive you!' he shouted. 'My lord Ceska is a man of honour and he will abide by his promise.'

'Go home and die!' said Ananais, turning on his heels and striding back to his men.

'Death will come to you before me,' screamed Breight, 'and his coming will be terrible.' Then the old man wheeled his horse and cantered downhill.

'I think the war will start tomorrow,' muttered Thorn.

Ananais nodded and waved Decado to him. 'What do you think?'

Decado shrugged. 'We could not pierce the screen the Templars mounted.'

'Did they pierce ours?'

'No.'

'Then we start even,' said Ananais. 'But they have tried to win us with words. Now it will be swords and they will try to demoralise us by a sudden attack. The question is where, and what are we going to do about it?'

'Well,' said Decado, 'the great Tertullian was once asked what he would do if he was attacked by a man stronger, faster and infinitely more skilful than he.'

'What did he say?'

'He said he would cut off his damned head for being a liar.'

'Sounds good,' put in Thorn, 'but words are not worth pigs' droppings now.'

'You are right there,' said Ananais, grinning. 'So what do you suggest, mountain man?'

'Let's cut off their damned heads!'

*

The hut was bathed in a soft red glow as the log fire

burned low. Ananais lay on the bed, his head resting on his arm. Valtaya sat beside him rubbing oil into his shoulders and back – kneading the muscles, loosening the knots of tension around his spine. Her fingers were strong and the slow rhythmic movements of her hands soothing. He sighed and fell into a half-sleep, dreaming dreams of brighter days.

As her fingers began to burn with fatigue, she lifted them from his broad back, pushing pressure on to her palms for a while. His breathing deepened. She covered him with a blanket and then pulled a chair alongside the bed and sat staring at his ruined face. The angry scar below his eye seemed cooler now, and dry; she gently smoothed oil on the skin. His breath made a snuffling sound as it was sucked through the oval holes where his nose should have been. Valtaya leaned back, sadness a growing ache within her. He was a fine man and did not deserve his fate. It had taken all her considerable nerve just to kiss him, and even now she could not gaze on his features without feeling revulsion. Yet she loved him.

Life was cruel and infinitely sorrowful.

She had slept with many men in her life. Once it had been a vocation, once a profession. During the latter time many ugly men had come to her and with them she had learned to hide her feelings. She was glad now of the lessons, for when she had removed Ananais' mask two sensations had struck her simultaneously. One was the awful horror of his mutilated face. The other was the terrible anxiety in his eyes. Strong as he was, in that moment he was made of crystal. Now she transferred her gaze to his hair – tightly curled gold thread, laced with silver. The Golden One! How handsome he once must have been. Like a god. She pushed a hand through her own fair hair, sweeping it away from her eyes.

Tired, she stood and stretched her back. The window was part open and she pushed it wide. Outside the valley was silent beneath a scimitar moon.

'I wish I was young again,' she whispered. 'I would have married that poet.'

*

Katan soared above the mountains and wished that his body could fly as high as his spirit. He wanted to taste the air, feel the harsh winds upon his skin. Below him the mountains of Skoda reared like spearpoints. He flew higher and now the mountains took on another image. Katan smiled.

Skoda had become a stone rose with jagged petals on a field of green. Rings of towering granite, interlinking to create a gargantuan bloom.

To the north-east Katan could just make out the fortress of Delnoch, while to the south-east were the glittering cities of the Drenai. It was all so beautiful. From here there was no cruelty, no torture, no terror. No room here for men with small minds and limitless ambition.

He turned again to the rose of Skoda. The outer petals concealed nine valleys through which an army could march. He scanned them all, gauging the contours and the gradients, picturing lines of fighting men, charging horsemen, fleeing infantry. Committing the facts to memory, he moved on to the second ring of mountains. Here there were only four main valleys, but three treacherous passes threaded their way through to the open pastures and woodlands beyond.

At the centre of the rose the mountains bunched with only two access points from the east – the valleys known as Tarsk and Magadon.

His mission completed, Katan returned to his body and reported to Decado. He could offer no hope.

'There are nine main valleys and a score of other narrow passes on the outer ring. Even on the inner ring around Carduil there are two lines of attack. Our force could not hold even one. It is impossible to plan a defence that stands a one-in-twenty chance of success. And by success I mean standing off one attack.'

'Say nothing to anyone,' ordered Decado. 'I will speak to Ananais.'

'As you wish,' said Katan coolly.

Decado smiled gently. 'I am sorry, Katan.'

'For what?'

'For what I am,' answered the warrior, moving away up the hill until he reached the high ground overlooking several spreading valleys. This was good country – sheltered, peaceful. The ground was not rich, like the Sentran Plain to the north-east, but treated with care the farms prospered and the cattle grew fat on the grass of the timberlands.

Decado's family had been farmers far to the east and he guessed that the love of growing things had been planted in him at the moment of conception. He crouched down, digging his strong fingers into the earth at his feet. There was clay here and the grass grew lush and thick.

'May I join you?' asked Katan.

'Please do.'

The two men sat in silence for a while, watching distant cattle grazing on fertile slopes.

'I miss Abaddon,' said Katan suddenly.

'Yes. he was a good man.'

'He was a man with a vision. But he had no patience and only limited belief.'

'How can you say that?' asked Decado. 'He believed enough to form The Thirty once more.'

'Precisely! He decided that evil should be met with raw force. And yet our faith claims that evil can only be conquered by love.'

'That is insane. How do you deal with your enemies?'

'How better to deal with them than to make them your friends?' countered Katan.

'The words are pretty, the argument specious. You do not make a friend of Ceska – you become a slave or die.'

Katan smiled. 'And what does it matter? The Source governs all things and eternity mocks human life.'

'You think it doesn't matter if we die?'

'Of course it does not. The Source takes us and we live for ever.'

'And if there is no Source?' asked Decado.

'Then death is even more welcome. I do not hate Ceska. I pity him. He has built an empire of terror. And what does he achieve? each day brings him closer to the grave. Is he content? Does he gaze with love on any single thing? He surrounds himself with warriors to protect him from assassins, then has warriors watching the warriors to sniff out traitors. But who watches the watchers? What a miserable existence!'

'So,' said Decado, 'The Thirty are not Source warriors at all?'

'They are if they believe.'

'You cannot have it all ways, Katan.'

The young man chuckled. 'Perhaps. How did you become a warrior?'

'All men are warriors, for life is a battle. The farmer battles drought, flood, sickness and blight.

The sailor battles the sea and the storm. I didn't have the strength for that, so I fought men.'

'And who does the priest fight?'

Decado turned to face the earnest young man. 'The priest fights himself. He cannot look at a woman with honest lust without guilt burning into him. He cannot get drunk and forget. He cannot take a day just to soak in the glory of the world's beauty, without wondering if he should be engaged on some worthy deed.'

'For a priest, you have a low opinion of your brothers.'

'On the contrary, I have a very high opinion of them,' said Decado.

'You were very hard on Acuas. He really believed he was rescuing Abaddon's soul.'

'I know that, Katan. I admire him for it – all of you, in fact. I was angry with myself. It was not easy for me, for I don't have your faith. For me the Source is a mystery I cannot solve. And yet I promised Abaddon I would see his mission fulfilled. You are fine young men and I am merely an old warrior in love with death.'

'Do not be too hard on yourself. You are chosen. It is a great honour.'

'Happenstance! I came to the Temple and Abaddon read more into it than he should.'

'No,' said Katan. 'Think on this: you came on the day when one of our brothers died. More than that – you are not just a warrior, you are possibly the greatest swordsman of the age. You defeated the Templars single-handed. Even more, you developed talents with which the rest of us were born. You came to our rescue in the Castle of the Void. How can you not be the natural leader? And if you are . . . what brought you to us?'

Decado leaned back, staring at the gathering clouds.

'I think we are in for rain,' he remarked.

'Have you tried praying, Decado?'

'It would still rain.'

'Have you tried?' persisted the priest.

Decado sat up and sighed deeply. 'Of course I have tried. But I get no answers. I tried on the night you journeyed into the Void . . . but He would not answer me.'

'How can you say that? Did you not learn to soar on that night? Did you not find us through the mists of non-time? You think you did that in your own strength?'

'Yes I do.'

'Then you answered your own prayers?'

'Yes.'

Katan smiled. 'Then keep praying. Who knows the heights to which it will carry you?'

Now it was Decado's turn to chuckle. 'You mock me, young Katan! I will not have it. Just for that you can lead the prayers this evening – I think Acuas needs a rest.'

'It will be my pleasure.'

Across the fields Ananais spurred his black gelding into a gallop. Bending low over the beast's neck he urged it on, hooves drumming on the dry ground. For those few seconds of speed he forgot his problems, revelling in the freedom of the race. Behind him Galand and Thorn were neck and neck, but their mounts were no match for the gelding and Ananais reached the stream twenty lengths ahead. He leapt to the ground and patted the horse, keeping him from the water and walking him round to cool down. The others dismounted.

'Unfair!' said Galand. 'Your mount is hands higher and bred for speed.'

'But I weigh more than both of you together,' said Ananais.

Thorn said nothing, merely grinned crookedly and shook his head. He liked Ananais and welcomed the change which had come over him since the fair-haired woman had moved into his hut. He seemed more alive – more in tune with the world.

Love was like that. Thorn had been in love many times, and even at sixty-two he hoped for at least another two or three romances. There was a widow woman who had a farm in the high, lonely country to the north; he stopped there often for breakfast. She hadn't warmed to him yet, but she would – Thorn knew women. There was no point in rushing in . . . Gentle talk, that was the answer. Ask them questions about themselves . . . Be interested. Most men travelled through life determined to rut as swiftly as the woman would allow. Senseless! Talk first. Learn. Then touch, gently, lovingly. Care. Then love and linger. Thorn had learned early, for he had always been ugly. Other men disliked him for his success, but they could never be bothered to learn from it. Fools!

'Another caravan from Vagria this morning,' said Galand, scratching his beard. 'But the treasury gold is running low. Those cursed Vagrians have doubled their prices.'

'It's a seller's market,' said Ananais. 'What did they bring?'

'Arrowheads, iron, some swords. Mostly flour and sugar. Oh yes – and a quantity of leather and hide. Lake ordered it. There should be enough food to last a month . . . but no more.'

Thorn's dry chuckle stopped Galand in full flow.

'What's so funny?'

'If we are still alive in a month I will be happy to go hungry!'

'Are the refugees still coming in?' asked Ananais.

'Yes,' said Galand, 'but the numbers are shrinking. I think we can handle it. The army now musters at two thousand, but we are being stretched thin. I don't like sitting around waiting to react. The Dragon operated on the premise that the first blow was vital.'

'We have no choice,' answered Ananais, 'since we must hold as wide a line as possible during the next few weeks. If we draw back they will simply ride in. At the moment they are undecided what to do.'

'The men are getting edgy,' said Thorn. 'It's not easy just to sit – it makes them think, wonder, imagine. Rayvan's performing miracles, travelling from valley to valley, fuelling their courage and calling them heroes. But it may not be enough.

'The victory was heady stuff, Ananais, but those who missed the battle now outnumber the men who fought in it. They are untried. And they're nervous.'

'What do you suggest?'

Thorn grinned his crooked grin. 'I'm not a general, Darkmask. You tell *me*!'

15

Caphas moved away from the tents and spread his black cloak on the dry earth as a blanket. He removed his dark helm and settled himself down. The stars were bright, but Caphas had no eyes for them. The night was cool and clean, but he hated the emptiness. He longed for the sanctuary of the Temple and the drug-induced orgies. The music of the torture room, the sweet sound of a victim's plea. Joy was what he missed here in this barren land. Laughter.

A special relationship came into being between the torturer and his victim. First there was defiance and hatred. Then tears and screams. Then begging. And finally, after the spirit was broken, there was a kind of love. Caphas cursed loudly and stood up, arousal creating anger within him. He opened the small leather pouch on his hip and removed a long Lorassium leaf. Rolling it into a ball, he placed it in his mouth and began to chew slowly. As the juices took hold and his mind swam, he became aware of the dreams of the sleeping soldiers and the slow, hungry thoughts of a badger in the undergrowth to his right. He screened them out, forcing his memory to replay a scene from the recent past when they had brought a girl-child to the torture room . . .

Uneasiness flooded him and he jerked his mind to the present, eyes flickering to the dark shadows in the trees.

A bright light grew before him, shimmering and coalescing into the shape of a warrior in silver armour. A white cloak was draped across his shoulders, the edges fluttering in the winds of Spirit.

Caphas closed his eyes and leapt from his body, black soul-sword in hand, dark shield upon his arm. The warrior parried the blow and stepped back.

'Come here and die,' offered Caphas. 'Twelve of your party are dead already. Come and join them!'

The warrior said nothing and only his blue eyes could be seen through the slit in the silver face-helm. The eyes were calm and the quiet confidence emanating from them seeped into Caphas' heart. His shield shrank.

'You cannot touch me!' he screamed. 'The Spirit is stronger than the Source. You are powerless against me!'

The warrior shook his head.

'Damn you!' shouted Caphas as his shield disappeared. He charged forward, slashing wildly.

Acuas parried the blow with ease and then slid his own blade deep into the Templar's chest. The man gasped as the icy sword cloved his spirit flesh. Then his soul guttered and died and, beyond it, his body toppled to the earth.

Acuas vanished. Two hundred paces into the wood he opened the eyes of his body and sagged into the supporting arms of Decado and Katan.

'All the Templar guards are dead,' he said.

'Good work!' praised Decado.

'I feel strained by their evil. Even to touch them is to be as one accursed.'

Decado moved back silently to where Ananais waited with one hundred warriors. Thorn crouched to his left, Galand to his right. Fifty of the warriors were legion men of whom Ananais was unsure.

Though he trusted Decado's instincts, the talents of The Thirty left him sceptical still. Tonight he would see whether these men were with him. he was uncomfortably aware of their swords around him.

Ananais led the force to the edge of the trees. Beyond lay the tents of the Delnoch army – one hundred of them – each giving shelter to six men. Beyond the tents were the picket ropes where the horses were tethered.

'I want Breight alive and I want those horses,' whispered Ananais. 'Galand, take fifty men and lead the mounts clear. The rest can follow me.' He moved forward, crouching low, his dark-armoured warriors spreading out behind him.

As they reached the tents the force split up, armed men silently lifting the front flaps and stepping stealthily inside. Daggers were drawn across sleeping throats and men died without a sound. At the edge of the camp, a sleeping soldier was awakened by the pressure of a full bladder; he rolled from his blanket and stepped out into the night air. The first thing he saw was a black-masked giant bearing down on him, followed by twenty swordsmen. He screamed once . . . and died.

Suddenly all was chaos as men surged from the tents with swords in hand. Ananais cut two warriors from his path and cursed loudly. Breight's tent was just ahead, blue silk bearing the White Horse emblem of the Drenai herald.

'To me, Legion!' he bellowed and ran forward. A soldier ran at him with a spear but Ananais side-stepped the weapon, his own sword sweeping viciously in a tight arc that smashed the man's ribs to shards. Ananais ran on, wrenching open the tent-flap and stepping inside. Breight was hiding below his bed, but Ananais dragged him out by his hair and hurled him into the night.

Old Thorn ran to Ananais as he emerged. 'We are in a little trouble, Darkmask,' he said.

The Legion fifty had closed ranks by Breight's tent, but all around them the Delnoch warriors stood ready, waiting the order to move in. Ananais dragged Breight to his feet and pushed his way to the front of the line.

'Order your men to lay down their weapons or I will cut your miserable throat,' he hissed.

'Yes, yes,' whimpered the greybeard, holding up his hands. 'Men of Ceska, lay aside your weapons. My life is too valuable to be thrown away in such a fashion. Let them go, I command you!'

A Dark Templar stepped from the line. 'You are worth nothing, old man! You had one mission – to talk these dogs from the hills. You failed.' His arm swept back, then down, and a black dagger hammered into Breight's throat. The old man staggered and fell to his knees. 'Now take them!' yelled the Templar and the Delnoch men surged forward. Ananais cut and thrust as the forces met, drawing the enemy to him like moths to a candle. His swords flickered among them faster than the eye could follow. Around him the Legion fought hard and well, and old Thorn ducked and cut cunningly.

Suddenly the thunder of hooves overrode the sounds of clashing steel and the Delnoch line waved as men glanced back to see a fresh force racing into the fray.

Galand's group hit the rear of the Delnoch force like a hammer-blow, scattering the enemy. As Ananais ran forward, yelling for the men to follow him, a sword lanced into his side. He grunted and back-handed a cut that swept the attacker from his feet. Decado spurred his horse towards Ananais, holding out his left arm. Ananais grasped it and vaulted to the saddle behind the priest. Other Legion men followed suit and the Skoda warriors galloped from the camp. Ananais glanced back, seeking Thorn and spotted him clinging to Galand.

'He's certainly a tough old man!' said Ananais.

Decado said nothing. He had just received a report from Balan, whose talk had been to scout the land over Drenan in order to study the marshalling of Ceska's main force. The news was not good.

Ceska had wasted no time.

The Joinings were already on the march and there was no way Tenaka Khan could bring a Nadir force to intercept them.

According to Balan the army would be camped by the Skoda valleys in four days.

All Tenaka could do was avenge them, for no force on earth was going to hold the werebeasts of Ceska.

*

Ananais rode into the city, holding himself straight in the saddle though weariness sat upon him like a boulder. He had spent a day and two nights with his lieutenants and their section leaders, informing them of Ceska's lightning march. Many leaders would have disguised the threat, fearing desertions and loss of morale, but Ananais had never subscribed to that theory. Men waiting to die had every right to know what lay in store.

But now he was tired.

The city was quiet, for dawn was only two hours old, but even so children gathered to play in the street, halting their game to watch Darkmask ride by. His horse almost lost its footing on the shiny cobbles and Ananais pulled up its head and patted its neck.

'Almost as tired as me – eh, boy?'

An old man, thickset and balding, stepped from a garden to the right. His face was flushed and angry.

'You!' he shouted, pointing at the rider. Ananais halted his mount and the man came forward, some twenty children bunching behind him.

'You want to talk to me, friend?'

'I am no friend to you, butcher! I just wanted you to see these children.'

'Well, I have seen them. They are a fine bunch.'

'Fine, are they? Their parents were fine, but now they're rotting in the Demon's Smile. And for what? So that you can play with a shiny sword!'

'Have you finished?'

'Not by a damn sight! What is going to happen to these children when the Joinings arrive? I was a soldier once and I know you can't hold those hell-beasts – they will come into this city and destroy every living thing. What will happen to these children then?'

Ananais touched his heels to his mount and the horse moved away.

'That's right!' yelled the man. 'Ride away from the problem. But remember their faces – you hear me?'

Ananais rode on through the winding streets until he reached the Council building. A young man came forward to take his horse and Ananais mounted the marble steps.

Rayvan sat alone in the hall staring – as she often did – at the faded mural. She had lost weight in the last few days. Once more she was wearing the chain-mail shirt and broad belt, her dark hair swept back and tied at her neck.

She smiled as she saw Ananais and gestured him to a chair beside her. 'Welcome, Darkmask,' she said. 'If you have bad news, hold on to it for a little while. I have enough of my own.'

'What happened?' asked Ananais.

She waved her hand and closed her eyes, unable to speak. Then she took a deep breath, exhaling slowly. 'Is the sun shining?' she asked.

'It is, lady.'

'Good! I like to see the sun on the mountains. it carries a promise of life. Have you eaten?'

'No.'

'Then let us go to the kitchen and find something. We will eat in the tower garden.'

They sat in the shade of a thick flowering shrub. Rayvan had picked up a black loaf and some cheese, but neither of them ate. The silence itself was comforting.

'I hear you were lucky to escape with your life,' said Rayvan at last. 'How is your side?'

'I heal fast, lady. The wound was not deep and the stitches will hold.'

'My son, Lucas – he died last night. we had to remove his leg . . . gangrene.'

'I'm so sorry,' said Ananais lamely.

'He was very brave. Now there is only Lake and Ravenna. Soon there will be no one. How did we come to this, Darkmask, tell me?'

'I don't know. We let a crazy man come to power.'

'Did we truly? It seems to me that a man has only as much power as we allow him. Can Ceska move mountains? Can he put out the stars? Can he tell rain to fall? He is only a man and if everyone disobeyed him he would fall. But they don't, do they? It is said that he has an army of forty thousand men. MEN. Drenai men! ready to march on other Drenai men. At least in the Nadir Wars we were sure of our enemy. Now there is no enemy. Only failed friends.'

'What can I say?' asked Ananais. 'I have no answers. You should have asked Tenaka. I am just a warrior. I remember a tutor who told me that all of the world's hunters had eyes that faced front: lions, hawks, wolves, men. And all the world's prey had eyes on either side to give them a greater chance of spotting the hunter. He said Man was no different from the tiger. We are nature's killers and we have great appetites for it. Even the heroes we remember show our love of war. Druss, the greatest killing machine of all time – it is his image you stare upon in the council chamber.'

'True enough,' said Rayvan. 'But there is a difference between Druss and Ceska. The legend fought always for others to be free.'

'Don't fool yourself, Rayvan. Druss fought because he loved to fight – it was what he did well. Study his history. He went east and battled for the tyrant Gorben; his army razed cities, villages, nations. Druss was part of it, and he would have offered no excuses. Neither should you.'

'Are you saying there never were true heroes?'

'I wouldn't know a hero if he bit my buttocks! Listen Rayvan, the beast is in all of us. We do our best in life, but often we are mean, or petty, or needlessly cruel. We don't mean to be, but that's the way we *are*. Most of the heroes we remember – we remember because they won. To win you must be ruthless. Single-minded. Druss was like that, which was why he had no friends – just admirers.'

'Can we win, Ananais?'

'No. But what we can do is to make Ceska suffer so greatly that someone else might win. We shall not live to see Tenaka return. Ceska is already on the march; but we must tie him down, give him losses – crack the aura of invincibility he has built around his Joinings.'

'But even the Dragon could not stand against the beasts.'

'The dragon was betrayed, caught on open ground. And many of them were old men. Fifteen years is a long time. They were not the real Dragon. We are the real Dragon – and by the Gods, we'll make them suffer!'

'Lake has devised some weapons he wants you to see.'

'Where is he?'

'In the old stables at the southern quarter. But take some rest first – you look exhausted.'

'I will.' He pushed himself to his feet, staggered slightly and then laughed. 'I'm getting old, Rayvan.' He moved away several paces, then returned and placed his huge right hand on her shoulder. 'I am not good at sharing, lady. But I'm sorry about Lucas. He was a good man – a credit to you.'

'Go and get some rest. The days are growing shorter and you will need your strength. I'm relying on you – we are all relying on you.'

After he had gone she wandered to the wall and gazed out over the mountains.

Death felt very close.

And she didn't care.

*

Tenaka Khan was sick with fury. His hands were tied tightly with rawhide thongs and his body was lashed to the trunk of a slender elm. Before him five men sat around a camp-fire searching through his saddlebags. His small cache of gold had been discovered and now lay next to the leader – a one-eyed rogue, thickset and surly. Tenaka blinked away the thin stream of blood that trickled into his right eye and closed his mind to the pain of his bruises.

He had been too preoccupied as he rode into the forest and a stone from a sling had hammered into his temple, toppling him from his horse semi-conscious. Even then, as the outlaws rushed him he had drawn his sword and killed one before they bore him down, hitting him with clubs and sticks. The last words he heard before darkness fell were, 'He killed my brother. Don't kill him – I want him alive.'

And here he was, less than four days out of Skoda, tied to a tree and moments away from a gruesome death. Frustration tore at him and he wrenched at the ropes, but they were expertly tied. His legs ached and his back burned.

The one-eyed outlaw stood up and walked to the tree, his face a mask of bitterness.

'You pig-rutting barbarian – you killed my brother!'

Tenaka said nothing.

'Well, you will pay for it. I shall cut you into tiny pieces, then cook your flesh on that fire and force you to eat it. How do you like that?'

Tenaka ignored him and the man's fist lashed out. Tenaka tensed the muscles of his stomach just as the blow struck, but the pain was terrible. As his head sagged the man hit him in the side of the face.

'Speak to me, Nadir dung!' hissed the outlaw.

Tenaka spat blood to the ground and licked his swollen lip.

'You will talk to me; before dawn I will have you singing a sweet song.'

'Cut out his eyes, Baldur!' said one of the outlaws.

'No. I want him to see everything.'

'Just one, then,' urged the man.

'Yes,' said Baldur. 'Maybe just one.' He drew his dagger and moved forward. 'How would you like that, Nadir? One of your eyes dangling from your cheek?'

A ghostly cry echoed into the night, high-pitched and eerie.

'What in the seven Hells was that?' said Baldur, spinning round. The others made the sign of the Protective Horn and reached for their weapons.

'It sounded close,' said one, a short man with a sandy beard.

'Cat, maybe. Sounded like it could be a cat,' said Baldur. 'Build up the fire.' Two men scurried forward, gathering up dry wood as Baldur turned back to Tenaka. 'You ever heard that sound before, Nadir?'

Tenaka nodded.

'Well, what is it?'

'Forest demon,' said Tenaka.

'Don't tell me that! I've lived in forests all my life.'

Tenaka shrugged.

'Whatever it is, I don't like it,' said Baldur. 'So you don't die so slow. I'll just open up your belly and you can bleed to death. Or maybe the forest demon will get you!'

His arm drew back . . .

A black feathered arrow appeared in his throat and for a moment he just stood there, as if stunned. Then he dropped his knife and slowly reached up to feel the shaft. His eyes widened, then his knees gave way and he pitched to the earth. A second arrow flashed across the clearing, taking the sandy-haired outlaw in the right eye. He fell screaming. The remaining three raced for the sanctuary of the forest, their weapons forgotten. For a while there was silence, then a little figure stepped from the trees with bow in hand.

She was wearing a tunic and troos in light brown leather, and a green burnoose covered her hair. A short, slender sword hung at her side.

'How are you, Tenaka?' asked Renya sweetly.

'I am certainly happy to see you,' he answered. 'Loose me.'

'Loose you?' she said, squatting by the fire. 'A big strong man like you. Come, now! Surely you don't need a woman's help?'

'Now is the wrong time for this conversation, Renya. Untie me.'

'And then do I come with you?'

'Of course,' he said, knowing he had no choice.

'You're sure I won't be a hindrance?'

Tenaka gritted his teeth, struggling to control his anger as Renya walked round the tree and slashed the rawhide with her shortsword. Tenaka stumbled and fell as the ropes gave way and she helped him to the fire.

'How did you find me?'

'It wasn't hard,' she hedged. 'How are you feeling?'

'Alive. Just! I shall have to be more careful once we cross the mountains.'

Renya's head came up, nostrils flaring. 'They're coming back,' she said.

'Damn! Get me my sword.' He glanced round but she had gone, vanished into the trees. He cursed and staggered to his feet, scooping up his sword from the far side of the fire. He felt in no condition to fight.

The terrible howling began again and his blood froze. Then Renya walked back into the clearing with a broad smile on her face.

'They're running so fast now, I don't think they will stop until they reach the sea,' she said. 'Why don't you get some sleep?'

'How do you do that?'

'It is a talent I have,' said Renya.

'I underestimated you, woman,' said Tenaka, stretching himself out beside the fire.

'The cry of men down the ages,' muttered Renya.

*

Night was falling once more when Renya and Tenaka sighted the deserted fortress of Dros Corteswain, nestling in the shadows of the Delnoch mountains. Built as a defence against Vagrian invasion during the days of Egel, the first Earl of Bronze, the fortress had been disused for more than forty years. The town that had sprung up around it was also deserted.

'Eerie isn't it?' said Renya as she guided her grey mare close in to Tenaka.

'Corteswain was always folly,' answered Tenaka, gazing up at the bleak battlements. 'Egel's only mistake. It is the one fortress in the Drenai that has never seen a battle.'

Their horses' hooves echoed in the night as they walked towards the main gates. The wood had been removed and the stone opening beckoned to them like a toothless mouth.

'Couldn't we camp in the open?' asked Renya.

'Too many forest demons,' said Tenaka, ducking as she swiped a blow at his head.

'Halt!' called a quavering voice and Tenaka's eyes narrowed.

In the open gateway stood an old man in rusty mailshirt. In his hands was a spear with a broken point. Tenaka reined in his mount.

'Give your name, rider!' called the old man.

257

'I am Bladedancer. This is my wife.'

'Are you friendly?'

'We are no threat to any man who does not threaten us.'

'Then you can come in,' said the old man. 'The Gan says it's all right.'

'Are you the Gan of Dros Corteswain?' asked Tenaka.

'No. This is the Gan,' said the old man, pointing to the space beside him. 'Can't you see?'

'Of course, forgive me! My compliments to your commanding officer.'

Tenaka rode in to the gateway and dismounted. The old man limped towards him. He looked as if he must be over eighty and his hair was wispy and thin, clinging to his yellow skull like mountain mist. His face was sunken and blue shadows spread beneath his watery eyes.

'Make no false move,' he warned. 'Look you to the battlements. There are archers covering your every step.' Tenaka glanced up – the ramparts were deserted, save for sleeping pigeons.

'Very efficient,' he said. 'Is there food here?'

'Oh yes. For those that's welcome.'

'Are we welcome?'

'The Gan says you look like a Nadir.'

'I am indeed, but I have the honour to serve in the army of the Drenai. I am Tenaka Khan of the Dragon. Will you introduce me to the Gan?'

'There are two Gans,' said the old man. 'This is Gan Orrin – he is the first Gan. Hogun is our scouting.'

Tenaka bowed deeply. 'I have heard of Gan Orrin. My compliments on your defence of Dros Delnoch.'

'The Gan says you are welcome and may join him

in his quarters. I am his aide. My name is Ciall –
Dun Ciall.'

The old man put down his broken spear and wandered away to the darkened keep. Tenaka loosened
the saddle-cinch and left his horse to wander in
search of grass. Renya followed suit and they set off
after Dun Ciall.

'He's mad!' said Renya. 'There's no one else
here.'

'He seems harmless enough. And he must have
food. I'd as soon save as many of our supplies as I
can. Listen – the men he is referring to are the
original Gans of Dros Delnoch when my ancestor
fought Ulric. Orrin and Hogun were the com-
manders before Rek became the Earl of Bronze.
Humour him – it will be a kindness.'

In the Gan's quarters Ciall had set out a table for
three. A jug of red wine was placed at the centre
and a stew was bubbling in a pot over the fire. With
trembling hands the old man filled their plates, said
a prayer to the Source and set to with a wooden
spoon. Tenaka tried the stew; it was bitter, but not
unpleasant.

'They're all dead,' said Ciall. 'I am not mad – I
know they're dead but they're here just the same.'

'If you see them, then they are here,' said Renya.

'Don't humour me, woman! I see them and they
tell me stories . . . Wonderful stories. They forgave
me. People didn't, but ghosts are better than people.
They know more. They know a man can't be strong
all the time. They know there are some times when
he can't help running away. They forgave me – said
I could be a soldier. They trust me to look after the
fortress.'

Ciall winced suddenly and gripped his side. Renya

looked down and saw blood flowing into the rust and dripping to the bench seat.

'You are hurt,' she said.

'It's nothing. I don't feel it. I am a good soldier now – they tell me that.'

'Remove your mailshirt,' said Tenaka softly.

'No. I am on duty.'

'Remove it, I say!' thundered Tenaka. 'Am I not a Gan? There will be no lack of discipline while I am here.'

'Yes sir,' said Ciall, fumbling with the ancient strap. Renya stepped forward to help him and slowly the mailshirt came away. The old man made no sound. His back was raw with the marks of a whip. Renya searched the drawers and cupboards, finding an old shirt. 'I'll get some water,' she said.

'Who did this to you, Ciall?' asked Tenaka.

'Riders . . . yesterday. They were looking for someone.' The old man's eyes glittered. 'They were looking for you, Nadir prince.'

'I expect they were.'

Renya returned carrying a copper bowl brimming with water. Gently she washed the old man's back, then tore the shirt into strips to place over the worst of the wounds.

'Why did they whip you?' Did they think you knew of my whereabouts?'

'No,' said Ciall sadly. 'I think they just enjoyed it. The ghosts could do nothing. But they were sorry for me – they said I bore it bravely.'

'Why do you stay here, Ciall?' asked Renya.

'I ran away, lady. When the Nadir were attacking I ran away. There was nowhere else to go.'

'How long have you been here?'

'A long, long time. Years probably. It's very nice

here, with lots of people to talk to. They forgave me, you see. And what I do here is important.'

'What is it you do?' asked Tenaka.

'I guard the stone of Egel. It is placed by the gate and it says that the Drenai empire will fall when Corteswain is manned no more. Egel knew things. He's been here, you know, but I wasn't allowed to see him when he came; I hadn't been here long then and the ghosts didn't trust me yet.'

'Go to sleep, Ciall,' said Tenaka. 'You need your rest.'

'First I must hide your horses,' said Ciall. 'The riders will be coming back.'

'I will do that,' promised Tenaka. 'Renya, help him into bed.'

'I can't sleep here – it's the Gan's bed.'

'Orrin says that you can – he's going to meet Hogun and will share his quarters tonight.'

'He's a good man,' said Ciall. 'I'm proud to serve under him. They're all good men – even though they're dead.'

'Rest, Ciall. We will talk in the morning.'

'Are you the Nadir prince who led the charge on the Ventrian raiders near Purdol?'

'I am.'

'Do you forgive me?'

'I forgive you,' said Tenaka Khan. 'Now sleep.'

*

Tenaka awoke to the sound of galloping hooves on the cold stone of the courtyard. Kicking aside his blanket, he woke Renya and together they crawled to the window. Below some twenty riders were grouped together; they wore the red capes of Delnoch and shining helms of bronze topped with black horse-hair plumes. The leader was a tall man with a trident beard and beside him was one of the outlaws who had captured Tenaka.

Ciall limped out into the courtyard, broken spear in hand.

'Halt!' he said. His arrival broke the tension and the riders began to laugh.

The leader raised his hand for silence and then leaned forward over his horse's neck.

'We seek two riders, old man. Are they here?'

'You are not welcome at the fortress. The Gan commands you to leave.'

'Did you not learn your lesson yesterday fool?'

'Must we force you to go?' countered Ciall.

The outlaw leaned over to whisper something and the leader nodded. He turned in the saddle. 'The tracker says that they are here. Take the old man and get him to talk.'

Two riders began to dismount. Ciall screamed a battle cry and ran forward; the officer was still half turned when the broken spear rammed into his side. He screamed and half-fell. Ciall dragged the spear loose and hacked at him once more, but a rider to the left dipped his lance and spurred his mount forward and Ciall was lifted from his feet as the iron tip plunged into him. The lance snapped and the old man fell to the stones.

The officer hauled himself upright in the saddle. 'Get me away from here; I'm bleeding to death!' he said.

'What about the riders?' asked the tracker.

'Damn them! We have men spread out from here to Delnoch and they can't escape. Get me away from here!' The tracker took the officer's reins and the troop cantered back through the gates. Tenaka raced out to the courtyard, kneeling beside the mortally wounded Ciall.

'You did well, Dun Ciall,' he said, lifting the man's head.

Ciall smiled. 'They've done it now,' he said. 'The stone.'

'You will still be here. With the Gan and the rest.'

'Yes. The Gan has a message for you, but I don't understand it.'

'What does he say?'

'He says to seek the King Beyond the Gate. You understand?'

'Yes I do.'

'I had a wife once . . .' whispered Ciall. And died.

Tenaka closed the old man's eyes; then lifted the frail body and carried it to the shade of the gate tower, laying it to rest beneath the stone of Egel. He placed the broken spear in the dead man's hand.

'Last night,' he said, 'he prayed to the Source. I don't know enough to believe in any god, but if you are there then I pray you will take his soul into your service. He was not an evil man.'

Renya was waiting in the courtyard when he returned.

'Poor man,' she said. He took her in his arms and kissed her brow.

'Time to go,' he told her.

'You heard what they said – there are riders everywhere.'

'First they must see us. Secondly they must catch us. We are only an hour's ride from the mountains, and where I go they will not follow.'

Throughout the long morning they rode, hugging the tree-line and moving carefully out on to open ground, avoiding the sky-lines. Twice they saw riders in the distance. By midday they had reached the base of the Delnoch peaks and Tenaka led them up into the high country. By dusk the horses were exhausted and the riders dismounted, seeking a place to camp.

'Are you sure we can cross here?' asked Renya, wrapping her cloak tightly about her.

'Yes. But we may not be able to take the horses.'

'It's cold.'

'It will get colder. We have maybe another three thousand feet to climb yet.'

Throughout the night they huddled together beneath their blankets. Tenaka slept fitfully. The task he had set himself was awesome. Why should the Nadir follow him? They hated him more than the Drenai did. The two-worlds warrior! He opened his violet eyes and watched the stars, waiting for the dawn.

It arrived in garish splendour, bathing the sky in crimson – a giant wound that seeped from the east. After a hurried breakfast they set off once more, moving ever higher into the peaks.

Three times during the morning they dismounted to rest the horses, leading them on over the patchy snow. Far below them Renya glimpsed the red cloaks of the Delnoch riders.

'They've found us!' she shouted.

Tenaka turned. 'They're too far back. Don't worry about them.'

An hour before dusk they breasted a rise. Before them the ground dropped away alarmingly. To the left a narrow trail hugged a sheer wall of icy rock; nowhere was the trail wider than six feet.

'We're not going to cross that?' asked Renya.

'Yes.'

Tenaka touched his heels to his mount and moved out. Almost at once the horse slipped, then righted itself. Tenaka kept up its head and began talking to the beast in a low soothing voice. His left leg was touching the rock wall, his right over the awesome drop; he did not dare swing his weight to see if Renya was following. The horse moved on slowly, its ears flat against its skull and its eyes wide in fear. Unlike the Nadir or Sathuli ponies, it had not been bred for mountain work.

The trail wound round the mountains, widening in some places and narrowing sickeningly in others, until at last they came to a slanting sheet of ice across their path. Tenaka had just enough room to slide from the saddle and he moved forward slowly, kneeling to examine the ice. The surface was powdery with fresh-fallen snow, but beneath it was glossy and sheer.

'Can we go back?' called Renya.

'No, there is nowhere to turn the horses. And the Delnoch riders will have reached the trail. We must go on.'

'Across that?'

'We must lead the horses,' said Tenaka. 'But if it starts to go, don't hold on. You understand?'

'This is stupid,' she said, staring down at the rocks hundreds of feet below.

'I couldn't agree more,' he answered with a wry grimace. 'Keep to the cliff face and don't curl the reins around your hand – hold them loosely. Ready?'

Tenaka stepped out on to the sloping ice, placing his foot carefully on the powdery snow.

He tugged on the reins, but the horse refused to budge; its eyes were wide with fear and it was close to panic. Tenaka stepped back, curling his arm over the beast's neck and whispering in its ear.

'There is no problem for you, noble heart,' he whispered. 'You have courage in your soul. It is merely a difficult path. I will be here with you.' For some minutes he spoke thus, patting and stroking the sleek neck. 'Trust me, great one. Walk with me for a little while.'

He stepped out on to the slope and pulled the reins and the horse moved forward. Slowly, and with great care, they left the safety of the trail.

Renya's horse slipped, but recovered its footing. Tenaka heard the commotion but could not look back. Solid rock was only inches away, but as Tenaka stepped on to it his horse slithered suddenly, whinnying in terror. Tenaka grabbed the reins tightly with his right hand, his left snaking out to the cliff face and hooking round a jutting edge of rock.

As the horse slid back towards the drop, Tenaka felt the muscles across his back tighten and tear. It seemed his arms were being torn from their sockets. He wanted to let go of the reins, but could not; instinctively he had curled the leather round his wrist and if the horse fell, he would be drawn with it.

As suddenly as it had lost its footing the beast found a solid section of rock, and with Tenaka's help struggled back to the trail. Tenaka sagged against the cliff face. The horse nuzzled him and he patted it. His wrist was bleeding where the leather had burned through the skin.

'Stupid!' said Renya, leading her horse to the safety of the trail.

'I cannot deny it,' he said, 'but we made it. From here on the trail widens and there are few natural dangers now. And I do not think the Drenai will follow us over this path.'

'I think you were born lucky, Tenaka Khan. But don't use up all your luck before we reach the Nadir.'

They made camp in a shallow cave and fed the horses before lighting a fire with brushwood they had strapped to their saddles. Tenaka stripped off his leather jerkin and lay down on a blanket by the fire while Renya massaged his bruised back. The struggle to keep the horse from falling had taken its toll and the Nadir prince could hardly move his right arm. Renya gently probed the shoulder-blade and the swollen muscles around it.

'You are a mess,' she said. 'Your body is a patchwork of bruises.'

'You should feel them from this side.'

'You are getting too old for this,' she said mischievously.

'A man is as old as he feels, woman!' he snapped.

'And how old do you feel?'

'About ninety,' he admitted. She covered him with a blanket and sat staring out at the night. It was peaceful here, away from war and the talk of war. Truthfully she did not care about overthrowing the Ceska – she did care about being with Tenaka Khan. Men were so stupid; they didn't understand the reality of life at all.

Love was what mattered. Love of one for one. The touching of hands, the touching of hearts. The warmth of belonging, the joy of sharing. There would always be tyrants. Man seemed incapable of existing without them. For without tyrants there would be no heroes. And Man could not live without heroes.

Renya wrapped herself in her cloak and added the last of the wood to the fire. Tenaka lay asleep, his head resting on his saddle.

'Where would you be without Ceska, my love?' she asked him, knowing he could not hear her. 'I think you need him more than you need me.'

His violet eyes opened and he smiled sleepily.

'Not true,' he said. Then his eyes closed once more.

'Liar,' she whispered, curling up beside him.

16

Scaler, Belder and Pagan lay on their bellies overlooking the Drenai camp. There were twenty soldiers sitting around five camp-fires. The prisoners sat back-to-back at the centre of the camp and sentries patrolled near them.

'Are you sure this is necessary?' asked Belder.

'It is,' Scaler told him. 'If we rescue two Sathuli warriors, it will give us a great advantage in seeking aid from the tribesmen.'

'They look too well-guarded to me,' muttered the older man.

'I agree,' said Pagan. 'There is one guard within ten paces of the prisoners. Two others patrol the edge of the trees and a fourth has positioned himself in the forest.'

'Could you find him?'

Pagan grinned. 'Of course. But what of the other three?'

'Find the one in the forest and bring me his armour,' said Scaler.

Pagan slipped away and Belder slithered across to lie beside Scaler. 'You're not going down there?'

'Of course. It's a deception – that's something I am good at.'

'You won't be able to pull it off. We shall be taken.'

'Please, Belder, no morale-boosting speeches – you will make me conceited.'

'Well, I'm not going down there.'

'I don't recall asking you.'

It was almost half an hour before Pagan returned. He was carrying the sentry's clothes wrapped in the man's red cloak.

'I hid the body as best I could,' he said. 'How soon will they change the guards?'

'An hour – maybe a little less,' said Belder. 'There's not enough time.'

Scaler opened the bundle, examined the contents and then buckled on the breastplate. It was a poor fit but better too large than too small, he thought.

'How do I look? he asked, placing the plumed helm upon his head.

'Ridiculous,' said Belder. 'You won't fool them for a minute.'

'Old man,' hissed Pagan, 'you are a pain in the ears! We have only been together three days and already I am sick of you. Now close your mouth.'

Belder was about to whisper a cutting reply, but the look in the black man's eyes stopped him dead. The man was ready to kill him! His blood froze and he turned away.

'What is your plan?' asked Pagan.

'There are three guards, but only one near the prisoners. I intend to relieve him.'

'And the other two?'

'That's as far as I have worked it out.'

'It is a beginning,' said Pagan. 'If the first part works, and the man takes to his blankets, move across to the other two. Keep your knife handy and make your move when I make mine.'

Scaler licked his lips. Keep your knife handy? He wasn't sure he would have the nerve to plunge the blade into someone's body.

Together the two men crept through the undergrowth towards the camp. The moon was bright, but the occasional cloud masked it, plunging the clearing into darkness. The fires had burned low and the warriors were sleeping soundly.

Pagan put his mouth close to Scaler's ear and whispered: 'It's about ten paces to the first sleeping soldier. The next time a cloud passes the moon, move forward and lie down. When the clouds clear, sit up and stretch. Make sure the sentry sees you.' Scaler nodded.

Minutes passed in silent tension until at last darkness fell once more. Immediately Scaler was up and moving, hitting the ground just as the moon shone clear again.

He sat up and stretched his arms wide, waving to the sentry. Then he stood, looked around and gathered up a lance from beside a sleeping warrior. Taking a deep breath he walked across the clearing, yawning.

'Couldn't sleep,' he told the man. 'Ground is damp.'

'You should try standing here for a while,' grumbled the sentry.

'Why not?' offered Scaler. 'Go on – get some sleep. I'll take the watch.'

'Mighty large of you,' said the man. 'I'm due to be relieved soon.'

'Your choice,' said Scaler, yawning once more.

'I haven't seen you before,' said the man. 'Who are you with?'

Scaler grinned. 'Picture a man with the face of a pig with warts, and the brain of a retarded pigeon.'

'Dun Gideus,' said the man. 'Bad luck!'

'I've known worse,' commented Scaler.

'I've not,' said the man. 'I think there's a special place where they breed the fools. I mean – why

270

attack the Sathuli? As if there are not enough pox-ridden problems in the Skoda. Baffles me!'

'Me too,' said Scaler. 'Still, as long as the pay comes through . . .'

'You had yours then? I've been waiting four months,' said the man, outraged.

'It was a joke,' said Scaler. 'Of course I haven't!'

'Don't joke about that, man. There's enough trouble brewing as it is.'

A second sentry joined them. 'Cal, is that the relief?'

'No, he just couldn't sleep.'

'Well, I'm going to wake them up. I've had enough of standing around,' said the second soldier.

'Don't be a fool,' advised the first. 'You wake up Gideus and we'll be for a flogging!'

'Why don't you go off and get some rest?' offered Scaler. 'I can stand watch – I'm wide awake.'

'Damn it, I think I will,' said the first man. 'I'm dead on my feet. Thanks, friend,' he said, clapping Scaler on the shoulder before wandering away to lie down with the others.

'If you want to put your head down in the forest, I'll wake you when I see the relief getting ready,' suggested Scaler.

'No, thanks anyway. The last time a watchman was found asleep, Gideus had him hanged. Bastard! I won't take that risk.'

'Whatever you like,' said Scaler indifferently, his heart hammering.

'Bastards have cancelled leave again,' said the sentry. 'I haven't seen my wife and youngsters in four months.' Scaler eased his knife into his hand. 'Farm's not doing too well. Bastard taxes! Still, at least I'm alive, I suppose.'

'Yes, that's something,' agreed Scaler.

'Life's a pig, isn't it? Any time now they're going to send us into the Skoda, killing a few more of our own. Life's a pig and no mistake!'

'Yes.' Holding the knife behind his back, Scaler adjusted his grip, ready to hammer the blade into the man's throat.

Suddenly the man swore. 'I will take you up on that offer,' he said. 'This is the third night they've put me on watch. But promise you'll wake me?'

'I promise,' said Scaler, relief washing over him.

But then Pagan moved from the shadow, whipping his knife across the other sentry's throat. Scaler reacted instantly – his own blade slashing upwards, entering the man's neck under the jaw-line and plunging on into the brain. He sank without a sound, but Scaler caught the look in his eyes as he died and looked away.

Pagan ran across to him. 'Good work. Let's free the prisoners and get away from here.'

'He was a good man,' whispered Scaler.

Pagan gripped him by the shoulders. 'There are a lot of good men dead in Skoda. Get a hold . . . Let's move.'

The two prisoners had watched the killings in silence. Both wore the robes of Sathuli tribesmen and had their faces part hidden by flowing burnooses. Pagan moved to them, his knife slashing through their bonds; Scaler joined them, kneeling by the first warrior as the man pulled the burnoose sash from his face and took a deep breath. His face was strong and dark, a curved nose above a full black beard; his eyes were deep-set and seemingly black in the moonlight.

'Why?' he said.

'We'll talk later,' said Scaler. 'Our horses are over there. Move quietly.'

The two Sathuli followed as they moved into the darkness of the forest. Minutes later they found Belder and the mounts.

'Now tell me why,' repeated the Sathuli.

'I want you to take me to your camp. I need to speak to the Sathuli.'

'You have nothing to say to which we would listen.'

'You cannot know that,' said Scaler.

'I know that you are Drenai and that is enough.'

'You know nothing,' said Scaler, lifting the helm from his head and hurling it into the undergrowth. 'But I will not argue with you now. Get on a horse and take me to your people.'

'Why should I?'

'Because of who I am. You owe me a debt.'

'I owe you nothing. I did not ask to be freed.'

'Not that debt. Listen to me, child of man! I have returned from the Mountains of the Dead, across the mists of the centuries. Look in my eyes. Can you see the horrors of Sheol? I dined there with Joachim, the greatest of Sathuli princes. You will take me into the mountains and let your leader decide. By the soul of Joachim, you owe me that much!'

'It is easy to speak of the great Joachim,' said the man uneasily, 'since he has been dead more than one hundred years.'

'He is not dead,' said Scaler. 'His spirit lives and it is sickened by Sathuli cowardice. He asked me to give you a chance to redeem yourselves – but it is up to you.'

'And who do you say you are?'

'You will find my likeness in your burial chambers, standing beside Joachim. Look at my face, man, and tell me who I am.'

The Sathuli licked his lips, uncertain and yet filled with superstitious fear.

'You are the Earl of Bronze?'

'I am Regnak, the Earl of Bronze. *Now* take me into the mountains!'

They rode through the night, cutting left into the Delnoch range and up through many passes, winding into the heart of the mountains. Four times they were intercepted by Sathuli scouts, but always they were allowed on. At last, as the morning sun reached the heights of midday, they rode into the inner city – a thousand white stone buildings filling the bowl of a hidden valley. Only one building stood higher than a single storey and this was the palace of Sathuli.

Scaler had never been here. Few Drenai had. Children gathered to watch them pass and as they approached the palace some fifty white-robed warriors carrying curved tulwars joined them, lining up on either side. At the palace gates a man waited, arms folded across his chest. He was tall and broad-shouldered and his face was proud.

Scaler halted his horse before the gates and waited. The man unfolded his arms and walked forward, dark brown eyes fixed firmly on Scaler's.

'You say you are a dead man?' asked the Sathuli. Scaler waited, saying nothing. 'If that is so, you will not mind if I pass my sword through your body?'

'I can die like any man,' said Scaler. 'I did it once before. But you will not kill me, so let us stop playing these games. Obey your own laws of hospitality and offer us food.'

'You play your part well, Earl of Bronze. Dismount and follow me.'

He led them to the west wing of the palace and left them to bathe in a huge marble bath, attended by male servants who sprinkled perfumes into the water. Belder said nothing.

'We cannot tarry here too long, Lord Earl,' said Pagan. 'How much time will you give them?'

'I have not decided yet.'

Pagan eased back his giant frame into the warm water, ducking his head below the surface. Scaler summoned a servant and asked for soap. The man bowed and backed away, returning with a crystal jar. Scaler poured the contents on his head and washed his hair; then he called for a razor and a glass and shaved his chin. He was tired, but he felt more human for the bath. As he mounted the marble steps, a servant ran forward with a towelling robe which he placed over Scaler's shoulders. Then he led him to a bedchamber, where Scaler found his clothes had been brushed clean. Taking a fresh shirt from his saddlebag, he dressed swiftly, combing his hair and placing his headband carefully over his brow. Then on impulse he removed the leather band and searched his saddlebag to find the silver circlet with the opal centrepiece. He settled it into place and another servant brought him a mirror. He thanked the man, noting with satisfaction the awe in the tribesman's eyes.

Lifting the mirror, he gazed at himself.

Could he pass himself off as Rek, the Warrior Earl?

Pagan had given him the idea when he said that men were always willing to believe that other men were stronger, faster, more capable than themselves. It was all a matter of portrayal. He had said that Scaler could appear to be a prince, an assassin, a general.

Then why not a dead hero?

After all, who could prove otherwise?

Scaler left the room; a tribesman carrying a spear bowed and requested him to follow. The man led him to a wide chamber in which sat the young man from the gates, the two Sathuli he had rescued and an old man in robes of faded brown.

'Welcome,' said the Sathuli leader. 'I have someone here who is anxious to meet you.' He pointed to the old man. 'This is Raffir, a holy man. He is of the line of Joachim Sathuli, and a great student of history. He has many questions concerning the siege of Dros Delnoch.'

'I will be happy to answer his questions.'

'I am sure you will. He also has another talent we find of use – he speaks with the spirits of the dead. Tonight he will enter into a trance and you will be delighted, I am sure, to attend.'

'Of course.'

'For myself,' said the Sathuli, 'I am looking forward to it. I have listened to Raffir's spirit voice many times and often questioned him. But to have the privilege of bringing together such friends . . . well, I feel great pride.'

'Speak plainly, Sathuli!' said Scaler. 'I am in no mood for children's games.'

'A thousand apologies, noble guest. I was merely trying to tell you that Raffir's spirit guide is none other than your friend, the great Joachim. I shall be fascinated to listen to your conversation.'

*

'Stop panicking!' said Pagan as Scaler paced the room. The servants had been dismissed and Belder, dismayed at the news, was strolling in the rose garden below.

'There is a time for panic,' said Scaler, 'when all else fails. Well, it has – so I'm panicking.'

'Are you sure the old man is genuine?'

'What difference does it make? If he is a fake, he will have been schooled by the prince to deny me. If he is genuine, the spirit of Joachim will deny me. There is no way round it!'

'You could denounce the old man as a fake,' offered Pagan, without conviction.

'Denounce their holy man in their own temple? I don't think so. It stretches the laws of hospitality to breaking point.'

'I hate to sound like Belder, but this was your idea. You really should have thought it through.'

'I hate you sounding like Belder.'

'Will you stop that pacing? Here, have some fruit.' Pagan tossed an apple across the room but Scaler dropped it.

The door opened and Belder entered. 'It's a real mess and no mistake,' he said glumly.

Scaler sank into a wide leather chair. 'It should be quite a night.'

'Are we allowed to go armed?' asked Pagan.

'If you like,' said Belder, 'though I cannot see even you fighting your way through a thousand Sathuli!'

'I don't want to die without a weapon in my hand.'

'Bravely spoken!' said Scaler. 'I will take this apple. I don't want to die without a piece of fruit in my hand. Will you put a stop to this talk of dying? It's extremely unsettling!'

The conversation struggled on pointlessly until a servant tapped on the door, entered and requested them to follow him. Scaler asked the man to wait while he moved to the full-length mirror on the far wall and gazed at his reflection; he was surprised to find himself smiling. He swung his cloak over his shoulder dramatically and adjusted the opal headband on his brow.

'Stay with me, Rek,' he said. 'I shall need all the help there is.'

The trio followed the servant through the palace until they reached the porch to the temple, where the man bowed and backed away. Scaler walked on into the cool shadows and out into the temple proper. Seats on all sides were filled with silent tribesmen, while the prince and Raffir sat side by side on a raised dais. A third chair was placed at Raffir's right. Scaler drew himself upright and marched down the aisle, removing his cloak and settling it carefully over the back of his chair.

The prince stood and bowed to Scaler. There was, Scaler thought, a malevolent gleam in his dark eyes.

'I welcome our noble guest here this evening. No Drenai has ever stood in this temple. But this man claims to be the Nadir Bane, the living spirit of the Earl of Bronze, brother in blood to the great Joachim. Therefore it is fitting that he should meet Joachim again in this holy place.

'Peace be on your souls, brothers, and let your hearts open to the music of the Void. Let Raffir commune with the darkness . . .'

Scaler shivered as the vast congregation bowed their heads. Raffir leaned back in his seat; his eyes opened wide and then rolled back under the sockets. Scaler began to feel sick.

'I call upon you, spirit friend!' shouted Raffir, his voice high-pitched and quavering. 'Come to us from the holy place. Give us of your wisdom.'

The candles in the temple guttered suddenly, as if a breeze had sprung up in the midst of the building.

'Come to us, spirit friend! Lead us.'

Once more the candle-flames danced – and this time many went out. Scaler licked his lips; Raffir was no fake.

'Who calls Joachim Sathuli?' boomed a voice, deep and resonant. Scaler started in his seat, for the voice came from the scrawny throat of Raffir.

'Blood of your blood calls upon you, great Joachim,' said the prince. 'I have here a man who claims to be your friend.'

'Let him speak then,' said the spirit, 'for I have heard too often your whining voice.'

'Speak!' ordered the prince, turning on Scaler. 'You heard the command.'

'You do not command *me*, wretch!' snapped Scaler. 'I am Rek, the Earl of Bronze, and I lived in a day when the Sathuli were men. Joachim was a man – and my brother. Tell me, Joachim, how do you like these sons of your sons?'

'Rek? I cannot see. Is it you?'

'It is I, brother. Here among these shadows of you. Why could you not be here with me?'

'I cannot tell . . . So much time. Rek! Our first meeting. You remember your words?'

'I do. "And what is your life worth, Joachim?" And you answered, "A broken sword." '

'Yes, yes, I remember. But at the last, the words of importance. The words that brought me to Dros Delnoch.'

'I was riding towards death at the fortress and I told you so. Then I said, "Before me I have nothing but enemies and war. I would like to think I have left at least a few friends behind me." I asked you to take my hand as a friend.'

'Rek, it is you! My brother! How is it you enjoy the life of blood once more?'

'The world has not changed, Joachim. Still evil rises like pus in a boil. I fight a war without allies and with few friends. I came to the Sathuli, as I did in the past.'

'What do you need, my brother?'

'I need men.'

'The Sathuli will not follow you. Nor should they. I loved you, Rek, for you were a great man. But it would be an obscenity for a Drenai to lead the chosen tribe. You must be desperate even to ask. But in your great need I offer you the Cheiam to use as you will. Oh Rek, my brother, would that I could walk beside you once more, tulwar in hand! I can still see the Nadir breasting the last wall, hear their cries of hatred. We were men, were we not?'

'We were men,' said Scaler. 'Even with the wound in your side, you were mighty.'

'My people fare badly now, Rek. Sheep led by goats. Use the Cheiam well. And may the Lord of All Things bless you.'

Scaler swallowed hard. 'Has he blessed you, my friend?'

'I have what I deserve. Goodbye, my brother.'

A terrible sadness overcame Scaler and he sank to his knees, tears coursing his cheeks. He tried to stifle the sobs but they forced their way through as Pagan ran to him, pulling him to his feet.

'So much sorrow in his voice,' said Scaler. 'Take me away from here.'

'Wait!' ordered the prince. 'The ceremony is not yet over.'

But Pagan ignored him and half-carried the weeping Scaler from the temple. Not one Sathuli barred his path as the trio returned to their rooms. There Pagan helped Scaler to a wide satin-covered bed and fetched him water from a stone jug; it was cool and sweet.

'Have you ever heard such sadness?' Scaler asked him.

'No,' admitted Pagan. 'It made me value life. How

did you do it? By all the gods, it was a performance unparalleled.'

'It was merely another deception. And it made me sick! What skill is there in deceiving a tormented, blind spirit? Gods, Pagan, he's been dead for over a hundred years. He and Rek met very rarely after the battle – they were of two different cultures.'

'But you knew all the words . . .'

'The Earl's diaries. No more, no less. I am a student of history. They met when the Sathuli ambushed my ancestor and Rek took on Joachim in single combat. They fought for an age and then Joachim's sword snapped. But Rek spared him and it was the start of their friendship.'

'You have chosen a difficult part to play. You are no swordsman.'

'No, I don't need to be. The act is enough. I think I will sleep now. Gods, I'm tired . . . and so damned ashamed.'

'You have no reason to feel shame. But tell me, what are the Cheiam?'

'The sons of Joachim. It is a cult, I think; I'm not sure. Let me sleep now.'

'Rest well, Rek, you have earned it.'

'There is no need to use the name in private.'

'There is every reason – we must all live the part from now on. I don't know anything about your ancestor, but I think he would have been proud of you. It took iron nerve to go through that.'

But Scaler missed the compliment, for he had fallen asleep.

Pagan returned to the outer room.

'How is he?' asked Belder.

'He is all right. But a word of advice for you, old man: no more cutting remarks! From now on he is the Earl of Bronze and will be treated as such.'

'How little you know, black man!' snapped Belder. 'He is not playing a role, he *is* the Earl of Bronze. By right and by blood. He thinks he is playing a part. Well, let him. What you see now is the reality. It was always there – I knew it. That was what made me so bitter. Cutting remarks? I am proud of the boy – so proud I could sing!'

'Well, don't,' said Pagan, grinning. 'You have the voice of a sick hyena!'

*

Scaler was wakened by a rough hand clamping over his mouth. It was not a pleasant awakening. The moonlight made a silver beam through the open window and the breeze billowed the curtain of lace. But the man leaning over his bed was in silhouette.

'Do not make a sound,' warned a voice. 'You are in great danger!' He removed his hand and sat down on the bed.

Scaler sat up slowly. 'Danger?' he whispered.

'The prince has ordered your death.'

'Nice!'

'I am here to help you.'

'I am glad to hear it.'

'This is not jest, Lord Earl. I am Magir, leader of the Cheiam, and if you do not move you will find yourself in the Halls of the Dead once more.'

'Move where?'

'Out of the city. Tonight. We have a camp higher in the range where you will be safe.' A slight scratching noise came from beyond the window, like a rope rubbing on stone. 'Too late!' whispered Magir. 'They are here. Get your sword!'

Scaler scrambled across the bed, dragging his blade from its scabbard. A dark shadow leapt through the window but Magir intercepted it, his curved dagger flashing upwards. A terrible scream rent the silence of the night. As two more assassins clambered into the room, Scaler screamed at the top of his voice and leapt forward, swinging the sword. It hammered into flesh and the man fell without a sound. Scaler tripped over the body just as a dagger flashed over his head but rolled onto his back, thrusting his blade into the man's belly. With a grunt of pain he staggered back and pitched out of the window.

'Magnificent!' said Magir. 'Never have I seen the tumbler's roll so brilliantly executed. You could be of the Cheiam yourself.'

Scaler sat back against the wall, sword dropping from nerveless fingers.

Pagan crashed open the door. 'Are you all right, Rek?' he said. Scaler turned to see the giant black man filling the doorway like an ebony statue, while the door itself sagged on broken hinges.

'You could have merely opened it,' said Scaler. 'Gods, the drama around here is killing me!'

'Speaking of which,' said Pagan, 'I have just killed two men in my room. Belder is dead – they cut his throat.'

Scaler pushed himself to his feet. 'They killed *him*? Why?'

'You shamed the prince,' said Magir. 'He must kill you – he has no choice.'

'And what of the spirit of Joachim? What was the point of bringing him back?'

'I cannot answer that, Lord Earl. But you must leave now.'

'Leave? He killed my friend – probably the only friend I ever had. He was like a father to me. Get out and leave me alone – both of you!'

'Don't do anything foolish,' warned Pagan.

'Foolish: It's all foolish. Life is a farce – a stupid,

sickening farce played out by fools. Well, this is one fool who has had enough. So get out!'

Scaler dressed swiftly, buckling on his sword-belt and taking his blade in his hand. Moving to the window, he leaned out. A rope swung in the night breeze and Scaler took hold of it, leaping from the window and sliding hand-over-hand to the courtyard below.

Four guards watched him in silence as he landed lightly on the marble flagstones. He walked out into the centre of the courtyard and stared up at the windows of the prince's chamber.

'Prince of cowards, come forth!' he shouted. 'Prince of lies and deceit, show yourself. Joachim said you were a sheep. Come out!'

The sentries exchanged glances but did not move.

'I am alive, prince. The Earl of Bronze is alive! All your assassins are dead and you are about to join them. Come out – or I will shrivel your soul where you hide. *Come out!*'

The curtains of the window moved and there stood the prince, his face flushed and angry. He leaned on the carved stone sill and shouted to the sentries.

'Kill him!'

'Come and do it yourself, you jackal!' yelled Scaler. 'Joachim called me his friend and so I am. In your own temple you heard him, yet you send assassins to my room. You spineless pig! You defile your ancestor and break your own laws of hospitality. Offal! Get down here!'

'You heard me – kill him!' screamed the prince. The sentries moved forward, lances levelled.

Scaler lowered his sword, his bright blue eyes fixed on the leading warrior.

'I will not fight you,' he said. 'But what will you have me tell Joachim when next I meet him? And what will you tell him when you walk the road to Sheol?' The man hesitated as behind Scaler Pagan ran across the courtyard, two swords in his hands. Magir was beside him.

The sentries braced themselves for the charge.

'Leave him be!' yelled Magir. 'He is the Earl and his challenge is laid down.'

'Come down, prince of cowards,' shouted Scaler. 'Your time is come!'

The prince clambered over the sill and leapt the ten feet to the flagstones, his white robes flaring out in the breeze. Walking to a sentry he took the man's tulwar, testing it for balance.

'Now you will die,' said the prince. 'I know you are a liar. You are not the long-dead Earl – you are a deceiver.'

'Prove it!' snapped Scaler. 'Step forward. I am the greatest swordsman ever to walk the earth. I turned back the hordes of the Nadir. I broke the blade of Joachim Sathuli. Step forward and die!'

The prince licked his lips and stared into the blazing eyes. Sweat trickled down his cheeks and in that moment he knew he was doomed. Life was suddenly very precious and he was far too important a man to allow some demon from the deep to trick him into combat. His hand began to shake.

He felt the stares of his men upon him and glanced up to see the courtyard ringed with Sathuli warriors. And yet he was alone; not one of them would come to his aid. He had to attack, but to do so meant death. With a wild scream he threw himself forward, tulwar raised. Scaler buried his sword in the prince's heart, then dragged it clear and the body sagged to the flagstones.

Magir stepped to Scaler's side. 'Now you must

leave. They will allow you to pass from the mountains, then they will follow to avenge this killing.'

'That's of no importance to me,' said Scaler. 'I came here to win them. Without them we are lost anyway.'

'You have the Cheiam, my friend. We will follow you back into Hell itself.'

Scaler looked down at the dead prince. 'He didn't even try to fight – he just ran forward to die.'

'He was a dog and the son of a dog. I spit on him!' said Magir. 'He was not worthy of you, Lord Earl, though he was the greatest swordsman in all of Sathuli.'

'He *was*?' said Scaler, astonished.

'He was. But he knew you were a greater man and the knowledge destroyed him before your sword could do so.'

'The man was a fool. If he only . . .'

'Rek,' said Pagan, 'it is time to leave. I will fetch the horses.'

'No. I want to see Belder buried before we leave this place.'

'My men will see to it,' said Magir. 'But your friend speaks wisely and I will have horses brought to the courtyard. It is only an hour to our camp, where we can rest and speak of your plans.'

'Magir!'

'Yes, my Lord.'

'I thank you.'

'It was my duty, Lord Earl. I thought I would hate this duty, for the Cheiam bear no love for Drenai warriors. But you are a man.'

'Tell me, what are the Cheiam?'

'We are the Drinkers of Blood, the sons of Joachim. We worship only one god: Shalli, the spirit of Death.'

'How many of you are there?'

'One hundred only, Lord Earl. But judge us not by our number. Rather, watch the numbers of dead we leave behind us.'

17

The man was buried up to his neck, the dry earth packed tightly around him. Ants crawled on his face and the sun beat down on his shaven head. He heard the sound of approaching horses, but could not turn.

'A pox on you and all your family!' he shouted.

Then he heard someone dismount and a merciful shadow fell across him. Glancing up, he saw standing before him a tall figure in black leather tunic and riding boots; he could not see his face. A woman led the horses round to the front and the man squatted down.

'We are seeking the tents of the Wolves,' he said.

The buried man spat an ant from his mouth. 'Good for you!' he said. 'Why tell me? You think I have been left here as a signpost?'

'I was contemplating digging you out.'

'I shouldn't bother. The hills behind you are full of Pack-rats. They would not take kindly to your intrusion.'

'Pack-rats' was the name given to members of the Green Monkey tribe following a battle some two hundred years before, when they had been deprived of their ponies and forced to carry their possessions on their backs. The other tribes never forgot the humiliation, nor allowed the Monkeys to forget.

'How many are there?' asked Tenaka.

'Who knows? They all look alike to me.'

Tenaka held a leather canteen of water to the man's lips and he drank greedily.

'What tribe are you?' asked Tenaka.

'I'm glad you asked that after offering me water,' said the man. 'I am Subodai of the Spears.'

Tenaka nodded. The Spears were hated by the Wolfshead on the ample grounds that their warriors were equally as vicious and efficient as their own.

For the Nadir there was seldom respect for an enemy. Weaker foes were treated with contempt, stronger regarded with hatred. The Spears, though not exactly stronger, fell into the latter category.

'How did a Spear fall to the Pack-rats?' asked Tenaka.

'Luck,' answered Subodai, spitting more ants from his mouth. 'Pony broke a leg and then four of them jumped me.'

'Only four?'

'I have not been well!'

'I think I will dig you free.'

'Not a wise move, Wolfshead! I may be forced to kill you.'

'I am not concerned by any man who is captured by a mere four Pack-rats. Renya, dig him out.'

Tenaka moved back to sit down cross-legged on the ground, staring at the hills. There was no sign of movement, but he knew they were watching him. He stretched his injured back – over the last five days it had eased greatly.

Renya scraped away the hard-packed earth, freeing the man's arms which were bound behind him. Once free, he pushed her away and struggled until he had pulled himself clear. Without a word to Renya he walked to Tenaka and squatted down.

'I have decided not to kill you,' said Subodai.

'You have great wisdom for a Spear,' said Tenaka, without taking his gaze from the hills.

'This is true. I see your woman is a Drenai. Soft!'

'I like soft women.'

'There is something to be said for them,' agreed Subodai. 'Will you sell me a sword?'

'With what will you pay me?'

'I will give you a Pack-rat pony.'

'Your generosity is matched only by your confidence,' observed Tenaka.

'You are Bladedancer, the Drenai half-blood,' observed Subodia, removing his belted fur jacket and brushing more ants from his squat, powerful body.

Tenaka did not bother to reply; he was watching the dust swirl up in the hills as men took to their horses.

'More than four,' said Subodai. 'About that sword . . . ?'

'They are leaving,' said Tenaka. 'They will return in greater numbers.' Rising to his feet, he walked to his horse and vaulted to the saddle. 'Goodbye, Subodai!'

'Wait!' called the Nadir. 'The sword?'

'You have not paid me the pony.'

'I will – given time.'

'I have not time. What else can you offer?'

Subodai was trapped. Left here without a weapon, he would be dead within the hour. He contemplated leaping at Tenaka, but dismissed the idea – the violet eyes were disconcerting in their confidence.

'I have nothing else,' he said. 'But you have a thought, I can tell.'

'Be my bondsman for ten days and lead me to the Wolves,' suggested Tenaka.

Subodai hawked and spat. 'That sounds marginally more appealing than dying here. Ten days, you say?'

'Ten days.'

'With today counting as one?'

'Yes.'

'Then I agree.' Subodai raised his hand and Tenaka took it, hauling him into the saddle behind him. 'I'm glad my father is no longer alive to see this day,' muttered the Nadir.

As they cantered off to the north Subodai thought about his father. A strong man and a fine rider – but such a temper.

It was his temper that killed him. After a horse-race, which Subodai won, his father had accused him of loosening the saddle-cinch on his own mare. The argument had blown up into a full-scale fight with fists and knives.

Subodai still remembered the look of surprise on his father's face as his son's knife rammed home in his chest. A man should always know when to control his temper.

The Nadir twisted in the saddle, his black eyes resting on Renya. Now there was a good woman! Not good for the Steppes, maybe – but good for plenty else.

For nine days more he would serve Bladedancer. After that he would kill him and take his woman.

He turned his gaze to the mounts. They were fine beasts. He grinned suddenly as the full joy of life settled over him once more.

The woman he would take.

The horses he would keep.

For they would be worth riding more than once.

*

Lake was sweating heavily as he cranked the thick wooden handle, dragging the bow-arm and the twined leather back to the hook. A young man in a leather apron passed him a loosely tied bundle of fifty arrows, which Lake placed in the bowl of the device. Thirty feet down the room, two assistants lifted a thick wooden door into place against the far wall.

Ananais sat in a corner with his back against the cool grey stone wall of the old stable. The machine had so far taken more than ten minutes to load. He lifted his mask and scratched his chin. Ten minutes for fifty arrows! One archer could let fly twice that number in half the time. But Lake was trying hard and Ananais could see no reason to demoralise him.

'Ready?' Lake asked his assistants at the far end of the room. Both men nodded and hurried away behind large sacks of oats and grain.

Lake glanced at Ananais for approval and then tugged the release cord. The massive arm flashed forward and fifty arrows hammered into the oak door, some passing through and striking sparks from the wall beyond. Ananais strode forward, impressed by the killing power. The door was a mess, having given way at the centre where more than a third of the shafts had struck home.

'What do you think?' asked Lake anxiously.

'It needs to spread more,' said Ananais. 'If this had been loosed at a charging mass of Joinings, fully half the shafts would have hit only two beasts. But it needs to spread laterally – can you do that?'

'I think so. But do you like it?'

'Do you have any slingshot?'

'Yes.'

'Load that in the bowl.'

'It will ruin the cap,' protested Lake. 'It's designed to shoot arrows.'

Ananais put his hand on the young man's shoulder. 'It's designed to kill, Lake. Try the shot.'

An assistant brought a sack of shot and poured several hundred pebble-sized rounds of lead into the copper bowl. Ananais took over the cranking of the device and they hooked the leather into place within four minutes.

Then Ananais moved to one side, taking the release thong in his hand. 'Stand clear,' he ordered. 'And forget about the sacks. Get outside the door.' The assistants scurried to safety and Ananais tugged the release. The giant bow-arm leapt forward and the slingshot thundered into the oak door. The sound was deafening and the wood split with a groan, falling to the floor in several pieces. Ananais gazed down at the leather cap on the bow – it was twisted and torn.

'Better than arrows, young Lake,' he said as the young man ran to his machine, checking the cap and the leather drawstring.

'I will make a cap in brass,' he said, 'and increase the spread. We shall need two cranks, one on either side. And I'll have the slingshot filed to give points on four sides.'

'How soon can you have one ready?' asked Ananais.

'One? I already have three ready. The adjustments will take only a day and then we shall have four.'

'Good work, lad!'

'It's getting them up to the valleys that concerns me.'

'Don't worry about that – we don't want them in the first line of defence. Take them back into the mountains; Galand will tell you where to place them.'

'But they could help us to hold the line,' argued Lake, his voice rising. Ananais took him by the arm, leading him out from the stable, and into the clear night air.

'Understand this, lad: *nothing* will help us hold the first line. We don't have the men. There are too many passes and trails. If we wait too long we shall be cut off, surrounded. The weapons are good and we will use them – but further back.'

Lake's anger subsided, to be replaced by a dull, tired sense of resignation. He had been pushing himself hard for days without rest: seeking something, anything, that could turn the tide. But he was not a fool and secretly he had known.

'We cannot protect the city,' he said.

'Cities can be rebuilt,' answered Ananais.

'But many people will refuse to move. The majority, I wouldn't wonder.'

'Then they will die, Lake.'

The young man removed his leather work apron and sat back on a barrel top. He screwed the apron into a tight ball and dropped it at his feet. Ananais felt for him then, for Lake was staring down at his own crumpled dreams.

'Damn it, Lake, I wish there was something I could say to lift you. I know how you feel . . . I feel it myself. It offends a man's sense of natural justice when the enemy has all the advantages. I remember an old teacher of mine once saying that behind every dark cloud the sun was just waiting to boil you to death.'

Lake grinned. 'I had a teacher like that once. A strange old boy who lived in a hovel near the west hill. He said there were three kinds of people in life: winners, losers and fighters. Winners made him sick with their arrogance, losers made him sick with their whining and fighters made him sick with their stupidity.'

'In which category did he put himself?'

'He said he had tried all three and nothing suited him.'

'Well, at least he tried. That's all a man can do, Lake. And we shall try. We will hit them and hurt them. We will bog them down in a running war. Knuckle and skull, steel and fire. And with luck, when Tenaka gets back, he will mop them up with his Nadir riders.'

'We don't seem to be exactly overflowing with luck,' Lake pointed out.

'You make your own. I put no faith in gods, Lake. Never have. If they exist, they care very little – if at all – about ordinary mortals. I put my faith in me – and you know why? Because I have never lost! I've been speared, stabbed and poisoned. I've been dragged by a wild horse, gored by a bull and bitten by a bear. But I have never lost. I've even had my face ripped away by a Joining, but I'm still here. And winning is a habit.'

'You are a hard act to follow, Darkmask. I won a foot-race once, and was third in the Open Wrestling at the Games. Oh . . . and a bee stung me once when I was a child and I cried for days.'

'You'll do, Lake! Once I have taught you how to be a good liar! Now, let's get back in there and work on the weapons you have devised.'

*

From dawn to dusk for three days, Rayvan and scores of helpers toured the city preparing the people for evacuation into the depths of the mountains. The task was thankless. Many were those who refused to consider moving and some even scoffed at the threat Rayvan outlined. Why should Ceska attack the city, they asked? That's why it was built without walls – there was no need to sack it. Arguments developed and doors were slammed. Rayvan endured insults and humiliation, yet still she tramped the streets.

On the morning of the fourth day the refugees gathered in the meadows to the east of the city; their possessions were piled on carts – some drawn by mules, others by ponies or even oxen. The less fortunate carried their belongings on their backs in canvas bundles. In all there were fewer than two thousand people – twice that number had elected to stay.

Galand and Lake led them out on the long hard trek to the highlands, where already three hundred men were building crude shelters in hidden valleys.

Lake's weapons of war, covered in oiled leather, had been placed on six wagons which headed the column.

Rayvan, Decado and Ananais watched the refugees set out. Then Rayvan shook her head, cursed and marched back to the council chamber without another word. The two men followed her. Once inside, her anger burst into the open.

'What in the name of Chaos is going on in their heads?' she raged. 'Have they not seen enough of Ceska's terror? Some of those people have been friends of mine for years. They are solid, intelligent, reasoning people. Do they want to die?'

'It is not that easy, Rayvan,' said Decado softly. 'They are not used to the ways of evil and they cannot conceive why Ceska would want to butcher the city's population. It makes no sense to them. And you ask as if they have not seen enough of Ceska's terror. In short, they have not! They have seen men with their arms lopped off, but the spectators can ask: Did he deserve it? They have heard of starvation and plague in other areas, but Ceska has always had an answer for that. He slides the blame from himself with rare skill. And truly they do not *want* to know. For most men life is their home and their families, watching the children grow, hoping next year will be better than this.

'In southern Ventria an entire community lives on a volcanic island. Every ten years or so it spews ash, dust and burning rock, killing hundreds. Yet they stay, always convincing themselves that the worst is over.

'But do not torment yourself, Rayvan. You have done all that you could. More than could have been asked for.'

She sagged back in her seat and shook her head. 'I could have succeeded. About four thousand people are going to die down there. Horribly! And all because I started a war I could not win.'

'Nonsense!' said Ananais. 'Why are you doing this to yourself, woman? The war began because Ceska's men poured into the mountains and massacred innocent people. You merely defended your own. Where the Hell would we be if we just allowed such atrocities to occur? I don't like the situation; it smells worse than a ten-day-dead pig in summer, but it's not my doing. Nor is it yours. You want blame? Blame the people who voted him into power. Blame the soldiers who follow him still. Blame the Dragon for not putting him down when they could. Blame his mother for giving birth to him. Now, enough of this! Every man and woman down there had a choice, given to them freely. Their fate is in their hands. You are not responsible.'

'I don't want to argue with you, Darkmask. But somewhere along this dreadful line someone must claim responsibility. The war is not of my making, as you say. But I elected myself to lead these people and every one of them that dies will be on my head. I would have it no other way. Because I care. Can you understand that?'

'No,' said Ananais bluntly. 'But I accept it.'

'I understand it,' said Decado. 'But your care must now be for those people who have trusted you and moved to the mountains. What with refugees from outside Skoda, and the city folk, we will have over seven thousand people up there. There will be problems with food, sanitation, sickness. Lines of communication must be set up. Stores, supplies and medicines. That all takes organisation and manpower. And every man we lose to that side of the war is one fewer warrior standing against Ceska.'

'I shall be there to organise that,' said Rayvan. 'There are maybe twenty women I can call on.'

'With respect,' said Ananais, 'you will also need men. Penned up like that, tempers can flare and some people will become convinced they are getting less than their ration. Many of the men among the refugees are cowards – and often that makes them bullies. There will be thieves, and among so many women there will be men who seek to take advantage.'

Rayvan's green eyes blazed. 'All that I can handle, Darkmask. Believe it! No one will question my authority.'

Beneath his mask Ananais grinned. Rayvan's voice had an edge of thunder and her square chin jutted pugnaciously. She was probably right, he thought. It would be a brave man who went against her. And all the brave men would be facing a more formidable foe.

During the days that followed Ananais divided his time between the small army manning the outer mountain ring, and the setting-up of a passable fortress on the inner ring. Minor trails into the valleys were blocked and the main entrances – the valleys of Tarsk and Magadon – hastily walled with boulders. Throughout the long hours of daylight the mountain-hardened men of Skoda added to the fortifications, rolling huge boulders from the hills and wedging them into place across the mouths of the valleys. Slowly the walls increased in size. Pulleys and wooden towers were erected by skilled builders and larger rocks were lifted by ropes and swung into place, cemented by a mix of clay and rock-dust.

The main builder – and wall architect – was a Vagrian immigrant named Leppoe. He was tall, dark, balding and indefatigable. Men walked warily around him, for he had an unnerving habit of looking through a man, ignoring him totally as his mind wrestled with some problem of stress or structure. And then, with the problem solved, he would smile suddenly and become warm and friendly. Few workers could keep up with his pace and often he would work long into the night, planning refinements or taking over as foreman of a work party and pushing his men hard under the moonlight.

As the walls neared completion, Leppoe added yet another refinement. Planks were laid and cunningly fitted to create ramparts, while the outer walls were smeared with mortar and smoothed, making it more difficult for an enemy to scale them.

Leppoe had two of Lake's giant bows placed near the centre of each wall; these were tested for range and spread by Lake himself and the twelve men he had trained to handle them. Sacks of lead shot for slings were placed by the weapons, along with several thousand arrows.

'It all looks strong enough,' Thorn told Ananais. 'But Dros Delnoch it is not!'

Ananais strode along the ramparts of Madagon, gauging the possible lines of attack. The walls negated Ceska's cavalry, but the Joinings would have no trouble in scaling them. Leppoe had worked miracles getting them up to fifteen feet in height, but it was not enough. Lake's weapons would create havoc to within thirty feet of the walls, but nearer than that they would be useless.

Ananais sent Thorn to ride the two miles across the valley to Tarsk. Then he despatched two other men to run the same distance. It took Thorn less than five minutes to make the journey, while the runners took almost twelve.

The general's problem was a tough one. Ceska was likely to strike at both valleys simultaneously and if one was overrun, the second was doomed. Therefore a third force had to be held in check somewhere between the two, ready to move the instant a breach looked likely. But walls could be breached in seconds and they didn't have many minutes. Signal fires were useless, since the Skoda range loomed between the valley mouths.

However, Leppoe solved the problem by suggesting a triangular system of communication. By day, mirrors or lanterns could be used to send a message back into the valley, where a group of men would be constantly on the lookout. Once the message was received, the group would relay it back to the second valley in the same way. A force of five hundred men would camp between the valleys and once a signal was received, they would ride like the devil. The system was practised many times, both in daylight and in darkness, until Ananais was convinced it had reached its peak of efficiency. A call for help could be transmitted and a relief force arrive within four minutes. Ananais would have liked to halve the time, but he was content.

Valtaya had moved back into the mountains with Rayvan and taken control of the medical supplies. Ananais missed her terribly; he had a strange feeling of doom which he could not shake off. He was never a man to give a great deal of thought to death; now it plagued him. When Valtaya had said goodbye the previous night, he had felt more wretched than at any time in his life. Taking her in his arms, he had fought to say the words he felt, desperate to let her know the depth of his love for her.

'I . . . I will miss you.'

'It won't be for long,' she said, kissing his scarred cheek and averting her eyes from the ruined mouth.

'You . . . er . . . look after yourself.'

'And you.'

As he helped her to her horse, several other travellers cantered towards the hut and he scrambled to replace his mask. And then she was gone. He watched her until the night swallowed her.

'I love you,' he said at last, too late. He tore the mask from his face and bellowed at the top of his voice.

'I LOVE YOU!' The words echoed in the mountains as he sank to his knees and hammered the ground with his fist. 'Damn, damn, damn! I love you!'

18

Tenaka, Subodai and Renya had an hour's start on the tribesmen, but this was gradually whittled back for, despite the strength of the Drenai mounts, Tenaka's horse now carried double. At the top of a dusty hill Tenaka shaded his eyes with his hand and tried to count the riders giving chase, but it was not easy for a swirling dust-cloud rose up around them.

'I would say a dozen, no more,' said Tenaka at last.

Subodai shrugged. 'Could be a lot less,' he said.

Tenaka remounted, casting about for a likely ambush site. He led them up into the hills to a low outcropping of rock which jutted over the trail like an outstretched fist. Here the trail curved to the left. Tenaka stood up in the saddle and leapt to the rock. Startled, Subodai slid forward and took up the reins.

'Ride forward to that dark hill, then slowly circle until you come back here,' Tenaka told him.

'What are you going to do?' asked Renya.

'I'm going to get a pony for my bondsman,' said Tenaka, grinning.

'Come woman!' snapped Subodai and cantered off in the lead. Renya and Tenaka exchanged glances.

'I don't think I shall enjoy being the docile woman of the Steppes,' she whispered.

'I said as much,' he reminded her with a smile.

She nodded and heeled her horse after Subodai.

Tenaka lay flat on the rock, watching the horsemen approach; they were some eight minutes behind Subodai. At close range Tenaka studied the riders; there were nine of them, wearing the goatskin-hide jerkins of the Steppes rider and rounded leather helms fringed with fur. Their faces were flat and sallow, their eyes black as night and coldly cruel. Each carried a lance, and swords and knives were strapped to their belts. Tenaka watched them come, waiting for the back marker.

They thundered up the narrow trail, slowing as they came to the curve by the rock. As they passed Tenaka slid out, drawing up his legs under him; then, as the last rider cantered below him, he dropped like a stone to hammer his booted feet into the man's face. He catapulted from the saddle. Tenaka hit the ground, rolled, came upright and lunged for the pony's rein. The beast stood still, nostrils quivering with shock. Tenaka patted him gently and then led him to the fallen warrior. The man was dead and Tenaka stripped off his jerkin, pulling it over his own. Then he took the man's helm and lance and, vaulting to the saddle, set off after the others.

The trail wound on, veering left and right, and the riders became less bunched. Tenaka cantered close to the man in front, just before another bend.

'Hola!' he called. 'Wait!' The man drew back on the reins as his comrades moved out of sight.

'What is it?' enquired the rider. Tenaka drew up alongside him, pointing up in the air. As the man glanced up, so Tenaka's fist thudded into his neck and without a sound he fell from the saddle. Up ahead came the sound of triumphant yells. Tenaka cursed and heeled his mount into a gallop, rounding the bend to see Subodai and Renya facing the seven riders, swords in hand.

Tenaka hit their line like a thunderbolt, his lance

punching a rider from the saddle. Then his sword was out and a second man fell screaming.

Subodai bellowed a war-cry and kicked his mount forward; blocking a wild cut, he swept down his sword, cleaving his opponent's collar-bone. The man grunted, but he was game and attacked once more. Subodai ducked as the tribesman's sword slashed through the air, then gutted the man expertly.

Two of the riders now charged at Renya, determined to gain some spoils. However, they were met by a feral snarl as she leapt from the saddle at the first, bearing man and pony to the ground. Her dagger sliced his throat so fast that he felt no pain and could not understand his growing weakness. Renya came up quickly, letting forth the blood-curdling shriek that had terrified the outlaws back in Drenai. The ponies reared in terror and her nearest opponent dropped his lance and grabbed the reins with both hands. Renya leapt, hammering a fist to his temple; he flew from the saddle, struggling to rise, then slumped to the ground unconscious.

The remaining two tribesmen disengaged and raced from the battleground as Subodai cantered to Tenaka.

'Your woman . . .' he whispered, tapping his temple. 'She is crazy as a moon-dog!'

'I like them crazy,' said Tenaka.

'You move well, Bladedancer! You are more Nadir than Drenai, I think.'

'There are those who would not see that as a compliment.'

'Fools! I have no time for fools. How many of these horses do I keep?' asked the Nadir, scanning the six ponies.

'All of them,' said Tenaka.

'Why so generous?'

'It stops me having to kill you,' Tenaka told him. The words moved through Subodai like ice knives but he forced a grin and returned the cool stare of Tenaka's violet eyes. In them Subodai saw knowledge, and it frightened him. Tenaka knew of his plan to rob and kill him – as sure as goats grew horns, he knew.

Subodai shrugged. 'I would have waited until after my bond was completed,' he said.

'I know that. Come, let us ride.'

Subodai shuddered; the man was not human. He gazed at the ponies – still, human or not, he was growing rich in Tenaka's presence.

For four days they moved north, skirting villages and communities, but on the fifth day their food ran out and they rode into a village of tents nestling by a mountain river. The community was a small one, no more than forty men. Originally they had been of the Doublehair tribe far to the north-east, but a split had developed and now they were Notas – 'No Tribe,' and fair game for all. They greeted the travellers with care, not knowing if they were part of a larger group. Tenaka could see their minds working – the Nadir law of hospitality meant that no harm could come to visitors while they stayed in your camp. But once out on the Steppes . . .

'Are you far from your people?' asked the Notas leader, a burly warrior with a scarred face.

'I am never far from my people,' Tenaka answered him, accepting a bowl of raisins and some dried fruit.

'Your man is a Spear,' said the leader.

'We were pursued by Pack-rats,' answered Tenaka. 'We slew them and took their ponies. It is a sad thing for Nadir to kill Nadir.'

'But it is the way of the world,' commented the leader.

'Not in Ulric's day.'

'Ulric is long dead.'

'Some say he will rise again,' observed Tenaka.

'Men will always say that about kings of greatness. Ulric is forgotten meat and dusty bones.'

'Who leads the Wolves?' asked Tenaka.

'Are you Wolfshead then?'

'I am what I am. Who leads the Wolves?'

'You are Bladedancer.'

'Indeed I am.'

'Why have you come back to the Steppes?'

'Why does the salmon swim upstream?'

'To die,' said the leader, smiling for the first time.

'All things die,' observed Tenaka. 'Once the desert in which we sit was an ocean. Even the ocean died when the world fell. Who leads the Wolves?'

'Saddleskull is the Khan. So he says. But Knifespeaks has an army of eight thousand. The tribe has split.'

'So, now it is not only Nadir who kills Nadir, but Wolf who rends Wolf?'

'The way of the world,' said the leader once more.

'Which is the nearest?'

'Saddleskull. Two days north-east.'

'I will rest here with you tonight. Tomorrow I will go to him.'

'He will kill you, Bladedancer!'

'I am a hard man to kill. Tell that to your young men.'

'I hear you.' The leader rose to leave the tent but stopped at the flap. 'Have you come home to rule?'

'I have come home.'

'I am tired of being Notas,' said the man.

'My journey is perilous,' Tenaka told him. 'As you say, Saddleskull would desire my death. You have few men.'

'In the coming war we will be destroyed by one or other faction,' said the man. 'But you – you have the look of eagles about you. I will follow you, if you desire it.'

A sense of calm settled over Tenaka. An inner peace seemed to pulse from the very earth at his feet, from the distant blue mountains, to whisper in the long grass of the Steppes. He closed his eyes and opened his ears to the music of silence. Every nerve in his body seemed on edge as the land cried out to him.

Home!

After forty years Tenaka Khan had learned the meaning of the word.

His eyes opened. The leader stood very still, watching him; he had seen men in a state of trance many times, and always it brought a sense of awe, and a feeling of sadness that he could never experience this himself.

Tenaka smiled. 'Follow me,' he told the man, 'and I will give you the world.'

'Are we to be wolves?'

'No. We are the Nadir Rising. We are the Dragon.'

*

At dawn the forty men of the Notas, less the three outriding sentries, sat in two lines outside Tenaka's tent. Behind them were the children: eighteen boys and three girls. Lastly sat the women, fifty-two of them.

Subodai stood apart from the group, baffled by this new turn of events. There was no point to it. Who would wish to start a new tribe at the dawn of a civil war? And what could Tenaka possibly gain from this shoddy band of goat-breeders? It was all beyond the Spear warrior; he wandered into an empty tent and helped himself to some soft cheese and a loaf of gritty black bread.

What did it matter?

When the sun was high he would ask Tenaka to release him from his bond, take his six ponies and ride home. Four ponies would buy him a fine wife and he would relax for a while in the western hills. He scratched his chin, wondering what would happen to Tenaka Khan.

Subodai felt strangely uncomfortable at the thought of riding away. Few were the moments of original interest in the harsh world of the Steppes. Fight, love, breed, eat. There was a limit to the amount of excitement these four activities could generate. Subodai was thirty-four years old and he had left the Spears for a reason none of his peers could understand:

He was bored!

He moved out into the sunlight. Goats were milling at the edge of the camp-site near the pony picket line, and high above a sparrowhawk circled and dived.

Tenaka Khan stepped out into the sunlight and stood before the Notas – arms folded across his chest, face impassive.

The leader walked towards him, dropped to his knees, bent low and kissed Tenaka's feet. One by one every member of the Notas followed him.

Renya watched the scene from within the tent. The whole ceremony disturbed her, as did the subtle change she sensed in her lover.

The previous night, as they lay together under fur rugs, Tenaka had made love to her.It was then that the first tiny sparks of fear had flashed in her subconscious. The passion remained, the thrill of the touch and the breathless excitement. But Renya sensed a newness in Tenaka which she could not read. Somewhere inside him one gate had opened and another closed. Love had been locked away. But what had replaced it?

Now she gazed at the man she loved as the ceremony continued. She could not see his face, but she could see the faces of his new followers: they shone.

When the last of the women backed away, Tenaka Khan turned without a word and re-entered the tent. Then the sparks within Renya became a fire, for his face reflected what he had become. He was no longer the warrior of two worlds. His Drenai blood had been sucked from him by the Steppes and what was left was pure Nadir.

Renya looked away.

By midday the tribesmen had seen their women dismantle the tents and pack them on wagons. The goats were rounded up and the new tribe headed north-east. Subodai had not requested to be free of his bond and he rode beside Tenaka and the Notas leader, Gitasi.

That night they camped on the southern slopes of a range of wooded hills. Towards midnight as Gitasi and Tenaka talked by a camp-fire, the pounding of hooves sent tribesmen rolling from their blankets to grab at swords and bows. Tenaka remained where he was, seated cross-legged by the fire. He whispered something to Gitasi and the scarred leader ran to his men, calming them. The hoofbeats grew louder and more than a hundred warriors rode into the camp, bearing down on the fire. Tenaka ignored them, calmly chewing on a strip of dried meat.

The horsemen dragged on their reins. 'You are in the land of the Wolfshead,' said the lead warrior, sliding from the saddle. He wore a helm of bronze, rimmed with fur, and a lacquered black breastplate edged with gold.

Tenaka Khan looked up at him. The man was close to fifty years old and his massive arms were criss-crossed with scars. Tenaka gestured to a place by the fire.

'Welcome to my camp,' he said softly. 'Sit and eat.'

'I do not eat with Notas,' said the man. 'You are on Wolfshead land.'

'Sit down and eat,' said Tenaka, 'or I shall kill you where you stand.'

'Are you a madman?' asked the warrior, taking a firmer grip on the sword in his hand. Tenaka Khan ignored him and, furious, the man swung the sword. But Tenaka's leg shot out, hooking his feet from under him, and he fell with a crash as Tenaka rolled to his right with his knife flashing in his hand. The point rested gently on the warrior's throat.

An angry roar went up from the riders.

'Be silent among your betters!' bellowed Tenaka. 'Now, Ingis, will you sit and eat?'

Ingis blinked as the knife was withdrawn. He sat up and recovered his sword.

'Bladedancer?'

'Tell your men to dismount and relax,' said Tenaka. 'There will be no bloodshed tonight.'

'Why are you here, man? It is insane.'

'Where else should I be?'

Ingis shook his head and ordered his men to dismount, then turned back to Tenaka.

'Saddleskull will be confused. He will not know whether to kill you or make you a general.'

'Saddleskull was always confused,' said Tenaka. 'It surprises me that you follow him.'

Ingis shrugged. 'He is a warrior, at least. Then you have not come back to follow him?'

'No.'

'I will have to kill you, Bladedancer. You are too powerful a man to have for an enemy.'

'I have not come to serve Knifespeaks.'

'Then why?'

'You tell me, Ingis.'

The warrior looked into Tenaka's eyes. 'Now I know you are insane. How can you hope to rule? Saddleskull has eighty thousand warriors. Knifespeaks is weak, with only six thousand. How many do you have?'

'All that you see.'

'How many is that? Fifty? Sixty?'

'Forty.'

'And you think to take the tribe?'

'Do I look insane? You knew me, Ingis; you watched mc grow. Did I seem insane then?'

'No. You could have been . . .' Ingis cursed and spat into the fire. 'But you went away. Became a Lord of the Drenai.'

'Have the shamen met yet?' asked Tenaka.

'No. Asta Khan has called a council for tomorrow at dusk.'

'Where?'

'At the tomb of Ulric.'

'I shall be there.'

Ingis leaned in closer. 'You don't seem to understand,' he whispered. 'It is my duty to kill you.'

'Why?' asked Tenaka calmly.

'Why? Because I serve Saddleskull. Even sitting here talking to you is an act of betrayal.'

'As you pointed out, Ingis, my force is very small. You betray no one. But think on this: you are pledged to follow the Khan of Wolves, yet he is not chosen until tomorrow.'

'I will not play with words, Tenaka. I pledged my support to Saddleskull against Knifespeaks. I will not go back on it.'

'Nor should you,' said Tenaka. 'You would be less a man. But I also am against Knifespeaks, which makes us allies.'

'No, no, no! You are against them both, which makes us enemies.'

'I am a man with a dream, Ingis – the dream of Ulric. These men with me were once Doublehair. Now they are mine. The burly one by the far tent is a Spear. Now he is mine. These forty represent three tribes. United, the world is ours. I am an enemy to no one. Not yet.'

'You always had a good brain and a fine sword-arm. Had I known you were coming, I might have waited before pledging my force.'

'You will see tomorrow. For tonight – eat and rest.'

'I cannot eat with you,' said Ingis, rising. 'But I will not kill you. Not tonight.' He strode to his pony and climbed into the saddle. His men ran to their mounts and with a wave Ingis led them out into the darkness.

Subodai and Gitasi ran to the fire, where Tenaka Khan was quietly finishing his supper.

'Why?' asked Subodai. 'Why did they not kill us?'

Tenaka grinned, then yawned theatrically. 'I am tired. I will sleep now.'

Out in the valley beyond, Ingis was being asked the same question by his son, Sember.

'I cannot explain it,' said Ingis. 'You would not understand.'

'Make me understand! He is a half-blood with a

rag-tag following of Notas scum. And he did not even ask you to follow him.'

'Congratulations, Sember! Most of the time you cannot grasp the simplest subtlety, but on this occasion you surpass yourself.'

'What does that mean?'

'It is simple. You have stumbled on the very reasons why I did not kill him. Here is a man with no chance of success, faced by a warlord with twenty thousand warriors under his banner. Yet he did *not* ask for my help. Ask yourself why.'

'Because he is a fool.'

'There are times, Sember, when I could believe your mother had a secret lover. Looking at you makes me wonder if it was one of my goats.'

19

Tenaka waited in darkness and silence as the sounds of movement in the small camp ceased. Then he lifted the flap of his tent and watched the sentries. Their eyes were scanning the trees around the camp and they were not interested in what went on within. Tenaka slid from the tent, hugging the moon shadows from the twisted trees as he silently edged into the deeper darkness of the woods.

Walking cautiously, he made his way for several miles, as the ground dipped and rose towards the distant hills. He cleared the edge of the wood some three hours before dawn and slowly began to climb. Far below, and to the right, lay the marble-covered tomb of Ulric – and the armies of Knifespeaks and Saddleskull.

Civil war was inevitable and Tenaka had hoped to convince whoever was the Khan that it would be profitable to aid the Drenai rebels. Gold was a scarce commodity on the Steppes. Now things would have to be different.

He continued to climb until he saw a cliff face, pock-marked by caves. He had been here once before, many years ago when Jongir Khan had attended a shamen council. Then Tenaka had sat with Jongir's children and grandchildren outside the caves while the Khan journeyed into the darkness. It was said that hideous rites were performed in these ancient places, and that no man could enter uninvited. The caves were, the shamen promised, the very gates of Hell where demons lurked at every corner.

Tenaka reached the mouth of the largest cave, where he hesitated, calming his mind.

There is no other way, he told himself.

And entered.

The darkness was total. Tenaka stumbled. He pushed on, hands stretched out before him.

As the caves wound on – twisting and turning, splitting and rejoining – Tenaka quelled the panic rising in him. It was like being in a honeycomb. He could wander lost in this blind gloom until he died of hunger and thirst.

He moved on, feeling his way along a cold wall. Suddenly the wall ended, cutting away at right-angles to his hand. Tenaka walked on, hands outstretched. Cool air touched his face. He stopped and listened. He had the impression of space all around him, but more than that he felt the presence of people.

'I seek Asta Khan,' he said, his voice booming in the cavern.

Silence.

A shuffling sound came from left and right of him and he stood still, folding his arms across his chest. Hands touched him, scores of hands. He felt his sword being drawn from its scabbard, his knife from its sheath. Then the hands withdrew.

'Speak your name!' commanded a voice as dry and hostile as a desert wind.

'Tenaka Khan.'

'You have been gone from us for many years.'

'I have returned.'

'Obviously.'

'I did not leave willingly. I was sent from the Nadir.'

'For your own protection. You would have been slain.'

'Perhaps.'

'Why have you returned?'

'That is not a simple question to answer.'

'Then take your time.'

'I came to aid a friend. I came to gather an army.'

'A Drenai friend?'

'Yes.'

'And then?'

'Then the land spoke to me.'

'What were its words?'

'There were no words. It spoke in silence, heart to soul. It welcomed me as a son.'

'To come here unsummoned is death.'

'Who decides what is a summons?' asked Tenaka.

'I do.'

'Then you tell me, Asta Khan – was I summoned?'

Darkness fell away from Tenaka's eyes and he found himself in a great hall. Torches shone on every side. The walls were smooth, embedded with crystals of every hue, while stalactites hung like shining spears from the vast dome of the roof. The cavern was packed with people, shamen from every tribe.

Tenaka blinked as his eyes grew accustomed to the light. The torches had not sprung up instantly. They had been alight all the time – only he had been blind.

'Let me show you something, Tenaka,' said Asta Khan, leading him from the cavern. 'This is the path you took to reach me.'

Directly ahead was a yawning chasm, crossed by a slender stone bridge.

'You walked that bridge in blindness. And so, yes, you were summoned. Follow me!'

The ancient shaman took him back over the bridge to a small room close to the main cave entrance. There the two men sat on a goatskin rug.

'What would you have me do?' asked Asta Khan.

'Initiate the Shamen Quest.'

'Saddleskull has no need of the Quest. He outnumbers his enemy and can win it by battle alone.'

'Thousands of brothers will die.'

'That is the Nadir way, Tenaka.'

'The Shamen Quest would mean the deaths of only two,' said Tenaka.

'Speak plainly, young man! Without the Quest you have no chance to rule. With it your chances rise to one in three. Do you truly care about a civil war?'

'I do. I have the dream of Ulric. I want to build the nation.'

'And what of your Drenai friends?'

'They are still my friends.'

'I am no fool, Tenaka Khan. I have lived many, many years and I can read the hearts of men. Give me your hand and let me read your heart. But know this – if there is deceit in you, I shall kill you.'

Tenaka held out his hand and the old man took it.

For several minutes they remained thus, then Asta Khan released him.

'The power of the shamen is maintained in many ways. There is generally very little direct manipulation of tribal directions. You understand?'

'I do.'

'On this occasion I will grant your request. But when Saddleskull hears he will send his executioner. There will be a challenge – it is all he can do.'

'I understand.'

'Do you wish to know of him?'

'No. It is immaterial.'

'You are confident.'

'I am Tenaka Khan.'

*

The Valley of the Tomb stretched between two ranges of iron-grey mountains; these were known as the Ranks of Giants and Ulric himself had named this place as his burial ground. It amused the great warlord to think of these ageless sentries standing guard over his mortal remains. The tomb itself was built of sandstone, covered with marble. Forty thousand slaves had died building this monolith, shaped like the crown Ulric never wore. Six pointed towers ringed the white dome and giant runes were carved upon every surface, telling the world and all succeeding generations that here lay Ulric the Conqueror, the greatest Nadir warlord of them all.

And yet, typically, Ulric's humour came through even this corpse-white colossus. The only carving to show the Khan depicted him riding his pony and wearing the crown of kings. Set sixty feet above the ground and back beyond a curving gateway, the statue was meant to depict Ulric waiting beyond the walls of Dros Delnoch, his only defeat. On his head was the crown, placed there by Ventrian sculptors who did not realise that a man could command an army of millions without being a king. This was a subtle jest, but one which Ulric would have enjoyed.

To the east and west of the tomb camped the armies of the two enemy kinsmen: Shirrat Knifespeaks and Tsuboy Saddleskull. More than 150,000 men waited for the outcome of the Shamen Quest.

Tenaka led his people down into the valley. Ramrod-straight on his Drenai stallion he rode, and beside him Gitasi felt a surge of pride. He was Notas no longer – he was a man again.

Tenaka Khan rode to a point south of the tomb and dismounted. Word of his coming had spread to both camps and hundreds of warriors began to drift towards his camp-site.

The women of Gitasi busied themselves erecting the tents while the men attended to their ponies and settled themselves down around Tenaka Khan. He sat cross-legged on the ground, staring at the great tomb, his eyes distant and his mind closed to the drifters.

A shadow fell across him. He waited for long seconds, letting the insult build, then he smoothly rose to his feet. This moment had to come – it was the opening move in a none-too-subtle game.

'You are the half-blood?' asked the man. He was young, in his middle twenties, and tall for a Nadir. Tenaka Khan looked at him coolly, noting the balanced stance, the slim hips and the wide shoulders, the powerful arms and the depth of chest. The man was a swordsman and confidence blazed from him. He would be the executioner.

'And who would you be, child?' said Tenaka Khan.

'I am a true-born Nadir warrior, the son of a Nadir warrior. It galls me that a mongrel should stand before the tomb of Ulric.'

'Then move away and continue your yapping elsewhere,' said Tenaka Khan. The man smiled.

'Let us cease this nonsense,' he said smoothly. 'I am here to kill you. It is obvious. Let us begin.'

'You are very young to wish for death,' said Tenaka. 'And I am not old enough to refuse you. What is your name?'

'Purtsai. Why do you wish to know it?'

'If I have to kill a brother, I like to know his name. It means that someone will remember him. Draw your sword, child.'

The crowd drew back, forming a giant circle around the combatants. Purtsai drew a curved sabre and a dagger. Tenaka Khan drew his own shortsword, and deftly caught the knife Subodai tossed to him.

And so the duel began.

Purtsai was good, skilled beyond the vast majority of tribesmen. His footwork was extraordinary and he had a suppleness unseen among the squat, bulky warriors of the Nadir. His speed was dazzling and his nerve cool.

He was dead within two minutes.

Subodai swaggered forward and stood with hands on hips, staring down at the body. He kicked it savagely, then spat upon it. Then he grinned at the watching warriors and spat again. Tucking his toe under the body, he flipped the corpse on to its back.

'This was the best of you?' he asked the crowd. He shook his head in mock sorrow. 'Whatever will become of you?'

Tenaka Khan walked to his tent and ducked under the flap. Inside Ingis was waiting, seated cross-legged on a fur rug and drinking a goblet of Nyis, a spirit distilled from goats' milk. Tenaka seated himself opposite the warlord.

'That did not take you long,' said Ingis.

'He was young, with much to learn.'

Ingis nodded. 'I advised Saddleskull against sending him.'

'He had no choice.'

'No. So . . . you are here.'

'Did you doubt it?'

Ingis shook his head. He removed his bronze helm

and scratched at the skin beneath his thinning, iron-grey hair. 'The question is, Bladedancer, what am I to do about you?'

'Does it trouble you?'

'Yes.'

'Why?'

'Because I am trapped. I want to support you, for I believe you are the future. Yet I cannot, for I have sworn to uphold Saddleskull.'

'A thorny problem,' agreed Tenaka Khan, helping himself to a goblet of Nyis.

'What shall I do?' asked Ingis and Tenaka Khan stared at his strong honest face. He had only to ask and the man was his – he would break his oath to Saddleskull and pledge his warriors to Tenaka instead. Tenaka was tempted, but he resisted with ease. Ingis would not be the same man if he broke his oath for it would haunt him for the rest of his life.

'Tonight,' said Tenaka, 'the Shamen Quest begins. Those who stand for leadership will be tested and Asta Khan will name the Warlord. That is the man you are pledged to follow. Until that time you are bound to Saddleskull.'

'And what if he commands that I kill you?'

'Then you must kill me, Ingis.'

'We are all fools,' said the Nadir general bitterly. 'Honour? What does Saddleskull know of honour? I curse the day I swore to serve him!'

'Go now. Put these thoughts from your mind,' ordered Tenaka Khan. 'A man makes mistakes, but he lives by them. Foolish it may be, on occasion. But in the main it is the only way to live. We are what we say, only so long as our words are iron.'

Ingis rose and bowed. After he had gone Tenaka

refilled his goblet and leaned back on the thick cushions scattered round the rug.

'Come out, Renya!' he called. She stepped from the shadows of the sleeping section and sat beside him, taking his hand.

'I feared for you when the warrior made his challenge.'

'My time is not yet.'

'He would have answered the same,' she pointed out.

'Yes, but he was wrong.'

'And have you so changed? Are you now infallible?'

'I am home, Renya. I feel different. I cannot explain it, and I have not yet tried to rationalise it. But it is wonderful. Before I came here I was incomplete. Lonely. Here I am whole.'

'I see.'

'No, I do not think that you do. You think I criticise you; you hear me talking of loneliness and you wonder. Do not misunderstand me. I love you and you have been a source of constant joy. But my purpose was not clear, and therefore I was what the shamen called me as a child: the Prince of Shadows. I was a shadow in the world of stone reality. Now I am a shadow no longer. I have a purpose.'

'You want to be a king,' she said sadly.

'Yes.'

'You want to conquer the world.'

He did not answer.

'You have seen Ceska's terror and the folly of ambition. You have seen the horror that war brings. Now you will bring a greater horror than Ceska could ever dream of.'

'It does not have to be horror.'

'Do not fool yourself, Tenaka Khan. You have

merely to look beyond this tent. They are savages – they live to fight . . . to kill. I don't know why I'm talking like this. You are beyond my words. After all, I am just a woman.'

'You are my woman.'

'I was. Not any longer. You have another woman now. Her breasts are mountains, and her seed waits out there to spill across the world. What a hero you are, great Khan! Your friend is waiting for you. In the blindness of his loyalty, he expects to see you riding on a white horse at the head of your Nadir. Then the evil will fall and the Drenai will be free. Imagine his surprise when you rape his nation!'

'You have said enough, Renya. I will not betray Ananais. I will not invade the Drenai.'

'Not now, maybe. But one day you will have no choice. There won't be anywhere else.'

'I am not yet the Khan.'

'Do you believe in prayer, Tenaka?' she asked suddenly, tears in her eyes.

'Sometimes.'

'Then think on this: I pray that you lose tonight, even if it means your death.'

'If I lose, it will,' said Tenaka Khan.

But she had already moved away from him.

*

The ancient shaman squatted in the dust, staring intently into a brazier of coals on an iron stand. Around him sat the chieftains of the Nadir, the warlords, the masters of the Horde.

Away from the crowd, within a circle of stones, sat the three kinsmen: Tsuboy Saddleskull, Shirrat Knifespeaks and Tenaka Khan.

The warlords studied each other with rare interest. Saddleskull was a blocky, powerful figure, with a braided top-knot and a wispy forked beard. He was stripped to the waist and his body gleamed with oil.

Knifespeaks was slimmer and his long hair, streaked with silver, was tied at the nape of the neck. His face was oblong accentuated by the drooping moustache, and mournful. But his eyes were sharp and alert.

Tenaka Khan sat quietly with them, staring up at the tomb which was shining silver in the moonlight. Saddleskull cracked his fingers noisily and tensed the muscles of his back. He was nervous. He had planned for years to take control of the Wolves. And now – with his army stronger than his brother's – he was forced to gamble his future on a single throw. Such was the power of the shamen. He had tried to ignore Asta Khan, but even his own warlords – respected warriors like Ingis – had urged him to seek their wisdom. No one wanted to see wolf rend wolf. But what a time for Tenaka the Mongrel to come home. Saddleskull cursed inwardly.

Asta Khan pushed himself to his feet. The shaman was old, older than any man living among the tribes, and his wisdom was legend. He moved slowly round to stand before the trio; he knew them well – as he had known their fathers and grandfathers – and he could see the resemblance between them.

He lifted his right arm. 'Nadir we!' he shouted, and his voice belied his age; resonant and powerful it floated above the massed ranks and the men echoed the shout solemnly.

'There is no going back from this quest,' said the shaman, addressing the trio. 'You are all kinsmen. Each of you claims blood link to the great Khan. Can you not agree amongst you who should lead?'

He waited for several seconds, but all three remained silent.

'Then hear the wisdom of Asta Khan. You expect to fight one another – I see that your bodies and your weapons are sharp. But there will be no battle of the blood. Instead I shall send you to a place that is not of this world. He that returns will be the Khan, for he will find the helm of Ulric. Death will be closer to you, for you will be walking within his realm. You will see terrible sights, you will hear the screams of the damned. Do you still wish this quest?'

'Let us begin!' snapped Saddleskull. 'Get ready to die, mongrel,' he whispered to Tenaka.

The shaman stepped forward, placing his hand on Saddleskull's head. The warlord's eyes closed and his head dropped. Knifespeaks followed . . . then Tenaka Khan.

Asta Khan squatted down before the sleeping trio, then he closed his eyes.

'Stand!' he ordered.

The three men opened their eyes and stood, blinking in surprise. They were still before the tomb of Ulric, only now they were alone. Gone were the warriors, and the tents, and the camp-fires.

'What is the meaning of this?' asked Knifespeaks.

'There is the tomb of Ulric,' answered Asta Khan. 'All you must do is fetch the helm from the sleeping Khan.'

Knifespeaks and Saddleskull loped off towards the tomb. There were no entrances visible – no doors, only smooth white marble.

Tenaka sat down and the shaman squatted beside him.

'Why do you not search with your cousins?' he asked.

'I know where to look.'

Asta Khan nodded. 'I knew you would come back.'

'How?'

'It was written.'

Tenaka watched his kinsmen circling the tomb, waiting for the moment when both of them were out of sight. Then he rose slowly and sped to the dome. The climb was not difficult, for the marble fascia had been pinned to the sandstone and this left handholds where the blocks joined. He was half-way to the statue of Ulric before the others spotted him. Then he heard Saddleskull curse, and knew they were following.

He reached the arch. It was seven feet deep and the statue of Ulric nestled at the rear.

The King Beyond the Gate!

Tenaka Khan moved forward carefully. The door was hidden behind the archway. He pushed at it and it creaked open.

Saddleskull and Knifespeaks arrived almost together, their enmity forgotten in their fear that Tenaka was ahead. Seeing the open door they pushed forward, but Saddleskull pulled back just as Knifespeaks entered. As Knifespeaks' foot crossed the threshold there was a loud crack and three spears hammered through his chest, punching through his lungs and jutting from his back. He sagged forward. Saddleskull moved round the body, seeing that the spears had been attached to a board, and the board to a series of ropes. He held his breath and listened carefully; he could hear the whispering fall of sand trickling on the stone. He dropped to his knees – there inside the doorway was a broken glass. Sand trickled from it.

As soon as Knifespeaks had broken the glass, the balance was lost and the death-trap released. But how had Tenaka avoided death? Saddleskull cursed and carefully moved into the doorway. Where the half-blood walked, he could surely follow? Immediately he disappeared, Tenaka stepped out from behind the ghostly statue of the Khan. He paused to study the trap which had killed Knifespeaks and then silently moved into the tomb.

The corridor beyond should have been in total darkness, but a strange green light glowed from the walls. Tenaka dropped to his hands and knees and crawled forward, scanning the walls on either side. There must be more traps. But where?

The corridor ended at a circular stair, dipping down into the bowels of the tomb. Tenaka studied the first few steps – they seemed solid. The wall alongside was panelled with cedar. Tenaka sat on the top stair. Why panel a stairwell?

He ripped a section of cedar from the wall and moved on down the stairs, testing each step. Halfway down he felt a slight movement beneath his right foot and withdrew it. Taking the cedar plank, he laid it flat against the edges of the steps and then lay back upon it and lifted his feet. The plank began to slide. It hit the rigged steps at speed and Tenaka felt the 'whoosh' of a steel blade slice above his head. The plank increased speed, hurtling down the stairs. Thrice more it triggered death-traps, but such was the speed of the makeshift sled that Tenaka was untouched. He thrust his booted feet against the walls to slow himself down, his arms and legs being battered and bruised as the journey continued.

The plank hit the ground at the foot of the stairs, pitching Tenaka through the air. Instantly, he relaxed, curling his body into a ball. The air was punched from him as he hit the far wall. He grunted and rolled to his knees. Gingerly he touched his ribs; at least one felt broken. He glanced round the chamber. Where was Saddleskull? The answer came seconds later: hearing the clatter on the stairs, Tenaka grinned and moved away from the stairwell. Saddleskull hurtled by him – his plank smashing to shards, his body cartwheeling into the far wall. Tenaka winced at the impact.

Saddleskull groaned and staggered to his feet; spying Tenaka, he drew himself upright.

'It didn't take me long to work out your plan, half-blood!'

'You surprise me. How did you get behind me?'

'I hid by the body.'

'Well, we are here,' said Tenaka, pointing to the sarcophagus on the raised dais at the centre of the chamber. 'All that remains is to claim the helm.'

'Yes,' said Saddleskull warily.

'Open the coffin,' said Tenaka smiling.

'You open it.'

'Come now, cousin. We cannot spend the rest of our lives here. We will open it together.'

Saddleskull's eyes narrowed. The coffin would almost certainly be rigged and he did not want to die. But if he allowed Tenaka to open the coffin, he would gain not only the helm but, more importantly, Ulric's sword.

Saddleskull grinned. 'Very well,' he said. 'Together!'

They moved to the coffin and heaved at the marble lid, which creaked open. The two men gave a final push and the lid fell to the floor, breaking into three pieces. Saddleskull lunged for the sword that lay on the chest of the skeleton within. Tenaka seized the helm and leapt to the far side of the coffin. Saddleskull chuckled.

'Well, cousin. Now what will you do?'

'I have the helm,' said Tenaka.

Saddleskull leapt forward, slashing wildly, but

Tenaka jumped clear, keeping the coffin between them.

'We could do this for ever,' said Tenaka. 'We could spend eternity running round and round this coffin.'

His opponent hawked and spat. There was truth in what Tenaka said – the sword was useless unless he could get within range.

'Give me the helm,' said Saddleskull. 'Then we can both live. Agree to serve me and I will make you my Warmaster.'

'No, I will not serve you,' said Tenaka. 'But you can have the helm if you agree to one condition.'

'Name it!'

'That you let me lead thirty thousand riders into the Drenai.'

'What? Why?'

'We can discuss that later. Do you swear?'

'I do. Give me the helm.'

As Tenaka tossed the helm across the coffin, Saddleskull caught it deftly and pushed it on his head, wincing as a sharp edge of metal pricked his scalp.

'You are a fool, Tenaka. Did Asta not say that only one would return? Now I have it all.'

'You have nothing, numbskull. You are dead!' said Tenaka.

'Empty threats,' sneered Saddleskull.

Tenaka laughed. 'Ulric's last jest! No one can wear his helm. Did you feel the sharpness, cousin, when the poison needle pierced your skin?'

The sword fell from Saddleskull's hand and his legs gave way. He struggled to rise, but death pulled him down into the pit. Tenaka recovered the helm and replaced the sword in the coffin.

Slowly he climbed the stairs, squeezing past the

blades jutting from the panels. Once into the open air he sat back, cradling the helm in his lap. It was bronze, edged with white fur and decorated with silver thread.

Far below Asta Khan sat watching the moon and Tenaka climbed down to him. The old man did not look round as he approached.

'Welcome, Tenaka Khan, Lord of Hosts!' he said.

'Take me home,' ordered Tenaka.

'Not yet.'

'Why?'

'There is someone you must meet.' A white mist billowed from the ground, swirling around them; from its depths strode a powerful figure.

'You did well,' said Ulric.

'Thank you, my Lord.'

'Do you mean to keep your word to your friends?'

'I do.'

'So the Nadir will ride to the aid of the Drenai?'

'They will.'

'It is as it should be. A man must stand by his friends. But you know that the Drenai must fall before you? As long as they survive, the Nadir cannot prosper.'

'I know this.'

'And you are prepared to conquer them . . . end their empire?'

'I am.'

'Good. Follow me into the mist.'

Tenaka did as he was bid and the Khan led him to the banks of a dark river. There sat an old man who turned as Tenaka approached. It was Aulin, the former Source priest who had died in the Dragon barracks.

'Were you true to your word?' he asked. 'Did you look after Renya?'

'I did.'

'Then sit beside me, and I shall be true to my word.'

Tenaka sat and the old man leaned back, watching the dark water bubble and flow.

'I discovered many machines of the Elders. I scanned their books and notes. I experimented. I learned much of their secrets. They knew the Fall was imminent and they left many clues for future generations. The world is a ball, did you know that?'

'No,' said Tenaka.

'Well, it is. At the top of the ball is a world of ice. And at the base, another. Round the centre it is hellishly hot. And the ball spins around the sun. Did you know that?'

'Aulin, I have no time for this. What do you wish to tell me?'

'Please, warrior, listen to me. I so wanted this knowledge shared – it is important to me.'

'Go on, then.'

'The world spins and the ice at the poles of the world grows daily: millions of tons of ice, every day for thousands of years. At last the ball begins to wobble as it spins, and then it tips. And as it tips, the oceans rise up and cover the land. And the ice spreads to cover whole continents. That is the Fall. That is what happened to the Elders. Do you see? It makes the dreams of men a nonsense.'

'I see. Now what can you tell me?'

'The machines of the Elders – they do not operate as Ceska thinks. There is no physical joining of beasts and men. Rather is it a harnessing of vital forces, held in delicate balance. The Elders knew it was important – vital – to allow the spirit of man to remain in the ascendant. The horror of the Joinings is the result of allowing the beast to emerge.'

331

'How does this help me?' asked Tenaka.

'I saw a joining revert once; it became a man again and died.'

'How?'

'When it saw something which jolted it.'

'What did it see?'

'The woman who had been its wife.'

'Is that it?'

'Yes. Is that helpful?'

'I don't know,' said Tenaka. 'It may be.'

'Then I shall leave you,' said Aulin. 'I shall return to the Grey.'

Tenaka watched him shuffle away into the mist. Then he stood and turned as Ulric stepped forward.

'The war has already begun,' said the Khan. 'You will not arrive in time to save your friends.'

'Then I shall be in time to avenge them,' answered Tenaka.

'What was the old man trying to tell you about the Fall?'

'I don't know – something about ice spinning. It wasn't important,' said Tenaka

*

The old shaman bade Tenaka sit down and the new Khan obeyed. His eyes closed. When he opened them, he was sitting before the tomb as before, watched by the massed ranks of Nadir generals. To his left lay Shirrat Knifespeaks – his chest ripped apart, blood staining the dust. To his right was Saddleskull, a small trickle of blood on his temple. Before him was the helm of Ulric.

Asta Khan stood and turned to the generals.

'It is over and it has begun. Tenaka Khan rules the Wolves.'

The old man took the helm, returned to the brazier, swept up his cloak of ragged skins and walked from the camp. Tenaka remained where he was, scanning the faces before him and sensing the hostility. These were men prepared for war, supporters of Knifespeaks or Saddleskull. Not one man among them had considered Tenaka as Khan. Now they had a new leader and from this moment on Tenaka would need to walk with extreme care. His food would have to be tasted . . . his tent guarded. Among the men before him would be many who would desire his death.

And swiftly!

It was easy to become a Khan. The real trick lay in staying alive thereafter.

A movement in the ranks caught his eye and Ingis rose and walked towards him. Taking his sword from its scabbard and reversing the blade, he handed it hilt-first to Tenaka.

'I become your man,' said Ingis kneeling.

'Welcome, warrior. How may brothers do you bring?'

'Twenty thousand.'

'It is good,' said the Khan.

And one by one the generals trooped forward. It was dawn before the last backed away and Ingis approached once more.

'The families of Saddleskull and Knifespeaks have been taken. They are being held near your campsite.'

Tenaka rose and stretched. He was cold, and very tired. With Ingis beside him, he walked from the tomb.

A great crowd had assembled to watch the deaths of the prisoners. Tenaka looked at the captives as they knelt in silent ranks, their arms tied behind them. There were twenty-two women, six men and a dozen boy-children.

Subodai came forward. 'You wish to kill them yourself?'

'No.'

'Gitasi and I will do it then,' he said with relish.

'No.' Tenaka walked on, leaving Subodai baffled and surprised.

The new Khan halted before the women, the wives of the dead warlords.'

'I did not kill your husbands,' he told them. 'There was no blood feud between us. Yet I inherit their property. So be it! You were part of that property and I name you as wives of Tenaka Khan. Release them!' he ordered.

Muttering under his breath, Subodai moved along the line. A young woman ran forward as he freed her and threw herself at Tenaka's feet.

'If I am truly your wife, then what of my son?'

'Release the children also,' said Tenaka.

Only the six men remained now, close relatives of the dead warlords.

'This is a new day,' Tenaka told them. 'I give you this choice. Promise you serve me and you live. Refuse and you die!'

'I spit on you, half-blood,' shouted one man. Tenaka stepped forward, held out his hand for Subodai's sword and with one sweep severed the man's neck.

Not one of the five remaining prisoners spoke, and Tenaka moved along the line, killing them all. He called Ingis to him and the two men sat quietly in the shadows of the tent.

There they stayed for three hours while the Khan outlined his plans. Then Tenaka slept.

And while he slept twenty men ringed his tent, swords in hand.

20

Parsal continued to crawl, dragging himself through the long grass. The pain from his mutilated leg had faded from the searing agony of the previous afternoon to a throbbing ache which occasionally flared, causing him to lose consciousness. The night was cool, but Parsal was sweating freely. He no longer knew where he was going, only that he had to put as great a distance between himself and the horror as he could.

He crawled over an area of earth pitted with pebbles, and a sharp stone dug into his leg. Groaning, he rolled over.

Ananais had told them to hold on for as long as they could, then to draw back and make for Magadon. He had then gone to another valley with Galand. The events of the afternoon kept flooding Parsal's mind and he could not push them away . . . With four hundred men he had waited in a tiny pass. The cavalry had come first, thundering up the incline with lances levelled. Parsal's archers had cut them to pieces. The infantry were harder to repel, well-armoured and with their round bronze shields held high. Parsal had never been the swordsman his brother was but, by all the gods, he had given a good account of himself!

The Skoda men had fought like tigers and Ceska's infantry were forced back. That was the point when he should have ordered his men to withdraw.

Foolish, foolish man!

But he had been so uplifted. So proud! Never in his life had he led a fighting force. He had been turned down for the Dragon, while his brother had been accepted. Now he had repelled a mighty enemy.

And he waited for one more attack.

The Joinings had surged forward like demons of the pit. If he lived to be a hundred, he would never forget that charge. The beasts sent up a terrifying wall of sound, howling their blood-lust as they ran. Giant monsters with slavering maws and blood-red eyes, sharp talons and bright, bright swords.

Arrows scarce pierced their flesh and they swept aside the fighting men of Skoda as a grown man scatters unruly children.

Parsal gave no order to run – it was unnecessary. The Skoda courage vanished like water on sand and the force scattered. In his anguish Parsal ran at a Joining, aiming a mighty blow for the beast's head, but his sword bounced from the thick skull and the creature turned on him. Parsal was thrown back and the Joining dived, its great jaws closing on Parsal's left leg and ripping the flesh from the bone. A gallant Skoda fighter leapt to the beast's back, driving a long dagger into its neck; it turned away from Parsal to rip the throat from the warrior. Parsal rolled clear over a rise and tumbled down and down into the valley. And so his long crawl began.

He knew now that there was no victory for the Skoda men. Their dreams were folly. Nothing could stand against the Joining. He wished he had stayed on his farm in Vagria, far away from this insane war.

Something seized his leg and he sat up, waving a dagger. A taloned arm smashed it from his grip and three Joinings squatted around him – their eyes gleaming, saliva dripping from open maws.

Mercifully he blacked out.

And the feeding began.

*

Pagan edged forward until he was less than one hundred yards from the western quarter of the city. His horse was hidden in the woods behind him. Smoke from the burning buildings was swirling like mist and it was hard to see for any distance. Bodies were being dragged from the city by groups of Joinings, and the feast started in the meadows beyond. Pagan had never seen the beasts before and he watched them in grim fascination. Most were over seven feet tall and mightily muscled.

Pagan was at a loss. He had a message for Ananais from Scaler – but where would he now deliver it? Was the dark-masked warrior still alive? Was the war over? If it was, then Pagan must change his plan. He had sworn to kill Ceska and he was not a man to take an oath lightly. Somewhere among this army was the tent of the emporer – all he had to do was find it and gut the son of a whore.

That was all!

The deaths of Pagan's people weighed heavily on him and he was determined to avenge them. Once he killed Ceska, the emperor's shade would be consigned to the Land of Shadow to serve the slain. A fitting punishment.

Pagan watched the beasts feed for a while, noting their movements, and learning all he could against the day when he must fight them. He was under no illusion – the day would come. Man against beast, head to head. The beast might be strong, swift and deadly. But then Kataskicana the King had earned the title Lord of War. For he was too strong, swift and deadly. But added to this, he was cunning.

Pagan eased his way back into the woods. Once there he froze, his wide nostrils flaring. His eyes narrowed and he slid his axe into his hand.

His horse was standing where he had left it, but the beast was quivering in fear, its ears flat against its skull and its eyes wide.

Pagan delved into his leather tunic, pulling clear a short, heavy throwing-knife. Licking his lips, he scanned the undergrowth. Hiding places close by were few; he was in one such, which left three other obvious places. So, he reasoned, he was facing a maximum of three opponents. Did they have bows? Unlikely, for they would have to stand, draw and loose at a swiftly moving target. Were they human? Unlikely, for the horse was terrified and mere men would not create such fear.

So then – a possible three Joinings crouched in the bushes ahead of him.

His decision made, Pagan stood up and walked towards his horse.

A Joining leapt from the bushes to his right and another rose from the left. They moved with incredible speed. Pagan spun on his heel, his right arm flashing down; the knife plunged into the right eye-socket of the first beast. The second was almost upon him when the black man dropped to his knees and dived forward, crashing into the creature's legs. The Joining pitched over him and Pagan rolled, lashing the axe-blade deep into the beast's thigh. Then he was up and running. He tore the reins clear of the branches and vaulted to the saddle as the Joining ran at him. As Pagan leaned back in the saddle, tugging on the reins, the horse reared in terror, its hooves lashing at the beast and catching it full in the face. The Joining went down and Pagan heeled away his horse through the woods, ducking under overhanging branches. Once clear, he galloped to the west.

The gods had been with him, for he had seriously miscalculated. Had there been three Joinings he would have been dead. He had aimed the knife for the beast's throat, but so swift had been its charge that he had almost missed the target altogether.

Pagan slowed his horse as the burning city fell away behind him.

All over the lowlands would be the scouts of Ceska. He had no wish to gallop into a greater danger than that from which he fled. He patted the horse's neck.

He had left Scaler with the Cheiam. The new Earl of Bronze had grown in stature and his plans for taking the fortress were well-advanced. Whether or not they would work was another matter, but at least Scaler was tackling them with confidence. Pagan chuckled. The young Drenai was more than convincing in his new role and Pagan could almost believe that he really was the legendary Earl.

Almost. Pagan chuckled again.

Towards dusk he moved into a section of trees near a stream. He had seen no sign of the enemy and he scouted the area carefully. But a surprise lay in wait for him as he rode into a small hollow.

Some twenty children were seated around the body of a man.

Pagan dismounted and tethered his horse. A tall boy stepped forward, a dagger in his hand.

'Touch him and I will kill you!' said the boy.

*

'I will not touch him,' said Pagan. 'Put up the knife.'

'Are you a Joining?'

'No, I am merely a man.'

'You don't look like a man – you're black.'

Pagan nodded solemnly. 'Indeed I am. You, on the other hand are white and very small. I don't doubt your bravery, but do you really think you can stand against me?'

The boy licked his lips, but stood his ground.

'If I was your enemy, boy, I would have killed you by now. Stand aside.' He walked forward, ignoring the lad as he knelt by the body. The dead man was thickset and balding, his large hands locked on his jerkin.

'What happened?' Pagan asked a little girl sitting closest to the body. She looked away and the boy with the knife spoke.

'He brought us here yesterday. He said we could hide until the beasts went away. But this morning, as he was playing with Melissa, he clutched his chest and fell.'

'It wasn't me,' said Melissa. 'I didn't do anything!'

Pagan ruffled the child's mousy-blonde hair. 'Of course you didn't. Did you bring food with you?'

'Yes,' answered the boy. 'It's over there in the cave.'

'My name is Pagan and I am a friend of Darkmask.'

'Will you look after us?' asked Melissa. Pagan smiled at her, then stood and stretched. The Joinings would be on the loose now and he had no chance of avoiding them on foot with twenty children in tow. He strode to the top of a nearby hill, shading his eyes to view the mountains. It would take them at least two days to walk that distance – two days out in the open. He turned to see the boy with the knife sitting on a rock behind him. He was tall and about eleven years of age.

'You didn't answer Melissa's question,' said the boy.

'What is your name, lad?'

'Ceorl. Will you help us?'

'I don't know that I can,' answered Pagan.

'I cannot do it all by myself,' said Ceorl, his grey eyes locked on Pagan's face.

Pagan sat down on the grass. 'Try to understand, Ceorl. There is virtually no way that we can make it to the mountains. The Joinings are like beasts of the jungle; they track by scent, they move fast and range wide. I have a message to deliver to Darkmask; I am involved in the war. I have my own mission and have sworn to see it through.'

'Excuses!' said Ceorl. 'Always excuses. Well, I will get them there – trust me.'

'I will stay with you for a little while,' said Pagan. 'But be warned: I don't much like children chattering around me – it makes me irritable.'

'You can't stop Melissa chattering. She is very young and very frightened.'

'And you are not frightened?'

'I am a man,' said Ceorl. 'I gave up crying years ago.'

Pagan nodded and smoothly rose to his feet. 'Let's get the food and be on our way.'

Together they gathered together the children. Each child carried a small rucksack of food and a canteen of water. Pagan lifted Melissa and two other toddlers to the horse's back and led them out on to the plain. The wind was at their backs, which was good . . . unless there were Joinings ahead of them. Ceorl was right about Melissa; she chattered on and on, telling Pagan stories he could scarcely follow. Towards the evening she began to sway in the saddle and pagan lifted her clear and held her to his chest.

They had covered maybe three miles when Ceorl ran alongside Pagan and tugged his sleeve.

'What is it?'

'They are very tired. I just saw Ariane sit down beside the trail back there – I think she's gone to sleep.'

'All right. Go back and get her – we will camp here.'

The children huddled in together around Pagan as he laid Melissa down on the grass. The night was cool, but not cold.

'Will you tell us a story?' asked the girl.

Keeping his voice soft, he told them of the Moon Goddess who came down to earth on silver steps to live the life of a mortal. There she met the handsome warrior prince Anidigo. He loved her as no man has loved a woman since, but she was coy and fled from him. Up into the sky she rose in a silver chariot, perfectly round. He could not follow and went to see a wise wizard who made him a chariot of pure gold. Anidigo swore that until he had won the heart of the Moon Goddess he would never return. His golden chariot, also perfectly round, soared into the sky like a gleaming ball of fire. Round and round the earth he went, but always she was ahead of him. Even to this day.

'Look up!' said Pagan. 'There she rides – and soon Anidigo will send her fleeing from the sky.'

The last child fell into a dreamless sleep and Pagan eased himself through them, seeking Ceorl. Together they walked some paces away.

'You tell a good story.'

'I have many children,' replied Pagan.

'If they irritate you, why have so many?' the boy asked.

'That's not easy to explain,' said Pagan, grinning.

'Oh, I understand,' snapped Ceorl. 'I am not so young.'

Pagan tried to explain.

'A man can love his children, yet be annoyed by them. I was delighted with the births of all my children. One of them stands now in my place at home, ruling my people. But I am a man who has always needed solitude. Children do not understand that.'

'Why are you black?'

'So much for the philosophical conversation! I am black because my country is very hot. A dark skin is a protection against the sunlight. Does your skin not darken during summer?'

'And your hair – why is it so tightly curled?'

'I don't know, young man. No more do I know why my nose is wide and my lips thicker than yours. It is just the way it is.'

'Does everybody look like you where you come from?'

'Not to me.'

'Can you fight?'

'You are full of questions, Ceorl!'

'I like to know things. Can you fight?'

'Like a tiger.'

'That's a kind of cat, isn't it?'

'Yes. A very *large* cat and distinctly unfriendly.'

'I can fight,' said Ceorl. 'I am a good fighter.'

'I'm sure that you are. But let us hope that we don't have to prove it. Go and sleep now,'

'I am not tired. I'll stand watch.'

'Do as I tell you, Ceorl. You can stand watch tomorrow.'

The boy nodded and went back to the children. Within minutes he was fast asleep. Pagan sat for a while thinking of his homeland. Then he too moved to where the children lay. Melissa was still sleeping soundly, cuddling a rag doll. The doll was ancient; it had no eyes and only two thin strands of yellow thread for hair.

Scaler had told him of his own strange religious belief. The gods, said Scaler, were all so old that they had grown senile. Their vast power was now employed in senseless japes upon humans, misdirecting their lives and leaving them in appalling situations.

Pagan was fast becoming a believer.

A distant howl echoed in the night. Then a second and a third added to the noise. Pagan cursed softly and drew his sword. Taking a small whetstone from his leather pouch, he spat upon it and honed the sword-blade; then he unstrapped the axe from his saddlebag and sharpened that also.

The wind shifted, carrying their scent to the east. Pagan waited, counting slowly. He had reached eight hundred and seven when the howling increased in intensity. Considering variations in the wind speed, that put the Joinings between eight and twelve miles behind them – it was not enough.

The kindest action would be to creep forward and cut all the children's throats as they slept, saving them the horror that ran behind. But Pagan knew he could take three of the smallest on his horse.

He drew his dagger and crept among them.

But which three?

With a soft curse he rammed his dagger home in its scabbard and woke Ceorl.

'The Joinings are close,' he said. 'Wake the children – we're moving out.'

'How close?' asked Ceorl, eyes wide in fear.

'An hour behind – if we're lucky.'

Ceorl rolled to his feet and moved among the youngsters. Pagan lifted Melissa to his shoulder. She

344

dropped the doll and he retrieved it, tucking it into his tunic. The children huddled around him.

'See that peak yonder?' he said to Ceorl. 'Make for it! I shall be back.'

'You promise?'

'I promise.' Pagan climbed into the saddle. 'Put two of the smaller children behind me.' Ceorl did as he was bid. 'Now hold on tight, little ones – we're going for a ride.'

Pagan dug his heels into the stallion and he leapt forward into the night, eating the distance between the mountains. Melissa woke up and began to cry, so Pagan pulled out the doll and pushed it into her arms. After riding for some minutes at a fast run, he saw an outcropping of rock away to the right. Hauling on the reins, he directed the stallion up and into the boulders. The pathway was narrow, less than five feet, widening at the top into a shallow bowl. There was no exit but by the path.

Pagan helped the children down. 'Wait here for me,' he said and rode down into the plain once more. Five times he made the journey, and by the last Ceorl and the remaining four older boys had almost reached the rocks as he rode out. Jumping from the saddle, he handed the reins to the boy.

'Take the horse up into the bowl and wait there for me.'

'What are you going to do?'

'Do as I say, child!'

Ceorl stepped back a pace. 'I just wanted to help.'

'I'm sorry, boy! Keep your dagger handy – I intend to hold them here, but if they come through use your dagger on the youngest children. You understand?'

'I don't think that I can,' Ceorl faltered.

'Then do as your heart bids you. Good luck, Ceorl!'

'I . . . I don't really want to die.'

'I know. Now get up there and comfort them.'
Pagan pulled his axe clear of the saddle and untied
his bow and a quiver of arrows. The bow was of
Vagrian horn and only a very strong man could draw
it. Pagan settled himself down on the trail, watching
the east.

It was said that the Kings of the Opal Throne
always knew when their day was done.

Pagan knew.

He strung his bow and removed his tunic, letting
the night air cool his body.

In a deep voice he began to sing the Song of the
Dead.

*

At a prearranged meeting place Ananais and his
captains sat together discussing the day's action.
Once thrown back from the first ring of mountains,
the Skoda force had split into seven, moving to high
ground and ambushing the invading force as they
swarmed into the heights. Hit-and-run raids harassed
Ceska's troops, slowing the advance, and Skoda
casualties had been remarkably light – with the
exception of Parsal's force, of which not one man
had escaped.

'They are moving faster than we had estimated,'
said Katan. 'And their numbers have been swelled
by Delnoch troops.'

'I'd say there were as many as fifty thousand in
the invading force,' said Thorn. 'We can forget about
holding anywhere but Tarsk and Magadon.'

'We shall keep hitting them,' maintained Ananais.
'How long can you hold the power of those damned
Templars, Katan?'

'I think even now they are finding ways through.'

'Once they do, our raids could become suicidal.'

'I know that well, Darkmask. But we are not dealing here with an exact science. The battle in the Void is unceasing, but we are being pushed back.'

'Do your best, boy,' said Ananais. 'All right – we shall hit them for one more day, then pull everyone back to the walls.'

'Do you get the feeling we are spitting into the eye of a hurricane?' asked Thorn.

Ananais grinned. 'Maybe, but we've not lost yet! Katan is it safe to ride?'

The priest closed his eyes and the men waited for several minutes. Then Katan jerked suddenly, his eyes flaring open.

'To the north,' he said. 'We must go now!'

The priest lurched to his feet, half-fell, recovered and ran to his horse. Ananais followed him.

'Thorn!' he shouted. 'Take your men back to the group. The rest of you follow me!'

Katan led them in a headlong gallop to the north, followed by Ananais and twenty warriors. It was almost dawn and the tips of the mountains to their right were bathed in red.

The priest lashed his mount and Ananais, close behind, bellowed, 'You'll kill the beast, you fool!' Katan ignored him, bending low over the horse's neck. Ahead was an outcropping of rock; Katan dragged on the reins and leapt from the saddle, racing into a narrow cleft. Ananais drew his sword and followed him.

Inside the cleft lay two dead Joinings, black-feathered arrows jutting from their throats. Ananais ran on. Another dead beast, shot through the heart. He rounded a bend and heard the sound of bestial growling and the clash of steel on steel. Hurdling three more bodies, he turned a corner with sword raised. Two dead Joinings lay before him, a third live beast was attacking Katan, and two others were engaged in a grim struggle with a man Ananais could not see.

'To me, Dragon!' yelled Ananais. One of the two Joinings turned on him, but he blocked a savage cut and plunged his sword into the beast's belly. Its talons lashed out and he threw himself back as his men raced in, hacking and cutting. The beast went down under a score of blows. Katan despatched his opponent with consummate ease and ran forward to assist the warrior, but it wasn't necessary. Pagan hammered his axe through the beast's neck and sagged back to the path.

Ananais ran to him, to find Pagan's body was a mass of wounds: his chest was ripped open, flesh hanging in bloody strips.

His left arm was almost severed and his face had been mauled.

The black man's breathing was ragged, but his eyes were bright and he tried to smile as Ananais cradled his head in his lap.

'There are children above,' whispered Pagan.

'We will fetch them. Lie still!'

'For what, my friend?'

'Just lie still.'

'How many did I get?'

'Nine.'

'That's good. I am glad you came – the other two would have been . . . difficult.'

Katan knelt beside Pagan, laying his hand on the bloody head. All pain vanished from the dying warrior.

'I failed in my mission,' said Pagan. 'I should have gone after Ceska back at the city.'

'I will get him for you,' Ananais promised.

'Are the children all right?'

'Yes,' Katan assured him. 'We are bringing them out now.'

'Don't let them see me. It will frighten them.'

'Have no fear,' said Katan.

'Make sure you have Melissa's rag doll . . . she would be lost without it.'

'We will make sure.'

'When I was young I ordered men into the fire! I should not have done it. It is a lasting regret. Well, Darkmask, now we will never know, will we?'

'I already know,' said Ananais. 'I could not have felled nine Joinings. I would not have thought it possible.'

'All things are possible,' said Pagan, his voice sinking to a whisper. 'Except the passing of regret.' He paused. 'Scaler has a plan.'

'Can it work?' asked Ananais.

Pagan grinned. 'All things are possible. He gave me a message for you, but it is useless now. He wanted you to know that ten thousand Delnoch men were on the march. But they arrived before I could.'

Ceorl pushed his way through to Pagan, kneeling by his side with tears in his eyes.

'Why?' he said. 'Why did you do this for us?'

But Pagan was dead.

Ananais took the lad by the arm. 'He did it because he was a man – a very great man.'

'He didn't even like children.'

'I think you are wrong there, boy.'

'He said so himself. We irritated him, he told me. Why did he let himself get killed for us?'

Ananais had no answer but Katan stepped forward.

'Because he was a hero. And that is what heroes do. You understand?'

Ceorl nodded. 'I didn't know he was a hero – he didn't say.'

'Maybe he didn't know,' said Katan.

*

Galand took the death of his brother hard. He withdrew into himself, suppressing his emotions, his dark eyes giving no hint of the agony he felt. He led his men on several raids against Drenai cavalry, hitting them fast and withdrawing at speed. Despite his desire to wreak vengeance upon them he remained a disciplined warrior – not for Galand the reckless charge, only the calculated risk. Among his three hundred men, losses were light and they cantered to the walls of Magadon having left only thirty-seven of their comrades buried back in the hills.

There was no gate at Magadon and the men released their horses and scaled rope ladders let down by the defenders. Galand was the last to climb the ramparts and at the top he turned, gazing back to the east. Somewhere there the body of Parsal was rotting on the grassland. No grave, no marker.

The war had claimed Galand's daughter and now his brother.

Soon it would claim him, he mused.

Strange how the thought struck no terror in him.

Among his men were another forty who had suffered wounds. He went down with them to the timber hospital where Valtaya and a dozen women tended them. Galand waved to the blonde woman and she smiled, then returned to her work stitching a shallow cut in a warrior's thigh.

He wandered out into the sunlight where one of his men brought him a loaf of bread and a jug of wine. Galand thanked him and sat down with his back to a tree. The bread was fresh, the wine young. One of his section leaders, a young farmer named

Oranda, joined him. He had a thick bandage on his upper arm.

'They said the wound was clean – only six stitches. I should still be able to hold a shield.'

'Good,' said Galand absently. 'Have some wine?'

Oranda took a mouthful. 'It is a little young,' he said.

'Maybe we should lay it down for a month or two!'

'Point taken,' said Oranda, tilting the jug once more.

For a while they sat in silence, and the tension grew in Galand as he waited for the inevitable comment.

'I'm sorry about your brother,' said Oranda at last.

'All men die,' answered Galand.

'Yes. I lost friends in his force. The walls look strong, don't they? It's strange to see walls across this valley. I used to play here as a child and watch the wild horses run.'

Galand said nothing. Oranda handed him the wine-jug, wishing he could just get up and walk away, but he didn't want to be rude. When Valtaya joined them, Oranda greeted her with a grateful smile and slipped away.

Galand glanced up and smiled.

'You are looking lovely, lady. A vision.' She had removed the blood-drenched leather apron and now wore a dress of light blue cotton which moulded to her figure beautifully.

'Your eyes must be tired, blackbeard. My hair is greasy and there are purple rings under my eyes. I feel wretched.'

'In the eye of the beholder,' he said. She sat beside him, laying her hand on his arm.

'I am truly sorry about Parsal.'

'All men die,' he said, tired of the repetition.

'But I am glad you are alive.'

'Are you?' he asked, his eyes cold. 'Why?'

'What a strange question for a friend to ask!'

'I am not your friend, Val. I am the man who loves you. There is a difference.'

'I am sorry, Galand. There is nothing I can say – you know that I am with Ananais.'

'And are you happy?'

'Of course I am – as happy as anyone can be in the middle of a war.'

'Why? Why do you love him?'

'I cannot answer that question. No woman could. Why do you love me?'

He tilted the wine-jug, ignoring the logic.

'What hurts is that there is no future for any of us,' he said, 'even if we should survive this battle. Ananais will never settle down to married life. He's no farmer, no merchant . . . He will leave you in some lonely city. And I shall return to my farm. None of us will be happy.'

'Don't drink any more, Galand. It is making you melancholy.'

'My daughter was a joyous creature and a real rascal. Many's the smack I laid on her leg and many the tear I wiped away. Had I known how short her life was to be . . . And now Parsal . . . I hope he died swiftly. I feel it in a very selfish way,' he said suddenly. 'My blood runs in not a single living being, bar me. When I am gone, it will be as if I never was.'

'Your friends will care,' she said.

He pulled his arm from her comforting touch and glared at her through angry eyes.

'I *have* no friends! I never had.'

21

The emperor sat within his tent of silk surrounded by his captains. His warmaster, Darik, was beside him. The tent was huge, split into four sections: the largest, where the warriors now sat, had room for fifty men though only twenty were present.

Ceska had grown fat over the years and his skin was pasty and blotched. His dark eyes glittered with feral intelligence and it was said that he had learned the ways of the Dark Templars and could read minds. His captains lived in a state of cold dread around him, for often he would suddenly point at a man and scream 'Traitor!' That man would die horribly.

Darik was his most trusted warrior, a general of great guile, second only to the legendary Baris of the Dragon. A tall man in his early fifties, slender and wiry, Darik was clean-shaven and looked younger than his years.

Having heard the reports, and the numbers of the slain, Darik spoke: 'The raids seem casual, haphazard, yet I sense unity of thought behind them. What do you say, Maymon?'

The Dark Templar nodded. 'We are almost through their defences, but already we can see a great deal. They have walled the two passes known as Tarsk and Magadon. And they expect aid from the north, though without great confidence. The leader, as you expected, is Ananais, though it is the woman Rayvan who binds them together.'

'Where is she?' asked the emperor.

'Back in the mountains.'

'Can you get to her?'

'Not from the Void. She is protected.'

'They cannot protect all her friends?' suggested Ceska.

'No, my lord,' agreed Maymon.

'Then soul-take someone close to her. I want the woman dead.'

'Yes, my lord. But first we must break through the Void wall of The Thirty.'

'What of Tenaka Khan?' snapped Ceska.

'He escaped to the north. His grandfather, Jongir, died two months ago and there is civil war brewing.'

'Send a message to the Delnoch commander, ordering him to watch closely for any Nadir army.'

'Yes, my lord.'

'Leave me now,' said the emperor. 'All except Darik.'

The captains gratefully obeyed, walking out into the night. Around the tent stood fifty Joinings, the largest and most ferocious beasts in Ceska's army. The captains did not look at them as they passed.

Inside the tent Ceska sat silently for several minutes.

'They all hate me,' he said. 'Small men with small minds. What are they without me?'

'They are nothing, sire,' said Darik.

'Exactly. And what of you, general?'

'Sire, you can read men like an open book. You can see into their hearts. I am loyal, but the day you doubt me I shall take my life the instant you order it.'

'You are the only loyal man in the empire. I want

them all dead. I want Skoda to be a charnel-house that will be remembered for eternity.'

'It shall be as you command, sire. They cannot hold against us.'

'The Spirit of Chaos rides with my forces, Darik. But it needs blood. Much blood. Oceans of blood! It is never satisfied.'

Ceska's eyes took on a haunted look and he lapsed into silence. Darik sat very still. The fact that his emperor was mad worried him not at all, but Ceska's deterioration was another matter. Darik was a strange man. Almost totally single-minded, he cared only for war and strategy and what he had told the emperor was the literal truth. When the day came – as come it must – that Ceska's madness turned on him, he would kill himself. For life would have nothing more to offer. Darik had never loved a single human being, nor been entranced by things of beauty. He cared not for paintings, poetry, literature, mountains nor storm-tossed seas.

War and death were his concerns. But even these he did not love – they merely maintained his interest.

Suddenly Ceska giggled. 'I was one of the last to see his face,' he said.

'Who, my lord?'

'Ananais, the Golden One. He became an arena warrior and a great favourite with the crowds. One day as he stood there acknowledging their cheers, I sent in one of my Joinings. It was a giant beast, a three-way breed of wolf, bear and man. He killed it. All that work and he killed it.' Ceska giggled again. 'But he lost face with the crowd.'

'How so, sire? Did they like the beast?'

'Oh no. He just *lost face*. It's a jest!'

Darik chuckled dutifully.

'I hate him. He was the first to sow seeds of doubt.

He wanted to lead the Dragon against me, but Baris and Tenaka Khan stopped him. Noble Baris! He was better than you, you know.'

'Yes, sire. You have mentioned it before.'

'But not as loyal. You will stay loyal, won't you, Darik?'

'I will, sire.'

'You wouldn't want to become like Baris, would you?'

'No, sire.'

'Isn't it strange how certain qualities remain?' mused Ceska.

'Sire?'

'I mean – he is still a leader, isn't he? The others still look to him – I wonder why?'

'I don't know, sire. You look cold – can I fetch you some wine?'

'You wouldn't poison me, would you?'

'No, sire, but you are right – I ought to taste it first.'

'Yes. Taste it.'

Darik poured wine into a golden goblet and drank a little. His eyes widened.

'What is it, general?' asked Ceska, leaning forward.

'There is something in it, sire. It is salty.'

'Oceans of blood!' said Ceska, giggling.

*

Tenaka Khan awoke in the hour before dawn and reached for Renya, but the bed was empty. Then he remembered and sat up rubbing the sleep from his eyes. He seemed to recall someone saying his name, but it must have been a dream.

The voice called again and Tenaka swung his legs from the bed and gazed around the tent.

'Close your eyes, my friend and relax,' said the voice.

Tenaka lay back. In his mind's eye he could see the slender, ascetic face of Decado.

'How long before you reach us?'

'Five days. If Scaler opens the gates.'

'We will be dead by then.'

'I can move no more swiftly.'

'How many men do you bring?'

'Forty thousand.'

'You seem changed, Tani.'

'I am the same. How fares it with Ananais?'

'He trusts you.'

'And the others?'

'Pagan and Parsal are dead. We have been forced back to the last valleys. We can hold for maybe three days – no more. The Joinings are everything we feared.'

Tenaka told him of his ghostly meeting with Aulin and the words of the old man. Decado listened in silence.

'So you are the Khan,' he said at last.

'Yes.'

'Farewell, Tenaka.'

Back at Tarsk, Decado opened his eyes. Acuas and The Thirty sat in a circle around him, linking their powers.

Each of them had heard the words of Tenaka Khan, but more importantly each had entered his mind, sharing his thoughts.

Decado took a deep breath. 'Well?' he asked Acuas.

'We are betrayed,' answered the warrior priest.

'Not yet,' said Decado. 'He will come.'

'That is not what I meant.'

'I know what you meant. But let tomorrow look

after itself. Our purpose here is to aid the people of Skoda. None of us will live to see the events thereafter.'

'But what is the point?' asked Balan. 'Some good should come of our deaths. Are we merely helping them to exchange tyrants?'

'And what if we are?' said Decado softly. 'The Source knows best. If we do not believe that, then it is all for nothing.'

'So you are now a believer?' said Balan sceptically.

'Yes, Balan, I am a believer. I think I always was. For even in my despair I railed at the Source. That itself was an admission of belief, though I could not see it. But tonight has convinced me.'

'Betrayal by a friend has convinced you?' asked Acuas, astonished.

'No, not betrayal. Hope. A glimmer of light. A sign of love. But we will talk of this tomorrow. Tonight there are farewells to be said.'

'Farewells?' said Acuas.

'We are The Thirty,' said Decado. 'Our mission is near completion. As the Voice of The Thirty I am the Abbot of Swords. But I am to die here. Yet The Thirty must live on. We have seen tonight that a new threat is growing and that in the days to come the Drenai will have need of us again. As in the past, so shall it be now. One of us must leave, take on the mantle of Abbot and raise a new group of Source warriors. That man is Katan, the Soul of The Thirty.'

'It cannot be me,' said Katan. 'I do not believe in death and killing.'

'Exactly so,' said Decado. 'Yet you are chosen. It seems to me that the Source always chooses us to perform tasks against our natures. Why, I do not know . . . but He knows.

'I am a poor man to be a leader. And yet the Source has allowed me to see His power. I am content. The rest of us will obey his will. Now, Katan, lead us in prayer for the last time.'

There were tears in Katan's eyes as he prayed and a great sadness rested upon him. At the end he embraced them all and walked away into the night. How would he manage? Where would he find a new Thirty? He mounted his horse and rode into the high country towards Vagria.

On a ridge overlooking the refugee settlement he saw the boy Ceorl sitting by the path. He reined in his horse and stepped down.

'Why are you here, Ceorl?'

'A man came to me and told me to be here – to wait for you.'

'What man?'

'A dream man.'

Katan settled down beside the boy. 'Is this the first time the man has come to you?'

'This man, you mean?'

'Yes.'

'Yes, it is. But often I see others – they talk to me.'

'Can you do magical things, Ceorl?'

'Yes.'

'Such as?'

'Sometimes when I touch things I know where they came from. I see pictures. And sometimes, when people are angry with me I hear what they are thinking.'

'Tell me of the man who came to you.'

'His name is Abaddon. He said he was the Abbot of Swords.'

Katan bowed his head and covered his face with his hands.

'Why are you sad?' asked Ceorl.

Katan took a deep breath and smiled. 'I am not sad . . . Not any more. You are the First, Ceorl. But there will be others. You are to ride with me and I will teach you many things.'

'Are we to be heroes, like the black man?'

'Yes,' said Katan. 'We are to be heroes.'

*

The armies of Ceska arrived with the dawn, marching in ranks ten deep and led by the Legion riders. The long column wound across the plain, splitting into two as it breasted the valley pass of Magadon. Ananais had ridden in with Thorn, Lake and a dozen men only an hour before. Now he leaned on the ramparts watching the force spread out and pitch their tents. Half the army rode on towards Tarsk.

Twenty thousand battle-hardened veterans remained. But there was no sign as yet of the emperor or his Joinings.

Ananais squinted against the rising sun. 'I think that's Darik – there in the centre. Now that's a compliment!'

'I don't think I would be comfortable with too many of his compliments,' muttered Thorn. 'He's a butcher!'

'More than that, my friend,' said Ananais, 'he is a warmaster. And that makes him a master butcher.'

For a while the defenders watched the preparations in grim, silent fascination. Wagons followed the army, piled high with crudely-made ladders, iron grappling-hooks, vine ropes and provisions.

An hour later, as Ananais was sleeping on the grass, the Joinings of Ceska marched into the plain.

A young warrior woke the sleeping general and he rubbed his eyes and sat up.

'The beasts are here,' whispered the man. Seeing his fear, Ananais clapped him on the shoulder.

'Don't worry, lad! Keep a stick in your belt.'

'A stick, sir?'

'Yes. If they get too close to the wall, hurl the stick and shout "Fetch!" '

The joke didn't help, but it cheered Ananais who was still chuckling as he mounted the rampart steps.

Decado was leaning on the wooden shaft of the giant bow when Ananais joined him. The leader of The Thirty looked haggard and drawn; his eyes were distant.

'How are you feeling, Dec? You look tired.'

'Just old, Darkmask.'

'Don't you start with the Darkmask nonsense. I like my name.'

'The other suits you better,' said Decado, grinning.

The Joinings had settled down beyond the tents, creating a vast circle around a single black tent of silk.

'That will be Ceska,' said Ananais. 'He's taking no chances.'

'It seems we are to keep all the Joinings to ourselves,' concluded Decado. 'I see no sign of them splitting the force.'

'Lucky us!' said Ananais. 'It makes sense from their viewpoint, though. It doesn't matter which wall they take – just one and we are finished.'

'Tenaka will be here in five days,' Decado reminded him.

'We shall not be here to see him.'

'Perhaps, Ananais . . . ?'

'Yes?'

'It doesn't matter. When do you think they will attack?'

'I hate people who do that – what *were* you going to say?'

'It was nothing. Forget it!'

'What the hell is the matter with you? You look sadder than a sick cow!'

Decado forced a laugh. 'Yes – as I grow older so I become more serious. It's not as if there's anything to worry about after all – a mere twenty thousand warriors and a pack of hell-beasts.'

'I suppose you're right,' agreed Ananais. 'But I'll bet Tenaka mops them up in a damned hurry.'

'I would like to be here to see it,' said Decado.

'If wishes were oceans, we would all be fish,' said Ananais.

The huge warrior wandered away to the grass once more, settling down to finish his nap. Decado sat on the ramparts and watched him.

Was it wise to withhold from Ananais that Tenaka was now the Khan of the Drenai's greatest enemy? But what would it achieve to tell him? He trusted Tenaka, and when a man like Ananais gave his trust it was forged stronger than silver steel. It would be inconceivable to Ananais that Tenaka could betray him.

It was a kindness to let him die with his belief intact.

Or was it?

Did a man not have a right to know the truth?

'Decado!' called a voice in his mind. It was Acuas and Decado closed his eyes, concentrating on the voice.

'Yes?'

'The enemy has arrived at Tarsk. There is no sign of the Joinings.'

'They are all here!'

'Then we will travel to you. Yes?'

'Yes,' answered Decado. He had kept eight priests with him at Magadon and sent the other nine to Tarsk.

'We did as you suggested and entered the mind of one of the beasts, but I don't think you will like what we found.'

'Tell me.'

'They are Dragon! Ceska began rounding them up fifteen years ago. Some of the more recent came from amongst men captured when the Dragon reformed.'

'I see.'

'Does it make a difference?'

'No,' said Decado. 'It only increases the sorrow.'

'I am sorry. Does the plan go ahead?'

'Yes. Are you sure we must be close?'

'I am,' said Acuas. 'The closer the better.'

'The Templars?'

'They have breached the Void Wall. We almost lost Balan.'

'How is he?'

'Recovering. Have you told Ananais about Tenaka Khan?'

'No.'

'You know best.'

'I hope so. Get here as soon as you can.'

On the grass below, Ananais slept dreamlessly. Valtaya saw him there and prepared a meal of roasted beef and hot bread. She carried it to him after about an hour and together they walked into the shade of some trees where he lifted his mask and ate.

She couldn't watch him eat and moved away to

gather flowers. When he had finished she returned to him.

'Put on your mask,' she said. 'Someone might come by.'

His bright blue eyes burned into hers, then he looked away and pulled on the mask.

'Someone just did,' he said sadly.

22

Towards the middle of the morning bugles sounded in the enemy camp and some ten thousand warriors began to move purposefully around the wagons – pulling ladders clear, tying ropes to grappling hooks, hitching shields in place.

Ananais ran to the wall where Lake was bent over the giant bow, checking the ropes and ties.

The army lined up across the valley, sunlight flashing from swords and spears. A drum-beat began and the force moved forward.

On the wall, defenders licked dry lips with dry tongues and wiped sweating palms on their tunics.

The slow drum-beat echoed in the mountains.

Terror hit the defenders like a tidal wave. Men screamed and jumped from the wall, rolling on to the grass below.

'The Templars!' screamed Decado. 'It's only an illusion.'

But panic continued to well up in the Skoda ranks. Ananais tried to rally them, but his own voice was shaking with fear. More men leapt from the walls as the drums grew closer.

Hundreds of men now streamed back, skidding to a halt as they saw the woman standing before them in her rusty mailshirt.

'We don't run!' bellowed Rayvan. 'We are Skoda! We are the sons of Druss the Legend. *We don't run!*'

Drawing a shortsword, she walked through them

towards the walls. Only a handful of men remained by the ramparts, and these were ghost-faced and trembling. Rayvan mounted the steps, fear growing as she reached the battlements.

Ananais staggered towards her, holding out his hand which she accepted gratefully.

'They can't beat us!' she said through gritted teeth, her eyes wide.

The Skoda men turned and saw her standing defiantly at the centre. Gathering their swords they moved forward again, pushing against the wall of fear before them.

Decado and The Thirty fought back against the force, holding a shield around Rayvan.

And then the fear vanished!

The Skoda warriors surged back to the walls, angry now. Shamed by the courage of the warrior woman who led them, they stood their ground, determination on every face.

The drum-beat stopped. A bugle sounded.

With a savage roar ten thousand warriors surged forward.

Lake and his workers hauled back the bowstrings on the two weapons, filling their bowls with filed lead shot. At fifty paces Lake lifted his arm. At forty he dropped it and tugged the release. The arm whipped forward. The second machine let fly a moment later.

The first ranks of the enemy were scythed down and a great cheer rose from the defenders. Taking up their bows, the Skoda men sent volley after volley of arrows into the charging warriors. But they were heavily armoured and they held their shields before them.

Ladders thudded against the wall and grappling-hooks sailed over the ramparts.

'Now it begins!' said Ananais.

The first warrior to reach the ramparts died with Ananais' sword in his throat. As he fell, he dislodged the man below him.

And then they were over and the battle became hand-to-hand.

Decado and The Thirty fought together as a unit to the right of Ananais. Not one warrior gained the ramparts there.

But to the left the invaders forged an opening. Ananais charged among them, cutting and slashing, hacking and slaying. Like a lion among wolves he hammered his way through their ranks, and the Skoda men gathered behind him roaring their defiance. Slowly they pushed back the soldiers. At the centre Rayvan plunged her blade into a warrior's chest, but as he fell he lashed out, his sword slicing her cheek. She stumbled as another man ran at her and Lake, seeing his mother's danger, hurled his dagger to hit the assailant hilt-first, behind the ear. He half-fell and dropped his sword, whereupon Rayvan finished him with a two-handed cut to the neck.

'Get away from here, mother!' yelled Lake.

Decado, hearing the cry, left The Thirty and ran to Rayvan, helping her to her feet.

'Lake is right,' he said. 'You are far too important to risk yourself here!'

'Behind you!' she yelled, as a warrior leapt over the wall with axe raised. Decado spun on his heel and lunged. His sword skewered the man's chest – and snapped. Two more warriors climbed into view and Decado dived forward, scooping up the fallen axe and rolling to his feet. He blocked an overhead cut, then back-handed the warrior from the wall. The second man lanced his blade into Decado's shoulder but Lake, running in behind, hammered his sword through the attacker's skull.

The attackers drew back.

'Get the wounded from the wall,' shouted Ananais. 'They'll return at any moment.'

Ananais moved along the wall, hastily checking the wounded and dead. At least a hundred men would fight no more. Ten more attacks like this and they were finished.

Galand made his way from the far left, meeting Ananais at the centre.

'We could do with a thousand more men and a higher wall,' said Galand sourly.

'They did well. Losses will be fewer next time. The weakest of our men fell during this assault.'

'Is that all they are to you?' snapped Galand. 'Units with swords. Some good, some bad?'

'There is no time for this, Galand.'

'You make me sick!'

'I know Parsal's death . . .'

'Leave me alone!' said Galand, pushing past him.

'What was that about?' asked Thorn, climbing the rampart steps. A bandage had been wrapped around a shallow cut to his head.

'I don't know.'

'I brought some food,' said Thorn, handing Ananais a loaf filled with creamed cheese. Ananais had taken one bite when the drums began beating once more.

*

Five attacks were launched and repulsed before dusk, and one night attack was turned back with heavy losses among the Drenai.

Ananais remained on the wall until two hours before dawn, but Decado assured him no further attacks were planned and the general finally staggered away from the ramparts. Valtaya had a room in the hospital, but he resisted the impulse to go to her; instead he moved into the trees and fell asleep on a grassy knoll.

Four hundred men had been removed from the battle; the wounded overflowed the hospital and had been laid on blankets on the grass around the building. Ananais had sent for reinforcements, two hundred and fifty men of the reserve force.

At Tarsk, he learned from Acuas, the losses had been fewer, but then only three attacks had been launched. Turs, the young warrior who led the Tarsk troops, had done well by all accounts.

It was now obvious that the main thrust would be aimed at Magadon. Ananais hoped the Joinings would not be sent in tomorrow, but in his heart he knew that they would be.

Across from the hospital buildings a young warrior tossed in his sleep as the nightmare grew. Suddenly he stiffened and a strangled scream died in his throat. His eyes opened and he sat up, reaching for his knife. Reversing the blade, he slowly pushed it into his chest between the ribs until it sliced into his heart. Then he withdrew it and stood up. No blood ran from the wound . . .

Slowly he walked to the hospital building, staring through the open window. Inside Valtaya was working into the night, fighting to save the worst of the wounded.

He moved away from the window to the woods beyond, where some two hundred refugees had pitched their makeshift tents. By a camp-fire sat Rayvan, cradling a babe and talking to three women.

The dead man walked towards them.

Rayvan looked up and saw him – she knew him well.

'Can you not sleep, Oranda?'

He did not reply.

Then Rayvan saw the knife and her eyes narrowed. When the man knelt beside her, she looked into his eyes. Blank and dead, they stared back unseeing.

The knife flashed up and Rayvan twisted and dived, turning her body to protect the sleeping babe as the blade raked her hip. Letting the child roll clear, she blocked the next blow with her forearm and smashed a right cross to the man's chin. He fell, but rose again. Rayvan pushed herself to her feet. The other women were screaming now and the babe had begun to wail. As the corpse approached, Rayvan backed away; she could feel the blood oozing down her leg. Then a man ran forward, holding a blacksmith's hammer which he brought down savagely on the dead man's head. The skull cracked, but still no expression crossed his face.

An arrow flashed into the dead man's chest; he merely gazed down at it and then slowly pulled it clear. Galand ran forward just as the corpse reached Rayvan. As the knife came up, Galand lashed out and the knife-arm sailed from the body. The corpse staggered . . . And fell.

'They want you dead pretty badly,' said Galand.

'They want us all dead,' replied Rayvan.

'Tomorrow they will get their wish,' he observed.

*

Valtaya finished stitching the nine-inch cut on Rayvan's hip and then smeared a thick ointment along the wound.

'It will help to prevent an ugly scar,' said Valtaya, covering the wound with gauze.

'A matter of indifference to me,' said Rayvan.

'When you get to my age, no one is going to notice a scar on the nip – if you take my meaning?'

'Nonsense, you are a handsome woman.'

'Exactly. It is a rare man who notices a handsome woman. You are Darkmask's lover, are you not?'

'Yes.'

'Known him long?'

'No, not long. He saved my life.'

'I see.'

'What do you see?'

'You are a nice girl, but maybe you take debts too seriously.'

Valtaya sat down beside the bed, rubbing her eyes. She was tired, too tired for sleep.

'Do you always make snap judgements of people you meet?'

'No,' said Rayvan, sitting up carefully and feeling the pull of the stitches. 'But love is in the eyes and one woman knows when another woman is in love. When I asked you about Darkmask you showed your sadness. And then you said he had saved your life. It was not difficult to reach the obvious conclusion.'

'Is it so wrong to want to repay someone?'

'No, it isn't wrong – especially now. Anyway, he is a fine man.'

'I have hurt him,' said Valtaya. 'I didn't mean to, I was tired. Most times I try to ignore his face, but I told him to put on his mask.'

'Lake caught a glimpse of him once without his mask. He told me Ananais' face was hideously scarred.'

'There is no face,' said Valtaya. 'The nose and upper lip have been ripped away and the cheeks are a mass of scar tissue. One scar will not heal and oozes pus. It is a horror! He looks like a dead man.

I have tried . . . I can't . . .' Tears fell and the words died.

'Don't think badly of yourself, my girl,' said Rayvan softly, leaning forward and patting her back. 'You *tried* – most women would not even have done that.'

'I am ashamed of myself. I told him once that a face was not a man. It was the man I tried to love, but the face keeps coming back to haunt me.'

'You were not wrong. The answer lies in your words – the man you *tried* to love. You took on too much.'

'But he's so noble and so tragic. He was the Golden One . . . He had everything.'

'I know. And he was vain.'

'How can you know that?'

'It's not hard. Consider his story: the rich young patrician who became a Dragon general. But what happened then? He entered himself in the arena games, and there he killed people to thrill the crowds. Many of the men he fought were prisoners, forced to fight and die. They had no choice, he did. But he couldn't stay away from the applause. There is nothing noble in that. Men! What do they know? They never grow up.'

'You are being very hard on him – he is willing to die for you!'

'Not for me. For himself. He is after revenge.'

'That's unfair!'

'Life is unfair,' said Rayvan. 'Don't misunderstand me, I like him. I like him a great deal. He is a fine man. But men don't come in just two groups, one of gold and the other of lead. They are a mix of both.'

'And what about women?' asked Valtaya.

'Pure gold, my girl,' answered Rayvan with a chuckle.

Valtaya smiled.

'That's better!' said Rayvan.

'How do you do it? How do you stay so strong?'

'I fake it.'

'That can't be true. You turned the tide today – you were magnificent.'

'That was easy. They killed my husband and my sons and they have nothing left to make me suffer. My father used to say that you can't stop a man who knows he is right. At first I thought it was a nonsense. An arrow through the gizzard stops anyone. But now I know what he meant. Ceska is unnatural, like a snowstorm in July. He cannot succeed just so long as enough people stand up to oppose him. All over the empire word of the Skoda rebellion will be spreading and other groups will rise up. Regiments will mutiny, honest men will take up their swords. He cannot win.'

'He can win here.'

'It will be shortlived.'

'Ananais believes that Tenaka Khan will return with a Nadir army.'

'I know,' said Rayvan. 'I don't feel too comfortable about that.'

In the next room Decado lay awake, his wounded shoulder throbbing. He smiled as he heard Rayvan's words. You can't fool a woman like her, he thought.

He stared at the wooden ceiling, ignoring the pain from his wound. He was at peace. Katan had come to him, telling him of the boy Ceorl, and Decado had been close to tears. All things were falling into place. Death was no longer a living fear.

Decado eased himself into a sitting position. His

armour lay on a table to his right. Serbitar's armour. The Delnoch Thirty.

Serbitar was said to have been filled with doubts and Decado hoped that at the end these had been resolved. It was so good to *know*. He wondered how he could have been so blind to the truth when the facts shone before him with such crystal simplicity.

Ananais and Tenaka, drawn together near the Dragon bar-racks. Scaler and Pagan. Decado and The Thirty. Rayvan.

Every one a link in a web of mystery and magic. And who knew how many other links there were of equal importance?

Valtaya, Renya, Galand, Lake, Parsal, Thorn, Turs?

Pagan had been drawn from a far country to save one special child. But who would the child save?

Webs within webs within webs . . .

Perhaps the events themselves were merely links. The legendary battle for Dros Delnoch conspired after two generations to create Tenaka Khan. And Scaler. And the Dragon.

It was all too vast for Decado.

The pain in his shoulder flared once more and he grunted as it washed over him.

Tomorrow the pain would end.

*

Three more attacks began with the dawn. On the last the line almost gave way but Ananais, wielding two swords, hurled himself at the invaders in a berserk charge, cutting and cleaving his way through them. As they were thrown back a single bugle sounded in the enemy camp and the Joinings assembled, five thousand of them.

The beasts loped forward and the men of the

Legion moved back through their ranks, leaving the way clear for the Joinings to advance.

Ananais swallowed hard and gazed left and right along the wall. This was the moment of dread. But there was no give in these Skoda men and he felt a surge of pride.

'There will be a warm fur rug for every man tonight!' he bellowed.

Grim laughter greeted the jest.

The beasts waited as the Dark Templars gathered among them – pulsing visions of blood and carnage, inflaming their bestial natures.

The howling began.

On the wall Decado called Balan to him. The dark-eyed priest approached and bowed formally.

'It is near the time,' said Decado.

'Yes.'

'You will remain behind.'

'What?' said Balan, stunned, 'Why?'

'Because they will need you. To link with Tarsk.'

'I don't want to be alone, Decado!'

'You will not be alone. We will all be with you.'

'No. You are punishing me!'

'It is not so. Stay close to Ananais and protect him as best you can. Also the woman Rayvan.'

'Let someone else stay. I am the worst of you – the weakest. I need you all. You cannot leave me alone.'

'Have faith, Balan. And obey me.'

The priest stumbled back from the ramparts, running headlong into the shadows of the trees beyond.

On the plain the howling grew to a terrible crescendo.

'Now!' cried Decado.

The seventeen warrior priests slid over the ramparts and dropped to the ground below, walking towards the beasts now some hundred paces distant.

'What in thunder?' said Ananais. 'Decado!' he bellowed.

The Thirty advanced in a wide line, their white cloaks flapping in the breeze, their swords in their hands.

The beasts charged, the Templars running behind them and spurring them on with mind-blasts of fearful power.

The Thirty dropped to their knees.

The leading Joining, a giant beast almost eight feet tall, staggered as the vision hit him. Stone. Cold stone. Shaped.

Blood, fresh blood, dripping from salty meat.

The beast ran on.

Stone. Cold stone. Wings.

Blood.

Stone.

Wings. Shaped wings.

Thirty paces separated the beasts from The Thirty. Ananais could watch no longer and turned his back upon the scene.

The Joining leader bore down on the silver-garbed warriors kneeling before it.

Stone. Shaped stone. Wings. Marching men. Stone . . .

The beast screamed.

Dragon. Stone Dragon. MY DRAGON!

All along the line the Joinings slowed. The howling faded. The image grew in strength. Long-lost memories struggled to surface. Pain, terrible pain burned in the awesome bodies.

The Templars pushed hard, sending searing mind-bolts at the beasts. One Joining turned and lashed out, his talons ripping a Templar's head from his shoulders.

The massive Joining leading the others halted before Decado, its great head hanging down, its tongue lolling. Decado looked up. Holding the image in the beast's mind, he saw the sorrow in its eyes. It *knew*. Its taloned arm came up and tapped its chest. The long tongue rolled around a single word that Decado could only just make out:

'Baris. Me Baris!'

The beast turned and ran back screaming towards the Templars. Other Joinings followed it and the Templars stood rooted to the spot, unable to comprehend what was happening. And then the beasts were upon them. But not all the Joinings were former Dragon and scores of them milled in confusion until one focused on the silver-garbed warriors.

It ran forward, followed by a dozen of its fellows.

In their trance state The Thirty were defenceless. Only Decado had the power to move . . . And he did not. The Joinings fell upon them, snarling and lashing out.

Decado closed his eyes and his pain ended.

The Templars fell in their hundreds as the beasts rampaged through the camp. The giant Joining that had been Baris, the Lord of the Dragon, leapt upon Maymon as he tried to run. With one bite he tore the man's arm from his shoulder. Maymon screamed, but a lashing blow from a taloned paw tore away his face, drowning the scream in blood.

Baris lunged to his feet and ran at the tent of Ceska.

Darik hurled a spear that took him in the chest, but it did not penetrate deeply and the Joining pulled the weapon clear and charged on.

'Legion, to me!' yelled Darik. Archers peppered the beast with arrows, but still it came on.

All over the field Joinings were collapsing, screaming in their death throes.

Still Baris pushed on. Darik watched in amazement as the giant Joining seemed to shrink before his eyes. An arrow pierced the beast's chest and it stumbled, then Darik ran forward to plunge his sword into the Joining's back. It tried to roll over . . . And died. Darik turned it with his foot. The beast quivered and he stabbed once more. Then he noticed that the movement had nought to do with life – it was reverting to human form. He turned away.

All over the plain the beasts were dying – all but the small group ripping at the silver-garbed warriors who had brought this chaos upon them.

Ceska sat within his tent. Darik entered and bowed.

'The beasts are dead, sire.'

'I can make more,' said Ceska. 'Take the wall!'

*

Scaler gazed down at the dead Templar. Two Sathuli warriors ran ahead to catch the dead man's horse, while Magir ripped the arrow from the man's throat and stuffed a cloth into the wound, staunching the blood.

Hastily they unbuckled the man's black breastplate, pulling it clear. Scaler wiped spots of blood from the straps. Two warriors carried on stripping the Templar as Scaler opened the leather pouch hidden inside the breastplate. Within it was a scroll, sealed with the sign of the Wolf. Scaler pushed it back into the pouch.

'Hide the body,' he said, and ran back into the haven of the trees.

For three days they had waited for a messenger on the lonely road through Skultik. Magir had downed him with a single arrow – it was fine marksmanship.

Back at the camp Scaler examined the seal. The wax was green and marbled; there was nothing like it among the Sathuli. He toyed with the idea of opening it, then thrust it back in the pouch.

Sathuli outriders had brought news of Tenaka Khan. He was less than a day from the fortress and Scaler's plan had to be put into effect immediately.

Moving to the armour, Scaler tried on the breast-plate. It was a little large. Removing it, he pierced the leather strap with his dagger point, tightening the buckle. Better.

The helm was a good fit, but Scaler would have been happier had the man not been a Templar. It was said they could communicate mind to mind. He hoped there were no Templars at Delnoch.

'When do you go in?' asked Magir.

'Tonight. After midnight.'

'Why so late?'

'With luck the commander will be sleeping. He will be drowsy and less inclined to question me.'

'This is a great risk, Lord Earl.'

'Don't remind me.'

'I wish we could have descended on the fortress with ten thousand tulwars.'

'Yes,' agreed Scaler uneasily. 'That would have been nice. Still, never mind!'

'You are a strange man, my Lord. Always the jest.'

'Life is sad enough, Magir. Laughter is a thing to be treasured.'

'Like friendship,' said the Sathuli.

'Indeed.'

'Was it hard being dead?'

'Not as hard as it is to be alive without hope.'

Magir nodded solemnly. 'I hope this venture is not in vain.'

'Why should it be?'

'I do not trust the Nadir.'

'You are a suspicious man. Magir. I trust Tenaka Khan. When I was a child, he saved my life.'

'Then he too is reborn?'

'No.'

'I do not understand.'

'I did not rise full-grown from the grave, Magir. I grew like any other child.'

'There is much I do not understand. But we shall leave it for another day. Now it is time to prepare.'

Scaler nodded, amazed at his own stupidity. How easily could a man betray himself.

Magir watched Scaler don the black armour, and he wondered. He was not a stupid man and he sensed the unease in the Earl, knowing in that moment that all was not as he had believed. And yet the spirit of Joachim had trusted him.

It was enough.

Scaler tightened the saddle-cinch on the black gelding and swung to the saddle, hooking the helm over the pommel.

'Farewell, my friend,' he said.

'May the god of fortune rest with you,' answered Magir.

Scaler heeled the gelding away through the trees. He rode for over an hour until at last the southern gates of Delnoch appeared before him, the great wall spanning the pass. It was so long since he had been home.

Two sentries saluted as he rode under the portcullis gate, turning left to the doors of the keep. A soldier came forward and took the reins as he dismounted.

Scaler marched forward and another sentry approached.

'Take me to the Gan,' ordered Scaler.

'Gan Paldin is asleep, sir.'

'Then wake him!' snapped Scaler, keeping his voice bleak and cold.

'Yes, sir. Follow me, sir,' said the man.

He led Scaler down the long torch-lit corridor, through the Hall of Heroes lined with statues and on up the marble staircase to Paldin's quarters. Once they had belonged to Scaler's grandfather. The sentry rapped on the door several times before a sleepy voice answered; the door swung open. Gan Paldin had pulled on a woollen robe. He was a short man of middle years, with large. protruding dark eyes. Scaler disliked him instantly.

'Could this not have waited?' asked Paldin testily.

Scaler handed over the scroll and Paldin ripped it open and read it swiftly.

'Well,' he said, 'is that it? Or is there a personal message?'

'I have another message, my Lord. From the emperor himself. He is expecting aid from the north and you are to allow the Nadir general through the gates. You understand?'

'How strange,' murmured Paldin. 'Let them through, you say?'

'That is correct.'

Paldin swung round, seizing a dagger from his bedside table. The blade swung up, resting on Scaler's throat.

'Then perhaps you would explain the meaning of this message?' he said, holding up the scroll for Scaler to read.

'*Watch out for Nadir army. Hold at all costs. Ceska.*'

'I do not intend to stand here for much longer with a knife at my throat,' said Scaler stonily. 'I do not wish to kill a general. Remove it this instant – or face the fury of the Templars.'

Paldin blanched but he removed the knife. The sentry had drawn his sword and was standing behind Scaler.

'Good,' said Scaler. 'Now read the message again. You will note that it says,"Watch out for Nadir army." Hence my message to you. "Hold at all costs" refers to the rebels and the damned Sathuli. What the emperor required of you is that you obey him. He needs the Nadir – you understand?'

'It is not clear.'

'It is clear enough to me,' snapped Scaler. 'The emperor has arranged a treaty with the Nadir. They are sending a force to help him stamp out the rebels, there and elsewhere.'

'I must have confirmation,' argued Paldin.

'Indeed? Then you refuse the emperor's orders?'

'Not at all. I am loyal, always have been. It is just that this is so unexpected.'

'I see. You criticise the emperor for not bringing you into all his plans?'

'Don't put words in my mouth. That is not what I said.'

'Do I look like a fool to you, Paldin?'

'No, that's . . .'

'What kind of a fool would I be, coming here with a letter that proved me a liar?'

'Yes, I see that . . .'

'Well, there are only two possibilities. I am a fool or . . . ?'

'I understand,' mumbled Paldin.

'However,' said Scaler, his voice taking on a more kindly tone, 'your caution is not without reason. I could have been a traitor.'

'Exactly.'

'Therefore I will allow you to send a message to confirm.'

'Thank you.'

'It is nothing. You have fine quarters here?'

'Yes.'

'Have you checked them thoroughly?'

'For what?'

'Hidden places where spies can lurk and listen.'

'There are no such places here.'

Scaler smiled and closed his eyes. 'I will search for you,' he said.

Gan Paldin and the sentry stood in silence as Scaler slowly turned on his heel. His finger stabbed out. 'There!' he said and Paldin jumped.

'Where?'

Scaler opened his eyes. 'There, by the panel. A secret passage!' He walked to the carved oak panelling and pressed a switch. The panel slid open to reveal a narrow walkway and a flight of stairs.

'You really should be more careful,' said Scaler. 'I think I will sleep now and travel back with your message tomorrow. Or would you prefer another messenger to go tonight?'

'Er . . . no!' said Paldin, peering into the web-shrouded chamber. 'How did you do that?'

'Question not the power of the Spirit!' said Scaler.

23

Ananais stepped down from the wall and joined Thorn, Lake and Galand on the grass below. Jugs of wine and plates of meat had been set out and the group ate in weary silence. Ananais had not watched as his old friend was torn apart, but he had turned back in time to see the power of the Templars ripped asunder by the awful ferocity of the dying beasts.

After that the Legion had attacked again, but half-heartedly. They were repulsed with ease. Darik called a halt while the bodies were cleared away: five thousand Joinings, three hundred Templars and another thousand soldiers had died in those terrifying minutes.

Ananais saw Balan sitting alone near the trees; taking a jug of wine, he joined him. Balan was a picture of misery, sitting with head bent staring at the ground. Ananais sat beside him.

'Tell me!' he ordered.

'What is to tell?' answered the priest. 'They gave their lives for you.'

'What did they do?'

'I cannot describe it to you, Darkmask. But simply they projected a picture into the minds of the beasts. The picture awakened that within them which was still human – it tore them apart.'

'Couldn't they have done it from the safety of the walls?'

'Perhaps. But the closer you are to a man, the

stronger is your power. They had to get close in order to be sure.'

'And now only you are left.'

'Yes. Only Balan!'

'What is happening at Tarsk?'

'I shall find out for you,' said Balan, closing his eyes. Moments later he opened them again. 'All is well. The wall holds.'

'How many men did they lose?'

'Three hundred will not fight again. Only one hundred and forty have died.'

'*Only*,' muttered Ananais. 'Thank you.'

'Don't thank me,' said Balan. 'I loathe everything to do with this insane venture.'

Ananais left him and wandered back into the trees, pulling off his mask and allowing the cool night air to soothe his burning skin. Stopping by a stream he dunked his head, then he drank deeply. Rayvan saw him there and called out, giving him time to replace his mask.

'How goes it?' she asked.

'Better than we expected. But more than four hundred men are dead at both walls. At least another four hundred will not fight again.'

'How many does that leave us?'

'Around three hundred here. Five hundred at Tarsk.'

'Can we hold?'

'Who the Hell knows? Maybe one more day. Maybe two.'

'Still a day short,' said Rayvan.

'Yes. Tantalising, isn't it?'

'You look weary. Get some rest.'

'I will, lady. How are your wounds?'

'The scar on my face will enhance my looks. The hip is sore.'

'You have done well.'

'Tell that to the dead.'

'I don't need to,' said Ananais. 'They died for you.'

'What will you do if we win, Darkmask?'

'A strange question in the circumstances.'

'Not at all. What will you do?'

'Stay a soldier, I suppose. Re-form the Dragon.'

'What about marriage?'

'No one would have me. I am not exactly pretty under this mask.'

'Show me!' she said.

'Why not?' He pulled the mask clear.

'Yes,' she said, 'that is ghastly. I am surprised you survived. The fang-marks are almost at your throat.'

'Do you mind if I put this on again? I feel uncomfortable.'

'Not at all. It is said that you were once the most handsome man in the empire.'

'True, lady. In those days I would have swept you from your feet.'

'That's not saying much. I always had trouble saying no . . . And that was with ugly men. I even slept with Thorn once, though I daresay he wouldn't remember. It was thirty years ago – before I married, I might point out.'

'You must have been very young.'

'How gallant! But yes, I was. We are in the mountains, Darkmask, and there is precious little entertainment. But tell me, do you love Valtaya?'

'It's no business of yours,' he snapped.

'Indeed it is not. But answer me anyway.'

'Yes, I do.'

'This is going to sound hurtful, Ananais . . .'

'I wondered what we were leading up to.'

'Well, it is this: if you love her, leave her alone.'

'Did she ask you to come to me?'

'No. But she is confused, uncertain. I don't think she loves you. I think she is grateful and trying to prove it.'

'I take what I can get these days,' he said bitterly.

'I don't think that's true.'

'Leave me alone, Rayvan. Please!'

When she had gone Ananais sat alone for some hours, unable to sleep. His mind relived his triumphs, but strangely there was no longer any satisfaction in his memories. Cheering crowds, pliant women, envious men – he wondered if he had genuinely enjoyed any of it.

Where were the sons he should have bred?

Where was the woman of his heart?

Valtaya?

Be honest with yourself, man. Was it ever Valtaya? If you were still the Golden One, would you give her a second look? Dawn tinted the eastern sky and Ananais chuckled, then laughed aloud.

What the hell? He had lived as hard as a man could.

No use in morbid regret. The past was a dead beast anyway, and the future was a bloody sword in a Skoda valley.

You are nearing fifty years of age, he told himself, and you are still strong. Men follow you. The Drenai people depend on you. Your face may be gone, but you know who you are.

Ananais, the Golden One.

Darkmask, the Ceska Bane.

A bugle sounded. Ananais heaved himself to his feet and walked back to the ramparts.

*

Renya lay awake for the third night, angry and uncertain. The walls of her small tent crowded in on her and the heat was oppressive. For two days now the Nadir had been preparing for war; gathering provisions, choosing their ponies with care. Tenaka had selected two warlords to accompany him, Ingis and Murapi. Renya had learned this from Subodai, for not one word had passed between Tenaka and herself since the night before the Shamen Quest.

She sat up, hurling the sheepskin blanket across the floor. She was tired, yet tense as a bowstring. She knew why, yet knowledge was useless. She was in limbo, caught between her love of the man and her hatred of his mission. And she was lost, for her mind dwelt on him ceaselessly.

Renya's childhood had been built on rejection, for she was deformed and could not take part in children's games. They mocked her lame leg and twisted back and she withdrew into her room . . . and into her mind. Aulin had taken pity on her, giving her the gift of beauty through the machines of terror. But though outwardly she had changed, the inner Renya remained the same – fearful of affection lest it turned on her, afraid of love because it meant opening the heart and removing the defences. Yet love had taken her like an assassin's blade and she felt tricked. Tenaka had been a hero, a man she could trust. And she had welcomed the blade. Now she found it was tipped with poison.

She could not live with him.

She could not live without him.

The drab tent depressed her and she walked out into the night. The camp sprawled over almost half a mile, with Tenaka's tent at the centre. Subodai groaned and rolled over as she passed him. 'Sleep, woman!' he muttered.

'I cannot.'

He cursed and sat up, scratching his head. 'What's wrong with you?'

'None of your business.'

'His wives bother you,' decided Subodai. 'Natural for a Drenai woman. Greedy.'

'It has nothing to do with his wives,' snapped Renya.

'So you say! How come he put you out of his tent, eh?'

'I put myself out.'

'Mm. You're a good-looking woman, I will say that.'

'Is that why you sleep outside my tent? Waiting to be invited in?'

'Shhh, don't even whisper it!' said Subodai, his voice rising. 'A man could lose his head – or worse. I don't want you, woman. You are strange, crazy even. I heard you howl like an animal, watched you leap on those dumb Pack-rats. I wouldn't want you in my bed – I would never sleep for worrying!'

'Then why are you here?'

'The Khan ordered it.'

'So now you are his dog. Sit, stay, sleep outside the tent!'

'Yes, I am his dog. I am proud to be his dog. Better the hound of a king than a king among jackals.'

'Why?' asked Renya.

'What do you mean, why? Is it not obvious? What is life but a betrayal? We start out young, full of hope. The sun is good, the world awaits us. But every passing year shows how small you are, how insignificant against the power of the seasons. Then you age. Your strength fails and the world laughs at you through the jeers of younger men. And you die. Alone. Unfulfilled. But sometimes . . . sometimes there will come a man who is not insignificant. He can change the world, rob the seasons of their power. He is the sun.'

'And you think Tenaka is such a man?'

'Think?' said Subodai. 'What do I know of think? A few days ago he was Bladedancer. Alone. Then he took me. A Spear. Then Gitasi. Then Ingis. Then the nation. You understand? There is nothing he cannot do. Nothing!'

'He cannot save his friends.'

'Foolish woman. Still you do not see.'

Renya ignored him and walked away towards the centre of the camp. He followed her discreetly, keeping some ten paces behind. This was no hardship, for it allowed him to gaze at her with undisguised pleasure. His dark eyes lingered on her long legs and the subtle swing of her hips. Gods, what a woman! So young and strong. Such animal grace.

He began to whistle, but the sound died in an instant as he saw the tent of the Khan. There were no guards. He ran forward to Renya, pulling her to stop.

'Don't touch me,' she hissed.

'Something is wrong,' he said.

Her head came up, her nostrils catching the scents of the night. But the stench of the Nadir was all around her and she could detect nothing.

Dark shadows moved towards the tent.

'Assassins!' yelled Subodai, dragging clear his sword and running forward; the dark shapes converged on him. Tenaka Khan opened the flap of his tent, sword in hand, to see Subodai hacking and slashing his way forward. Tenaka watched him stumble and go down under the swinging blades.

He stepped out to meet the killers.

An eerie howl echoed through the camp and the assassins slowed in their advance.

Then the demon was upon them. A back-handed blow sent a man ten feet through the air. A second fell as her taloned hand opened his throat. Her speed was awesome. Tenaka ran forward, parried a thrust from a squat warrior, and slid his own blade between the man's ribs.

Ingis raced in with forty warriors and the assassins lowered their weapons, standing sullen-eyed before the Khan.

Tenaka cleaned his sword and then sheathed it.

'Find out who sent them,' he told Ingis, then strode to where Subodai lay. The man's left arm was gushing blood and there was a deep wound in his side above the hip.

Tenaka bound the arm. 'You'll live!' he said. 'But I am surprised at you, allowing yourself to be over-come by a few night-stalkers.'

'Slipped on some mud,' muttered Subodai defensively.

Two men came forward to carry the injured warrior to Tenaka's tent. The Khan stood up and looked for Renya, but she was nowhere to be seen. He questioned the warriors nearby and two of them claimed to have seen her running towards the west. Tenaka called for his horse.

Ingis approached him. 'It is not safe to go after her alone.'

'No. Yet I must do it.'

He climbed into the saddle and galloped through the camp. It was too dark to see a trail, but he rode on and out on to the Steppes. There was no sign of her.

Several times he slowed his horse and called out, but there was no response. Finally he stopped his mount and sat quietly staring at the land around him. Ahead to the left was a small grove of trees, screened by thick bushes. He turned his horse's head and cantered towards them, but suddenly the horse pulled up, whinnying in fear. Tenaka calmed the beast, stroking its neck and whispering soft words into its ear, but he could not make it move forward. He dismounted and drew his sword.

Logic told him that whatever was in the bushes could not be Renya, for the horse knew her. Yet something other than logic prevailed in his mind.

'Renya!' he called. The sound that greeted his call was like nothing he had ever heard: a keening, sibilant wail. He sheathed his sword and walked slowly forward.

'Renya! It is Tenaka.'

The bushes exploded outwards and her body hit him with immense force, hurling him from his feet to land on his back. One of her hands was locked about his throat; the other hovered above his eyes, the fingers curved into talons. He lay still, staring into her tawny eyes. The pupils had become slits, long and oval. Slowly he lifted his hand to hers. The feral gleam died in her eyes and the grip on his throat loosened. Then her eyes closed and she slumped forward into his arms. Gently he rolled her on to her back.

The sound of hooves on the Steppes caused him to push himself upright. Ingis galloped into sight, his forty warriors behind him, and leapt from the saddle. 'Is she dead?'

'No, sleeping. What news?'

'The dogs would say nothing. I killed all but one and he is being questioned now.'

'Good! And Subodai?'

'A lucky man. He will heal swiftly.'

'Then all is well,' said Tenaka. 'Now help me get my woman home.'

'All is well?' echoed Ingis. 'There is a traitor at large and we must find him.'

'He failed, Ingis. He will be dead by morning.'

'How can you be sure?'

'Wait and see.'

*

Tenaka saw Renya safely installed in his tent before accompanying Ingis to the place where the assassin was being questioned. The man had been tied to a tree and his fingers had been broken, one at a time. Now a fire was being prepared beneath his feet. Tenaka walked forward and stopped the torturers.

'Your master is dead,' he told the man. 'There is no further need of this. How do you wish to die?'

'I don't care.'

'Do you have family?'

'They know nothing of this,' said the man, fear in his eyes.

'Look in my eyes, man, and believe me. I shall not harm your family. Your master is dead and you have failed. It is punishment enough. All I want to know is: why?'

'I am pledged to obey,' said the man.

'You were pledged to me.'

'Not so. Only my warlord – *he* was pledged to you, but I broke no oath. How did he die?'

Tenaka shrugged. 'Would you like to see the body?'

'I would like to die beside it,' said the man. 'I will follow him even in death, for he was good to me.'

'Very well.' Tenaka cut the man loose. 'Do you need to be carried?'

'I can walk, damn you!' spat the man. Followed by Tenaka, Ingis and the forty warriors, he led them through the camp until he reached the tent of Murapi where two guards stood at the entrance.

'I have come to see the body,' said the man. The guards gazed at him nonplussed and realisation hit him like a blow.

He spun to face Tenaka. 'What have you done to me?' he shouted.

The tent-flap opened and Murapi stood forth. He was past middle age and stockily built. He smiled thinly.

'Of all men,' he said calmly, 'I did not think you could break this one. Life is full of such surprises!'

The man fell to his knees. 'I was tricked, Lord,' he sobbed.

'It doesn't matter, Nagati. We will speak of it on the journey.'

Tenaka stepped forward. 'You broke a life-oath, Murapi. Why?'

'It was a gamble, Tenaka,' replied the man evenly. 'If you are right the gates of Dros Delnoch will be open to us, and the entire Drenai empire with it. But you merely wish to rescue your Drenai friends. It was just a gamble.'

'You know the price of failure?'

'Indeed I do. Will I be allowed to kill myself?'

'Yes.'

'Then you will not harm my family?'

'No.'

'You are generous.'

'Had you stayed with me, you would have found out how generous.'

'Is it too late?'

'Indeed it is. You have one hour.'

As Tenaka turned to walk back to his tent, Ingis fell into step beside him. 'You are a subtle man, Tenaka Khan.'

'Did you think otherwise, Ingis?'

'Not at all, my lord. May I give my son, Sember, command of Murapi's wolves?'

'No, I will command them.'

'Very well, my lord.'

'Tomorrow they will guard my tent.'

'You like living dangerously?'

'Goodnight, Ingis.'

Tenaka stepped inside the tent and made his way to Subodai's bed. The warrior was sleeping soundly and his colour was good. Then he moved on into the rear section of the tent where Renya lay. He touched her brow and she woke, her eyes returned to normal.

'Did you find me?' she whispered.

'I found you.'

'Then you know?'

'I know.'

'Mostly I control it. But tonight there were so many of them and I thought you would die. I lost control.'

'You saved me.'

'How is Subodai? Did he live?'

'Yes.'

'He adores you.'

'Yes.'

'So . . . tired,' she said. Her eyes closed and, leaning forward, he kissed her lips.

Her eyes opened. 'You are trying to save Ananais, aren't you?' Her lids drooped once more. He lifted the blanket around her and returned to the centre of the tent.

There he sat down and poured himself a goblet of Nyis, sipping it slowly.

Was he trying to save Ananais?

Truly?

Or was he glad that the decision had been taken from him?

If Ananais were to die, what would stop him from continuing his war deep into the Drenai lands?

True he was not hurrying, but then what was the point? Decado had told him they could not hold. What purpose would it serve, driving his men day and night to arrive exhausted at the battlefield?

What purpose?

He pictured Ananais standing defiantly before Ceska's hordes, sword in hand, blue eyes blazing.

He cursed softly.

And sent for Ingis.

24

The Legion swept forward and Lake's giant bows let fly with the last of the lead shot. Scores of men went down, mostly with leg injuries, for the infantry were more wary now and advanced with their shields held high. Archers sent a black cloud of arrows into their advancing ranks, then the ladders crashed against the walls.

The men of Skoda had moved beyond weariness and they fought like automatons. Their swords were blunted, their arms aching. Yet still they held.

Lake swept up a battle-axe, cleaving the blade through a helm that appeared over the battlements. The axe lodged in the skull and was torn from his grip as the man fell. Another soldier heaved his way over the wall, but Ananais ran forward to pitch the invader head-first to the ground below. He handed one of his two swords to Lake, then ran to the right where the line was bending back.

Balan joined him. And Galand. The defenders steadied, and rallied. To the left three Legion warriors broke through, leaping from the ramparts to the grass below and sprinting towards the hospital building. The first fell, an arrow piercing his back. The second stumbled as another shaft glanced from his helm, stunning him. Then Rayvan stepped from the building with sword in hand.

The men grinned as they ran at her.

With surprising speed she blocked the first blow

and then dived into them, her great weight hurling them to the ground. Her sword snaked out, slicing the throat of the first.

The second man rolled clear. 'You fat sow!' he yelled.

Rayvan heaved herself upright as the man charged forward. Then Thorn loosed an arrow that thudded into the soldier's thigh; he shouted in pain and swung round. Rayvan's sword plunged into his back. She watched the battle on the wall for several moments . . . The line would not hold for much longer.

Galand fought beside Ananais now, moving where the battle was most deadly. The Legion, sensing victory close at hand, did not fall back but milled below the wall, pushing their ladders high. More and more Legion men gained the ramparts.

Ananais could feel the battle ebbing from them and a cold fury settled over him. Despite the odds against them, and his certain knowledge that they could not win, it still galled him terribly. He had done little with his life, save never to lose. Now even this small comfort was being stripped from him at the death.

He blocked a lunge, spun his blade and plunged it up and under a black helm. The man fell back, dropping his sword which Ananais swept up as he advanced into the mass, two swords now whirling and killing. He was bleeding from a score of minor cuts, but his strength was unimpaired.

A tremendous roar went up from behind the wall. Ananais could not turn, but he saw the consternation in the eyes of the invaders. Suddenly Rayvan was beside him, a shield on her arm and a sword in her hand. The Legion were pushed back.

The women of Skoda had arrived!

Lacking skill with weapons, they threw themselves

forward lashing out blindly, bearing the invaders before them by sheer weight of numbers.

The last Legion warrior was hurled from the wall and the Skoda men took up their bows, sending the invaders running back out of range.

'Clear the dead from the ramparts!' shouted Ananais.

For several moments there was no movement as men hugged their wives and daughters, sisters and mothers. Others knelt by still bodies, weeping openly.

'There is no time for this,' said Ananais, but Rayvan caught his arm.

'There is always time for this, Darkmask – it is what makes us human. Leave them be.'

Ananais nodded and sagged to the ramparts, pushing his aching back against the wall.

'You amaze me, woman!'

'You are easily amazed,' she said, sliding in beside him.

He glanced at her and grinned. 'I'll bet you were a beauty in your youth?'

'I've heard you were, too!'

He chuckled and closed his eyes.

'Why don't we get married?' he suggested.

'We shall be dead by tomorrow.'

'Then we should forget about a long engagement.'

'You are too old for me, Darkmask.'

'How old are you?'

'Forty-six,' said Rayvan.

'Perfect!'

'You must be desperate. And you are bleeding – get off and have those wounds seen to.'

'One proposal and already you are starting to nag.'

'Women are like that. Go on with you!'

She watched him walk to the hospital, then pulled

herself to her feet and transferred her gaze to the Legion. They were forming up again.

Rayvan turned to the defenders. 'Clear the dead from the walls, you numbskulls!' she shouted. 'Come on now. Move yourselves. You women, grab some swords. And find yourselves some helmets,' she yelled as an afterthought. A dead Legion soldier lay close to her and she tugged loose his helm before rolling the body from the ramparts. The helm was bronze with a black horse-hair plume. It fitted well, she thought, as she buckled the chin-strap.

'You looked damned fetching, Rayvan,' said Thorn, moving alongside her.

'Fancy people in helmets, do you, you old stag?'

'I have always fancied you, woman! Ever since that day in the north meadow.'

'Ah, you *do* remember? That is a compliment.'

Thorn laughed. 'I don't think any man would forget you.'

'Only you would talk about sex in the middle of a battle. You are a goat, old man! At least Ananais had the courtesy to ask me to marry him.'

'Did he now? Don't accept – he has a roving eye.'

'It won't rove far in a day,' she said.

The Legion charged again.

For an hour they fought to gain a toehold on the ramparts, but the defenders had found fresh strength and courage. Lake had gathered sacks of small stones which he poured into the bowls of his giant bows. Three times the missiles whistled and slashed into the Legion before one of the bows snapped under the strain.

The invaders fell back.

As the sun fell on the third day the wall still held.

*

Ananais called Balan to him. 'What news of Tarsk?'

'It is strange,' said Balan. 'There was one attack this morning, but since then nothing. The army merely sits.'

'I wish to Heaven they would do that here,' said Ananais.

'Tell me, Darkmask, are you a believer?'

'In what?'

'You mentioned Heaven.'

'I don't know enough to believe,' said Ananais. 'Decado promised me that I would not be alone. And yet I am. The others have gone. Either they arc dead and I am a fool, or they have been taken to the Source and I am refused.'

'Why should you be refused?'

Balan shrugged. 'I never had faith, I had talents. My faith was part of a corporate faith. You understand? The others believed and I felt their belief. With them gone . . . I don't know any more.'

'I cannot help you, Balan.'

'No. No one can.'

'I think maybe it is better to believe than not to believe. But I couldn't tell you why,' said Ananais.

'It creates hope against the evil of the world,' said Balan.

'Something like that. Tell me, do husbands and wives stay together in your heaven?'

'I don't know. That has been a debating point for centuries,' said the priest.

'But there is a chance?'

'I suppose so.'

'Then come with me,' said Ananais, pulling the man to his feet. They walked across the grass to the tents of the refugees where Rayvan sat with her friends.

She watched them approach, then Ananais halted before her and bowed.

'Woman, I have a priest with me. Do you wish to wed again?'

'You fool!' she said, chuckling.

'Not at all. I have always wanted to find a woman with whom I would like to spend the rest of my life. But I never have. Now it looks as though I am going to spend the rest of my life with you. So I thought I would make an honest woman of you.'

'This is all well and good, Darkmask,' she said, pushing herself to her feet, 'except that I don't love you.'

'Nor I you. But once you appreciate my great qualities, I am sure you will come round.'

'Very well,' said Rayvan with a broad smile. 'But there will be no consummation until the third night. Mountain custom!'

'Agreed,' said Ananais. 'Anyway, I have a headache.'

'This is a nonsense,' snapped Balan. 'I will have no part in it – it makes a mockery of a sacred bond.'

Ananais laid his hand on Balan's shoulder. 'No, it does not, priest,' he said softly. 'It is a light-hearted moment in the midst of horror. Look around you at the smiles.'

Balan sighed. 'Very well. Both of you approach.'

Refugees poured from the tents as the word spread and several women gathered flowers which they turned into garlands. Wine was brought forth. Word even reached the hospital, where Valtaya had just finished working; she wandered out into the night, unsure of her feelings.

Ananais and Rayvan walked back to the ramparts hand in hand, and the men there cheered themselves hoarse. As they reached the steps he swept her to his shoulder and carried her up to the wall.

'Put me down, you lummox!' she yelled.

'Just carrying you over the threshold,' he explained.

Men swarmed around them and the noise of their laughter drifted to the Legion camp.

Ceska called Darik to him.

'What is happening?' he demanded.

'I don't know, sire.'

'They are laughing at me! Why have your men not taken the wall?'

'They will, sire. At dawn, I promise you!'

'If they do not, you will suffer, Darik. I am tired of this pestilential place. I want to go home.'

*

For three bloody hours the battle continued on the morning of the fourth day, but the Legion could not gain the wall. Ananais could scarce contain his joy, for even through his weariness he could sense the battle had swung. Without the Joinings the Legion fought mechanically, reluctant to risk their lives, while the men of Skoda battled with fresh heart and confidence. The heady wine of victory pounded in Ananais' veins and he laughed and joked with the men, hurling curses at the fleeing enemy soldiers.

But just before noon a marching column was seen to the east, and the laughter died.

Twenty officers rode into Ceska's camp, bringing with them five hundred arena Joinings from Drenan, specially-bred beasts standing eight feet tall – blended from the souls of men, bears of the north, apes of the east, lions, tigers and the grey timberwolves of the west.

Ananais stood very still, his blue eyes scanning the horizon.

'Come on, Tani,' he whispered. 'By all that's holy, don't let it end like this.'

Rayvan joined him with Balan, Lake and Galand.

'There is no justice,' spat Rayvan. Silence greeted her comment, a silence that spread the length of the wall.

The giant Joinings did not hesitate in the camp but advanced in a wide line, their officers behind them.

Thorn tugged Ananais' sleeve. 'Got a plan, general?' he asked. Ananais glanced down at the old man, biting back the bitter reply as he saw the fear etched into Thorn's face. The man was grey and tight-lipped.

'No plans, my friend.'

The beasts did not charge but ambled forward bearing huge clubs, saw-edged swords, maces and axes. Their eyes were red as blood and their tongues lolled from gaping maws. They advanced in silence, a soul-sapping silence which ate away at the courage of the defenders. Men began to stir along the line.

'You must think of something to say, general,' urged Rayvan.

Ananais shook his head, his eyes bleak and empty. Once more he felt himself standing in the arena, tasting the bitterness of unaccustomed fear . . . watching the portcullis gate slowly lift . . . hearing the crowd fall strangely silent. Yesterday he could have faced these awesome beasts. But to have been in sight of victory – to have it so close that he could feel its sweet breath upon his brow . . .

One soldier leapt from the wall and Rayvan swung round.

'Olar! This is no time to leave!'

The man stopped and hung his head.

'Come back and stand with us, lad. We will all go down together – that's what makes us what we are. We're Skoda. We're family. We love you.'

404

Olar looked up at her, tears falling, and drew his sword.

'I wasn't running away, Rayvan. I was going to stand with my wife and son.'

'I know, Olar. But we must try at least to hold the wall.'

Lake nudged Ananais. 'Draw your sword, man!' But the giant did not move. He was no longer with them, but was fighting once more in a stone arena in another time.

Rayvan pulled herself up to stand on the battlements.

'Stand steady, my boys! Think on this: help is on the way. Turn back these creatures and we have a chance!'

But her voice was drowned in the terrifying blood-roar of the Joinings as they finally broke into a run. Behind them came the Legion.

Rayvan scrambled back as the beasts reached the wall. They needed no ropes and ladders – at full run they leapt, scrambling over the fifteen-foot rampart.

Shining steel met snarling fangs and ripping talons, but the first of the defenders were swept away. Rayvan thrust her sword into a gaping mouth and the Joining fell back, its teeth snapping the blade. Ananais blinked, dragging himself back to the present. Both his swords flashed in the bright sunshine. A beast towered over him but, stepping inside the first vicious sweep of an axe, Ananais plunged his right-hand sword into the creature's belly, twisting as the blade rammed home. A ghastly howl came from the Joining and it slumped forward, blood drenching the black-garbed warrior. Ananais pushed the beast clear, wrenching his blade from its body as another came to him, swinging a mace. He dropped his right-hand sword, took a double-handed grip on the left and sliced the blade through the creature's arm. Its taloned hand flew into the air, still clutching the mace as, screaming in pain and fury, it leapt at Ananais. The warrior ducked and drove his sword two-handed into the beast's belly as it went over him; it tore the sword from his hands.

Balan leapt from the battlements and ran back some twenty paces. Turning, he knelt on the grass and closed his eyes. Somewhere in all this pain and horror there had to be a purpose and a triumph. Yesterday the combined force of The Thirty had turned the Joinings back into men. Now there was only Balan.

He emptied his mind of all thought, reaching for the serenity of the Void, building his lack of thought into a channel to the beasts. He reached out . . .

And recoiled from the blood-lust and fury. Steeling himself he reached out once more.

Hate! Terrible, burning, all-consuming hate. He felt it and burned with it, hating the Joinings, their masters, Ananais, Rayvan and the world of untainted flesh.

No. Not hate. No hate. The horror washed over and past him. He was untouched, unsullied. He would not hate a man-made monster, nor even the man who had made them so.

The wall of hatred was all around him, but he pushed back.

He could not find a single memory to jolt the beasts, for they were not ex-Dragon, but he used the only emotion he could be sure they had known as men.

Love.

Love of a mother in a cold frightening night; love of a wife when all around you prove false; love of a daughter given so freely in a swift hug, in the first smile of a babe; love of a friend.

Growing in power, he sent out his feelings like a wave upon sand.

On the walls the carnage was terrible.

Ananais, bleeding from a dozen cuts and slashes, watched in horror as a Joining leapt at Rayvan and bore her from the battlements. He jumped after them. She twisted in the air and the Joining landed on its back with Rayvan above it. Her weight hammered the air from its lungs and, seeing her chance, she rammed her dagger into its neck, rolling clear as the beast lashed out with its talon. It reared drunkenly to its feet and Ananais plunged his blade into the creature's back.

Above them the line broke and the beasts swept on over the battlements. The Skoda survivors broke and ran, but the Joinings surged after them, hacking them down.

Suddenly the beast closest to Balan staggered, dropping its sword and holding its head. A howl of despair filled the air and everywhere the Joinings fell back as the Skoda warriors watched in disbelief.

'Kill them!' shouted Galand, running forward and hacking his sword through a furry neck. The spell broke and the Skoda men fell upon the dazed beasts, cutting them down in scores.

'No,' whispered Balan. 'You fools!'

Two Joinings turned on the kneeling priest. A mace thundered down, smashing him from his feet, then talons ripped away his chest and his soul was torn screaming from his flesh.

The fury of the beasts returned and their murderous roaring rose above the sound of clashing steel. Galand, Rayvan and Lake sprinted with a score of warriors to the timber-built hospital. As Ananais cut his way through to them, a talon raked across his back, ripping his leather jerkin and snapping a rib. He twisted and stabbed out and the beast fell back. Hands pulled him inside and the wooden door was slammed shut.

A hairy fist smashed the wooden shutters of the window and Galand ran forward, spearing his sword through the creature's neck. A taloned hand grabbed his jerkin and hauled him against the wooden frame. He screamed once as giant jaws closed around his face, then fangs fastened upon his skull and it burst like a melon. His body was dragged though the window.

An axe splintered the upper door, narrowly missing Ananais' head. Valtaya stepped from the ward within, her face bone-white with fear. In her hand was a needle and thread and a bloody swab, which dropped from her fingers as she saw the werebeasts climbing through the open window.

'Ananais!' she screamed and he jumped back as the door burst open and a huge Joining with an axe leapt forward. Ananais lashed out savagely opening a terrible wound across its belly which spilled its entrails to the wooden floor. The creature tripped and fell, dropping the axe which Ananais swept up.

Rayvan saw two Joinings running towards Valtaya and valiantly she leapt into their path, swinging her sword. A back-handed blow sent her reeling. Ananais beheaded a creature with the face of a lion and turned to aid Valtaya.

He hammered his axe into the back of the first Joining, tearing the weapon loose as swiftly as he could, but the second beast was towering over Valtaya.

'Here, you hellhound!' bellowed Ananais and the creature swung its great head, focusing on the puny black-masked figure. It backhanded the axe aside, ignoring the wound gashed in its forearm. Then its talons snaked out, ripping Ananais' mask from his face and hurling him from his feet. He hit the floor hard, losing hold of the axe. The creature leapt towards him and he rolled to a standing position to launch himself feet-first at the monster. Fangs snapped as his booted feet crunched home and the beast was thrown back into the wall. Ananais swept up the axe and whirled it in a murderous arc, caving in the creature's side.

'Behind you!' shouted Rayvan, but it was too late.

The spear entered Ananais' back, plunging through the lower chest.

He grunted, and twisted his powerful frame, tearing the weapon from the Joining's talons. The creatures leapt forward and he tried to back away, but the spear jammed against a wall. Ananais ducked his head and grabbed the beast, pulling it into him in a bear-hug.

Fangs tore at Ananais' face and neck, but his mighty arms continued to pull the creature forward on to the spear-point jutting from his own chest. The Joining howled in pain and fury.

Rayvan watched it all and time appeared to freeze.

A man against a monster.

A dying man against a creature of darkness. Her heart went out to him in that moment as she watched the muscles of his arms bunch and strain against the power of the beast. She lurched to her feet, ramming her dagger into the Joining's back. It was all the aid she could give . . . But it was enough. With one convulsive heave Ananais dragged back the beast and the spear-point plunged home.

Outside the rolling thunder of hooves echoed in

the mountains. Men of the Legion turned to the east, narrowing their eyes, trying to make out the riders in the dust-cloud.

At the tent of Ceska, Darik ran forward, screening his eyes. What the Hell was happening? Were they Delnoch cavalry? His mouth dropped as the first line of riders appeared from the dust-storm.

Nadir!

Screaming for his men to form a shield ring about the emperor, he dragged his sword from its sheath. It was impossible. How could they have taken Delnoch so swiftly?

Legion men raced into place, forming their shields as a wall against the riders. But there were too few, and none of them carried spears. The lead horsemen leapt over the shield wall, swinging their mounts to attack from the rear.

And then the wall collapsed, men running in all directions as the Nadir swept over them. Darik fell in the doorway of the emperor's tent with a lance through his chest.

Tenaka Khan leapt from the saddle and entered the tent with sword in hand.

Ceska was sitting on his silk-covered bed.

'I always liked you, Tenaka,' he said.

The Khan advanced, his violet eyes gleaming.

'You were to be the Earl of Bronze. You know that? I could have had you hunted down and killed in Ventria, but I did not.' Ceska wriggled his fat frame back on the bed and knelt before Tenaka, wringing his hands. 'Don't kill me! Let me go away – I will never trouble you.'

The sword lanced out, sliding between Ceska's ribs.

The emperor fell back.

'See?' he said. 'You cannot kill me. The power of

the Chaos Spirit is in me and I cannot die.' He began to laugh, high-pitched and shrill. 'I cannot die – I am immortal – I am a god.' He staggered to his feet. 'You see?' He blinked once, then sank to his knees.

'*No!*' he screamed and fell forward on his face. With one blow Tenaka severed the head. Gripping it by the hair, he walked out into the open and mounted his horse. Kicking the steed into a gallop, he rode to the wall where the Legion waited. On the plain every Legion soldier had been slain and the Nadir massed behind the Khan waiting for the order to attack.

Tenaka lifted the bloody head.

'This is your emperor! Lay down your arms and not one man will be slain.'

A burly officer leaned on the wall. 'Why should we trust your word, Nadir?'

'Because it is the word of Tenaka Khan. If there are any Joinings alive beyond that wall, kill them. Do it now if you want to live.'

Within the hospital building Rayvan, Lake and Valtaya struggled to break the lance pinning Ananais to the dead Joining. Thorn limped into the room, bleeding from a wound in the side.

'Get out of the way,' he said, taking up a fallen axe. With one blow he smashed the shaft. 'Now pull him off it.' With great care they eased Ananais from the spear and carried him to a bed where Valtaya plugged the wounds in his chest and back.

'Live, Ananais,' said Rayvan. 'Please *live!*'

Lake exchanged glances with Thorn.

Valtaya sat down beside Ananais and held his hand. The warrior's eyes opened and he whispered something, but no one could make out the words. Tears formed in Ananais' eyes, and he seemed to be staring beyond them. He made an effort to sit, but sagged back. Rayvan turned.

Tenaka Khan stood in the doorway. He came to the bed and leaned over the warrior, placing the mask carefully over his face. Rayvan moved aside as Ananais tried to speak and Tenaka leaned in close.

'Knew . . . you . . . would . . . come.'

'Yes, my brother. I came.'

'All . . . finished . . . now.'

'Ceska is dead. The land is free. You won, Ani! You held. As I knew you would hold. In the spring I will take you to visit the Steppes. I will show you some sights: Ulric's tomb, the Valley of Angels. Anything you would like.'

'No. No . . . lies.'

'No,' said Tenaka helplessly. 'No lies. Why, Ani? Why do you have to die on me?'

'Better . . . dead. No bitterness. No anger. Not much . . . of a hero now.'

Tenaka's throat seemed to swell and tears fell freely, splashing on the ruined leather mask. Ananais closed his eyes.

'*Ani*!'

Valtaya lifted his arm, feeling for a pulse. She shook her head. Tenaka stood, his face a mask of fury.

'You!' he stormed, pointing at Rayvan, his arm sweeping to take in the others. 'You miserable scum! He was worth a thousand of you.'

'Maybe he was, general,' agreed Rayvan. 'And where does that leave you?'

'In control,' he said, striding from the room.

Outside Gitasi, Subodai and Ingis waited with more than a thousand Nadir warriors. The Legion had been disarmed.

Suddenly a bugle sounded from the west and all heads turned. The warrior Turs and five hundred Skoda men came marching into the valley, followed by ten thousand Legion warriors, heavily armed and marching in fighting formation. Rayvan pushed past the Khan and ran to Turs.

'What happened?' she asked.

Turs grinned. 'The Legion mutinied and joined us. We came as fast as we could.' The young warrior looked around at the bodies littering the ramparts and the ground beyond.

'I see Tenaka was true to his word.'

'I hope so,' said Rayvan. Drawing herself upright, she walked back to Tenaka.

'My thanks, general, for your assistance,' she said formally. 'I want you to know that the entire Drenai nation will echo my words. I would like to offer you the hospitality of Dros Delnoch for a little while. While you are there, I shall journey to Drenan to gather a token of our appreciation. How many men did you bring?'

'Forty thousand, Rayvan,' he answered, smiling bleakly.

'Would ten gold Raq a head be acceptable as a token of our thanks?'

'It would indeed!'

'Walk with me a little way,' she said, and led him into the woods beyond the walls.

'Can I still trust you, Tenaka?' she asked.

He gazed about him. 'What is to stop me taking this land?'

'Ananais,' she said simply.

He nodded solemnly. 'You are right – it would be a betrayal at this time. Send the gold to Delnoch and I will leave for the north. But I will be back, Rayvan. The Nadir also have a destiny to fulfil.'

He turned to leave.

'Tenaka?'

'Yes?'

'Thank you for all you have done. I mean that.'

He smiled and a flash of the old Tenaka returned. 'Go back to your farm, Rayvan. Enjoy life – you have earned it.'

'You don't think politics would suit me?'

'It would suit you too well – I just don't want you for an enemy.'

'Time will tell,' she said.

She watched him return to his men.

Alone now, Rayvan bowed her head.

And wept for the dead.

Epilogue

Rayvan's rule was a popular one and the Drenai soon forgot the years of Ceska's terror. The machines at Graven were destroyed. Lake re-formed the Dragon, proving himself a skilled and charismatic general. Scaler married Ravenna, Rayvan's daughter, and took up his position as Earl of Dros Delnoch, Warden of the North.

Tenaka Khan fought many civil wars, absorbing each defeated tribe into his own army. Renya bore him three sons.

Ten years to the month after Ceska's defeat, Renya died in childbirth. Tenaka Khan gathered his army around him and rode south to Dros Delnoch.

Scaler, Lake and Rayvan were waiting for him.

And the gates were closed.